"SOPHIE." HE HELD HER BY THE SHOULDERS.
HIS VOICE WAS ROUGH. "YOU DON'T WANT THIS."

The shadows pressed in on her. The cold air bit her skin.
"You can't know what I want." She flung herself on him,
pulling at the buttons on his coat and waistcoat, tugging his
shirt free of his trousers.

"*Sacrebleu*, Sophie." His arms were around her again. His
lips were against her hair, her cheek, her throat. Where she had
been numb with cold and fear, her body came alive with sensation. She tugged off her gloves, cursing the slippery, damp
leather, ran her bare fingers over his chest, reached down for
the flap on his trousers. . . .

"Paul—"

"Yes." He pressed her backward, his mouth moving across
hers, until she was braced against something rough and solid.
Stone. One of the tombs. It didn't matter. It was enough to support her weight. It and Paul's hands, sure, compelling, anchoring her in the darkness. . . .

Shadows
of the
Heart

Tracy Grant

A Dell Book

Published by
Dell Publishing
a division of
Bantam Doubleday Dell Publishing Group, Inc.
1540 Broadway
New York, New York 10036

ISBN: 0-440-22164-1

Printed in the United States of America

Published simultaneously in Canada

November 1996

10 9 8 7 6 5 4 3 2 1

RAD

For Joan

Prologue

Paris
April 1794

PAUL CROUCHED ON THE FIRST-FLOOR LANDING, HIS FACE pressed to the cold window glass, and drank in the scene below. Torchlight glinted off musket barrels and sword hilts. Hooves thudded against the cobblestones. The steaming breath of the horses hovered over the courtyard like a thick mist.

Triumph surged through him. *He* had brought the soldiers here. *He* was the instrument of vengeance. For the first time in his ten years he had wielded power.

"What is happening?"

The voice of the Marquise de Ribard, high and strained, came from the foyer. Paul crawled across the landing and peered down through the gilded wrought-iron tracery of the balustrade. The marquise—Louisa, Paul defiantly called her in his head—stood below, her thin lips pale beneath their rouge, speaking to one of the footmen. "What is happening?" she repeated.

The footman swallowed. His face looked as green as his livery. "Soldiers, madame."

"Dear God in heaven."

Beyond the massive mahogany doors came the sound of shouts and running feet, the confused voices of the grooms, the sharp orders of the soldiers.

"Louisa?" The marquise's sister, Isabella de Milvery, rushed through the archway from the *petit salon*, her soft blond hair falling about her face, her white silk gown bunched up in her hands. "André has locked himself in the study. He won't speak to me. What—"

A heavy fist banged on the doors. "Open in the name of the Republic."

Isabella swayed and clutched a marble pillar for support. "They can't take us. We're English."

"We were English." Louisa was staring at the doors. "We married Frenchmen."

"But—"

"Don't be a fool." Louisa rounded on her sister. "They cut off Louis's head. They can cut off anyone's."

"Madame?" the footman asked, his voice tight. "Do we—"

"No." Louisa beat her fist against her palm. "In God's name, why isn't Daniel here?"

For the first time in his life Paul agreed with her. It was Daniel who should be paying for his crimes, not all these others. Daniel, Marquis de Ribard, Louisa's husband. And Paul's father, though Daniel had never acknowledged this fact. Just as he had not acknowledged Paul's mother during her final illness and death.

The voice beyond the doors sounded again. "We have warrants for the arrest of the Marquis de Ribard and the Comte de Milvery."

"No." Isabella ran toward the back of the house, stumbling over her full skirt.

Louisa hesitated a moment, then ran after her sister. The footman fled toward the service stairs.

The doors shuddered and groaned. Paul clutched the balustrade so tightly, the metal cut into his palms. He had unleashed this fury. He had brought the soldiers here to break down the doors of this powerful house. But he hadn't meant it to be this way. He hadn't wanted to hurt Isabella. He hadn't even wanted to hurt Louisa, though he knew she hated his presence under her roof. His target had been Daniel de Ribard—his *father*—and Daniel wasn't even here.

For a fleeting moment Paul wondered if he had done wrong

in going to the authorities. But killing was wrong, and Daniel and the Comte de Milvery and their friends were going to kill Monsieur Robespierre. Paul had heard them say so. That was why he had gone to the authorities. That and because he had sat alone at his mother's bedside while she lay coughing blood and calling for Daniel, who never came.

The doors gave way with a crash. The empty foyer suddenly seemed full of soldiers, though there were actually only four. Loud voices and the sound of booted heels against marble filled the air. The colors of the Revolution had invaded the Ribard house—blue coats, white breeches, blood-red facings. In the light of the chandelier their muskets seemed even larger than when he had glimpsed them in the courtyard.

A man wearing gold epaulets and a plumed bicorne hat issued a string of orders. One of the soldiers took up guard at the foot of the stairs. Two others made for the corridor at the left, while the man with the gold epaulets took the corridor on the right. The thud of doors being thrown open echoed through the house.

"Paul? What has happened?"

Paul looked round to see Isabella's four-year-old daughter Sophie crouching beside him. Her honey-colored hair and white nightdress caught the light from the wall sconce, but it was her face that caught Paul and held him. Her wide blue eyes were filled with confusion, and she looked at him as if he could make everything clear.

"Paul?" Sophie reached for his hand. "What is all that noise?"

Her hand was soft and warm. She sounded more puzzled than frightened, as if they were in the midst of a game. Paul hesitated, searching for the right words.

There was a splintering sound at the back of the house. A woman screamed.

"Maman!" Sophie sprang up and started for the stairs.

"No." Paul pulled her back into the shadows and put his

hand over her mouth. Whatever horror he had loosed on the Ribard house, he would at least protect Sophie from it.

Sophie went still. Two soldiers came through the archway on the left, dragging the Comte de Milvery between them. Isabella ran after them, sobbing. She tried to fling herself on her husband. Louisa, who was close on her heels, pulled her back.

The comte struggled like a roped animal. His claret-colored coat was rumpled beneath the soldiers' hands, his cravat untied, his hair released from its queue and hanging about his face in disorder. His eyes—blue like Sophie's—darted about the room, seeking escape.

Sophie twisted her head away from Paul's hand. "What are they doing to *Papa*?"

"Shush." Paul gripped her tightly. "Be quiet."

"Lieutenant," one of the soldiers shouted.

A moment later the lieutenant appeared in the archway on the right. He paused for a moment, a smile of satisfaction spreading across his fleshy face.

"He'd locked himself in the study," the soldier said. "He was burning papers."

The lieutenant's smile deepened. "So, *Monsieur le Comte*. Where's your friend Ribard?"

The comte stared at the lieutenant with the contempt he showed anyone of inferior station. "Away."

"We've arrested your other confederates already. You'll tell us where Ribard is." The lieutenant paused for a moment. Paul felt the menacing chill in the air. "Sooner or later."

"You can't take him." Isabella rushed forward and clutched at one of the soldiers holding her husband. "He's done nothing."

"Be quiet, woman." The soldier shook her off. She fell sprawling on the floor. The comte gave a cry of rage and jerked forward, breaking the soldiers' hold. The soldiers moved after him. The comte spun round and reached inside his coat. The candlelight glinted off the silver-mounted gun in his hand.

For a moment it seemed as if everyone in the foyer had

stopped breathing. Paul sucked in his breath. Sophie shrank back against him.

"Get out." The comte waved the gun in a drunken arc before him.

"Don't be a fool, Milvery." The lieutenant's voice was even but tense. "We have men all around the house. You'll never get away."

"Then neither will you." The comte leveled his arm at the lieutenant and fired.

Paul felt the report of the gun like a blow. The lieutenant dropped to his knees. The shot whizzed over his head, knocked his bicorne to the ground, and ricocheted off a statue of Eros. A green marble arm crashed to the floor. Isabella and Louisa cried out. Sophie was absolutely quiet.

"You can't take all of us, Milvery." The lieutenant got to his feet and jerked his head at his men. They began to close in on the comte, muskets drawn.

The comte waved the gun. The soldiers hesitated, then continued to approach. When they were little more than a handbreadth away, the comte lifted the muzzle to his own head.

"André!" Isabella stretched out her arms to him.

Paul reached out to put his hand over Sophie's eyes. A second report filled the foyer.

Paul let his hand fall to his side. It was too late to shield Sophie. All he could do was stare transfixed as the comte crumpled to the ground, a pool of claret-colored coat and dark-brown hair. Where the side of his head had been was a gaping hole that oozed blood and a sort of gray slime onto the veined white marble of the floor.

"No!" Isabella screamed, the word drawn out into a wail. She crawled past the soldiers and flung herself on her husband's body, encircling him with her arms, pressing her lips against what remained of his face. Patches of crimson seeped over the white silk of her dress.

"Paul?" Sophie said in a small voice.

Paul could not answer. He could not even move.

"Paul?" Sophie tugged on his shoulder.

Paul looked into her eyes and saw the horror he had brought about reflected back at him. Her lips were trembling. Her face was paler than the white muslin of her nightdress. Yet she still looked at him as if he would have an explanation for what they had both witnessed.

"When will *Papa* get up?" Sophie asked.

Paul's dinner rose up in his throat. He staggered to his feet, took a stumbling step backward, then turned and fled down the corridor.

He could still hear Isabella's sobbing and the voices of the soldiers. Footsteps sounded on the carpet behind him. "Paul!" Sophie's voice was high with fear. "Where are you going, Paul?"

The blood pounded in Paul's head. His chest felt as if it would burst. He reached the baize-covered door to the service stairs and fumbled with the handle, desperate for escape.

Sophie caught hold of his shirt. He wrenched himself from her grasp, tearing the fabric, and ran headlong down the narrow, winding stairs.

He could hear Sophie's bare feet slipping on the boards behind him. *"Paul!"* Her voice was shaking with full-fledged terror.

He could not let himself look back. He careened around a sharp bend, crashed into the wall, and fell down the last steps.

Sophie hurtled into him from behind, sobbing, clawing at his back. He pushed himself to his feet and lurched toward the area door. Sophie hung on to him, holding his leg in a viselike grip.

A chill blast of night air greeted him as he jerked the door open. Liberty. He shook his leg, but Sophie only clung more tightly.

"Get away from me, Sophie." He reached back and shoved her once, hard. He heard her fall with a thud against the floorboards, but her horrible cries did not cease. Seizing his moment of freedom, he pushed his way through the door and escaped into the cold, dark night.

Chapter 1

➤◄

Scotland
July 1817

THE TUG ON HIS POCKET WAS LIGHT BUT UNMISTAKABLE.
Paul reached out with his left hand and grasped the pickpocket's wrist.

The thief tensed and tried to pull away. Paul looked into
wary dark eyes set in a pinched, sharp-featured face. The face
held the wisdom and bitterness of years of experience, but the
pickpocket barely reached Paul's chest. The boy could be no
more than eleven or twelve. The same age as Paul's nephew.
Paul had seen many such children on the streets of Paris, but he
had not expected to encounter one at a village fair in the Scottish Highlands.

"You have light fingers." Paul raised his voice to make himself heard over the drunken shouts and hawkers' cries and wail
of bagpipes from the center of the village. "But I prefer to keep
my money."

The boy regarded Paul for a moment, then let out a wail that
was sharper than the notes of the bagpipes. "Oh, please, it's for
my mam, sir. She's verra sick and there's my three wee sisters
and my da took off last Hogmanay—"

"Bravo." Paul retained hold of the pickpocket's wrist. "You
have the makings of a fine actor."

The boy scowled. "It's true. If I dinna bring home some food
my four wee sisters—"

"I thought there were three," Paul said.

The boy drew a breath. "It's Mary, sir. We dinna like to talk about her 'cause she doesna aye come home. So sometimes there's three, and sometimes there's four, and there'll be five once the bairn comes."

"The bairn?" Paul asked.

"Mary's. Mam says I'm not to speak of it on account o' Mary doesna have a husband. She doesna ken how we'll manage to feed another mouth. Especially since there might be twa o' them."

"Two?" Paul studied the boy with fascination.

"Twins," the boy said. "Or maybe even triplets." He paused, as if wondering whether he had gone too far.

"You don't have any sisters, do you?" Paul said. "You don't even have a mother."

The boy drew himself up to his full height. The northern midsummer sun, still bright even at this late hour, fell across his face. For some reason, in this moment when he was trying to appear grown up, he looked younger than ever. "What's wrong wi' that?" he demanded. "I take care o' myself fine, I do."

A young couple brushed past them, hands clasped. The man's arm slipped around the waist of the woman's laced bodice. The woman slapped him away, then giggled and drew him closer.

Seeking an escape from the noise and confusion of the fair, Paul backed up toward a nearby lane, pulling the pickpocket with him.

The boy struggled against Paul's grip. "Here now, I didna take anythin'. Ye canna prove I did."

"I wasn't going to try." Paul stopped at the mouth of the lane. "What's your name?"

The boy regarded Paul for a long moment. "Dugal," he said at last. "Dugal Lumsden."

Paul smiled. "Well met, Dugal. My name is Paul Lescaut."

Dugal did not respond. He was staring at Paul's right hand. "What's the matter wi' yer hand?"

A clear tenor voice rose above the noise of the fair. Paul did not understand the Gaelic, but the mournful tone of the ballad needed no translation. Self-pity was a universal language. "It was broken," he told the boy, sticking to the literal truth.

"Dod." Dugal whistled. "It looks like a claw."

"So I've been told. I fear it's not as effective at shredding enemies to bits."

Dugal's eyes widened. Paul glanced over the boy's head. Farther down the street, banners and tartans flapped in the breeze, creating a stir of color. The air smelled of strong ale and hot spicy sausages and the thick oatmeal cakes the Scots called bannocks. He wondered if he could buy Dugal supper without the boy managing to make off with his purse.

"Look there, sir!" Dugal was staring past Paul into the lane. "That lady's bein' hurt!"

Paul laughed. "It's all right. I won't hand you over to the authorities."

"I'm no' lyin'." Dugal strained to break free of Paul's hold.

Paul turned. The lane was dark and twisting. The squat granite buildings on either side blocked out the light, but he could see movement at the far end. A man was pressing a woman up against the wall of a house, his arms encircling her. "I wouldn't call it hurting," Paul said.

"She was tryin' to get away," Dugal said. "I saw."

The noise from the main street was deafening. The man moved his arm as though to caress the woman's breast. Then Paul saw the glint of a knife blade.

Paul let go of Dugal and ran forward. The woman wrenched herself away from her assailant. The man seized her from behind. The knife blade flashed again, a relentless streak of brightness in the shadows of the lane.

The woman gave a high, terrified scream, twisting to take the knife in her side instead of her breast.

Paul launched himself at the man's back. He wrapped his right arm around the man's neck in a grip he had learned from a Gascon sergeant. With his left arm he reached across the man's body for the knife.

The man gave a grunt of surprise and released the woman. She collapsed on the cobblestones.

"Good work, Sassenach!" Dugal shouted.

"You bastard." The man twisted in Paul's grip, trying to break the choke hold with his free hand.

Paul struggled for possession of the knife. The man's booted foot caught him on the shin. He slipped. The man spun out of his grasp.

"Look out!" Dugal yelled.

The man lunged at Paul. Paul had a brief impression of red-brown side whiskers and a freckled, surprisingly youthful face. He grasped Red Whiskers by the lapels of his well-cut coat, brought up his knee, and rammed it hard into the man's groin.

Red Whiskers screamed, fell over backward, and rolled on the ground, clutching his balls. The knife flew in a glittering arc and clattered to the cobblestones. Dugal darted from the shadows and snatched it up. "No' bad for a one-armed Sassenach."

Paul dropped to his knees beside the woman. She lay slumped forward, her dark cloak spread around her, her dark hair spilling free of the hood and covering her face. Her arms curled protectively over her stomach. Her breathing was labored and shallow. Paul caught the sharp, sweet scent of blood. It was seeping through her cloak, forming a sticky, red-black pool on the cobblestones.

"We need a surgeon." Paul turned to Dugal, who was standing guard over Red Whiskers. But before the boy could answer, footsteps signaled a new arrival.

A fair-haired man in a light-blue coat, buckskin breeches, and a beaver hat ran up from the far end of the lane, then stopped, taking in the woman and Red Whiskers lying on the ground. "I thought I heard shouting. . . ." His voice—the voice of an educated gentleman with no trace of a Scots accent—trailed off. He dropped down beside the injured woman.

"She's been knifed," Paul said. "We stopped it just in time. She needs a surgeon. And a magistrate."

"In these parts they call it a baillie." The fair-haired man felt for the woman's pulse. He glanced from Paul to Dugal, as though weighing the truth of their story.

"She needs care," Paul said, his voice tight with impatience.

The fair-haired man got to his feet. "I know where to find a surgeon."

The woman moaned. Paul bent over her. "Tell him to hurry." He looked up and caught a fist in his face.

For a moment the world spun blackly. Paul pushed himself to his feet, ran full tilt at the fair-haired man, and sent him crashing against the house on the opposite side of the street. The fair-haired man yelped in pain and surprise. The beaver hat fell from his head. Paul punched his jaw and slammed his head into the stone. The fair-haired man went limp, slithered down the wall, and collapsed in a pile of refuse beside the house.

Paul heard a scream behind him. He spun round. Red Whiskers was on his feet, and Dugal was jamming the knife into his leg.

Red Whiskers threw Dugal to the ground and reached for the knife that was sticking out of his thigh. Paul lurched forward and aimed a blow at his head. Red Whiskers dodged, took the blow in his shoulder, and stumbled backward. With a grunt of pain and triumph he pulled the knife free and lashed out at Paul.

Paul blocked the blow with his left arm. The knife sliced through the skin and muscle of the arm, but missed his chest. Red Whiskers lunged again. Paul caught the man's wrist and tried to force the knife away. They were only inches apart. Paul could see the steely determination in the other man's eyes and the patches of sweat on his pasty skin. He smelled of whisky and Macassar oil.

Paul let his grip slacken, as though his strength were giving out. Red Whiskers grinned and pressed forward, turning the knife toward Paul and clawing at his eyes with his free hand. Paul raised his right arm to protect his face. Then he tightened his grip and twisted the other man's wrist, forcing the knife point away.

Red Whiskers growled in frustration and aimed a blow at Paul's face. Paul ducked, throwing the other man off balance. The knife between them, they fell together, locked in an obscene embrace.

"Bloody *slaoightire*." Dugal jumped on Red Whiskers and pummeled his head with both hands. Cursing fluently, Red Whiskers tried to shake the small demon from his back. His grip on Paul slackened. Paul wrenched the knife free.

Paul staggered to his feet, holding the knife in front of him, keeping the other man at bay. With a roar of rage Red Whiskers sprang up and launched himself at Paul, his hands reaching for Paul's throat. Dugal caught hold of his leg. Red Whiskers stumbled and fell against Paul.

Paul recognized the sound of steel slicing into flesh. Red Whiskers clung to him, a look of surprise of his face. "God damn you to hell."

"I expect He will," Paul said. "But not on your account."

Red Whiskers's fingers dug into Paul's arms, then went slack. He crumpled to the ground, legs twisted, arms stretched out on either side. Blood spilled from his mouth in a dark stream. The knife protruded from his chest.

Paul ran to the woman and knelt beside her. "A surgeon," he said to Dugal. "Where can we find one?"

"Bloody hell." Dugal was staring down at Red Whiskers.

"Don't waste your sympathy on him." Paul stripped off his coat and laid it over the woman.

"It's no' that." Dugal swallowed. "It's him. Who he be. I didna get a good look at his face afore. He's Matt McAlpin."

"You know him?"

"Aye, everyone kens him. He's the baillie's son."

God in heaven. Paul glanced at the dead man, then at the woman and the fair-haired man who lay in the lane beyond.

"Ye mun go." Dugal ran to Paul. "I ken a place ye can hide."

"I can't go anywhere until I get this woman to a surgeon. Is there one in the village?"

"Aye, there's Dr. Moffat, but ye canna go back there. I dinna ken who the yellow-haired man be, but when he wakes up he'll be tellin' them it was ye killed McAlpin. There's no one but me to say McAlpin went for ye first, and nary a one will believe me."

"I'll take my chances," Paul said. "I can't leave her in the street."

"Dinna be daft. She's no' safe either." Dugal gripped Paul's arm. "McAlpin wanted her dead. Maybe his da does too."

His father the baillie. Dugal was right. Even if he could get the woman to a doctor, Paul did not know who in the village could be trusted with her care. Someone meant her harm, and the threat might not have died with Matt McAlpin.

Laughter and snatches of song and a torrent of Gaelic spilled into the alley. Throngs of people were all too close. Paul looked at Dugal. "It seems we're in your hands."

Dugal's worried expression relaxed into a grin. "That's it. I knew ye were a canny one."

Paul settled the woman's head against his right shoulder, aware of soft warm flesh and fresh damp blood. He clamped her body with his right arm, then slipped his left arm beneath her legs and lifted her from the ground. A sharp pain lanced through his wound and he bit back a groan.

"This way." Dugal slipped through a gap between two buildings. The pathway was so narrow that Paul had to turn sideways, shifting the woman so she would not be scraped against the moss-covered granite of the houses on either side. The sounds of the fair receded, replaced by their own footfalls and the occasional scurrying of an animal. The houses seemed deserted. Everyone was at the fair.

Dugal led the way through a labyrinth of passages. Paul's arms began to throb. The woman's weight grew heavier with each step, but the feel of her breathing was sweet reassurance. Mercifully, she had not recovered consciousness. It was difficult to see her, for she was wrapped in both his coat and the voluminous folds of her cloak.

Dugal led the way unerringly until the buildings gave way to rolling green-brown land dotted with outcroppings of rock. They had reached the edge of the village. When he arrived that morning Paul would never have dreamed it could take so long to traverse its streets.

"Just a wee bit farther," Dugal said. "Ye're no' goin' to drop the lady, are ye?"

"That is one sin I have yet to commit," Paul told the boy. "I don't intend to start now."

The last stretch, across ground made brilliant by the red-gold remnants of the summer sunset, was the most dangerous of all. But though they saw an occasional sod-thatched cottage nestled in the folds of the land, the only living creatures they encountered were a pair of rabbits and a solitary fox.

They climbed over a small rise and down the other side. Paul's arm muscles screamed in protest.

"It's over yon." Dugal gestured toward a stand of pine. Behind the branches Paul caught a glimpse of weathered stone.

It proved to be a small barn, the walls thick with moss, the roof crumbling. Dugal opened a sagging wooden door. Narrow windows set high in one wall let in meager light. The air smelled of straw and damp and a faint, lingering scent of animals. "The cottage the barn belonged to burned down," Dugal said. "No one comes here anymore. Except me. I sleep here sometimes."

He stepped into the darkness with the confidence of familiarity. There was a rattle of metal and the sound of a flint striking steel, followed by a welcome flare of light. Dugal had lit a battered tin lamp, which cast flickering shadows over the interior. A rusting harness, a rotting cart, and other dilapidated farm equipment leaned haphazardly against the walls. Straw was strewn over the floor and more was piled deep in one corner. The sight was as welcome as a featherbed. Paul walked the last few feet, knelt in the pile of straw, and carefully set the woman down.

He had killed a man for her sake and carried her in his arms in one of the more arduous episodes of his far-from-uneventful life, but this was his first glimpse of her face. He smoothed back her disordered hair. In the light of the lamp he could see that it was a rich nut brown. It felt fine and silky beneath his fingers. Her skin was porcelain fair and soft to the touch. Pearls glimmered at her ears. A small lapis lazuli brooch was pinned at the neck of her dark-blue gown. A faint scent of roses mingled with the smell of blood and musty straw. This was no country maid or servant girl.

She was young, as he had expected, but not in the first blush of youth. The bones of her face were elegant and delicate, sharpened by the wavering light. There was a haunting quality about her. Deep inside him something shivered and trembled as though a long unplayed chord had been suddenly sounded in a quiet room.

Dugal knelt in the straw beside him. "She's no' dead, is she?"

Paul pushed back the folds of her cloak, intent on examining her wound. The swell of her belly rose before him.

"Dod," Dugal said. "She's carryin' a bairn."

"Yes," Paul said in a flat voice. Somehow the discovery was in keeping with the rest of the day's madness. No wonder she had felt so heavy in his arms. He remembered how she had twisted to take the knife in her side and how she had wrapped her arms around her stomach as she fell. She had been protecting her unborn child.

Her gown was plastered to her side where it had soaked through with blood. "Help me lift her," Paul said. "We have to get her dress off."

"Ye canna do that," Dugal said. "She be hurt. And she's carryin' a wean."

"I have to undress her to treat the wound." Paul unfastened her cloak and slipped his arm beneath her shoulders.

Though her gown was simple, the fabric was soft and finely textured. Only a woman accustomed to servants would have so many tiny fastenings on the back of her dress. Paul had learned to be skillful with his left hand, but he had never undressed a woman in such circumstances.

He eased her arms free of the dress and slipped the bodice down, save for where the blood-soaked fabric clung to her skin. Her chemise was drenched with blood as well. He hesitated a moment, then grasped the chemise at the neck where it was threaded through with pink ribbon and tore the muslin in two down the front.

Her breasts spilled free of the fabric, full and heavy because of the coming child. Paul drew a steadying breath and asked Dugal if he could find some water.

Dugal disappeared. Paul tore strips of fabric from the chemise. It was a mercy the attack and their escape through the village hadn't sent her into labor. Unless it still might. He studied the curve of her belly. He would guess she was close to eight months along.

He picked up her left hand, a slender hand with tapering fingers and well-tended nails. She wore no rings, save for a plain gold wedding band. So she had a husband. Or she used to have one.

"Here we be." Dugal reappeared, carrying a battered bucket filled with water. "Fresh from the burn."

Paul dipped a strip from the chemise into the cold water and pressed it against the woman's side. He eased the blood-soaked fabric away from her skin until at last the wound was visible. Dugal drew in his breath.

"Don't turn soft on me now," Paul said.

Dugal studied the woman's face. "I wonder who she be."

Paul cleansed the wound with a fresh cloth. "You've never seen her about the village?"

"Nay. And I ken everyone."

"Then she must be a visitor like me. We'll have to wait until she wakes up."

Dugal retreated into the shadows. Paul dried the wound and covered it with a pad of cloth torn from the chemise. The woman stirred once, but did not open her eyes. Paul took off his neckcloth and used the long strip of linen to fasten the makeshift bandage in place.

As he was tying the neckcloth he felt the woman stiffen. He looked into her face. She was awake. Her eyes were a clear, dark blue and wide with terror.

Chapter 2

≫≪

SHE WOKE TO DARKNESS AND CHOKING FEAR. HER HEART pounded in her chest. She could not remember the faceless demons of her nightmare, but they hovered near, just beyond recollection.

The blackness was pierced by a single rude lamp perched on a rough-hewn block of wood. She could not see beyond its meager light. The air was dank and had a musty smell. She had never been in this place before.

She turned her head, and her heart gave a sudden jolt. A man was squatting on his haunches by her side. His features were harsh, his look guarded and intent. She couldn't tell whether he meant her well or ill.

She looked down. Her gown was half off and her chemise was ripped to the waist. Panic returned. She scrabbled in the straw on which she lay, seeking some purchase to raise herself, to stand and run, to escape this horror. A sharp pain lanced her side. She gasped. The nightmare was closing in.

"Lie still. You've been hurt." The man pointed to her lower ribs. "A knife wound. A rather nasty one. There was a lot of blood. I've cleaned it and improvised a bandage, but you'd best not move for a while."

She looked over the swell of her breast and saw that at least part of what he spoke was the truth. A heavy pad of white cloth was clamped against her side, held in place by a long strip of white material that wound round her lower ribs. A dark stain in the center of the pad was visible through the binding.

The man leaned toward her. "Let me help you with your dress."

"No." She mouthed the word, but no sound came forth. She pushed herself further into the straw, trying to put distance between them.

The man settled back. "Very well. You'd best do it yourself. You'll be cold."

He meant her no immediate harm. The thought did little to allay her fear. She tugged at the dark fabric of her gown, pulling it up over her naked breasts and the torn remnants of her chemise. Her right arm was half-imprisoned in the sleeve and she tugged again, bringing it over her shoulder. The movement drew the fabric taut and she saw the swelling mound of her belly.

No, it could not be. One did not forget such a thing.

She slid her hand over the protruding mass. It was solid, warm, pulsing with life. God in heaven, she was with child. Why hadn't she remembered?

A flicker of terror edged her consciousness. She shook her head, unwilling to acknowledge its presence. If she faced the beckoning abyss she was lost.

"You need a surgeon," the man said, "but we don't dare risk it. The men who came after you weren't common footpads. One was the baillie's son. Do you know him?"

She stared at him, trying to sort through his words. She could remember neither the men nor the knife. But there was the evidence of the blood-soaked bandage beneath her dress. Someone had done that to her. The man before her? She had only his word that she was in danger from someone other than himself. His eyes were very dark, almost black. There were secrets behind them, she was sure of it.

She opened her mouth to speak and heard herself utter a harsh, croaking noise.

The man turned his head. "Dugal, she needs water. Empty the bucket and get some fresh. And if you're up to a miracle, find something that will serve for a cup."

There were two men. Her situation was worse than she had imagined. She peered into the darkness beyond the faint circle of light cast by the lamp, but could see nothing at all. There was a rustling of straw, then the sound of a door being opened and shut. The man sitting beside her did not stir. Exhausted, she closed her eyes.

She must have dozed, for in her next moment of awareness she was propped up while someone fumbled at her back. She looked up, mouth dry with fear, and saw a new face, thin and narrow, under a shock of dark hair.

"Just doin' up yer buttons, lady. Ye'll catch yer death."

His voice was high and light, a child's voice, not yet deepened to manhood. She felt the tension leave her body.

"This is Dugal," the man said. "He's made a miracle and found a cup and fresh water. Try to drink a little."

He held the cup to her lips. The water was pure nectar, cooling her parched throat, moistening her cracked lips. She drank greedily, grasping the cup with her hand, careless of the water dribbling out the corners of her mouth and dampening her dress. Sated, she pushed the cup away, aware for the first time that her fingers had been tightened around the warm flesh of the man's hand, not the cold metal of the cup.

"Where am I?" she asked, looking up and meeting his eyes.

"A barn of sorts. Dugal found it. It isn't used now. No one's likely to come here."

He was being stupid. She knew what the building was. That wasn't what she had asked. "No. Where *am* I?"

The man stared at her for a long moment. Something like comprehension grew in his eyes. Or perhaps it was pity. She clenched her fists. She would not accept his pity.

"You're in Kinrie," he said at last. "It's a village in Argyllshire. In the Highlands. In Scotland. I'd venture you're not a Scotswoman. I daresay you're a traveler, like myself. Am I right?"

She looked from side to side, seeking escape from his inquisition. There was none.

"Dugal here is Scots," he went on, quite as though he expected no answer from her. "He lives in Kinrie. We met this evening when he tried to pick my pocket."

She looked up at the boy who squatted near her head. He was grinning. "I'm no' from Kinrie, lady, but I ken it well enough."

"There was a fair in the village and crowds of people," the man went on. "Perhaps you heard the pipes. I was wandering about when Dugal caught up with me. We were talking—"

"No' bleedin' likely," Dugal said. "He had me by the wrist and I couldna get away. He's a grip like iron."

The man ignored him. "Dugal saw you in a lane just beyond where we were standing. You were pushed up against a wall and a man had his arms around you. I thought he was your lover till I saw the gleam of his knife."

"Ye shoulda seen him—Paul, I mean. This here is Paul Lescaut. He tears up the wynd like a greased pig and jumps on the man wi' the dirk and dings him proper, and all the time ye're bleedin' fit to die. Then along comes the other man with a fine blue coat and hair like corn silk. His voice is all soft and smooth and he says he's tryin' to help. But he dings Paul a blow and Paul fights back and lays him out on the ground. Then the first man comes to, but I go after him wi' the dirk, and then he and Paul go at it and the next minute he's laid out too, only he's dead."

At these words her body went taut again. She had begun to trust them, the cheerful boy and the man he called Paul. But how could she be sure that things had happened as they claimed? They admitted Dugal was a thief, and Paul had killed a man. Paul was dangerous. She could see it in his eyes.

Dugal took a deep breath and continued his story. "I take a look, just to see he's proper out of it, and Dod, it's the baillie's son and he'll no' go itchin' after the skirts no more. So I tell Paul we ha' to run for it, and here we be."

"That's more or less the way it happened," Paul said, a dry note in his voice. He leaned forward and explored her skull with gentle fingers. "You have a lump the size of an egg."

Dugal leaned over her. "Ye mun ha' smashed yer head when the man threw ye on the ground. Does it hurt much, lady?"

"No," she said, though the spot was exquisitely tender, the pain sharp enough to cut through the dull throbbing that had been with her since she returned to consciousness.

Paul laid her back against the straw. "You need a doctor and you need rest. Do you have friends nearby? Family?"

She turned her head away and plucked at her dress with nervous fingers.

Paul persisted. "Can you tell us your name?"

He had said it. He had breached the dikes, and a new terror came flooding in. She didn't know how to answer him.

Dugal leaned over her, his brow wrinkled with worry. "We dinna ken what to call ye. It's no' decent." Paul put out a hand to restrain him, but the boy would not be stopped. "Lady, ye ha' to be *someone*."

At his words she felt hot tears coursing over her face.

"It doesn't matter," Paul said. "It will come to you." He turned to Dugal. "No more questions."

"But she doesna ken—"

"A blow on the head takes some people that way. We have to give her time." He pulled Dugal aside.

There was nowhere to hide. They had stripped away her defenses and left her naked and chilled in a world in which she had no place. She had never felt so vulnerable, so isolated, so alone.

She watched the boy sitting at the edge of the circle of light, his arms round his legs, his chin resting on his knees. "It's no' right," he muttered. "We canna call her no name at all."

Paul regarded the boy a moment. "No, I suppose we can't." He turned to her. "You need a name for the moment, just to make things easy among us. Until you get your own name back. What shall we call you?"

She stared at him, unable to answer. Her hand sought the mound of her belly. Her child was nameless too. There must be some name she had chosen for the life that grew within her.

Yet that knowledge, too, had vanished. She looked away, her throat tight with sorrow. "I don't know."

"Lady," Dugal said.

She turned her head to look at him. Surely she could trust a child. "You choose a name for me."

Dugal took a deep breath. "I'll try. It would ha' to be right for ye. Ye're no' a Margaret. No more a Janet or an Alice. Catriona? No. Fiona? No, that's no' quite right." He bent his chin to his knees again, his brows contracting, giving him the look of a puzzled gnome. Then he raised his head and a wide grin split his face. "Fenella, that's who ye be." His eyes grew misty and he moved to kneel beside her. "I knew a Fenella once. She lived i' the house where my mam worked. She was kind to me." He paused, an anxious look on his face. "Is that all right, lady?"

She tried it out, like a badly cut garment that did not quite fit. Yet it covered the worst of her nakedness. "Fenella," she whispered. It was not a name she recognized, but it had a sweet-flowing sound. She looked up into Dugal's dark eyes. "Fenella," she said again, loud enough so he could hear. "It will do."

Dugal sat back, his face relaxing into a broad grin. He turned to Paul. "That's done then." He thought a moment and the worried look came back. "They'll be lookin' for us. We canna stay here."

Paul glanced at her, his eyes dark and appraising.

Dugal nodded in understanding. "Dod, that's a rare pickle." He clutched a fistful of straw and let it drop through his fingers. "I tell ye what, mate. I'd best be goin' back and see what's about. Maybe someone kens somethin' about Fenella."

"No," Paul said. "It's dangerous. You'll have been seen. I'll go."

"Dinna be daft. They'll ken ye for a stranger and ye'll stick out like a twa-headed ram, what wi' yer claw for a hand."

She gave a start at these last words. Her gaze went to Paul's hands.

Paul's mouth tightened. He held up his right hand. "An all too accurate description, I'm afraid."

The bones of his hand were bent at an awkward angle, the skin ridged with scars. She flinched, not because the sight was so hideous, but because of the lilt of bitter mockery in his voice.

Dugal had disappeared into the recesses of the barn. He emerged now with a cap on his head that reached the tops of his ears and a torn strip of cloth that might once have been a scarf wound round his neck. "See?" he said to Paul. "I dinna think the man wi' the blue coat got a good look at me, and i' he did it doesna matter. He willna ken me."

Paul leaned forward as though he would restrain the boy. Then he sat back and nodded. "Take care, Dugal."

Dugal moved away from the circle of light. "Take care yerself. Better douse the glim."

She saw Paul reach for the lamp. In the next instant everything went black. She heard a faint scrape of wood against wood, and then the sound was repeated. Dugal must have left the barn.

Paul's voice came out of the darkness. "Will you be all right? I can light the lamp again if you like."

"No, I don't mind the dark." In truth she found it comforting. It matched the awful darkness within her.

"We'll have to stay here for a time. It's as safe as on the road. There's a man likely to be looking for you. Fair-haired, well-dressed, soft-spoken. Blue coat and buckskin breeches. I don't suppose you remember him either."

"No."

"There'll be men looking for me too. Because of McAlpin, the man I killed." He made a sound that might have been a laugh. "I don't think much of your protectors, but we're all you've got. We'll try to get you somewhere you'll be cared for, someplace you can be safe. But for now you should rest. Perhaps tomorrow you can remember—"

"Please," she said, ... voice. "I'm so tired."

"All right." He was silent ... enough? Would you like some wa...

"No, nothing."

To her relief he said no more. Her e... grown accustomed to the darkness. She looke... windows to judge the progress of the night. The... smudges of gray, as though someone had tried to erase... rounding blackness. She could make out the darker ma... Paul's body. She watched him, thinking she could hear hi... breathing. Then she heard him move farther away from her.

Pulling the cloak around her, she tried to ease her position. The throbbing pain in her side grew more intense. She put her hand on the distended swell of her belly and let it rest there till it was jarred by the unmistakable kick of the child she carried within her. Tenderness for her unborn babe welled up in her chest.

Perhaps Paul was right. She had had a shock, but she would remember in time. She closed her eyes. Perhaps tomorrow, in the morning, when she woke.

PAUL SAT QUIETLY UNTIL FENELLA'S BREATHING SLOWED into the steady rhythm of sleep. Then he stood and stretched his cramped muscles. The sudden pain in his left arm reminded him that he had failed to attend to his own wound. He lit the lamp and washed the wound as best he could, then bound it with some remnants of Fenella's chemise. It was a clumsy job, managed with teeth and a right hand that was nearly useless. The effort left him shaking with rage at his infirmity.

He blew out the lamp. Fenella had not stirred. He moved without sound to the door, eased it open, and stepped outside.

The moon had risen, but it was barely more than a quarter full and there was scant light. He stared toward the steep peaks of the Grampian Hills to the east. The silence grated on his nerves. In Paris it was never so quiet, nor so dark. Wheels

amps and
the cafés
ll hours. In

this land of
s element. He
in a scant two
with a wounded
was. In the name
Where was he to
, people who spoke
a guide save a half-
? For all he knew Du-
gal would ... iers. Or not come back
at all.

Yet even as the thought cr... mind, Paul knew that he wronged the boy. Dugal reminded him of his own childhood. After he fled the Ribard house he had spent weeks on the streets before finding refuge with his uncle and aunt. He had learned to lie and cheat, but he had acquired his own loyalties. He suspected that Dugal was the same. The boy would not deliberately play him false.

There was a hint of dampness in the air. With luck there would be a mist tomorrow morning, giving them some cover if they had to leave. Nothing moved in the gray landscape. The silence was absolute. Paul took a last look round, then returned to the barn.

SHE WOKE SUDDENLY, STIFLING A SCREAM. SHE COULD NOT remember her dream, but her heart was pounding and her face was covered with sweat. She lay still as a trapped animal. Straw prickled her hands and her bare neck. She was in a barn. She could remember that at least. But nothing more.

Strange that she knew where she was when she knew so little else. She waited, and memory returned—not her name nor her home nor where she had come from, but an image. A man's face, lit from below by a lamp that accentuated its harshness and lines of pain. He had tousled hair that showed glints of gold; dark, guarded eyes that gave nothing away; sharp, slanting brows. His voice had a rough edge that was not unpleasant. She remembered his name now. Paul.

There was a boy too, an eager, dark-haired child called Dugal. They'd undressed her and bandaged her wound. They said she'd been knifed.

She lifted her hand and placed it against her side, feeling the wad of cloth beneath her dress and the ever-present pain. That much was true, she'd been hurt.

But by whom? There were two attackers, Paul had told her. He'd killed one of them and run away with Dugal, who was a thief. They'd taken her with them because it wasn't safe to leave her in the village. The fair-haired man would be looking for her; perhaps he wanted to kill her.

She wrapped her arms around her swollen belly. She was carrying a child, and the man would have killed it as well. She broke into a fresh sweat. Fragments of her dream returned but were gone before she could grasp them.

There was a stir in the air and the scrape of wood against wood. It must be Dugal, returned from the village. "Paul?" he said in a voice she could scarcely hear.

"Over here. Any trouble?"

There were soft footsteps and a rustle of straw. "None as I couldna handle," Dugal said. She could hear him more clearly now. "I cribbed some cloths for bandages and near got caught. And some bannocks to break our fast. We'd best be away afore light. Half the village has turned out to find ye. There's talk o' hangin'. The baillie's called i' the soldiers from Dounfries. Sassenachs. A Captain Cotter and a dozen or more men. They'll be goin' house to house now. I' the mornin' they'll start searchin' beyond the village."

A chill went through her like a sudden blast of wind. Soldiers. Hanging. But Paul had been trying to help her. Or so he said. Who was this man who at once offered protection and led her further into danger? She lay very still, afraid to make a sound. She must hear what they were saying.

PAUL LISTENED TO DUGAL'S STORY WITH A SINKING heart. In his youth in France he'd seen enough of what mobs could do, and he had little faith in justice, human or divine. "Did you hear anything of Fenella?" he asked.

"Nay. There are Sassenachs from Dounfries and the big houses hereabouts come to visit the fair, but nary a one makin' a fuss over missin' a woman carryin' a bairn i'side her." Dugal glanced toward the far end of the barn. "Is she—"

"Asleep, I trust."

"What are we goin' to do wi' her?"

Paul heard the worry in the boy's voice though he could not see his face. "See her safe as quick as possible. Curse the woman, she didn't come out of nowhere. Someone must be looking for her."

"Like the man wi' the blue coat?"

Paul groaned. "There's that. We can't leave her to his mercy."

"I' yer way, is she?"

"Of course she's in my way. So are the soldiers and the baillie and the man who's lying dead and the man who got away. But I can't wish them on the moon. We can't stay here, and she's not fit to walk."

"Is she bad?"

"Not as bad as she might be. The wound's long and she lost a good deal of blood, but it's not deep. If it doesn't go putrid she'll be all right. I'll take a look at it when it's light. If she's able I'll take her away. There must be someplace I can leave her."

"We'll take her. I'm goin' wi' ye."

It was a generous offer, but Paul could not endanger the boy as well as the woman. "You can't," he said after a moment. "You belong here."

"I dinna belong anywhere."

Paul heard the touch of bravado in Dugal's voice, but he also heard the undercurrent of bitterness. "How old are you?" he asked him.

"Eleven, I think, last Martinmas."

"Your mother's dead, isn't she? How long since?"

Dugal sniffed. "Twa years and more," he said after a moment.

Paul could barely hear him. "Do you have a father? Brothers and sisters? Aunties?"

"No one. Just my mam and me. She was i' service, see, and they let her keep me wi' her. Things was all right till she got sick and they sent us away. We went to the workhouse i' Dunkeld, but she didna last. After she'd gone I ran away."

In Paris a boy like Dugal could survive on the streets. If he wasn't caught no one would bother about him. Paul supposed it was the same in London and the other large British cities. But in the Highland villages it would be harder to pass unnoticed. "How do you live?" he asked.

"How d'ye think?"

"Lie about your age. Take what work you can. Keep one step ahead of the authorities. Move on when people ask too many questions."

"Ye've got it, mate." Dugal sounded almost cheerful. "I tend sheep and cut hay and muck out stables. If I can crib what I need to eat, I dinna work at all. I've had enough o' Kinrie. It's time I moved on." He was silent for a time. Then Paul heard a stirring in the straw. "Here now, ye'll not be goin' off and leavin' me behind? Ye're daft i' ye do. Ye dinna ken the land and ye dinna ken the tongue. How will ye take care o' Fenella and the bairn, let alone yerself? Ye'll bungle the business for sure."

The boy was right. Paul would have chanced flight on his own, but not with Fenella. He needed Dugal, both as guide and translator. "It won't be easy," he said.

"Easy as pissin' the bed. They willna find us."

"You're a liar, boy, but I'll be glad of your company."

"That's all right, then." Dugal gave a huge yawn. "Dod, I need some snooze."

"Sleep while you can," Paul said. "I'll wake you if I hear anything."

Dugal made a sound of assent. There was a rustling in the straw as he settled down. He yawned again. "Paul? Where d'ye come from? London?"

"Paris."

"Paris?" There was more rustling. Dugal had sat up. "Ye're a Froggy?"

"A harmless one."

"Ye speak English like a Sassenach."

"I grew up in a house where English was spoken. You speak English well yourself. Where did you learn?"

"At the big house, where my mam worked. They didna like to hear the Gaelic, so we only talked it 'tween ourselves and wi' the other servants." There was more rustling as Dugal settled down again. "A Frog," he murmured. "I'm goin' on the road with a Sassenach lady and a Frog."

There was no sound from the end of the hut where Fenella lay. Dugal was snoring quietly. Paul wrapped his arms around his knees and prepared to wait out the night.

THE TALKING HAD STOPPED. SHE WILLED HER HEART TO slow its rapid beat. There was danger on all sides. If she stayed with Paul they would be hunted. They would have to hide and there would be no way of learning who and what she was. She would have to trust Paul with her life and the life of her child. She would have to trust a man of whom she knew nothing save what he had told her. He had made it clear he did not relish the burden of looking after her.

If she returned to the village she risked meeting the man in the blue coat. But he must at least know who she was. If she could reach the soldiers, surely they would protect her from him. Perhaps they could force him to speak. She must have family or friends near the village.

She pushed herself into a sitting position, wincing at the sharp stabs of pain in her side as she moved. She could not bear to be dependent on others. She had to learn who she was. It was the only way to protect herself, the only way to protect her child. She would go to the village.

Slowly, fearful of making a sound, she got to her feet. She felt awkward and heavy. She bent to retrieve her cloak, aware of the bulk of her swollen belly.

She fastened the cloak round her neck, then lifted its heavy folds lest it brush against the straw and give her away. She stood very still, listening. Her hearing seemed unusually acute. There was breathing and the sound of someone snoring softly. Paul and Dugal were off to her right, somewhere in the darkness, and providence be praised, they were asleep. To her left were the faint oblongs of gray that were the windows. The door must be straight ahead.

She moved carefully, pausing after each step to listen for some change in the sounds in the barn. Opening the door would be a problem, but with luck the man and boy would not wake. With each step her confidence grew. A moment more and she would be free of them.

"Are you all right?"

It was Paul's voice. She stopped, her heart pounding. She had not heard him rise, but she knew he was standing nearby, close enough to touch her. "I need to relieve myself," she said softly, surprised that her voice held no hint of tremor.

"I'll show you where to go." Paul moved past her and opened the door. "There's a stand of oak just ahead. It will give you some privacy. Shall I walk part of the way with you?"

"No!" Her voice went sharp with panic. "I need to be alone."

"Of course." He stood aside and let her pass.

She took a few steps toward the trees, then turned back to look at the barn. It was lighter outside, but there was a thick mist. She could just make out the doorway and the man standing in it. "Where did we run from?" she asked.

Paul looked at her for a moment, than raised his arm and pointed.

"And where will we run next?"

"As far in the other direction as we can." Paul went inside and shut the door behind him.

Picking up her skirt, she hurried to the shelter of the oak, pleased at her own cleverness. She had outwitted her captors. She had only to evade their pursuit, but that should not be beyond her. The moonlight was dim, the shadows were deep, and her cloak was dark. And she knew the direction of the village.

But as she moved into the trees she recognized the ache beneath her belly and realized she had told Paul no more than the truth. The pressure was intense and could not be denied. Picking up her skirts, she squatted and relieved herself. Her hands rested on her belly and she felt the warmth of the child within.

When she was done she moved through the trees. At their edge she found a shallow, brush-filled gully, no deeper than she was tall. She climbed down its side, clinging to the bushes to ease her descent. There were loose rocks along the bottom and a trickle of water that in winter must be a good-size stream. She knelt, cupped her hands, and drank. This must be where Dugal had come for water. The gully offered better cover than the open land above.

She dipped her hand once more into the water to test the direction of its flow. The stream ran toward the village. She rose and began to make her way downstream. The quiet of the night was broken by the distant bleating of a sheep, but there were no sounds of pursuit. She had perhaps five minutes before Paul would come looking for her.

The sky was lightening above her, making it easier to find her way. She scrambled over the rocky ground, aware of the sharp pain in her side and the ungainly weight she carried. She would have to move faster to elude pursuit, even if it meant leaving the shelter of the gully.

She clambered up the bank and looked around. The stand of oak near the barn was still in sight on the other side of the gully. Ahead of her the ground rose in a small hill. Once over it she would be out of view. Perhaps then she could get her bearings.

She climbed quickly, but stopped at the top of the rise and lowered herself to the ground lest she be seen. There were more hills beyond, but to her right, in the direction away from the trees and the barn, the land was relatively flat, with outcroppings of rock and small bushes. The village lay that way.

She got to her knees and scrambled partway down the hill, standing only when she was certain of being out of sight of the barn. She fought the temptation to move faster. The ground was rocky and treacherous, and she dared not risk a twisted ankle.

Suddenly a man loomed out of the mist below. She stopped, uncertain whether to go forward or retreat. Her heart thudded against her ribs.

The man stood at the base of the hill, perhaps a dozen yards away. His voice came to her through the mist, as indistinct as his features. "Sophie? I thought it was you. I've been searching for you these five hours."

He knew who she was. Sophie. That was her name. The nightmare was over. Flooded with relief, she moved toward him.

She could see him more clearly now. He was a gentleman, his voice had told her that, and he was dressed as a gentleman. White cravat, blue coat, polished boots, and buckskin breeches.

She stopped, recalling Paul's words. Fear shot through her. "How do you know I'm your Sophie?" she said, retreating up the hill.

The man stared at her, then began to climb toward her. "Sophie, it's Ned. Don't you know me?"

She continued her cautious retreat. "I've never seen you before."

"What's the matter with you? Are you ill or have you run mad?" He doffed his hat and threw it to the ground. "Look at me. You've known me all your life."

The growing light caught the gleam of his hair. Like corn silk, Dugal had said. Heaven defend her, Paul was right. If she had any lingering doubts they vanished as she saw the gleam of a blade in the man's hand. She felt a searing pain in her side, as if the knife had once more found its mark.

She turned and tried to run, then tripped over a protruding boulder and fell to her knees. He continued his relentless advance. She moved her hand frantically over the ground and found a good-size rock. It would be better than nothing.

"Stop this idiocy," the man said. "I'm trying to help you. Do you understand? You're coming with me."

He was so close that she could see the determined frown between his brows and the fog of his breath in the chill air. It was too late to run, too late even to stand. She straightened and raised her arm. She would not let him hurt her again. She would not let him harm her child. Tightening her fingers on her weapon, she drew back her arm and threw the rock at his groin with all the force she could muster.

The rock found its mark. The man let out a howl of rage and pain. He doubled over, staggered, fell to the ground with a great thud, and lay still.

He had hit his head on one of the boulders that littered the ground. She retched, tasting vomit in her throat. The nightmare was real and never-ending. She scrambled up the rest of the hill, reached its crest, and began her clumsy descent down the other side. She had one thought only, to reach the haven of the barn.

Chapter 3

PAUL SWORE UNDER HIS BREATH.

"What did ye say?" Dugal sat up with a rustle of straw.

"It was French." Paul pushed himself to his feet.

"Sounds dirty."

"It was."

"I thought so." Dugal sank back into the straw. "Where are ye goin'?"

"To find Fenella."

"She's gone?" Dugal sat up again. "Where?"

"Outside. She needed to—"

Dugal nodded in sudden comprehension. "How long?"

"Five minutes. Ten." Paul moved toward the door.

"I'll go wi' ye." Dugal scrambled to his feet.

"No. Stay here. In case she returns."

Paul put his hand to the door, but Dugal was beside him, clutching his sleeve. "Did yon man come after her?"

"I don't think so. We'd have heard something. I suspect she's run off."

"Run off? Why?"

"Because she doesn't trust us."

"But we're tryin' to help her."

"She doesn't seem to have grasped that fact. Keep watch." Paul squeezed the boy's shoulder, then slipped through the door, pulling it securely shut behind him.

Thick mist and the gray light of dawn hung over the country-side, giving it an unearthly aspect. Paul glanced toward the stand of oak. Fenella had started that way, but she might have changed her direction once he had gone back inside the barn. Curse the woman. She put them all in danger.

There were no footprints on the rocky ground and matted deer grass. Paul started for the trees, calling her name softly. He stopped when he reached their darkness and called again. Nothing, though he strained to hear. Not a sound, not even the chatter of birds.

"Fenella," he called again, his voice growing sharp with impatience. Mist swirled around the thick tree trunks. He picked his way through the damp, clinging darkness, stopping every few steps to look, to listen. Damn her, where had she run to? Where had she gone to earth?

When he emerged from the trees he found himself at the edge of a gully. He looked down, wondering if she would have attempted the descent. The ground was rough and rock-strewn. At the base, obscured by the mist, must be the stream where Dugal had found them water. Paul felt a moment of contrition. Perhaps she had only wanted to drink. Perhaps she had stumbled and fallen. He scrambled down the side of the gully, aware of the sudden sharp bite of fear.

He saw no one, though he looked upstream and down. Visibility was poor, but if she had gone for water she would not have gone far. It was flight then, or discovery by the fair-haired man. Paul stood and listened once more, pushing aside the impulse to action. There was no time for fruitless pursuit. He had to think himself into the skin of this frightened woman. Which way? Which way would she go?

He heard a barely perceptible scrabbling in the brush downstream. A mouse perhaps, or a vole. Then he heard another sound, a fall of rocks dislodged from their resting place. He raced down the streambed toward the sound and up the bank on the opposite side of the gully. The ground sloped upward, then rose more steeply. And there, midway down the hill before him, a cloaked figure was making an awkward descent with a quickness born of fear.

Breathing thanks to a God he did not believe in, Paul ran and caught her as she stumbled and fell. Her arms closed around him like a vise. He pushed her away from him to look into her face. "Where is he?"

Fenella's eyes held panic but not hysteria. "There." She gestured toward the other side of the hill. "He had a knife. I threw a rock at him. I think I may have killed him."

"I'll go see. Come, you mustn't stay here." He seized her hand and looked around the mist-shrouded landscape for cover. To the right was a cluster of birch, but the slender trunks would provide little protection. He pulled her to the left, toward a scatter of boulders and a tangle of gorse and bracken.

"Sophie?" a slurred voice shouted from the other side of the hill. "Where the devil have you gone, Sophie?"

Paul dropped to the ground behind the rocks and pulled Fenella down on top of him. Heavy footsteps crashed over the ground not twenty feet away. "I only wanted to talk to you, Sophie. Damn it, woman, where are you? This mist's so thick a man can scarce see his hand in front of him."

Fenella's breath was warm against Paul's face. The weight of the child pressed against him. The footsteps did not come closer, but neither did they retreat. Paul reached out with his good hand, searching for a rock large enough to make a sound that would distract the fair-haired man. His fingers met only prickly undergrowth.

The footsteps sounded again, closer this time, then gave way to a loud curse. Fenella eased herself off Paul and extended her arm. A moment later she pressed a small, jagged rock into his hand and raised her head to look into his eyes. A silent acknowledgment passed between them. For this instant she accepted him as her ally.

Paul pushed himself up on his elbow and hurled the rock as far as he could toward the cluster of birch. It landed with a satisfying crash. There was a sharp cry of "Sophie," followed by the sound of the fair-haired man lurching toward the trees.

Fenella released her breath in a harsh sigh. "Don't move," Paul whispered. The fair-haired man was still too close. They could not risk leaving their hiding place and venturing across the open ground of the gully.

There was a rustling in the gorse and bracken. Fenella stiffened. Paul pulled her tight against him.

"Paul?"

The whisper was high and breathless, but the voice was unmistakable. Dugal. Paul felt the tension rush from Fenella's body. "Here," he called softly.

There was more rustling, and Dugal slithered up beside them on his stomach, sprigs of gorse and bits of bracken sticking to his hair and shirt. "Ye found her," he said.

The fair-haired man let loose another string of invective. Apparently he had crashed into a tree.

"Is that him?" Dugal whispered.

Paul released Fenella and pushed himself up against the rock. "That's him. We can't go back to the barn without his seeing us."

"We canna go back anyway. There are soldiers fair swarmin' about the barn. That's what I came to tell ye."

"Bloody hell."

Fenella, propped on her elbows, regarded Dugal closely. "Are they looking for me?"

"I think they're lookin' for Paul. I didna stay to find out. I slipped away and went lookin' for Paul myself. I was down i' the burn when ye hid behind the rocks."

Fenella turned to Paul. Paul could read the thoughts flickering behind her eyes. Soldiers must seem blessedly safe beside the threat of the fair-haired man. "We can't trust them," he said. "They were called in by the baillie. His son was the man who attacked you."

He held her gaze while she looked at him in silence. Another test, another moment when she could give him her trust or refuse it.

She inclined her head the barest fraction of an inch. "What do we do?"

"I could run down the burn and draw him off while ye get Fenella away," Dugal suggested.

Paul looked at the boy. He couldn't risk Dugal, but the plan had merit. He stripped off his coat and turned to Fenella. "Give me your cloak."

Her eyes widened, but she unfastened the cloak, eased herself free of its folds, and handed it to him. Paul put his coat around her shoulders. "Stay here, both of you. If I don't return in a half hour . . . Dugal, do you know another safe place you can take Fenella?"

"I ken lots o' places. But what about the man wi' the yellow hair?"

Paul fastened Fenella's cloak about his throat and raised the hood over his head. "I'll take care of him."

The mist seemed to have grown heavier as morning came on, but the descent into the gully was plain enough. Paul ran, the cloak clutched about him, not taking any particular care to be quiet. As he reached the gully he heard a triumphant shout of "Sophie." The fair-haired man had given chase.

Paul splashed through the icy stream water and scrambled up the opposite bank. He could hear voices and the baying of dogs from the direction of the barn. The mist was thick about the stand of oak near the gully, perhaps so thick the soldiers would miss him altogether. To be sure they didn't he ran through a patch of underbrush, which made a satisfying crackling sound.

"Over there," a voice shouted from near the barn. "I heard something."

Paul dodged through the trees. He could hear the sound of running feet. There were at least two men coming toward him. More footsteps sounded on the bank behind him. The fair-haired man.

Moving now with the quiet he had learned in long-ago days as an army scout, Paul pushed back the folds of the cloak, found a purchase on a sturdy trunk, and climbed away from the mist and the pursuit.

The heavy folds of the cloak hampered him, the bark was rough and coarse and crusted with lichen, and he could only grasp the branches properly with one hand. He levered himself into an *L* formed by the trunk and a wide branch. Below him the mist swirled in a gust of wind. The footsteps grew louder and converged. There were shouts, the sounds of struggle, and a sudden, triumphant cry.

"Got him!"

"What the devil do you think you're doing? Let me go."

"Oh, no, you don't. We've been looking all night—" The soldier broke off and drew in his breath. "Mr. Rutledge."

"So I've been trying to tell you." The fair-haired man's voice was outraged, but Paul caught an undertone of fear.

"Forgive me, sir," said the second of the two soldiers. "We were looking for the man you told us about, the man who killed Mr. McAlpin. We believe he spent the night in an abandoned barn just over that way. You wouldn't happen to have seen or heard anything, would you, sir?"

Paul drew in his breath, praying he had read Rutledge right.

"No." Rutledge spoke almost too quickly. "Nothing at all."

"I see. Pity." There was a pause. Paul could practically smell Rutledge's unease. "Must say I'm surprised to see you about at this hour, sir," the soldier continued. "Especially after the shock you had yesterday."

"I couldn't sleep. I wanted to find the bastard who killed Matt myself."

"You'd best not go about on your own. Only lead to confusion. Perhaps you'll come back with us and have a word with the captain. I'm sure he'll be glad of your help. After all, you're the only one who got a look at the man."

Another pause. Paul could feel Rutledge bowing to the weight of the inevitable. "Of course. Anything I can do to help."

Paul stayed motionless, legs drawn up on the branch, back pressed against the trunk, while the footsteps faded into the distance. There were shouts from the direction of the barn and then an indistinguishable murmur of conversation as the soldiers and Rutledge arrived.

Moving carefully to ease his cramped limbs, Paul unfastened the cloak, tucked it under his arm, and climbed down the tree. Then, with as much silence and speed as he could muster, he made his way back into the gully and up the hill to the spot where he had left Fenella and Dugal.

They were huddled together, backs against the shelter of the rock. Fenella had her arm around Dugal, pulling him within the protection of Paul's coat. They looked up in unison at Paul's approach, and it occurred to him that never before had he been greeted with such relief.

"Where's the yellow-haired man?" Dugal asked.

"Explaining matters to the soldiers." Paul looked at Fenella. "He's a friend of McAlpin's. His name is Rutledge."

Her eyes showed no recognition. Whatever the name meant to her was lost along with the rest of her memory. "His given name is Ned," she said. "At least that's what he told me." She frowned, as if attempting to sort through the impenetrable fog in her mind. "I can't—"

"Don't worry about it now," Paul said.

"Ye led him to the soldiers?" Dugal asked.

"It seemed a good way to rid ourselves of the lot of them. But it's only a temporary respite, and the soldiers have dogs. We need to put distance between us and them. Preferably water as well. We're in your hands again, Dugal."

Dugal scrambled to his feet. "Right, mate."

FENELLA CONCENTRATED ON PUTTING ONE FOOT IN FRONT of the other. It took all her energy. Her side felt as if the knife was still twisting in it. The weight of the child pulled on her back. Pain shot through her legs with each step. She kept walking because there was no alternative.

Dugal led them up the slope of the hill into higher ground, which was mist-shrouded and purpled with heather. Avoiding open land, they zigzagged from stands of oak or birch or pine to outcroppings of rock and clusters of heather or gorse. Sometimes the land dipped down, but then it rose again in a series of ever higher hills, an undulating mass of green and brown and gray. The mist seeped through her cloak. The air smelled of pine needles and peat and cold.

None of them spoke. Paul helped her over the bits of ground that were particularly rough, but she was quick to shake him off. She could do this herself. She had to. If she stopped trying she knew she would not survive.

As they crested a rise she was dimly aware of the sound of running water. A stream lay below, its water shallow and brown with peat. "Take your shoes off," Paul said. "We need to break our scent."

The current pushed against them. The water was cold and biting, the rocky streambed slick underfoot. Paul took her arm, but she pulled away from him. "I'll do better on my own," she said. "There's no sense in both of us falling if one of us stumbles."

"I'm not planning on falling."

She gritted her teeth and kilted her skirt and cloak up higher. "Neither am I."

She trudged on without looking at him. She had come this far, she could go a little farther. The baby kicked, reminding her of all the reasons she could not give in to weakness.

Progress seemed agonizingly slow. Despite the chill in the water and air, she grew warm with exertion. The hood of her cloak fell back. Sweat trickled down her face and matted her gown to her skin. The blood pounded in her head in time with her harsh breathing.

Just when she was sure they would never be free of the stream, Paul called a halt. "This should be enough to throw them off our scent." He moved toward the bank, then turned and extended his hand.

She shook her head.

"You'd rather drown in the attempt?" His eyes held a glint of mockery.

"No one drowns in a foot and a half of water." She studied the bank, looking for a way to make her ascent. It was smooth and treacherously steep. Paul was already perched on a mossy granite slab that jutted over the edge of the stream. There was no help for it. She reached for his hand.

Dugal scrambled up beside them. "Dod. Who'd've thought water could be that cold and no' turn to ice?"

"We can rest here for a bit," Paul said.

Fenella pulled her stockings out from the toes of her half boots where she'd stuffed them. "Shouldn't we keep moving? What if Rutledge sends the soldiers after us?"

"I don't think he will." Paul tugged on his boots. "He didn't admit he was looking for you. He must have told the soldiers about me, and probably about Dugal as well, but he doesn't seem to have mentioned you at all."

"Why didna he?" Dugal asked.

Fenella looked at Paul. "Because he wants to find me first."

Paul met her gaze. "Exactly. But it's bought us time. I don't think he'll look for you as long as he's with the soldiers."

She nodded and shifted her position on the hard rock. The throbbing of her wound seemed worse now that she was sitting down. She put her hand to her side.

"Is the pain bad?" Paul asked.

She folded her arms across her chest. "No worse than last night."

"Gammon. We haven't time for heroics. Let me look at the wound."

"No. There's nothing you can do and we shouldn't stop for long."

He regarded her for a moment. She looked back at him, refusing to give way. "Very well," he said at last.

It was the first time he had given in to her. Satisfaction coursed through her, easing the river's chill.

Paul did not seem to recognize the significance of the moment. He turned to Dugal. "Where are you taking us?"

Dugal pointed to the next hill on their right. "Yon. I have

a mate who tends sheep there. He lets me stay i' his hut sometimes."

"I thought you stayed in the barn." Fenella struggled to reach over her swollen belly and pull on her boots. Paul didn't offer to help.

"I stay different places," Dugal said. "Ye ha' to keep movin' about, see. That way—"

"You don't get caught," Paul said.

Dugal grinned. "Ye've got the right of it."

After the brief rest it was harder than ever to start moving again. She wouldn't have thought it possible that her body could ache more than it had to begin with, but it did. At least the ground was easier going than the water.

The silent journey continued until Dugal gestured across a flat expanse of green to a small stone building. "That's the hut. Hamish'll be beyond it wi' the sheep. I'll go ahead and be sure it's safe."

Dugal set off at a brisk trot. Two roe deer who had been grazing in the meadow bounded off at the movement. Fenella glanced at the sky. The mist had begun to clear and a fitful sun shone through the clouds. Judging by the height of the sun, they had been walking little more than two hours. She could not remember when two hours had seemed so long.

The meadow was blessedly tranquil after the craggy ground they had crossed. A bubbling trickle of water cut across the ground. Purple-pink clusters of bell heather and golden bog asphodel dotted the grass. Strange that she knew the names of the flowers when she had forgotten so much else.

Paul gestured to a clump of gorse. "It's not much protection, but it will give us a few minutes' warning if anyone comes this way."

She nodded, though it seemed torture to move even a few more feet. It took all her willpower to sit up properly in the shade of the gorse bush rather than collapse on the loamy ground.

"All right," Paul said. "Let me look at the wound."

She swallowed an instinctive retort, unfastened her cloak, and reached up for the buttons at the back of her gown. White-hot pain lanced through her at the pull on the wound. She drew a breath and struggled with the buttons, but her fingers would not cooperate.

"I can't manage." The admission hurt almost as much as the wound. She turned her back to him and bent her head, keenly aware that it was a vulnerable position, a position of submission, of surrender.

Paul undid the first of the buttons. "You'd best tell me now if you're planning to run away again as soon as we're all asleep." She jerked her head up. Paul undid another button. "The odds are against us as it is. I can't afford to waste time running after you."

His voice stripped her as bare as the fingers that were unbuttoning her gown. "You expect me to trust you so easily?" she asked.

"I expect you not to behave like a bloody fool."

The gown, half-unbuttoned, slipped down over her shoulders. Cold, damp air cut against her skin. "I would think you'd as soon be rid of me."

"So would I. It seems I've more of a conscience than I credited."

She swallowed. "I'm sorry. You've risked a great deal for me. I didn't mean to jeopardize you or Dugal."

He undid the last of the buttons. "I don't want gratitude. I want to be damned sure you don't do it again."

He seemed to feel no further need for speech. With cool, efficient hands he removed the bandage and cleansed the wound. "It's healing cleanly," he said in a neutral voice as he replaced the bandage.

She longed to say something that would break his composure, but she knew she had been at fault. A peace offering was required. "Is that how your hand was injured?" she asked. "A wound that didn't heal cleanly?"

His fingers stiffened against her skin. "A battlefield wound," he said after a moment. "The bones weren't set properly."

"You're a soldier?"

"I was once." He was doing up her buttons briskly. "It's years since I've been fit to manage a rifle."

"You said you were a traveler. Are you from England?"

He fastened the last button. "No, I'm a rabid French Republican who hated Napoleon for betraying the Revolution but thought any government was better than a return of the monarchy."

She turned to look at him. He was watching her, a mocking challenge in his eyes. Something flickered in the recesses of her mind. "That's odd."

"Not to anyone who can remember the Bourbons."

"I mean it's odd that I know who Napoleon is." She plucked a bright yellow flower from the gorse bush and twisted the prickly stem between her fingers. "I don't know who I am or what I'm doing here, but I know that Wellington defeated Napoleon at Waterloo and that George III is King of England and his son is the Prince Regent and Lord Liverpool is Prime Minister. I know we're in Scotland, and France is across the Channel. I've forgotten everything about myself, but not about the rest of the world. I don't understand it."

For a moment Paul's eyes warmed with something like sympathy. "Nor do I, but I've seen the same with men who receive head wounds in battle."

A sparrow hawk soared in the wide gray sky above them. A gust of wind ruffled the grass and tugged at her hair. She shifted her position, easing the weight of her belly. "What are you doing in Scotland?"

"The new Government don't take kindly to criticism. They shut down the newspaper I run and threatened to throw me in the Conciergerie. I decided the time was ripe to pay a visit to my aunt and cousin in Edinburgh." He cocked an eyebrow as though to ask if the name of the city meant anything to her.

"I know where Edinburgh is. If we're in the Highlands you must have ventured away from your relatives."

"I came to collect information for a story. My cousin is a journalist as well. He runs the *Edinburgh Leader*." Paul stretched his legs out in front of him and rested his weight on his elbows. "A lot of Highlanders are being driven from their homes when the lairds clear the land and enclose it. Some go to America, some starve, some make their way to the cities. Even Edinburgh. I decided to see for myself. And to write about what I saw. If I can't voice my outrage at what's happening in Paris, I can be outraged by what I find here."

The words struck an unexpected chord. She pushed her fingers through her hair. "For a moment I thought I remembered something. As if you were echoing words I'd heard before. But it's gone now."

He gave a dry smile. "If it's anything to do with Clearances, perhaps it's just as well. Judging by your dress and speech we're bound to be on opposite sides of the question."

Anger stiffened her back. How dare he presume to know more about her than she did about herself? She bit back a retort. "So you simply happened to stumble into—what did you call the town—Kinrie?"

His gaze shifted to a steel-gray bank of clouds on the horizon. "Not stumbled exactly. I went looking for Kinrie. I was born there."

Just as she was beginning to form a picture of him, he shattered it to bits with this new piece of information. "But—"

His look froze the words on her lips. His face had gone shuttered. She knew he would reveal no more. At least not for now.

"It seems we should be calling you Sophie," he said after a moment, quite as though they hadn't been speaking of something else.

The name held no more resonance now than when Rutledge had used it. "No. I'd as soon be Fenella. I've begun to grow accustomed to it." In fact, she realized, she had already begun to think of herself that way. She curled her arms over her unborn child, savoring the one bond she had in the world. Unless she counted Rutledge, who one way or another must play an important role in her life.

She shivered for reasons that had nothing to do with the biting air. The thought that Rutledge might be her husband was too horrible to contemplate. "You don't think Rutledge told the soldiers anything about me at all? Not even that I was there when you fought?"

"What could he say? A strange man attacked my friend and me because we were trying to murder a pregnant woman?"

She flinched.

"That's what they were trying to do." Paul's voice was as brutal as a knife blade.

She met his gaze. Whatever else she thought about him, she could no longer doubt that in this he spoke the truth. "I don't think I really believed the story until Rutledge came after me this morning." She stared at the mountains that reared up in the distance, sheer walls of earth and rock. They made her feel disgustingly small and fragile. "If Rutledge didn't tell the soldiers about me, how could he account for the fight?"

Paul shrugged. "A street brawl. An attempted robbery. He had to offer me up as the villain to explain why he was found unconscious beside his friend."

"But if the soldiers find you they find me as well. You said Rutledge wouldn't want that."

"He can't know for certain that we're together. After meeting you alone last night he probably thinks we aren't."

"Then our traveling together is a sort of disguise. Rutledge will be looking for a woman alone."

"And the soldiers will be looking for a man, possibly accompanied by a young boy but certainly not by a pregnant woman."

"So I'm not the only one in need of help." A small glimmer of satisfaction warmed her. "You find me useful as well."

"You could say that."

She smiled. It was absurd how much better his admission

made her feel. "I don't like being helpless. I'm not—I don't think I'm used to it."

"No, I don't imagine you are." His voice lightened. It was almost teasing.

For a moment she felt easier with him. She might have tried to ask him more about himself, but before she could speak she caught sight of Dugal running across the meadow toward them.

"It's all right," Dugal said, his breath coming hard. "Hamish hasna seen any soldiers and he hates the bloody Sassenach, so i' they're chasin' ye he's happy to help."

They followed Dugal across the meadow to a crumbling stone building, four crude walls with an open archway for a door. A tall, slender, red-haired boy a few years older than Dugal stood waiting outside, a silky black-and-white dog beside him. "Chasin' a woman with a bairn," he said in a deliberate voice, more heavily accented than Dugal's. "The Sassenach will stoop to anythin' just."

"Whisht," Dugal said. "Fenella's a Sassenach."

"It's all right." Fenella smiled at Hamish. "Dugal's given me a Scottish name, and I'd as soon be Scots as anything else."

Hamish's serious face broke into a grin. He led them into the hut, which was lit only by the doorway and a hole cut in the roof to let out the smoke. When he offered them food Fenella realized she couldn't remember when she had last eaten. Bannocks and sheep's milk cheese tasted far better than she would have imagined.

After they had eaten, Hamish gestured to a pile of sheepskins in the corner. "I ha' to get back to the flock, but ye can sleep here. Dugal says ye've been up all the night."

Paul got to his feet. "I'll keep watch. The soldiers will be patrolling the hills."

"Dinna be daft." Dugal was spreading the sheepskins on the dirt floor. "I' ye dinna get some rest ye'll no' be fit to fight when ye need to. I'll watch."

Fenella looked up at Paul. "He's right, you know. Even you must have limits."

She expected Paul to argue and was looking forward to arguing back. Instead, he gave a twisted grin. "I'm all too aware of my limits." He reached for a sheepskin. "Wake me in two hours, Dugal."

Fenella sank down on the skins Dugal had arranged for her. Aching soreness oozed out of her body. Her wound throbbed, and her muscles, no longer called upon to support her, had turned to jelly. The skins were coarse and matted and smelled of sheep and dirt, but she was warm and fed and for a few hours she wouldn't have to move. And Paul had at least admitted to weakness. It made her own weakness seem more bearable.

PAUL WATCHED FENELLA THROUGH HALF-CLOSED LIDS. She was lying on her side, her head pillowed on her hands. Her thick brown hair spilled over her shoulders. Shorter curls framed her forehead, clinging damply to her skin. He recognized the remnants of a fashionable crop. There was a faint furrow between her brows. She darkened her lashes, he realized. The blacking had left smudges beneath her eyes. He knew now that the eyes themselves held intelligence and humor. Her generous mouth had a mocking curve to it. For all its fine-boned delicacy there was a hint of firmness, even stubbornness, in her face.

The frightened woman of last night wasn't the real Fenella at all. Or the real Sophie. Thank God she'd chosen to be called Fenella. Sophie was a common enough name, in England as well as France, but he could never hear it without feeling hot shame and cold, gut-twisting guilt.

He rolled onto his back and stared through the smoke hole at a patch of cloudy sky. Even if they managed to throw the soldiers and Rutledge off their trail, it would only be a temporary respite. Fenella's child would come soon. He had to learn what threatened her so he would know where she would be safe. And so he could clear his own name.

He could think no further. He closed his eyes on the sight of Dugal sitting in the doorway and let sleep take him.

The next thing he knew someone was shaking him furiously by the shoulder. "Paul, wake up!"

Paul opened his eyes. The light was coming through the doorway at a different angle and Dugal was leaning over him, his face contorted with excitement and fear. "Soldiers," Dugal told him. "Hamish's been up i' the braes. He saw them. They be ridin' this way. Think o' somethin', man. We canna let them take Fenella."

Chapter 4

>‹

"BLOODY SCOTS." CORPORAL JOSIAH WILKINS REINED IN his horse and stared across the meadow at the small stone hut that looked exactly like the five other shepherd's huts he had searched since morning. "Why do there have to be so damned many huts in such godforsaken places?"

"If this were England we'd have to search tenant cottages, and there'd be a devilish lot more of them." Ensign Peters spoke with what Wilkins thought was annoying reasonableness. Wilkins wasn't feeling reasonable. He and Peters had spent the entire day combing the hills, searching every sign of habitation for a man who might be English or might be a foreigner, who had hair that might be blond or might be brown, who had a hand that might be injured—though no one was quite sure how—and who might or might not be accompanied by a street urchin of indeterminate age. For their pains they'd been treated with everything from rudeness to downright hostility by all the Scots they'd encountered.

The wind carried the damp, foul stench of the undulating mass of sheep clustered around the hut. Raised in Bristol, Wilkins had never been particularly fond of sheep. After today he doubted if he could ever stand the sight of wool, let alone mutton, again.

The two dogs—sturdy foxhounds that he and Peters had been assigned by Captain Cotter—caught the smell of the sheep and barked with excitement. As they raced forward, a thin boy with carroty hair ran out of the hut, waving his arms and shouting. Wilkins couldn't make out the words, what with the dogs barking and the sheep bleating and half of it being in Gaelic anyway.

Peters, who always got on better with the locals, answered the boy in soothing tones, called to the dogs, then turned to Wilkins. "He says the dogs are bothering the sheep."

The dogs sat on their haunches but continued to bark. A black-and-white dog crouched beside the red-haired boy and barked back. "Tell him we aren't interested in sheep," Wilkins said. "We're looking for one scurvy fellow with a bad hand, and if he's not here nothing would please us better than to be on our way."

Peters swung down from his horse and spoke quietly to the boy. All three dogs continued to bark, ears back, teeth bared. A thick mist was settling over the meadow. The chill cut through the coat of Wilkins's uniform.

Peters turned back to Wilkins. "The boy says he hasn't seen anyone all day. He says he wouldn't help an outlander anyway. He doesn't want us to let the dogs get any closer. The sheep are edgy and they might bolt if they're frightened."

Wilkins stared at the flock. At the other huts they'd searched, the sheep had been grazing farther afield. But the day was closing and the shepherd must have gathered them in to count. Close up, looming in the mist, the animals looked larger than Wilkins would have thought. There was something menacing about their black faces. The rams had nasty-looking horns.

Wilkins got down from his horse. His own dogs leaped up at him, their barking intensified. "Down," Wilkins shouted. He was rewarded by sharp teeth sinking into his fingers.

Wilkins kicked the dog. The dog snarled at him. The red-haired boy made a sound that might have been a stifled laugh. Wilkins glared at him, then turned to Peters. "I'll look in the hut. Keep the dogs out here. They haven't been any use today anyway. And tell the boy that we'll hold him personally responsible if the blasted sheep don't behave themselves."

The boy glanced at Wilkins through narrowed eyes, then

called an order to his dog. The dog, far more obedient than Captain Cotter's bloody search dogs, ran to the sheep and nudged them. The sheep drew back so that a path of sorts was created to the door of the hut. Avoiding the steaming piles of sheep manure, Wilkins picked his way over the muddy ground and stepped inside.

It looked like all the other huts they had searched that day. A fire pit, a pile of sheepskins for sleeping, an open box that held some bannocks and strong-smelling cheese, a stack of peats that smelled even stronger. Christ, these shepherds lived worse than soldiers.

Wilkins crossed the earthen floor and stirred the sheepskins with his foot. There were fewer than in the other huts he'd searched. No room for a child to hide, let alone a grown man. The skins stank nearly as much as the sheep themselves. Even with the smoke hole and open doorway, the air seemed close and fetid. Eager to be gone, Wilkins tramped out of the hut.

The shepherd boy scowled at him. The sheep were bleating and stirring in what Wilkins thought was a menacing manner. The dogs, predictably, were still barking.

"Nothing," Wilkins told Peters, swinging back up onto his horse. "Same as all the others. Let's try the next one. And try to keep those blasted dogs quiet."

"YE CAN GET UP. THEY'RE GONE."

Hamish's voice seemed to come from a great distance above. Fenella lifted her head, aware of the weight of the sheepskin slipping back against her shoulders. She brushed against something rough and woolly. There was a stir of movement beside her and a bleating sound directly in her ear.

Paul helped her to her feet. Beside them Dugal was scrambling up, still half-wrapped in a sheepskin. Sheep milled around them, calm now that the dogs and soldiers were gone, seemingly oblivious to the strangers in their midst. Hamish stood by the hut, grinning.

"The dogs knew we were here, didn't they?" Fenella said. "That's why they wouldn't stop barking."

Paul nodded. "We were lucky."

"The soldiers were daft," Hamish said.

Paul searched her face. "Are you all right?"

"Considering I'm with child, I don't know who I am, and I've been lying facedown in a flock of sheep?"

He gave a grin that wiped the bitterness from his face and made him look unexpectedly boyish. His hair was ruffled and standing on end. His coat and trousers were stained with mud and perhaps worse. She looked down to see her gown in a similar condition. Muck oozed around her shoes. The smell of the sheep must be clinging to their skin. Yet they were safe. They had outwitted the soldiers. She looked back at Paul, and in the same moment they both burst into laughter.

Inside the hut Hamish and Paul got a fire going. Tired of feeling useless, Fenella helped Dugal lay out bannocks and cheese. The warmth of the fire was comforting, as were the food and the reprieve from danger, but she knew the comfort was only temporary. She looked across the fire at Paul, wondering why he put himself at risk again and again for her sake and how long he would continue to do so. She remembered nothing of her former life, but she knew she did not believe in heroes.

She had trusted Paul today because she had no choice. He had scalded her with his tongue, laughed with her, and saved her life. But she knew nothing about him, save what he chose to tell her.

The firelight lent a golden glow to his hair and his day's growth of beard, but it also lit the angles of his face, emphasizing its harshness. The man she had glimpsed briefly when they stood laughing amidst the sheep was gone. He had removed his coat and unbuttoned his waistcoat. The thin muslin of his shirt revealed the muscled strength of his arms and chest. He might have a crippled hand, but he was a powerful man. Far more powerful than she.

Paul met her gaze. A frisson went through her. His eyes

seemed to lay bare her thoughts. She drew her cloak more closely about her. She needed to ward off his probing, to keep some part of herself private. She must learn the secrets of her past before he discovered them himself. Else she would be wholly at his mercy. "What do we do next?" she asked, half hoping he wouldn't have a ready answer.

"Head for Edinburgh," he said at once. "My aunt and cousin will give us shelter, and in the city the baillie will have less influence. We'll stand a better chance of learning where you come from and why Rutledge wants you dead. And you need to be near a doctor when you—"

"Have the baby," she finished for him.

"Yes."

Dugal swallowed a large mouthful of cheese. "Fenella canna walk all the way to Edinburgh."

"No," Paul agreed. "We need a horse and cart and food and fresh clothes. Hamish, I have money. Can you—"

"Ye dinna need to buy them." Dugal wiped crumbs of cheese from his mouth. "I can prig anythin' we need."

"I'm sure you can, but we're being sought for enough crimes as it is."

"There's a croft or twa no' far from here," Hamish said. "If ye watch the sheep I'll go at first light."

"A bargain." Paul looked at Fenella. "That is, if you agree to the plan."

He had at least asked, but she still felt trapped. There was no getting around the fact that she needed him. With sudden, passionate certainty she knew that she hated to need anyone. "I don't have a choice, do I?"

"There's always a choice."

"Thank you, but I prefer to live." Then, because it seemed churlish not to put it into words, she added, "I'll go with you to Edinburgh."

"There." Paul's voice was brisk as he undid the last of the buttons on her gown. "Can you manage the rest?"

Fenella turned round, clutching her gown to her shoulders, and nodded. She *would* manage, one way or another.

Paul moved to the doorway. "Be sure to take your jewelry off. It would rouse suspicion."

When he had left the hut Fenella stepped out of her gown and pulled the remnants of her chemise over her head, wincing at the strain on her wound. The new clothes Hamish had brought for her were laid out on the sheepskins. She eased the fresh chemise over her head. It was coarse, unadorned linen, but it was clean and not torn. The gown was of sturdy, dark-green wool, cut loose like a smock to accommodate the bulk of the child. There were only two buttons at the neck and she managed to do them up herself. She felt an exaggerated pleasure at this small victory.

She removed her pearl earrings and used her lapis lazuli brooch to pin them inside the bodice of her gown. There was nothing she could do about her hair. She ran her fingers through it, trying to unravel the tangled knots. It was hopeless. With a cry of frustration she knelt and ripped a strip of fabric from her torn chemise and used it to bind the unruly mass into some semblance of order. Then she put her cloak round her shoulders, picked up her discarded garments, got heavily to her feet, and stepped out of the doorway.

The rough wooden wagon and rugged pony Hamish had brought stood in front of the hut. Hamish and Dugal were perched on the back of the wagon, dangling their legs over the edge. They were staring with fascination at Paul, who was kneeling on the ground, smearing his hair with a dark substance from a small pot.

"Ye missed a bit at the back," Dugal told him.

Paul smeared more of the substance on the back of his head and rubbed some over the stubble on his face. "Shoeblacking." He looked up at Fenella with a grin. "Sticky, but it makes for a crude disguise."

Indeed, with his hair darkened and slicked back from his face, Paul looked startlingly different: his face longer, his eyes darker, his features more angular. It was disconcerting. The man could change his appearance as readily as he could his demeanor.

Dugal sprang down from the wagon. "Ye look different too, Fenella. Yer hair's bonny like that."

Fenella laughed at the absurdity of his compliment, but she felt cheered.

"There be bannocks and cheese and apples i' the cart," Hamish said, coming to join them. "And blankets."

Paul wiped his hands on the grass and got to his feet. Like Dugal, he was dressed in wool breeches and a loose linen shirt. "You've done well, Hamish." He offered some coins to the boy.

Hamish shook his head. "Ye did give me enough already."

"Don't be a fool. We've used up half your supply of peat and more than half your food." Paul pressed the coins into Hamish's hand, then extended his hand again in man-to-man fashion.

A smile broke across Hamish's face. Then, very solemnly, he shook Paul's hand.

Within a matter of minutes they were off. Fenella was settled in the back of the cart with straw and sheepskins to lie on and blankets heaped over her. "You're my wife and you're ill and we're taking you home," Paul told her, arranging the blankets so they disguised the swell of her belly and half hid her face. "We know only a few words of English. If we're stopped lie still and don't speak."

There it was again, the quiet note of command, the inflexible voice of one in charge. Fenella pulled the scratchy wool away from her face. "If we're stopped your voice will give us away as much as mine."

"So it will if we're stopped by Highlanders. But I may be able to fool the soldiers. Dugal's been teaching me Gaelic."

The man was impossible. "Do you mean to tell me that in twenty-four hours you've learned enough—"

"Enough to suffice." He tucked the last blanket into place.

"My mother came from Brittany and I know a smattering of Breton. Gaelic's not so different."

"Is there anything," Fenella demanded, "that you can't do?"

Paul was silent for a moment. "Anything that requires the use of my right hand."

The boards creaked as Paul and Dugal climbed onto the front of the cart. Fenella pushed herself up to wave good-bye to Hamish and his dog, then settled back into the sheepskins and straw and drew the blankets over her. The baby kicked, as though protesting the movement of the cart. "Shush," Fenella murmured, wrapping her arms over her belly. "It's beastly to be so helpless, but we have to go where we're taken."

After that, coherent thought gave way to the feel of damp wind cutting through her blankets, the sound of rocks crunching beneath the wheels, the smell of pine needles and mist-dampened wool. Then suddenly they were no longer moving. She opened her eyes to see a midday sun attacking the mist and Paul bending over her. "Dugal and I agreed we were hungry," he said. "We thought you probably were too."

They had drawn the cart to the side of the road behind a stand of pines, but through the curtain of branches she could see that the road itself was surprisingly broad. As they sat on a carpet of damp pine needles, eating some of the food Hamish had provided, she heard the rumble of carriage wheels. She tensed, gripping a hunk of bannock so tightly that it crumbled in her fingers. A carriage drove by, its roof piled high with luggage, a many-caped coachman on the box.

When the sound of wheels and voices and hooves had faded into the distance, she looked at Paul. "This is a main road."

Paul cut some more cheese. "One of the main roads. At least as close to it as they have in these parts. There's no other way to reach Edinburgh."

She threw the crumbs of bannock onto the ground. "You aren't even trying to avoid the soldiers, are you? You expect to meet them."

Paul set down the knife. "There's a good chance we will."

"Dinna fash yerself, Fenella," Dugal said. "Paul and I be ready for them. We've been practicin' all the morning."

"If we can get past them we'll be safer," Paul said. "They'll still be looking in the area around Kinrie."

It made a sort of twisted sense. But the thought of the soldiers brought the thought of Ned Rutledge, and at the thought of Rutledge her insides threatened to disgorge the meal she'd just consumed. She swallowed hard and bit down on her lip, determined to maintain control over her body if nothing else.

Paul broke a bannock in half and added the piece of cheese to it. "If you're going to faint, wait until we're back in the cart. I'm not sure I'm up to carrying you again."

Fenella glared at him.

They set off again, but this time she lay wide awake, staring at clouds and branches and an occasional kestrel or merlin, her quickened heartbeat echoing in her ears. Dugal was reciting Gaelic phrases, which Paul repeated in tones that she was forced to admit sounded highly convincing.

"Dod," Dugal said. "Ye've fair got a knack for it. Ye sure ye dinna be part Scots, man?"

Paul gave a dry laugh. "I suppose you could say Scotland's in my blood."

"Hold there! Draw up!"

The voice was loud, authoritative, and unmistakably English. The soldiers. Fenella's arms tightened over the child.

Paul brought the cart to a halt. She heard the thud of hooves as the soldiers approached. "You. What's your business?" a brusque voice demanded.

An agitated stream of Gaelic—or Breton—followed. Fenella barely recognized the voice as Paul's.

"Speak English, man, we don't know your heathen tongue."

"We be takin' my wife home. Ill she be." Paul's voice had taken on Dugal's lilting tones.

"Mam has the fever," Dugal said. "Da willna let me near her. He says it may be—"

"Hold yer whisht, lad." Paul's voice sounded sharp with fear.

One of the soldiers drew in his breath. Fenella heard the horses stir. The riders must have pulled back a little. She held herself immobile. Straw cut into her cheek and sheepskin tickled her eyelid.

"He's got a boy with him," one of the soldiers said in a lowered voice.

"Don't be a fool. They're peasants. Rutledge said the man was dressed like a gentleman. And that he wasn't Scots."

"All the same," said a third voice, rougher, deeper. "We've a man and a boy of the right age. And there's something odd about the man's right hand."

"Oh, Christ." A fourth man spoke, a wary edge to his voice. "Our man wouldn't have a woman with him, let alone a sick woman."

"We don't know that she is sick. Or that there is a woman for that matter," said the rough voice. "Did anyone look inside the cart?"

"You do it if you're so keen," the wary voice said. "I'm not risking some fever from God knows where."

There was a murmur of agreement from the others. Fragments of prayers she had not realized she knew raced through Fenella's head.

"Damnation, are you soldiers or mice?" Rough Voice demanded. "You can tell the captain you were too lily-livered to look properly if you want. I have other ideas."

Fenella felt her muscles clench deep inside her. The baby shifted and kicked. Mary, Mother of God, please . . .

"Dinna frighten her." Paul reached back and put his hand on Fenella's shoulder. His touch was firm and strangely reassuring. "Sit up, *mo chridhe*. Let the Sassenach have a look at ye."

She grasped the side of the cart and pulled herself up. The sight of her should disarm the soldier's suspicions. But if he asked her questions, her bloody voice would give her away.

They'd likely find themselves hauled before the captain. And Rutledge would be with the captain.

Rough Voice drew his horse up to the cart. He had a beefy, pock-marked face and unruly dark hair. "Well, woman. Your husband says you're ill."

"My mam doesna speak English," Dugal said.

That was clever, save that she didn't speak Gaelic either. Perhaps she could try to stand, then collapse in a faint. That should convince them of her illness.

She struggled to her feet. Warm fluid spilled between her legs and spattered onto the straw and blankets. Dear God, she hadn't thought she would disgrace herself so thoroughly.

The soldiers gasped.

Paul leaped into the back of the cart and caught her about the waist.

"Bloody hell." Rough Voice drew his horse away. "It's her time."

Her legs damp and trembling, Fenella realized at last that she had not lost control of her bladder. It was far worse. Holy Mother protect her. Her water had broken.

Chapter 5

➤←

PAUL PULLED HER BACK AGAINST THE CART RAIL. FENELLA gripped her belly to drive home to the soldiers that she was in no condition to be interrogated. She felt at once chilled and flushed with heat. So much the better. Dugal had told the soldiers she had the fever.

The straw and blanket were dark where she had stood, fingers of damp seeping out beyond the wet circle. She was dimly aware of the voices of the soldiers, murmuring to each other in consternation and dismay. She had an absurd impulse to laugh. These rough men would have no desire to play midwife. They would have to let them go.

Her legs buckled. She clutched Paul's arm and let out a moan that was not wholly voluntary. *"Mo chridhe,"* she gasped in what she considered a fair imitation of his accent as she slid slowly to the straw at his feet.

Paul bent over her, chafed her hands, felt her forehead, then shook out the blanket and wrapped it round her. "Her hands be cold," he said, standing up and addressing Dugal, "but the fever be on her. And her time be soon." He turned to the soldiers. "She mun be home." His voice shook with emotion. "Now. I' God's name, give us leave to pass."

She could not see the soldiers' faces, but she heard the stamping of their horses and the jangle of spurs as though their mounts were being readied to move. Rough Voice rode forward and peered into the cart, suspicion and distaste warring on his face. She moaned again, this time without trying.

Rough Voice flinched. His face lightened with sudden decision. He made an abrupt gesture. "Move on. If you meet other parties of soldiers on the road, say that Sergeant Selden let you pass." He wheeled his horse, and the others fell in behind him.

Fenella tried to draw a deep breath to calm herself, but found she could not. Her mouth was dry, her chest tight with a fear she had not been able to feel while the soldiers were present. She watched Paul, his hands gripping the cart rail, his shoulders hunched and rigid with tension. Dugal stood on the seat of the cart, his face a mask of hatred and unease.

The sound of hoofbeats faded gradually till they could hear no more. The silence that followed was broken by a raucous cawing. Two crows were in flight above them, their sleek bodies etched sharply black against the gray sky. There was a sudden gust of wind and a spattering of raindrops fell on her face.

"Dod." Dugal's voice was expelled on a long sigh. "Fenella, be ye all right?"

She reached for the rail and pulled herself into a sitting position. She smiled at Dugal and took a deep breath, the tension in her chest miraculously gone. "Wet and miserable. It doesn't matter. The soldiers are gone." She stuck out her tongue to catch a raindrop. "And I'll soon be wet all over."

"Fenella." Paul was kneeling at her side, his eyes appraising. "Is this your first?"

Her moment of happiness was shattered. Without thought her hands sought her belly, that solid pulsing mound that was her future now and for years to come. She stared at the man who was at once her protector and tormentor. "I don't know," she said at last. It was a shameful admission. Surely she would remember if she had children. "I think so," she added, striving for a note of certainty. It was no use. She could not penetrate the gray nothingness in which she had lived for the past two days.

"What do you know about birthing?"

Anger stiffened her back. "What do you know?" She refused to accept that Paul knew more than she did about babies as well.

"I've seen births. Have you? Do you know what happens? Do you know what to expect?"

"My water broke. I know that. There'll be pain. I know that too. What is it to you?"

"I'll need to help."

"No." She clasped her hands more tightly around her belly, enfolding her child in an embrace that marked a boundary he would not dare cross. "This is my child. The seed was planted in me. I nourished it. I'll bring it into the world."

Paul sat back on his heels. She might as well not have spoken. He was ignoring her challenge. "We'll stay on the Edinburgh road," he said, "but as soon as possible we'll head east into the hills. I don't want to chance another party of soldiers, and you'll need shelter when the time comes."

"Dugal will make another miracle?"

He smiled, and some of her resentment washed away. "If he can. I'm hoping for an abandoned cottage. The Clearances are driving people from the Highlands."

"If I must I'll have the baby in the cart."

"It won't come to that."

The reassurance in his voice was meaningless. He could not know what lay a mile or an hour ahead. She shifted her position to ease the pain in her back and pulled the blanket over her head.

"Have the pains started?" he asked.

"No," she said, not sure whether or not it was true. The pain in her back had spread to the base of her belly, but she would not admit that her body was spiraling beyond her control.

"You must tell me when they do," he said, getting to his feet. "And how often they come. That way I'll know how much time we have before we need to stop. It may be several hours yet."

The confidence in his voice grated on her strained nerves. How can he know, she thought, appalled at the same time by her own ignorance. Had she never been told, or had this knowledge, too, vanished with the memory of her past life?

She watched Paul climb onto the seat beside Dugal and take up the reins. "Gee-hup!" he said, cracking the small pine bough he used for a whip. The cart lurched into motion. She grasped the rail to keep her balance and gave herself up to the rough movements of the cart and the sound of the rain.

The full force of what was about to happen washed over her. Dear God in heaven, she was actually going to have a baby. The mound in her belly would become a person in its own right, to be held and fed and cared for.

Her back ached and her dress clung damply to her legs, and she bore a name that was hers only by Dugal's intervention and the temporary grace of God. But somewhere beyond the confines of the cart was a man who had planted his seed in her body, a man who called her wife and perhaps longed for the child to which she would soon give birth. A man who would know her name, who would return her life to her for good or ill, to make of it what she must.

She stared at the backs of the man and boy sitting on the seat of the cart, swaying with its rough movements. They were strangers, but they had proven themselves safe. As Fenella she, too, was safe. For the moment. But as Sophie—was that truly her name? God help her, her husband, the man who fathered her child, might be a mortal danger. He might even be Rutledge.

She bit her lip to keep from crying out. A sudden cramp of pain brought her back to the present, scattering her morbid musings to the rain and the wind. So that's what it's like, she told herself as the pain receded. That wasn't too bad. I can manage.

When the second cramp came sometime later, it took her by surprise, sweeping away her certainty. How much worse would the pain grow before the baby came? Despite her brave words and braver thoughts she was chilled with terror at what lay ahead.

The swaying of the cart lulled her into uneasy slumber. She dozed, woke to pain, then dozed again. Her dreams eluded her. They held an answer, just out of reach, tantalizing and unattainable, but in her confused state between sleep and waking she was no longer sure of the question. Then the dreams dispersed, banished by the pain in her back and the waves of cramping in her belly.

FOR THE DOZENTH TIME DUGAL GLANCED BACK AT Fenella, then as swiftly looked away again. Paul half expected the boy to cross himself. There was a look of superstitious dread on his face, warring with an avid curiosity.

"Have you seen a birthing?" Paul asked.

"Oh, aye." He glanced at Fenella again. "Nay, no' this close I havena. I dinna ken much about women's business." He shuddered. "A bloody mess it be."

"Life's a bloody mess. I'd have thought you'd have learned that by now. Don't worry about Fenella. She'll manage."

"But will we? What will we do? Ha' ye ever birthed a bairn?"

Paul thought of the wives and other women who had followed the army in his days of soldiering. He had seen births and on occasion had offered his services, marveling at the resilience of womankind. "I'm no midwife," he said after a moment, "but I've a glimmering of what must be done."

A squall of rain burst above them, sending Dugal deeper into the shelter of the blanket he shared with Paul. "Ye'll need more than a glimmer, mate. Mayhap it's her first time."

Paul looked back at Fenella, wondering how much she knew and how much she feared. Her face told him nothing. Her eyes were closed, and she seemed in the grip of an uneasy slumber. A gentle moan escaped her parted lips.

"We need a midwife, that's for certain." Dugal made this assertion at intervals throughout the afternoon. It was a luxury they could not afford. Paul might have passed as a Scotsman for a few brief moments with the English soldiers, but neither he nor Fenella could move among the Scots for long without arousing curiosity.

They had long since left the Edinburgh road and moved into

the hills, taking a less traveled road that wound through a narrow glen. They followed a stream, its waters tumbling over mossy rocks. Paul was encouraged. Where there was water there would be habitation.

They found it two hours later, a cluster of mean stone huts thatched with sod and bracken. A goat was tethered before one of the huts. A half dozen children, barefoot and half-naked, played in the mud, heedless of the rain that was still falling. A gaunt-faced woman came to the door, an infant straddling her hip. Her belly was swollen with hunger or with child. Paul raised his left hand in greeting, careful to keep his right hand out of sight. The woman stared at him with vacant eyes, then retreated into the recesses of the hut.

"Stop here a wee bit," Dugal said. "I'll see what I can find out."

He slipped from the cart and made for the hut, stopping to pick up a howling boy who had been pushed by one of the others. The woman appeared once more, smacked the boy across the face, and sent him back to the other children. Dugal stood his ground, pouring forth a rapid stream of Gaelic. The woman listened reluctantly, then with grudging response, and at last with an animation that nearly matched Dugal's own.

"Drive on, mate," Dugal said when he returned to the cart. "We dinna want to bide here." He looked back as they left the village behind them, then drew the blanket over his head and huddled close to Paul. "They hold a bit o' land from the laird who lives beyond that hill." He pointed to a narrow track that led off to the right. "But the laird has brought in a fine breed o' sheep, and he's put up fences and the tenants ha' lost the common pasture, and they've lost the shielings. Half the folk ha' gone. The laird's men burned their houses to make sure they'd go and no' come back."

"Any sign of the soldiers?"

"She hasna seen them. Their cow died, she told me, and there's naught to eat but a few potatoes. Dod, life was better in Kinrie."

It was not a promising beginning to their search for shelter. Paul tightened his hands on the reins, conscious of the waning afternoon. They would have to stop before dark, and he was no longer confident that shelter was to be found. At this moment he would have settled for the crude comfort of Hamish's hut.

The rain had stopped. He glanced at Fenella. She was no longer sleeping, but her eyes were closed and her face contorted. She made no sound at all.

He gave the reins to Dugal and climbed into the back of the cart. He crouched by Fenella, waiting for the pain to cease. A moment later she expelled her breath in a harsh sigh and opened her eyes.

"How long have the pains been going on?" he asked.

She turned her head away as though she could not bear to look at him. "I don't know," she said in a deadened voice.

"You should have told me. You're a stubborn woman, Sophie."

Her head swung round and there was a welcome fire in her eyes. "Don't call me that."

"And just as stubborn as Fenella. For the next few hours our lives are bound with yours. You can't escape us, and we can't escape you. Tell me what's happening."

She had the grace to look abashed, as she had when he chastised her for running away. "They started not long after we left the soldiers. I don't know how often they come. More frequently now than at first. My back hurts and I'm thirsty and I need to relieve myself."

Paul signaled Dugal to stop, then helped Fenella down from the cart, a difficult process because of the ungainly weight she carried. "There'll be water when you return," he said. He watched her slow progress till she disappeared behind some bushes, then took the cup Hamish had provided and climbed down to the stream. The water was cold and blessedly clear. He cupped his hands and drank, filled the cup, and returned to the cart. A few moments later Fenella returned. She drank greedily and asked for more. When he brought the cup again she murmured a rare "Thank you." Paul understood there was now a truce of sorts between them.

"Where are we?" she asked, looking around the green and empty glen.

"God knows." The rocky hills rose steeply on either side, and there was no sign of man nor beast. Even the wind had died. It was beautiful country, but harsh and dangerous, even to those who had no cause to run from pursuit. "We passed a village a while back," Paul said as he helped her back into the cart.

"I know. Dugal said it was no place for us."

Paul was tempted to offer reassurance once more, but Fenella's face told him that only honesty would serve between them. "I'll try to do better, but I make no promises. Try to relax when the pains come. Cry out if you must. Then I'll know what's happening."

He untethered the pony, who had used the interval for grazing, and called to Dugal, who was exploring the stream. "The pains have started," he told the boy.

"How soon will the bairn come?"

"I don't know. But we'll have to stop before nightfall."

They drove on. The clouds, once more sopping wet, let down their accumulated burden of rain. Fenella, huddled beneath her blanket, uttered occasional groans, but Paul judged that their timing did not indicate an imminent delivery.

As they neared a sharp bend in the road, they heard the welcome sound of voices. Paul urged the pony to greater effort, then pulled up short. A cart, not unlike their own, lay on its side in a ditch, its burden of babes and a meager array of household goods spread over the verge of the road. A woman had gone to the assistance of the frightened children. A goat, escaped from its tether, stood in the grassland beyond. A short, burly man was striving to right the cart, while a young boy struggled to untangle the fallen pony.

"They'll need help. Speak for me, Dugal." Paul jumped from the cart and ran ahead. He gave the man a curt nod, then put his shoulder to the cart and his hands to the wheel. They lifted and shoved till they were streaming sweat and the cart was once more at the edge of the roadbed, though the wheels were mired in the mud.

The boy had got the pony to its feet. It seemed unhurt. Paul helped the burly man harness it to the rescued cart. With Dugal tugging at the reins and everyone else over the age of five save Fenella pushing from the rear and shouting encouragement all the while, the cart was finally brought to the relatively unchurned center of the roadbed.

Paul wiped his face with his sleeve. The burly man did the same, then held out his hand and spoke a few words of Gaelic. Paul hesitated, but he could not bring himself to ignore the offer of friendship. He held out his hand and the other man grasped it, showing neither surprise nor disgust. Dugal, scenting danger too late, ran up and replied to the man in his own tongue.

"So ye be strangers." The man cast a wary look at Paul. "I ken a bit o' the English. My name's Doon, and thanks it is I offer ye."

"Lester," Paul said, appropriating an English name similar to Lescaut. "I should tell you that I'm a hunted man. There are bands of soldiers looking for me, and they will know me by this." He held out his right hand. "I've done nothing of which I'm ashamed." He waited, praying his gamble would pay off.

Doon's face broke into a slow smile. "I ha' no use for soldiers. They will hear naught from me. 'Tis the least I owe ye."

"Then let me ask you for help. My wife is with child and her time is near. We need shelter this night." Paul led Doon to their cart, but it was empty. His breath caught in a moment of panic. Then he saw Fenella helping Doon's wife and children gather up their few possessions. Fenella was holding a small pane of glass, miraculously unbroken, set in a crude wooden frame. She laid it carefully in the Doons' cart, caught the side of the cart, and bent over, uttering a low groan.

Doon's wife, a thin, faded woman who might once have

been pretty, rubbed Fenella's back and spoke softly to her in Gaelic. When the pain had passed she led Fenella back to Paul's cart and helped her settle in it.

Doon watched the two women. "I was tenant to Sir James up yonder. He be bringin' i' the sheep. Improvin' his land, he says. Always has some daft notion."

"He burned you out?"

"Nay, he's no' so bad as some lairds. He says he wants us to stay. Claims his improvements will make a better life for our grandchildren. He doesna understand we canna afford to wait. We canna graze our animals and I canna feed my bairns. There be many gone already. There'll be huts aplenty standin' empty, but the roof timbers ha' been taken i' most and there's naught to keep out the rain."

He turned to his wife, who was piling children into the cart, and spoke in Gaelic. She nodded and went to retrieve the goat. "Ye can use our hut, though there be naught in it save the dirt we stand on. It's a distance from the big house and no one is likely to come that way. Or ye can use the hut where my wife's granny lived. We buried her yesterday and the bed still stands, i' ye no' be afeared to use it. She died o' grief and the passin' o' the years, no' the pestilence."

Doon crouched down, picked up a stick, and drew a crude diagram in the muddy road. "This be where ye turn, beyond the blighted pine." He continued with his directions, scratching lines as he talked. It was, Paul gathered, a matter of five or six miles off the road they now traveled. Sir James's house, and those of the families who still remained his tenants, lay well beyond.

Paul thanked Doon fervently and put out his hand. "Where are you going?"

Doon again took his hand without hesitation. "Glasgow. They say there be work i' the factories. We'd best be on our way." He picked up the pony's reins. "I wish ye well, Lester, ye and yer woman." He tugged at the reins and the cart lumbered into motion. Dugal called out a few words of Gaelic. Paul raised his arm in farewell.

"We have shelter," he told Fenella and Dugal when the Doons were out of sight. "A roof and perhaps a bed." He glanced at the sky and saw that it was darkening. "It should take us about two hours. Can you manage?" This last query was for Fenella, who was sitting in a corner of the cart, legs splayed, hands gripping the sides of the cart with such force that her skin was stretched near translucent across her knuckles.

She nodded, unable to spare the breath for speech.

"Dugal, stay with her. Her back hurts, low down. About here." Paul placed his open hand on Dugal to demonstrate. "Rubbing it may help, but when the pain comes on her, hold her firm. She can tell you if you're doing it right."

Dugal climbed into the back of the cart and sidled close to Fenella. Paul took the seat and picked up the reins. The pony, refreshed from the long rest and sated with grazing, took off with no further command. Paul peered into the gathering gloom, searching for the first landmark: the blighted pine.

The road became little more than a track with room only for a single cart. The rain was falling so softly that it might be disregarded, but a thick mist rose from the ground, obscuring vision. Paul could not say how many minutes or hours had passed since they had left the Doons.

He took mental note of their scant store of supplies. They had food for a few more days if they were frugal. Hamish had provided a crude lamp made of pierced tin holding a candle of molded animal fat. He had also brought them a pile of worn but clean linen to use as bandages. In his anxiety over the impending birth Paul had forgotten Fenella's injury. There had been no time to dress it since they left Hamish's hut. He wondered what the strain of her labor was doing to the wound. It might be bleeding afresh, one more complication in a task he feared might be beyond his meager skills. He could not bring himself to pray for guidance, but he hoped for a bit of sanity.

The handful of huts loomed round a bend in the road. Doon

had told him these lay at the farthest reaches of Sir James's property, most of the tenants farming rigs closer to the common ground, now enclosed and barred from their use. Paul pulled up the pony, jumped down from the cart, and asked Dugal to take the reins.

Fenella pulled herself to her knees and rested her arms on the side of the cart, her face wan but free of pain. "It has no roof," she said, staring at the nearest hut.

"It had one," Paul said, pointing to untidy piles of sod and dry bracken lying at the base of the small stone building. He looked up, searching for the beams that would have supported the roof. There was no sign of burning. There was nothing at all.

"The Doons took their window," Fenella said.

"And someone took the roof timbers. They'd be too valuable to leave. Wait here. I'll find Doon's hut."

Paul strode through the muck surrounding the pitiful collection of buildings. They were cut of the same pattern: rectangles of crudely dressed stone, perhaps twelve by fourteen feet. He pushed open the door of the nearest one, stooped to enter, and was met by an overpowering stench of urine. The animals must have bedded down with the hut's human occupants.

The single room had dirt for a floor and now the sky for a roof. There was no sign of a chimney, but a charred pile near one end suggested that a fire had been laid on the ground and the smoke allowed to escape through a hole in the roof. If there had been a grate, it would have been carried off with the roof timbers. There was no furniture, not a shelf, not a peg. How many men, women, and children had shared this bleak comfort? How many animals had been given shelter? Paul noted chicken dung in the dirt around him and was sure he caught the rancid smell of goats.

He backed out quickly, forgetting to stoop. He was rewarded by a sharp crack on the back of his head. He passed quickly by three more roofless huts, stopping only to open their doors and make sure that they were indeed empty. At the end of the row but one he found the Doons', its sod roof still intact. He swung open the door and peered inside. It was as bare as the others, but the stench was less pervasive, a tribute to the struggles of Doon's pale but resolute wife.

The last hut in the row would have belonged to the wife's granny. It, too, was roofed. Paul hoped against hope that Doon was right about the bed. It could easily have been taken in the interval since the Doons left home.

The bed was intact. It stood in solitary splendor in the center of the empty room, a box enclosed on four sides with access through folding doors in the front. Paul pushed these open. There was no bedding, but he had expected none. The bed frame consisted of rough slats of wood, which would have been covered, he expected, with straw. There was not much chance of clean straw in this deserted cluster of huts. No matter. They had blankets.

He closed the doors of the box bed and looked around. There was a hole in the roof above the fire pit. A broken grate stood on the pit, not considered worth the taking. The room was as clean as Doon's wife could make it. It would do. Thanks be to whatever gods there were, it would do very well.

He left Granny's hut and walked back to the cart. Dugal and Fenella watched him, their faces tight with anxiety. Paul raised his arms in a gesture of victory. "There be a place for us then," Dugal said when Paul reached them.

"A place indeed. A shelter, a refuge from the unforgiving rain, and wonder of wonders, a bed. Let's go."

Chapter 6

➤◆

THE FIRST THING FENELLA NOTED WHEN SHE ENTERED THE hut was that it was dry. Or as dry as could be expected in this land of constant rain. The second thing she saw was the bed. It was a huge boxlike structure with no visible means of entry. She was sure she had seen nothing like it before.

Dugal ran to the bed and flung open the folding doors. "Here it be," he said, as proud as if he had conjured it out of whole cloth. Fenella walked toward him, reluctant to confront this evidence of her further torment. The bed was covered with rough slats, a wisp of straw caught between two of them. She pulled it out. They would have used straw for a mattress, a luxury that would be denied her.

Dugal took it from her. "Dinna fash yerself. They wouldna leave old straw around because o' the rats."

The conjunction of rats with the pains that were tearing her apart struck her as funny. She gave a shout of laughter, a long, full-throated peal that turned into a gasping sound as pain tore through her.

"Fenella?" Dugal said.

Paul was beside her, his hand supporting her back. "It's all right," he said. "What can we do but laugh?"

She looked him full in the face and knew that he spoke of more than the baby struggling to be born. There were soldiers on their trail, a man who wanted to kill her, the inconvenient fog of her memory. The last few hours she had thought of none of these. Nor will I, she told herself, till this is over.

Paul pulled up the skirt of her dark green smock, checked

her wound, and replaced the bandage. "It hasn't begun to bleed again," he said. "Thanks for small mercies."

She nodded, unable to speak. The cramping grew worse, like a fist squeezing her. She doubled over. "You'll be better moving," Paul said. "Dugal, walk with her, as much as she's able. Keep your hand here, so."

They made several circuits of the small room, stopping when she felt she could move no more. She leaned against the wall, her fingers digging into the crumbling stone while the wind whistling through the cracks chilled her overheated body. Dugal talked to her all the while in a soft voice, lapsing sometimes into Gaelic. She asked him to speak to her in his language, for there was a soothing music in the harsh tongue.

Paul had lit the lantern and draped their sodden blankets over a rough slab laid across the open beams to serve as a shelf. He was now coaxing a fire from some dried peat that lay in a corner of the hut. The blankets steamed. Her throat choked on the rank smoke, but there was discernible heat. She sank to the floor near the grate and held out her hands to the warmth.

The pain in her back would not stop, even though the contractions had diminished. She was damp between her legs and wondered if she was bleeding. Or if she had now lost control completely. It didn't matter. She was tired, so tired, and she could not move to save herself.

"Dugal, fetch some water. And see to the pony." Paul slipped behind her and put his arms above the mound of her belly.

His touch warmed her where the fire would not. Strength seemed to flow into her from his arms. He was here, and there was no one else. She let herself lean back against him. "How long?"

"Ah, Fenella, I don't know."

Of course he didn't know, but that was not why she had asked the question. In those two words she had said "Help me. I need you." In those two words she had admitted she could not do this alone.

The cramping returned and she let herself scream. "Crouch down." Paul eased her onto all fours and rubbed her back with a firm pressure that distracted her from the pain.

The door shut as Dugal returned to the hut. She was dimly aware of him standing just beyond her field of vision. "Oh, lady," he said. "Dod, I be that worried. Is there aught I can do?"

"Sing to me, Dugal." She sank back into the haven of Paul's arms.

For a long time she was conscious of nothing but the pains that split her in two, accompanied by Dugal's wavering voice and the disembodied screams that filled the hut. "Tom, I can't bear it," she gasped after one long bout of cramping. Mother of God, what was happening to her? What was going wrong?

Fragments of half-remembered prayers raced through her mind. *Holy Mary, full of grace, virgin most glorious, virgin most wise, virgin most merciful. Protect me, protect me in my hour of need.*

Paul was helping her to her feet. She could not stand. He lifted her and carried her to the bed, now covered with the still-damp blankets. A pillow had been made of their cloaks. Her hair was plastered to her forehead with sweat. Paul took a cloth and sponged her face, then gave her a cup of water, which she drank greedily. When he left her side she asked Dugal the time.

"I dinna ken. It be night."

It was impossible to tell in the murky recesses of the hut, though her eyes had long since adjusted to the dark. "No sign of the day?" Surely she had passed the entire night in her torment.

Dugal walked to the wall and peered out through a chink in the stones. "Nary a sign."

"Lie back." Paul had returned with the lantern, which he fastened to a door of the bed. He peeled her damp dress and chemise away from her skin. Her legs were open before him, but she felt no shame. "You've bled," he said, wiping her gently with a cloth moistened with warm water.

There was a burning sensation between her legs. She felt a

renewed burst of energy. She grunted and pushed, certain the baby was now due to arrive. Her gaze met Paul's. The air between them tightened with expectation. He believed it too.

She pushed again, and again, till she had used up all her reserves of energy. She was dimly aware of Paul, speaking soothing words, wiping her face, giving her water to drink. She grew impatient with his useless efforts to help. She shook off his hands. It was his doing that it was so slow. "Leave me alone," she said between the pains. "You're in the way. God above, put an end to it! Why won't you come?"

"Push," Paul said.

"Damn you." He must know she could do no more.

"It be growin' light," Dugal said in a small voice. He came to the bed, but she could not see him clearly. Her eyes would not focus. The babe must be dead.

"Push," Paul said again in a voice that would not be denied.

Against her will, against all hope, Fenella made one last effort. "Dod," Dugal said. "I see the bairn's head."

THE SIGHT OF THE BABE'S HEAD BETWEEN FENELLA'S LEGS was the triumph of Paul's life. Victory in battle was nothing next to it. Taking a woman could not compare. He held the bloody, wrinkled mess of the babe's head as it emerged from Fenella's body. Its eyes were puffy and there was a cheesy coating in the folds of its face. It was small, surely too small to have come unprotected into the world.

Its head lay in his cupped hand, a weight so light he could not believe the child was real. Then it let out a squall and something broke free within him, a sheet of ice crackling with the strain of warmth, a barrier he had never known was there. He looked down at the agitated child. "Ah, beautiful. You are beautiful."

Fenella grunted. Paul raised his eyes, his mouth widening in a smile of pure joy. "Your babe is alive," he said, looking at her sweaty face. *And you, too, are beautiful.* But he did not say this last aloud.

He wiped the baby's face with a damp cloth, cradling its head in his clawed right hand. "The worst is over," he said. "Give me your hand." He guided it to the crown of the babe's head. "Feel it. This is your child. Push again. The shoulders come next."

"My child." Her face relaxed into a smile as she felt the babe's bloody head.

"Push."

"I can't. I'm so tired."

"You can."

She groaned and smiled and grimaced. And she pushed.

"The shoulders are out."

"Is it a boy or a girl?"

Paul laughed. "I don't know. Does it matter?"

"No. Yes. I'd like a girl." She panted. "I'd like it to come to an end."

"It will. It will. But you must finish it yourself."

She drew a deep breath, her face contorted with the effort she was making. A last push sent her babe into the world.

"You have your wish." Paul held the child in his hands so Fenella could see it was well and truly born. "It's a girl." He laid the impossibly small infant on Fenella's exposed belly. It continued to squall, its thin arms and legs making distressed and uncoordinated protests against the new world it had entered.

"Give her to me."

Paul wiped the girl child carefully with a damp cloth. "In a moment. We'll leave her here till the afterbirth comes. Then I'll cut the cord."

Fenella raised her head and stroked the child lying on her belly. "My daughter. My own."

The baby twisted her head, as though trying to find the source of the sound. "She knows your voice," Paul said.

Fenella smiled and continued to murmur to the child. Paul went to the fire and plunged his knife in the burning peat. When he returned to Fenella the afterbirth was lying, a bloody mass, between her legs. The cord that had given the child life for so many months was still throbbing. Paul waited till its motions had ceased, then cut the cord with one swift movement and tied it off with a piece of string. He wiped the babe once more, wrapped her in fresh linen, and laid her in Fenella's arms. Then he strode to the door and flung it open.

It was a glorious day. The rain had truly stopped, and the ground steamed lightly to rid itself of the accumulated damp. He turned back to look at Fenella, but she had eyes only for her child. In the sun streaming through the opened door, her face glowed with a light he had seen only on paintings of quattrocento madonnas as they held their babes up for all the world to see what they had wrought. It was triumph. It was the beginning of love.

"Ah, Dugal," Paul said to the boy who had come to stand beside him.

"She be right small." Dugal's face was creased with a frown. "And she be ugly as sin." He cast a backward look at Fenella. "Fenella doesna seem to mind."

"No, she doesn't." Paul wanted to howl for very joy. "She's besotted."

"Ye be fair besotted yerself."

Paul cuffed him. "Here, lad, it's not so bad. A few days and the babe won't be all red and wrinkled and bloody."

"She cries so. She hasna stopped cryin' since she set eyes on us."

"And wouldn't you if you'd been pushed out of a soft, warm body into the dubious comforts of an uncaring world? Use your imagination, lad."

Silence descended on the hut, startling them. Paul glanced at Fenella. She had managed to undo the buttons at the top of her dress and pull out a breast, swollen and blue-veined. It was too early for the milk to come, Paul had been told at another birth years ago, but there was some secretion that the infant craved. Fenella's child had lost the nipple and was thrashing about, trying to retrieve her source of sustenance. Fenella, the same absorbed smile on her face, urged the infant's head back to the nipple.

When he looked again a half hour later, Fenella was asleep, her child, satisfied at last, cradled within the curve of her arm.

There were chores to be done and the new day to savor. Paul and Dugal rubbed down the pony and tethered him in a spot where the sun would dry his still-damp coat. They gathered peat against the chill of the evening and broke their fast sitting cross-legged on the ground.

"Fenella?" Dugal asked.

"Will be famished, yes, but now she needs sleep more. We'll give her today to rest. Tomorrow, if she can, we'll make for Edinburgh."

"Be it safe? Stayin' here?"

Paul shrugged. "As safe here as elsewhere. For the moment we haven't much choice."

"I dinna fancy stayin'. But I'll put the day to use. I'll go huntin'. If ye'll wipe that daft grin off yer face."

Paul could no more do as Dugal asked than he could keep from bursting into song when his bubbling high spirits spilled over into sound. He was quiet only when he entered the hut and moved to the bed, drawn by the sight of the sleeping woman and child. He would have picked up the babe if he could, but he dared not disturb Fenella. And the child was hers, not his, no matter that he had helped bring her into the world.

Fenella slept for most of the day. When the infant stirred, Paul put her back at Fenella's breast. It was peaceful here inside Granny's hut. Paul could not remember spending a happier day.

An alien sound broke the stillness. His body tensed as it once had scouting enemy territory. Metal wheels—attached to an axle in want of grease—were moving over the rough ground. "Get the pony," he said to Dugal.

Dugal ran to the pony, who was grazing peacefully in full view. Paul stamped out the remains of the fire still smoldering beneath the grate. He hoped they had hidden the cart well enough from casual sight.

"What is it?" Fenella was sitting up in bed, the child at her breast.

"A carriage."

Her arms tightened around the babe. "Coming here?"

"I don't know."

Dugal pulled and pushed the pony into the hut. They closed the door as quietly as they could, then fastened the shutters on the bed so Fenella would be hidden from view.

"What do we do now?" Dugal asked.

"Wait," Paul said.

Chapter 7

><

THE SQUEAK OF THE WHEELS GREW LOUDER, THEN
stopped. Footsteps squelched on the mulchy ground. Dugal
sucked in his breath.

The door inched open, creaking in protest. "Is anyone there?
We saw smoke—Oh!"

A woman stood silhouetted in the doorway. She wore a
white dress trimmed with a great deal of pink ribbon and a
broad-brimmed straw hat tied with more ribbon. A basket with
yet another knot of ribbon on the handle dangled from one arm,
a fringed reticule from the other.

She was a vision from another time and place, a time and
place that had nothing to do with the crazy, dangerous world in
which they had been living for the past four days. But unless
she believed their story the woman with the ribbons could be as
dangerous as an armed man. "Forgive me," Paul said, speaking
in the well-bred English he had learned as a boy. "We know we
are trespassing, but we had no choice. My wife has just been
delivered of a child."

The woman's eyes widened in recognition of his accent. The
pony neighed from the shadows. The woman started and
dropped her basket.

"We thought it prudent to bring the animal inside when we
heard someone coming. We feared bandits." Paul opened the
doors of the bed. "It's all right, my dear. Nothing to fear." He
smiled at Fenella.

Fenella returned the smile. "Thank heavens, dearest. I was
so alarmed I could scarcely draw a breath."

The woman with the ribbons picked up her basket and

squinted against the murky light. Then she gave a shriek. "A bairn!" She ran across the room and peered into the bed. "You poor dear, how dreadful. To come to grief at such a time. Did you suffer an accident in the storm? No, never mind about that now. You must come to the house. My maid and I have only the pony cart, but we'll make room. Jeanie, don't just stand there. Fetch a blanket from the cart." She looked over her shoulder at a girl in a print dress and straw bonnet who was hovering in the doorway.

Paul felt his way carefully. "You're very kind, madam—"

"McClaren. Lady Margaret McClaren." Lady Margaret gave him a warm, toothy smile and extended a white-gloved hand.

Paul hesitated, then held out his own hand. Lady Margaret started to take it, looked down, and drew in her breath. "Oh, dear." She let her hand fall to her side. "Oh, I'm most terribly sorry." She made a helpless gesture. "But you must come and stay at the house. Mr.—"

"Paul Lester. My wife, Fenella. And Dugal, our servant."

"Mr. Lester. I'm very pleased to make your acquaintance. And you, Mrs. Lester." Lady Margaret dropped down on the end of the bed in a swirl of white muslin and violet scent. The baby had stopped suckling and was drifting off to sleep, her head falling back against Fenella's arm. "What a dear wee bairn. Is it a girl or boy?"

"A girl." Fenella's tone was guarded.

"A lassie. How lovely. I do so wish . . ." A look that was part longing, part envy crossed Lady Margaret's face, then was quickly banished. "But what you must have suffered, my dear. All alone and in this dreadful place. Are you in a great deal of pain? Do you feel well enough to be moved? What a mercy I have my herbs and simples with me." She began to hunt through her basket, the ribbons on her sleeves fluttering madly. "I'd been to visit the tenants, to be sure no one was hurt in that terrible storm, and then I heard that someone had seen smoke from this cottage. Well I was *sure* the Doons had left yesterday and poor Granny Doon went to her rest the day before, and I knew Sir James would be cross with me if I didn't look—Ah, here we are. Barley water." She held up a flask.

"Thank you. But I think I can manage a short journey. That is, if my husband—" Fenella looked at Paul.

"I think it would be the best thing for you, my love," Paul said. Events were moving as quickly as Lady Margaret's torrent of speech, but there were times to try to shape events and times to follow their flow. There was no reasonable excuse to refuse Lady Margaret's invitation. Besides, at the manor house Fenella and her babe could receive proper care. The risk of childbed fever weighed more heavily in the balance than the risk of discovery.

Lady Margaret sprang to her feet. "Thank goodness the rain stopped. Our weather is so unreliable, even in July. If you will permit me to hold the baby, Mrs. Lester, your husband can help you with your cloak."

Fenella stiffened. But after only a brief moment she placed the baby in Lady Margaret's arms. Lady Margaret cradled the child with the ease of a woman experienced with infants and tickled the baby's nose.

Paul put Fenella's cloak about her shoulders. Her skin was warm to the touch. Too warm? He had seen more than one soldier's wife survive the ordeal of childbirth only to lose her life to fever. "Shall I carry you?"

"Thank you, I can walk."

He fastened the ties beneath her chin. "I had a feeling you'd say that."

She gave him a smile that was brief, but meant solely for him. He felt something give way within him, a tension he hadn't even known he'd been feeling. They were about to reenter the wider world, but perhaps the bond they had forged in the hut would endure.

With difficulty he persuaded Lady Margaret that Fenella and the babe would be better off traveling in the farm cart, rough as it was, than in Lady Margaret's fragile, two-wheeled conveyance. This time Fenella sat on a folded blanket on the bench beside him, holding the baby, while Dugal perched in the back.

Fenella stared at Lady Margaret's white-painted cart as they squished through the mud and damp leaves. "She hasn't asked any questions."

"No, she hasn't."

"But she will."

"Undoubtedly."

"I hate to be difficult, but what are we going to tell her?"

"Aye." Dugal's voice sounded from the back. "Ye fair gave me a fright, agreein' to go off to the big house."

"It would have looked more suspicious if we'd resisted." Paul glanced at Fenella. "It was kind of you to defer the decision to me."

"Self-preservation. I wasn't sure what to do myself." In the light of day Fenella's skin looked translucent. It seemed to be stretched taut over the bones of her face. There were dark smudges of weariness around her eyes. But her gaze was as sharp as ever. "You haven't told us what our story is. Don't tell me you haven't thought of one. This isn't the time for you to start getting careless."

Paul slackened his grip on the reins, lengthening the distance between them and Lady Margaret. "We're from England. Devon, I think."

"What brought us to the Highlands? A visit to relatives?"

"Too risky. Lady Margaret's bound to know every wellborn family within a hundred miles. You have a Scots name because your mother was fascinated by the romance of the Highlands. But we came to Scotland to see your old nurse, a Scotswoman who retired to a village in the Grampians."

The straw in the back rustled as Dugal shifted his position. "What were ye doin' travelin' so far wi' Fenella about to ha' the bairn?"

"I wasn't supposed to have the baby for another month." Fenella's voice quickened, as though this were a drawing-room game. "I hoped to persuade my old nurse to return to service and look after my child."

"Very good," Paul said. "A mad freak, but expectant women are prone to them. Why didn't I fetch the woman and leave you safe at home?"

She flashed him a smile. "I couldn't bear to have you gone from my side."

"Of course. What a loving wife you are. And then the ungrateful woman wouldn't come with us. Her rheumatism was bothering her and she didn't feel equal to the task. But she asked if we could do something for her grandson, and we took him with us to help in the stable at home."

"Here now," Dugal said. "I dinna want a grandmother."

"Well, you've got one for the present. Dear old Elspbeth Pitcaple."

Fenella tucked Lady Margaret's blanket more closely around the baby. The babe stirred, but didn't open her eyes. "That gets us to Scotland. How did we lose our carriage, our luggage, and the clothes off our backs?"

"I'm coming to that. On our way home we were attacked by highwaymen. That's how you got your wound. How is it, by the way?" Paul turned his head to look at her.

"No worse than when you checked it an hour ago." Her gaze did not waver. "The highwaymen took all our luggage?"

"Exactly. We bought these clothes and the cart from a family of crofters. We were on our way to Edinburgh when you went into labor before your time."

The dirt track they were on gave way to a gravel drive overhung by an avenue of pleached limes, unexpectedly decorous in this rugged country. Lady Margaret gave an enthusiastic wave, nearly losing her balance in the process.

"Do you think Lady Margaret will believe the story?" Fenella asked.

"Why not? It's less improbable than the truth."

The rain-sodden trees swayed as they passed beneath. A shower of icy water came sluicing down on them. The baby woke with a loud protest. "Oh, darling, I'm sorry. There, we'll get you dry." Fenella patted the babe with the blanket. When she moved her hands the baby's head bobbled, too heavy to be supported by her slender neck. Fenella gave an exclamation of dismay and quickly slipped her hand back behind the baby's neck. "I'm still afraid she'll break."

Paul negotiated a sharp bend in the drive. "Only if you drop her."

The baby squirmed, her cries unabated. Fenella spared Paul a withering glance.

"Dod." Dugal whistled. "That looks like the workhouse i' Dunkeld."

Paul glanced up. They had come within view of the manor house, a somber, ungraceful mass of gray-brown stone. A four-story tower rose stolidly in the center. Two wings extended at stiff angles on either side. The windows were narrow and small-paned, giving the impression of enlarged arrow slits.

"I'm sure it's a good deal more comfortable inside," Paul said. "But you're right, it's not the sort of house you'd expect Lady Margaret to come from."

Fenella settled the baby against her shoulder. "She probably married into it." Her brows drew together, as though she had been reminded of her own marriage and the man who had fathered her child. She pressed her face against the baby's head.

Paul tightened his grip on the reins. The way her hands nestled the babe against her, the delicate bow of her neck, the curve of her head and the child's, blending into one, again put him in mind of a Renaissance madonna. He had little religious feeling, but he had always found the purity of the bond between mother and child strangely moving. If Fenella's husband lived, the blackguard damned well better appreciate what he had in his wife and child.

Lady Margaret drove through an open gate into a gravel-lined courtyard. Paul told himself he was a sentimental fool and forced his hands to relax. Grooms emerged from the stable to take charge of the ponies. Lady Margaret bustled up to the cart and led them through a second, smaller gate and across a second courtyard. A flight of stairs led to a heavy wooden door topped by an ornate pediment.

"I'm afraid there isn't a fire burning in the house. Sir James won't hear of it before November. But I've sent Jeanie to have a bedroom made up and the sheets warmed." Lady Margaret pushed the door open and ushered them into a flagstone entrance hall. They were met by an ecstasy of barking. At least a half dozen black-and-tan dogs hurled themselves on Lady Margaret.

"Perseus! Andromeda! Down. Theseus, Hippolyta, no. Pyramus, Thisbe, mind your manners." Lady Margaret gestured toward the back of the hall. The beagles retreated and sat on their haunches, but they thumped their tails on the floor and continued to look hopeful. "They're pining for Sir James," Lady Margaret said. "He insists that we give them the run of the house. It's such a gloomy old pile, but I've tried to make improvements, and dog hair shows so on the cream silk in the drawing room. I'm always telling Sir James that just because the English think we're barbarians doesn't mean we have to live as though we are. But here I am rattling on when you must be ready to drop." She turned to Fenella, who was standing within the shelter of Paul's arm. "What you'd really like is a bath, isn't it, my dear?"

Fenella gave a wholehearted smile. "Very much."

"I thought so. I felt just the same after my boys were born, and goodness knows I hadn't been through what you have. I'm having a tub filled in my room. Ah, there you are, Ronald." She nodded to a manservant in red-and-buff livery who had appeared in the hall. "Show Mr. Lester into the rose parlor and then take young Dugal to the kitchen and tell Cook to give him something to eat."

Fenella moved away from Paul without hesitation. Lady Margaret took her arm and the two women started up the dark wooden staircase, heads bent over the baby. Ronald threw open a door. It was a moment before Paul realized the footman was waiting for him to enter the room. He was not used to having servants wait on him. He glanced at Dugal, wondering how the boy felt about being sent off on his own. Dugal grinned.

There was nothing more he could do for the boy or for Fenella or the babe. He stepped into the parlor. Ronald pulled the door shut behind him. For the first time in the past four days, Paul found himself truly alone.

It was an odd sensation. He was accustomed to being alone. He preferred it that way. But for four days he had been absorbed with the needs of his two—now three—traveling companions. He felt a strange sort of hollowness, as when he had shut down his press and locked the door of his newspaper.

Too restless to sit, he prowled about the room. Lady Margaret's stamp was all over it. The walls were hung with pale-ivory silk patterned with roses. The windows, which looked so forbidding from the outside, were draped with the same silk, looped back with fringed cords. Sunlight, discreetly filtered by embroidered muslin subcurtains, fell softly on gilt-framed watercolors, a marquetry workbox, a silver dish of comfits. A thick Brussels carpet muffled the heavy tread of his boots. A faint smell of violets hung in the air.

It had been a long time since Paul was in such a room. He flipped through the stack of periodicals on the sofa table— the *Lady's Monthly Museum*, *Ackerman's Repository*—then moved toward the fireplace. The mantel was crowded with vases and figurines. A porcelain shepherd stood at one end, a shepherdess at the other.

A chill swept through him that had nothing to do with the faint draft from the windows. For a moment the walls were blue, not rose, the air smelled of hyacinth, not violets, and he was in the *petit salon* of his father's house, looking at another pair of figurines.

He had stared up at those figurines every morning when he made up the fire. They had come to symbolize Daniel de Ribard, who would not admit he was Paul's father, and Louisa de Ribard, who had kept Daniel from Paul's mother when she needed him most. He had often imagined smashing the shepherd and shepherdess against the creamy Italian marble of the mantel.

But when he finally struck out he had broken more than porcelain. And he had hurt not Daniel and Louisa, but the Comte de Milvery and his wife. Little Sophie's parents. Paul thought of the girl he had run from twenty-three years ago and then of the babe he had just helped bring into the world. Shame gripped him.

He drew a breath, longing for the cool, piney damp of the outdoors. He stared at the figurines and forced himself to note details and differences. The shepherdess wore a pink apron, not a white one, and carried a violin, not a basket of flowers. The shepherd's waistcoat was blue, not yellow, and he held a flute, not a shepherd's crook. The mantel on which they stood was lower by a foot or more—no, he had grown taller.

"Mr. Lester? I'm so sorry to have deserted you."

Paul spun around. Lady Margaret stood in the open doorway. She had wrapped a lace shawl around her shoulders and removed her hat, revealing honey-colored hair arranged in elaborate loops and braids and curls. Though the styles of her dress and hair were different, the soft frivolity reminded him of Louisa de Ribard and Isabella de Milvery.

Lady Margaret moved into the room. "Your wife is having a nice bath. My dear Mr. Lester, what an ordeal you have been through. Mrs. Lester told me about your dreadful encounter with the highwaymen. What sort of men could knife a pregnant woman? But do sit down. Your wife says you were injured as well." She sank onto the sofa and gestured Paul to a seat opposite her.

Paul glanced from the silk upholstery to his stained breeches. "I'm not sure—"

"Oh, my husband is in much more disreputable condition when he's been hunting. And so are my boys. That is, they are when they're home, which isn't nearly often enough. Take the armchair. I know men like to be comfortable."

Paul settled himself in the armchair with care. The back was stiff, but the padding was seductively luxurious.

Lady Margaret adjusted her shawl. "Does your wound pain you very much?"

"It's only a flesh wound."

"One must still guard against infection. I'll give you some of the comfrey salve I gave to Mrs. Lester." Lady Margaret shivered. "The countryside is so unsettled just now. Many of our own people have left and I don't understand it, for their families have been with us for years. That's why Sir James is away from home. There's been some unpleasantness on his property in Perthshire. But I know if he were here he'd insist that you stay as long as you wish."

"We're very grateful," Paul said. "We won't trouble you longer than necessary. I know my wife will be eager to be near her family once she is well enough to travel."

"Oh, but you mustn't think of rushing off too soon. And it's no trouble at all. Indeed, I shall be grateful for the company, what with Sir James gone and the boys away at school. It's so dreadfully quiet up here. I grew up in the Borders, you know. We had enormous house parties every summer. After thirteen years of marriage I still can't get used to the isolation."

Lady Margaret got to her feet and shook out her ruched skirt. "I'll show you to your room, Mr. Lester. I've had Ronald bring in hot water and lay out some of Sir James's clothes. I know it must be hard to believe after what you've been through, but you can stop worrying now."

Chapter 8

⇥⇤

FENELLA CLOSED HER EYES AND RESTED HER HEAD
against the rim of the tub. The warm, scented water lapped the
aches and soreness from her body along with the grime of the
past four days. Her scalp tingled from the scrubbing she had
given her hair. She could hear the reassuring footfalls of Beth,
the maidservant who was watching the baby. She opened her
eyes to see Beth, a slender, fair-haired girl, jiggling the babe in
her arms with enviable competence.

Reassured, Fenella reached for the amber-colored bar of
soap and ran it over her chest, luxuriating in the foaming lather
and the clean smell of thyme and rosemary. Pears soap. She
had known it the moment Jeanie handed her the bar.

An image rushed into her mind. A fragrant shop, a glass-
topped counter, a clerk handing her a paper-wrapped parcel.
Like her other recollections it was no more than a tantalizing
fragment. Disquiet prickled her skin. She set down the soap.
"I'd like to get out now."

"Of course, ma'am." Jeanie was beside the tub at once.
There was a familiarity to being helped from the bath, as there
was to being wrapped in soft white towels, smoothing her skin
with almond-scented lotion, untangling her hair with a silver
comb. Jeanie helped her cleanse and bandage her wound and
contrive a pad of cloths between her legs, for she was still
bleeding from the delivery. Lady Margaret had laid out one of
her own nightdresses. It was a few inches too short, but the
muslin felt right and the pin tucks and broderie anglaise were
familiar and comforting.

Fenella did up the last button and turned to the glass above

Lady Margaret's dressing table. She had combed her wet hair back from her face, throwing her features into harsh relief. The broad forehead, the high cheekbones, the long, full mouth. There were blue-black marks around her eyes that told of the last twenty-four hours. Surely, if she knew what to look for, she could read something of the more distant past in her face.

Her skin was very pale. She glanced at the crystal jars on the dressing table. Perhaps she had been accustomed to wearing rouge. Her eyebrows had been plucked into a fine arch. She must have devoted considerable time to her appearance. She reached up and traced the line of one of her brows, but the action brought no accompanying memory.

"Oh, you're out of the tub, my dear. Splendid. But you mustn't stand about in your nightdress. You'll catch a chill." Lady Margaret swept into the room. "Your room is ready. There's a fire lit so it's nice and warm. I've already taken Mr. Lester up. I was sure you'd want to share a bedchamber. You seem such a devoted couple. I know I always find it comforting to have Sir James nearby when I'm feeling poorly, even though half the time he isn't sure what to say or do."

Fenella checked an instinctive protest. She and Paul had shared straw on the floor of a barn and sheepskins in Hamish's hut. It was silly to cavil at occupying the same room. If Lady Margaret believed they were a devoted couple, so much the better. They needed to make their charade convincing.

Jeanie helped her into a trailing, full-sleeved dressing gown of blush-colored wool. Beth brought her the baby. "Here ye be, Mrs. Lester. I've given her a sponge bath and dressed her i' some o' Master Duncan's things."

"Doesn't she look sweet," Lady Margaret said. "I've never believed in swaddling bairns—so uncomfortable."

An embroidered muslin cap covered the baby's head, a matching gown was buttoned close to her throat, and she was swathed in a tartan blanket. Only the small face peeking out from all that fabric reassured Fenella that this was indeed her child. That and the babe's fretful cry as she was transferred from one pair of arms to another.

"I do hope you'll be comfortable," Lady Margaret said as she led Fenella into a side wing. "It's a bit removed from the rest of the house, but it gets the light." She opened a door onto a sunny room with lavender-sprigged wallpaper. "Here you are, Mr. Lester, I've restored your wife and child to you at last."

Paul was standing by the windows at the back of the room, but it was a moment before Fenella recognized him. He was dressed in tan breeches and a double-breasted, dark-brown coat, a trifle too large around the middle. Instead of the open-necked shirt she was used to, the coat revealed a pristine white cravat and a green-and-buff-striped waistcoat. His hair was washed of the last of the blacking and neatly combed. And for the first time since she had known him, he was clean-shaven. Would the man never stop changing?

"You're looking very fine, Mr. Lester," she said. "More like the man I married."

Paul raised his brows.

"Clothes make such a difference. I know I feel quite cross when I'm not properly dressed." Lady Margaret drew Fenella to a carved walnut cradle. "This was Sir James's when he was a boy. Both our sons used it. I do hope Baby will be comfortable. There are more blankets in the dresser. And a supply of clean napkins. My goodness, they go through them quickly, don't they?" She looked down with a smile as Fenella settled the baby in the cradle. "Such a wee darling. I do believe she has the look of you, Mrs. Lester. Though she has Mr. Lester's mouth, I'd swear it."

Fenella straightened up and met Paul's gaze. He smiled. "The Lester lower lip. It goes back for generations."

"Well." Lady Margaret glanced around the room, as though to be sure she had left nothing undone. "I know you both must be exhausted, so I'll have your dinner sent up. If you need anything you have only to ring."

The door closed behind Lady Margaret. Fenella turned to Paul. He had gone to poke up the fire. In its flickering light she could see that despite the shave there was still something rough about the planes of his face. It would take more than Sir James McClaren's clothes to make him entirely civilized.

They were alone together. No Dugal to act as a buffer, no imminent danger to turn their thoughts from all but the present. She drew a breath and found that her throat had gone tight. The intimacy that had seemed natural in the crofter's hut felt suffocating in this elegant bedchamber.

She moved to a chair, willing her body to relax. "How safe are we?"

Paul set down the shiny brass poker. "Safer than we've been these past four days."

"That's hardly reassuring." She sank into the armchair. The warmth of the fire curled round her toes and spread deliciously through her body. Instead of the peaty smell she had grown used to, the logs gave off the fragrant scent of pine. What a luxury it was just to be warm and clean and dry. She should enjoy it and not have missish scruples about being alone with the man who had delivered her child. "It feels safe here," she said, her eyes on the decorous blue-and-violet chintz that covered the chair arm. She looked up at Paul. "But I'm afraid the safety is an illusion."

He moved to a chair opposite her. "Lady Margaret believes our story. I don't think she's heard anything of the hunt for McAlpin's killer. Sir James might be harder to convince, but he's off subduing his tenants."

"He could return home knowing about McAlpin's death."

"He could. But he isn't expected until next week. We'll be gone by then."

Fenella glanced at the cradle. She could see the creamy muslin of the baby's cap and the brown-and-green plaid of the blanket. The past days should have taught her the meaning of fear, but since the baby's birth she had known a new terror, which at once chilled her with dread and made her burn with determination. No one was going to harm her child. "As far as I'm concerned we can leave tomorrow."

Paul stretched his legs out in front of him. "If I'd worked as hard as you did last night, I'd want a day or two to recover."

"If she was your baby you'd understand—" Fenella broke off.

Paul regarded her for a moment, his expression unreadable. "I'm rather fond of the little mite too. I wouldn't suggest staying if I didn't think it was safer than pushing on so soon after the birth."

She bit her lip. "We're holding you back, aren't we? If it wasn't for us you'd be halfway to Edinburgh by now."

His mouth twisted in a self-derisive smile. "If it wasn't for the baby's timely arrival the soldiers would have hauled me in for questioning yesterday. Don't worry about me, Fenella. I'm good at looking after myself. I've been doing it for a long time."

Some of the tension left her body. In truth, she was relieved that they would not have to travel again for a day or so. Her wound ached more than she would admit to herself, let alone to Paul. Not to mention the soreness she felt in more intimate places.

Paul's gaze drifted toward the fire. "Just before the baby was born, you called out the name Tom."

"Tom?" She repeated the name over and over in her mind, but it stirred no resonance. "He must be . . . I suppose he's the baby's father." How strange to be able to speak with such detachment about the man with whom she had created such a miracle.

"Rutledge's given name is Ned." Paul looked at her. "It seems at least you need not fear Rutledge is your husband."

"No." She leaned back into the chair. She should feel relief. She should want to think more about the unknown Tom. But she didn't want to think about any of it. She wanted to wrap herself in the mantle of Fenella Lester and burrow beneath the protective warmth of her assumed identity.

She glanced around the room that was to be her temporary

refuge. The four-poster bed was high and inviting, draped in the same chintz that covered the chairs. There was a thick bolster and mounds of fluffy pillows. She had no memory of actually sleeping in a bed, but she knew comfort when she saw it.

A heavy garment of burgundy brocade was laid out at the foot of the bed, looking incongruous against the delicate lilac embroidery on the counterpane. A dressing gown, she realized. A man's dressing gown. And the folded white garment beside it must be a nightshirt. For the first time she understood that Paul was expected to share the bed with her. Of course. Where else would he sleep?

Paul followed the direction of her gaze. "I'll tell Lady Margaret you need a room to yourself."

"No. It will look more natural if we want to be together. Lady Margaret thinks we're a devoted couple." Fenella fidgeted with the Mechlin lace on the sleeves of her dressing gown. The air had grown thick with awkwardness. The walls seemed to be pressing inward. She was keenly aware of the huge bed looming before them.

"Don't worry," Paul said. "I'll sleep on the sofa."

She stilled her hands and forced a smile to her lips. She would not let herself be foolish. "Believe me, Mr. Lescaut, after what we've been through that's the last thing I'm worried about."

THE SCREAM TORE PAUL FROM SLUMBER. HE PUSHED HIM-self up from the sofa, struggling to get his bearings in the darkened bedchamber. The embers of the fire glowed red-orange in the shadows. A shaft of moonlight seeped through the curtains and outlined the dark mass of the bed.

Fenella screamed again. He ran to the bed, stumbling against one of the chairs and knocking over a small table. Something porcelain smashed against the floor. He jerked back the bed-curtains and pulled Fenella into his arms. Her nightdress was drenched with sweat. She struggled like a trapped animal, clawing at his arms, twisting to break free of his hold.

"It's all right. You're safe now." He dredged up words his mother had used to him in childhood. Words he had learned were nothing but empty promises.

Fenella's palm smashed against his cheek. He drew back. She reached out blindly, caught hold of the bed-curtain, and ripped it halfway from the frame.

The silvered moonlight fell across her face. Her eyes were still closed. "Fenella." He gripped her by the shoulders. "Fenella, it's Paul."

Her eyes flew open. She stared up at him like a deer frozen by panic.

The baby's cry cut the air. The terror in Fenella's eyes gave way to realization. She made a move as though to get up. Paul pushed her back against the pillows. "I'll get her."

He lit the lamp on the bedside table and made his way to the cradle. Unlike her mother, the baby quieted as soon as he lifted her into his arms. He stroked her cheek and she grasped hold of his forefinger. Such utter trust. It was a frightening burden.

He carried the baby to the bed. Fenella was leaning against the chintz-covered headboard, drawing long, shuddering breaths. She held out her arms to take her daughter and settled the child at her breast. In the warm lamplight she looked a little less ashen, but fear still lurked in her eyes. The embroidery on the pillowcase had left a dark impression on her cheek.

"I'm sorry," she said, when the babe had begun to suckle. "I hit you, didn't I?"

"You've got a punishing right. Remind me not to fight with you when you're awake."

She gave a wan smile. He sat on the bed beside her. After the chaos of the last few minutes the room seemed very still, the only sound a faint hissing from the fireplace. "Do you remember the dream?" he asked.

Fenella gathered the baby closer. He could see the pulse beating above the frilled collar of her nightdress. "There was a fire. Smoke everywhere. I couldn't breathe."

"Were you alone?"

"Yes. No. I'm not sure. Later there was a man." Her brows drew together. She spoke quickly, with little expression. "He was being hanged. On a scaffold. I was trying to cut him down, but the knife kept slipping from my hand."

"Do you know who he was?"

She shook her head. "I couldn't see his face. There was a bag over it."

"Could he have been Tom?"

"He could have been anyone. I told you, I couldn't see." Her voice cut with sudden force.

"Why was he being hanged?"

"I don't know. I only know I wanted to save him. What's the sense in talking about it?"

"It frightened you. If we knew what you're frightened of, we might know how to protect you."

The baby stirred and made a protesting sound. Fenella adjusted her hold. "I'm sorry," she said. "I know you're trying to help. I just wish I could forget—" She gave a harsh laugh. "That's the problem, isn't it? I've forgotten too well. And sometimes I'm not sure I want to remember."

The ghosts of his own past stirred in his mind. "I can't say I blame you. There are any number of things I'd like to forget myself. But forgetting doesn't make them go away."

They sat in silence until the baby fell back into slumber. Paul carried her to the cradle, settled her against the pillow, tucked the tartan blanket around her. She stirred, but didn't open her eyes. When he returned to the bed Fenella was lying on her side, her eyes on the cradle, one hand beneath her cheek. Sweat-dampened tendrils of hair clung to her forehead. Against the expanse of white bed linen, her face looked as fragile as the porcelain he had smashed in his dash across the room.

"Will you be able to sleep?" he asked.

"I'll do my best." There was a note of bravado in her voice, but her eyes were open very wide, as though she was afraid of what she might see when she closed them. "Paul?"

"Yes?"

"You can't be comfortable on the couch. If you were going to ravish me you'd have done it by now. I don't mind if you sleep in the bed."

His chest tightened, as it had at the baby's touch. "Are you sure?"

"Yes." She was silent for a moment, then added in a small voice, "I'd rather not be alone."

He extinguished the lamp and moved to the far side of the bed. The sheets were smooth and soft and smelled of lavender. The featherbed felt like a drink of fine brandy after months of nothing but rotgut. He lay near the edge, not touching Fenella, but he could feel the stirring of her breath and the warmth of her body. Whatever else he did in a woman's bed, he usually left before he went to sleep. Sleep was too intimate a thing to be done in someone else's presence.

"Paul?" Fenella's voice sounded out of the darkness. "Thank you."

"DO HAVE SOME MORE SALMON, MRS. LESTER. YOU'RE still eating for two, you know." The knots of ribbon on Lady Margaret's sleeves—mauve tonight—fluttered dangerously close to the caper sauce as she handed Fenella the silver serving tray.

Paul studied Fenella across the damask-covered expanse of the table. This was their fifth night in the McClaren house, but the first that she had ventured downstairs. She seemed to be bearing up well. There was more color in her face. Or perhaps she was wearing rouge. She had spent nearly an hour getting ready.

Dressing for dinner was obviously a familiar process and one she enjoyed. She had piled her dark hair high on her head, emphasizing the fineness of her features and the long, elegant column of her throat. Carefully tousled curls framed her face. Her dress was a spun-sugar confection of rose-colored silk. The sleeves were sheer puffs banded in satin. The neck was trimmed with corkscrew twists of gauze. It should have looked ridiculous, but Fenella wore it with unconscious ease.

The Doons could live for a year on the price of that dress. Fenella probably had a dozen such in her wardrobe at home, wherever that might be. There were battle lines in British society clearer than any he had faced as a soldier. He knew which side he was on. Seeing Fenella reenter a world he despised should have helped break the seductive bond he had felt between them in the past days.

Instead, he found himself noticing other things. The way the candlelight reflected the rose-tinged glow of the gown onto her skin. The way her upswept hair made her eyes look even larger and more brilliant. The way the artfully draped fabric of her bodice was pulled taut across her breasts, full and swollen now that her milk had come in.

He set down his wineglass, sloshing the claret. He had tended Fenella's naked body, but as a doctor caring for a patient. Now he was a man looking at a woman. A beautiful woman.

"A little more wine, Mr. Lester?" Lady Margaret refilled his glass. "You deserve it after all your efforts. Beth tells me you're splendid about helping with the baby. I hope you appreciate how lucky you are, Mrs. Lester. Most men are so squeamish with bairns. Sir James avoided the nursery like the plague until the boys were out of leading strings. Then he couldn't wait to teach them to fish and hunt and all sorts of horrid things."

"Mr. Lester is a remarkable man. I'm very fortunate." Fenella smiled across the table at Paul. Her mouth curled with the familiar humor, but her eyes shone with warmth.

Paul took a swallow of wine. The claret was dry and slightly acidic. A good antidote to the errant turn his thoughts had taken. He twisted the stem between his fingers, studying the play of light on the finely faceted crystal. More than distance separated the McClarens' dining room from his favorite café in the Latin Quarter. The fact that he and Fenella were pretending to be husband and wife didn't change that.

Lady Margaret pushed a salmon bone to the edge of her plate. "Of course you're blessed with an angel of a bairn. To sleep four hours at a stretch. It was near a month before Ian would stay down so long, and Duncan had the most dreadful colic. Have you given any thought to a name for her?"

Fenella spread butter on a second piece of bread. "I'm afraid we've been too preoccupied with her immediate needs."

"There's plenty of time, of course. You'll want to be back in Devon for the christening. Do you come from a large family, Mrs. Lester?"

"No, I'm an only child," Fenella said without hesitation. She seemed to enjoy playacting her life as Mrs. Lester. She had had no nightmares since their first night at the McClaren house. Nor had she spoken of the man who was chasing her or the life that must be waiting somewhere for her to take it up again.

"You must have had a lonely childhood." Lady Margaret set down her fork and picked up her glass. "But you'll soon have a large family of your own."

Fenella met Paul's gaze across the table. Her color deepened, but there was amusement in her eyes. Paul swallowed. He didn't want children. He had never thought much about them. But for a fleeting moment he had an image of Fenella carrying his child. He clenched the stem of the wineglass, shaken to the soles of Sir James's Spanish leather shoes.

"Oh, dear." Lady Margaret glanced from Paul to Fenella. "I hope that didn't sound indelicate."

"Not at all." Fenella smiled at their hostess, then looked back at Paul. "Mr. Lester and I want a large family, don't we, Mr. Lester?"

Paul forced himself to draw a breath. His neckcloth felt tight around his throat. "My dear, you're braver than I if you can so easily consider undergoing the ordeal again."

"On the contrary. The second time couldn't possibly be more difficult."

Lady Margaret's answering laugh was drowned out by the sound of a door slamming shut in the hall. There was a flurry of running feet, raised voices, the sound of dogs barking. A booming voice rose above the noise. "What the devil do you mean Lady Margaret is dining with the guests? What guests?"

"Oh, good heavens." Lady Margaret pushed back her chair and sprang to her feet. "Sir James seems to have come home."

Chapter 9

>‹

THE DOOR OPENED AND THREE BEAGLES BOUNDED INTO the room. "See here, Meg, what's all this taradiddle about guests? We aren't entertaining." The door was flung wide and the dogs were followed by a tall, heavyset man with a thick, well-trimmed mustache showing none of the gray that sprinkled his dark hair. "Not unless I say—Oh. My word."

Sir James's gaze, which had gone directly to his wife, wavered and took in Fenella. Paul had risen when Lady Margaret did, but Fenella had shrunk back in her chair, her eyes wide, her face pale. Paul was sure her look of vulnerability was carefully calculated.

"I beg your pardon, ma'am—"

"Mrs. Lester," Lady Margaret informed her husband.

"Mrs. Lester," he repeated. "See here," he added, "you're wearing my wife's dress."

"But of course she's wearing my dress. The poor things didn't have a stitch to their names. They were staying in Granny Doon's hut and Mrs. Lester had a baby, the sweetest little girl you can imagine and you know how I've always longed for one. But it would never do—Granny's hut I mean— not for such a wee child and her milk not yet in, so I brought them here. Beth is helping look after the baby. I knew it's what you'd want me to do. This is Mr. Lester. Have you dined, my love?" Lady Margaret picked up a bell and rang for the footman who had been attending at table.

Sir James gave Paul a curt nod. "Sir."

"I'm afraid we're intruding," Paul said. "You'll want to speak with your wife."

"Not at all. Not at all. Sit down, Lester." Sir James pulled out a chair at the end of the table and settled into it with the contented sigh of a man who has spent long hours in the saddle. The dogs, who had been sniffing his boots, settled down by his feet. "Not a Scots name, is it?"

"We're from Devon."

"They came to Scotland to find Mrs. Lester's nurse." Lady Margaret conferred briefly with the footman who had slipped into the room, then bent the full force of her attention on her husband. "It was because of the baby, only they didn't expect it to come so soon, and the nurse had the rheumatism and couldn't come with them, but she sent her grandson, who's being a great help in the kitchen. His name is Dugal, and he reminds me so of Ian I want to weep. I do miss the children. I'm afraid we quite polished off the salmon, but there'll be a dish of meat in a few minutes, my love. I know how peevish you get when you haven't dined."

"Peevish? I'm never peevish."

"Of course not," Lady Margaret said, contradicting herself with practiced ease. "Out of sorts, perhaps, and who wouldn't be, riding about the countryside in this dreadful weather. The Lesters were on their way back to England when they were set upon by bandits."

"Bandits?" Sir James sat up abruptly.

"It was quite dreadful." Fenella's voice shook just the right amount. "I can't bear to talk about it."

Lady Margaret stretched out a hand to her. "Of course, dear. It was the shock, that's why the baby came so early, and what a mercy someone saw the smoke from the hut."

Sir James stared at Fenella as though trying to reconcile the beautiful and fashionable woman before him with the stories of bandits and giving birth in a crofter's hut. "I'm sure it was a trying experience." His gaze strayed to the swelling mounds of Fenella's breasts.

Lady Margaret gave her husband a sharp look. "It certainly was. This is the first night Mrs. Lester has felt well enough to dine downstairs, but she mustn't overtax her strength. Oh, good," she added as the footman reentered the room with a platter piled high with sliced meat. "It was a splendid joint and not the least overdone. I must remember to compliment Cook." She rose and put out her hand to Fenella. "Let's leave the men to their whisky and water and men talk. I'll take you up to your room."

Fenella smiled, as though she had nothing on her mind but rest and nursing her child. She was a consummate actress. Paul knew she must be feeling the same fear that had him taut as a bowstring. He forced himself to sit back in his chair and prepare for the inquisition that was bound to follow.

Fortunately, Sir James was sharp-set. He applied himself vigorously to meat and mustard, interrupted by the whining dogs—the full half dozen were now present—who were determined to share his dinner.

Paul took advantage of his host's preoccupation to tell his story without the interruption of inconvenient questions. Sir James chewed steadily, fed his dogs, and acknowledged Paul's tale with an occasional grunt or a lifted brow. Paul could not tell whether or not he believed him. The story sounded improbable enough to his own ears.

Sir James wiped his mouth, pushed back his plate, and rang for whisky. "Damned rum thing to have happened. Damned rum thing to take a woman in Mrs. Lester's condition on such a fool's errand."

"I couldn't agree with you more. My wife's a fragile woman, as you no doubt can tell, but when she gets a bee in her bonnet . . ."

"Ah. Women. Don't understand them. Never have. Don't get their way and they drown you in tears. Dogs now. Know where you are with dogs."

The footman brought in the whisky. Sir James filled two glasses and handed one to Paul. "Your health, sir."

Paul raised his glass. "And yours."

"We don't think much of Sassenachs in these parts. Not that

I've anything against the English, mind you, and we're grateful
enough for the soldiers to keep order, but you'd stand out as
fair game to anyone with a grudge." Sir James absently
scratched the ears of a soulful-eyed beagle whose head appeared on his lap. "And sometimes we have cause. There was a
murder up in Kinrie a few days since. The baillie's son. He was
knifed by an outlander, like yourself."

"A bad business," Paul murmured, taking what he hoped
was the right amount of interest in a lurid tale that had nothing
to do with him.

"Aye." Sir James added more whisky to his glass and passed
the decanter to Paul. "No one got a good look at him, but
they're agreed that his right arm is useless."

Paul met the unspoken challenge in his host's gaze. Despite
his bombast Sir James was not a stupid man, and he had certainly noticed Paul's reliance on his left hand. "Like mine?"
Paul set his right arm on the table and showed his damaged
hand. "A shell at Austerlitz. It was badly set and never healed
properly."

"Pity." Sir James relaxed back into his chair. "You were in the
army, then?"

The talk turned to war. Paul's injuries had forced him out of
the army long before the French fought against the British on
the Spanish Peninsula. But his cousin Robert had fought on the
Peninsula and had posed as an English officer on numerous intelligence missions. Paul had enough secondhand stories and information to pass himself off as a former soldier in the British
Army. He held Sir James's attention for the next half hour.

"I'd have liked to be a military man myself." Sir James filled
his glass for the fourth or fifth time. "There's something nice
and straightforward about battle. Running an estate now . . ."
He shook his head. "I've just had the devil of a time convincing my tenants in Perthshire that I don't mean to burn them out
of their homes."

"These are difficult times for Highland crofters." Paul kept
his voice neutral. It would not do to antagonize Sir James.

Sir James set down the decanter with the force of frustration. "Damme, I know that. But the old life died at Culloden, along with half our ancestors. The price of cattle has fallen pitifully. There's money to be made in sheep. And by God, this region needs money if we're ever to prosper again. In ten years they'll see the right of it."

Paul thought of the Doons. "I suspect most crofters count themselves fortunate if they can see their way through the winter, let alone ten years."

Sir James scowled into his whisky as though the answer lay in the pale gold liquid. "I've set up a kelp farm on the coast and a model village in Perthshire. Most of my tenants claim they can do better in the factories in the south."

Most of his tenants were starving. But Sir James was a more interesting man than Paul had at first supposed. At another time Paul would have been tempted to engage his host in a debate on reform. But though Sir James's suspicions seemed to have dissipated, Paul was not convinced they were out of the woods. It would be wise to beat a retreat. He pushed back his chair. "Thank you for the excellent whisky. If you'll excuse me, I should go up. My wife's health is still delicate."

Sir James rose and held out his hand. Paul grasped it.

"That's my coat and breeches you're wearing," Sir James said.

"I'm much indebted to you, sir. Your wife said you no longer wore them."

"I don't, eh?" Sir James patted the solid paunch around his midsection. "Well, I daresay she's right. You're welcome to them. Good night, Lester."

FENELLA SHIFTED THE BABY AT HER BREAST. THE CHILD was fretful tonight. Small wonder, for her mother could scarcely manage to sit still until Paul's return. Fenella leaned back in the chair and willed the tension from her arms and shoulders.

At last the door opened and Paul came into the room. "What

happened?" Fenella asked, the moment the door was closed again.

Paul tugged his neckcloth loose. "We drank whisky and talked about the war. I managed to pass myself off as a British soldier."

"And?"

He shrugged out of his borrowed coat. "I don't think we need fear Sir James will throw us from the house."

She drew a breath of frustration. "Paul—"

The baby turned her head from Fenella's breast and let out a wail of discomfort. "She needs a burp," Paul said. "I'll take her."

Fenella bit back the protest she had been about to make. It would be easier to talk when the baby had gone down. She gave the child to Paul and adjusted her dressing gown to cover her breast. After sharing the room—and the bed—with him for five days, she had lost all feelings of shame or modesty in his presence. Her qualms about their intimacy now seemed laughable.

She looked up to see Paul tucking the blanket round the baby. His face was bent low over the cradle so it was within the baby's narrow range of vision. He was smiling down at her with a look that Fenella would have called pure idiocy save that she knew she looked at the baby in precisely the same way.

Paul straightened up and caught her watching him. The smile gave way to a sheepish look. He had an unexpected tender side that sat oddly with his harsh and sometimes bitter self. She felt as though she had known him all her life, yet one day, when she had her own life back, she would walk away from him and he from her. The thought brought a tightness to her chest. She told herself it was fear.

"We have to leave," she said, more abruptly than she intended.

"Leave? Why?"

"Sir James. He's not blinded by fondness for the baby the way Lady Margaret is. We can't hope he won't find something odd in our being here. Do you think he truly believes our story?"

"No," Paul admitted. "He doesn't disbelieve it, but he's suspicious. And he's heard of McAlpin's murder."

"Mother of God." The tightness in her chest returned. "We have to leave, Paul. Tonight. I'm quite well enough to travel. We can't risk his bringing the soldiers down upon us. By morning we'll be far away."

"By morning we'll be fortunate to be ten miles off. Unless you plan to commandeer Sir James's coach and a team of horses. That would get the wind up."

Paul sat down in a chair and crossed his legs. Curse the man, he was not going to heed anything she had to say. "You'd have us sit here like rats in a trap, waiting to be put to death?" she asked.

"I have no intention of being put to death."

"And I have no intention of being taken by Ned Rutledge."

"Sir James has heard nothing of a woman being involved with McAlpin's killer. And if we leave tonight, it's an admission of guilt. Sir James would have no difficulty in catching us and turning us over to the authorities."

"If we leave tonight, we have a chance. If need be we'll abandon the cart and take to the hills. Dugal will know what to do."

Paul got to his feet, but made no move to come toward her. "With you still bleeding?"

"I'm strong. I can do it."

"You'd put the baby at risk."

He had stopped her. Unfair. Oh, unfair. But her child must be protected at all costs.

"We're anxious to get home," Paul said, his voice more gentle now that he had won the contest between them. "Lady Margaret will understand that. She'll persuade her husband to lend us their coach and coachman. We can leave in a day or two. Three at the most. We'll travel faster and in far greater safety. Even soldiers are cautious when faced with a crest."

He was right. Damn his soul to hell, he was right. And he had thought of the baby when she had not. "You promise?"

He smiled. "I promise."

He was humoring her. Why not? He had got his own way. Paul was an opponent she could not match. But his smile disarmed her, reminding her of all they had shared. Still, she would not let it end here.

"Because if you break your promise, Paul Lescaut," she said with the sweetest smile she could muster, "I'll cut your throat with a knife."

PAUL KEPT HIS WORD, AT LEAST TO THE EXTENT OF RAISING the subject of their leaving at the breakfast table the following morning. Lady Margaret's face fell. "Oh, my dear Mr. Lester, is that wise? It's been less than a week since Mrs. Lester's confinement, and surely the baby is much too young to travel. Besides, the boys will be home for their holidays soon and I do so want you to meet them."

Sir James wiped a trace of egg from his mustache. "You mustn't put yourself at risk, Mrs. Lester. My wife's delighted to have you here. Stay as long as you like. I insist upon it." He gave Fenella a broad smile, then turned his attention to a dish of broiled whiting.

Fenella did not trust his smile, still less his sudden cordiality. Paul was right. Sir James might not disbelieve their story, but neither did he fully accept it.

"My wife is very anxious to see her home again." Paul turned to Fenella. "Almost as anxious, my dear, as you were to leave it and come to Scotland." He smiled wryly at Sir James. "Women."

"Ah. Quite so. Still, we must insist on prudence." Sir James glanced at Lady Margaret, then looked away, as though unwilling to face an argument this early in the day.

Lady Margaret set down the marmalade spoon with a crisp clatter. "Mr. Lester, you cannot mean to take your wife and child all the way to Devon in a farm cart."

"We hope to find connections to the stage in Edinburgh," Fenella said.

"But you'll have to reach Edinburgh first. You won't find a stage in these parts. Not easily." Sir James pushed down one of the larger beagles whose head had appeared over the edge of the table.

"Surely not the stage. James, my love, we must send them to Edinburgh in one of our carriages. William Coachman can drive them, and Beth can go along to help with the baby. What a splendid idea! I'm so glad I thought of it."

The conversation had at least turned to the means of their departure, but Sir James continued to oppose their leaving. "Yes, yes, of course you will go in our carriage, but not just yet, Mrs. Lester. Must get your strength back, you know. I understand last night was the first time you'd ventured from your room. You'll forgive me if I say you look a bit peaked."

"Oh, but I gain strength every day. I feel in the best of health this morning. Mr. Lester and I plan to walk in the grounds after breakfast." Fenella gave Sir James a brilliant smile and vowed to use the rouge pot before she came down to dinner.

In truth she did not feel in the most robust health. The bleeding had diminished from a gushing of bright red blood to a watery pinkish flow, but she still suffered from cramping and she was miserably sore. Her breasts, which had taken Sir James's attention the night before—and small wonder, for they were twice or more their usual size—were sore and tight. The baby woke every four hours demanding food. Fenella was wretchedly tired. It was often an effort to dress or to make conversation. But she would complain of none of this to Paul. Both Paul and Sir James must be made to see that she was fit to travel.

The day was fresh and warm, wispy clouds contending with the sun for dominance of the sky. "You've made your point," Paul said when they had been walking for perhaps a quarter hour. "We're out of sight of the house, and there's a bench ahead where you can rest."

"I have no intention of resting. It's pure heaven to be out. I only wish we were on the road to Edinburgh."

"We will be, tomorrow or the day after. My wife has these odd crotchets, and I always indulge her caprices. It's the only way to keep peace in the family. Sir James will understand."

For the moment the knot of fear in her chest eased. Paul was so confident, and the day—glorious compared to most they had spent in Scotland—made it hard to think anything would go amiss. "I must confess the thought of a well-sprung carriage is tempting. I have bad memories of the cart. What do we do with it?"

"Leave it behind as a farewell gift. It's all we have to offer. That and the pony."

"I shall miss the pony."

"When I have more than a groat to my name, I'll buy you another."

"You're the most indulgent of husbands, Mr. Lester."

"I would spare my wife any pain."

Laughter bubbled up inside her. It was nonsense, of course, this playacting, but it made her lighthearted. And it hid something neither of them could yet put into words. For the moment she could savor their growing friendship. For the moment she did not have to think of their inevitable parting.

"Your arm, Mr. Lester. I find myself growing fatigued."

Paul raised his brows. She had learned to accept his help when she must, but she had never asked for it in so trivial a situation.

He held out his arm and tucked hers through it, his hand resting briefly on her own. She was startled by its warmth. They had lied for one another. They shared the same bed, though he was careful not to touch her. She had watched him shave and tie his cravat. He had changed the baby's napkins, helped with the buttons on her dress, fastened a borrowed necklace about her throat. There were moments when she could almost believe their charade was real and he was indeed her husband.

But this was different. She glanced up at his face, so familiar and harsh and—yes—even handsome. When he smiled, as he was doing now, she glimpsed a different person beneath the bitter facade. For the first time she was aware of them as man and woman. His touch brought something more than comfort, something that was sweet and perhaps dangerous.

She was careful not to remove her hand, lest that say more than she intended. They strolled, turning back only when she was hard put to deny the depths of her fatigue.

As they came in sight of the house Lady Margaret, who had been standing at the bottom of the front steps, ran down the path toward them. She was agitated beyond her usual state, and her hair threatened to come free of its pins. "We are in the most dreadful coil," she said, breathing hard from her exertion. "I saw you from the window and came out immediately. We've been closeted for the last half hour with the most extraordinary young man. Mrs. Lester, is it possible you have another husband?"

Chapter 10

❈

FENELLA'S THROAT WENT DRY. SHE FELT A DREADFUL hollowness in her chest. "Mr. Lester is my husband," she said, mustering all the firmness she could command.

"That's exactly what I told Mr. Hagerty, but he insists you are she—that is, his wife, Sophie—and that you were separated in Kinrie and he believes you are in a confused state of mind. He's heard that you are in the company of an unscrupulous man who abducted you, which I told him was preposterous, for you already have a husband and he is not in the least unscrupulous, and what reason would he have to abduct you in your condition? Besides, your mind is as clear as mine, and your name is Fenella, not Sophie, and you have just given birth to a daughter. I must say Mr. Hagerty became very agitated at this last. His wife was expecting, he said, though not so soon. Oh, my dear Mrs. Lester, I'm afraid Sir James takes the young man's story very seriously. You must come in at once and tell us which of the two husbands is truly yours."

Fenella heard her out. It would be impossible to answer Lady Margaret's request. Not unless the sight of the man who had fathered her child—who had most likely fathered it, for she was not sure on this point—triggered some rush of memory, or at least recognition. But the name Hagerty meant nothing to her. The man must be mistaken. Yet the coincidence of his losing his wife in Kinrie strained belief. No. Unless she knew him beyond any possibility of doubt, her only safety lay in insisting that Paul was her husband.

She glanced at Paul. His face was unreadable. She removed

her hand from his arm. "Very well. Then we must see this Mr. Hagerty. I'm sure he will soon realize his mistake."

Lady Margaret gave a sigh of relief and ran up the stairs, the flounces on her dress picking up stray twigs on the way. She was still breathless. "Of course you are right. But I don't know whatever I am to do with Sir James. Men."

Fenella could not help but smile. "My husband excepted."

"Oh, yes. That is, your present husband."

"Mr. Lester."

"Whoever else would I be thinking of?" Lady Margaret led them to a small room at the front of the house that was known as the morning room. It was flooded with sunlight, intensifying the yellow-patterned chintz that covered the chairs and the pair of settees that flanked the fireplace. Sir James was standing with his elbow on the white marble mantel. A small frown creased his forehead, but his face bore the look of triumph that comes from having been proved right against all opposition.

The other occupant of the room was seated on a settee with his back to the door, but he jumped up at their entrance. "Sophie. My dear girl." He came toward her, stumbling over the settee in his eagerness, and held out his hands. Fenella gripped Paul's arm and drew back.

A look of bewilderment crossed Hagerty's face. "Sophie, what's the matter? Don't you know me?"

It was what Ned Rutledge had asked her, and the answer was the same. She had no recollection of the man before her.

Sir James's frown deepened. Lady Margaret seemed disappointed and bewildered. Even the flounces on her gown and the ribbons on her sleeves had gone limp. Paul stood absolutely still. Fenella knew that he was giving her the choice of how to deal with Hagerty.

She left the security of Paul's arm and stepped forward, hands clasped loosely in front of her. "I don't believe I know you, sir. Come into the light where I may see you properly."

"Oh, yes. Absolutely." Hagerty moved backward, stumbling once more over the corner of the settee. "Will this do?"

"Turn a bit toward the windows. That's it." Fenella walked back and forth before Hagerty, who looked supremely uncomfortable at her scrutiny. He was a tall, thin man of perhaps thirty years with an amiable face and an awkward posture. His blond hair fell across his forehead, and he brushed it back repeatedly in a nervous gesture. His eyes were a pale brown, his nose long and narrow, his chin indeterminate.

"See here, Sophie, are you all right? Got hit in the head, they said, left you a bit confused, not sure what you're about. We'll sort this out. Splendid news about the baby. You're all right, aren't you? Look a bit pale to me. Not up to your usual twig."

Fenella stopped and looked up into his earnest face. His gaze wavered, as though he was reluctant to meet her own. She knew then, with a certainty that could not be denied, that he was not her husband. Amiable and weak, likable even, with no evidence of ill-intent on his vacuous face. But she would never have given herself to a man like Hagerty. She had forgotten her past, but she knew some core of herself. Hagerty was not a man she would have married.

She felt a sudden frisson of fear or anticipation. Her mind had conjured an image of a dark-haired man with a wicked smile. "You're an impostor, sir. Tom is my husband."

Hagerty's face broke into a broad smile. "That's it. Oh, jolly good. Tom Hagerty."

"But you are not my Tom."

Lady Margaret gasped. "Oh, merciful heavens. Three husbands."

Paul helped Lady Margaret to one of the settees. It was only then that Fenella realized what she had done. In denying Hagerty, she had denied Paul as well. It would all have to come out now. They might escape Lady Margaret, but Sir James would never let them go.

Damn them all. It was time to bring this to an end. She took a step toward Hagerty, backing him against the seat of a chair. He lost his balance and sat down abruptly. "Who are you? Who sent you? How do you know so much about me? The truth now. Who am I? Tell me my name."

Hagerty's round eyes grew rounder. He looked like a fish that found itself out of water, floundering on the alien earth. "See here—"

"No. I'll hear no more lies. What are you doing here? How did you find me?"

Hagerty's boneless body grew even more limp. He struggled to his feet. Fenella put a hand on his chest and pushed him back into the chair. "For the love of God, tell me who I am."

"You're Sophie, like I said." He swallowed. "Sophie Rutledge."

Rutledge. Mother in heaven, was she married to the unspeakable Ned? No, her husband had dark hair and his name was Tom. "You don't know me."

"Can't say that I do. Saw a miniature of you once. Lovely thing. Daresay you were in better health in those days. Roses in the cheeks, what? But I recognized you at once."

He tried again to get to his feet. Fenella suspected it was a question of good manners. She put out a restraining hand and he subsided in the chair. "Told him it was a rum thing to do," he muttered, "but he swore it would work."

"Swore? Who swore? Who sent you after me, Mr. Hagerty?"

"Why, Ned, of course. Ned Rutledge. Tom's brother. Would have come for you himself, but he said you were out of your mind. Well, in a manner of speaking. Didn't know him when he tried to help you. Threw a rock at him and hurt him most frightfully and then ran away. Then some cove who's wanted for murder abducted you. Had to get you back. Try anything. Ned told me all about it. I was staying with the Brideswells. Very decent people. They have a house near Loch Lomond. Had a party up for the fishing. Ned came to see me there. We were at Cambridge together. Couldn't help but oblige."

Hagerty took out a handkerchief and wiped the perspiration from his face. Sir James made a threatening noise and took a step toward Paul.

Lady Margaret moaned. "We *know* the Brideswells. My cousin Julianna is married to a connection of theirs. Surely they can't be mixed up in this?"

Paul walked to Fenella's side and looked down at Hagerty. "Where is Tom Rutledge? Why didn't he come for his wife himself?"

Hagerty glanced at Fenella, then looked left and right. He was imprisoned in the chair. "You heard me," Paul said. "Why didn't he come? Surely he was aware of his wife's condition."

"Not exactly. That is, he knew, but not recently. Oh, hang it all."

Fenella had grown light-headed with memories. Fragments, images too fleeting to hold. "He couldn't come," she said, certain of this at least. Her stomach twisted at the memory. "Tom's dead. He shot himself."

PAUL STARED AT FENELLA. SHE LOOKED BACK AT HIM, HER eyes wide with surprise. The room had gone very quiet. Somewhere a dog barked. Hagerty had burrowed into his chair, a schoolboy hoping he would not be called on to recite. Lady Margaret was pale with shock. Sir James stood with hunched shoulders and clenched fists, a bear of a man who didn't know where to turn.

Paul had known there was a husband, that someday he would come to claim his wife. He had once longed for that day, which would put an end to the burden he had assumed in Kinrie. Yet even Lady Margaret's announcement of Hagerty's arrival had not made it real. Still less the sight of Hagerty himself. Paul had gone quiet inside, suspending all feeling until Fenella announced that Hagerty was an impostor. Then he had allowed himself to breathe again, knowing she was speaking the truth.

But Tom was real. With her memory of her husband's death Fenella had gone through a door and stepped into another room, a room forbidden to him. They were only a few inches apart, but she seemed a vast distance away. He knew he had lost her. He had not expected it to hurt so much.

Paul looked from Lady Margaret to Sir James. "I think you should hear our story."

Sir James raised his fist. "By God, Lester, that we should."

"James, my love, come sit by me. I need you." The steel that underlaid Lady Margaret's fluttering ribbons was once more in evidence. Her husband hesitated, but the bear had long been tamed. He threw himself onto the settee next to his wife and took her hand.

Paul turned to Fenella. "Shall I? Or would you rather tell them yourself?"

"Please. Tell them." She sank into the nearest chair as if her legs would no longer support her. She looked up at him and mouthed the words "I'm sorry."

"Don't be," he said, in a voice nearly as quiet. "It's time this was in the open." He walked to the windows and faced the group. With the light behind him his face could not be clearly seen. His audience would strain to follow his words. "Mrs. Rutledge and I are not married," he began.

Lady Margaret gasped. No doubt she was thinking of the room they had shared.

Hagerty looked up from contemplation of the tassels on his boots. "I say, it ought to be Lady Rutledge. Tom was a baronet."

So she had a title. He might have known. "I called her Fenella," Paul went on, "because it was necessary to call her something. Ned Rutledge later called her Sophie, but we had no reason to trust him. Until this hour I did not know her real name. Nor did she. Mrs.—Lady Rutledge has lost her memory."

"Balderdash!" Sir James was not going to make this easy.

Lady Margaret held out her hand to Fenella. "Oh, my dear."

"Told you so," Hagerty said as though he had finally been justified. "Lost her mind. Worrisome thing to happen."

"Less worrisome than the reason for it. I found Lady Rutledge unconscious in a narrow side street in Kinrie. She'd been knifed and was bleeding heavily. A man we now know was Ned Rutledge appeared, prepared—I thought—to help her. Instead, he attacked me. I fought him off. Matt McAlpin, who had knifed Lady Rutledge, attacked me as well and was killed. McAlpin and Rutledge were both strangers to me. I'd only arrived in Kinrie that morning. But I was determined to save my life and the life of the woman they were trying to kill."

Paul stopped to let the brutish outlines of the story sink in. Hagerty stirred in his chair. "Must be some mistake," he said. "Ned and I were at Cambridge together. Put him up for my club."

Lady Margaret moaned and covered her mouth with her hand. Paul wondered if she was going to be sick.

Sir James sprang to his feet and took a turn about the room. "You claim Rutledge and McAlpin were accomplices?"

"I'm sure of it." Paul held Sir James with his eyes. "Rutledge told the soldiers I'd killed McAlpin, but said nothing of Lady Rutledge. If he'd truly been frantic to find her, why wouldn't he have enlisted the soldiers' aid?"

"Oh, that's easy. He—That is—" Hagerty broke off. He looked as if he'd just kicked aside a stone and glimpsed something ugly underneath.

Sir James looked sharply at Hagerty, then turned back to Paul. "Let's be very clear about this." He led Paul through all the tortuous steps of the journey that had brought them to the McClaren house. Fenella added her version of the story, particularly her encounter with Ned Rutledge on the hilltop.

"No," Hagerty objected. "You couldn't have seen a knife. Out of your head, said so yourself. Emotional creatures, women, bless them, at the best of times, and in your condition . . ." He waved his hands as though the matter was self-evident to every man present.

"I saw the knife." Fenella's voice did not waver.

Sir James took Paul through the story again and again, seeking always for other interpretations of the events he related. Paul answered him patiently. Sir James's certainty that Paul was the greatest villain on earth cracked, shattered, and gave way to bafflement. When he had no more to say he shook his head over and over, cleared his throat, and sat down heavily on the settee.

"I can't bring myself to believe it," he said at last. "God's mercy, Lady Rutledge is Ned Rutledge's brother's wife."

"Hagerty." Paul turned to the other man. "Who is Sir Thomas Rutledge's heir?"

"Why, Ned, of course. See here, you can't mean . . . Anyway, it would have gone to Lady Rutledge's child if it had been a boy, which it wasn't, and Ned had no way of knowing—Oh, my God." Hagerty put his face in his hands.

Paul looked at Fenella. You're safe, he wanted to tell her. There's no more danger. Her face was pale, her hands clenched. She did not seem to believe him.

"Where's Rutledge now?" Paul asked Hagerty.

"At an inn not ten miles from here. I was to bring Lady Rutledge and he would see her home." Hagerty shoved himself forward in his chair. "I should leave. He'll be wondering what's gone amiss."

Sir James sprang to his feet. "You'll go nowhere, Hagerty. By God, you've lied to us. You've lied to me. You've got to answer for that." He turned to Paul and squared his shoulders. "Lester, it seems I owe you an apology."

"Merciful heavens." Lady Margaret had risen and moved to the windows that commanded a view of the front drive. "There are *soldiers* out there trampling the borders. James, whatever have you done?"

Fear leaped into Fenella's eyes. She jumped to her feet, ran out of the room, and started up the stairs. Paul ran after her. He could hear Lady Margaret's indignant voice through the open door of the morning room and her husband's reassuring response. "Not to worry, Meg, I'll take care of it."

"Like you've already done? James, how could you be such a prime idiot?"

Fenella stopped and looked back. Her eyes were glassy, as

though she did not really see the room below. Paul reached her side. Lady Margaret was coming up the stairs behind them. Paul could still hear Sir James's voice.

"You'll go where I tell you, Hagerty, and do just as I say." Sir James stormed out of the morning room and slammed the door behind him, then took up a position in the center of the hall facing the front door. He signaled the footman on duty to be prepared to answer the expected summons. The dogs, who had been sleeping in the hall, pricked up their ears.

Fenella continued up the stairs. Paul followed. As they reached the first-floor gallery there was a heavy pounding at the door accompanied by unintelligible shouts. The dogs began to bark. The door was flung wide by the footman and a great number of red-coated soldiers burst into the hall, fanning out right and left as though they intended to seize the house and all who lived there. The soldier who seemed to be in charge came to an abrupt stop not three feet from Sir James. "Sir James McClaren?"

Fenella grasped the gallery railing for support. All the blood seemed to have drained from her face. *"Papa?"* she said in a bewildered whisper. She turned to Paul, the glassy look still in her eyes. "Paul? *Qu'est-ce qui s'est passé?"* Then, with an inarticulate cry, she fled toward the sanctuary of their room.

Paul stared after her, unable to move.

"Mr. Lester," Lady Margaret said in an urgent whisper, "come away from the railing. You'll be seen." She grasped Paul by the hand and pulled him down the corridor.

Paul followed, too shaken to make any protest. For a moment he had been in another house, watching other soldiers—in blue coats faced with red, he remembered that well—search for a man who was about to die. A girl with honey-colored hair crouched on the landing by his side, asking him to make sense of a world spinning out of control, a world he had helped create.

He saw Fenella's bewildered, panic-stricken face. Beneath the bones that stretched her skin taut he saw the rounder face of the child Sophie. Fenella had spoken in French. Her words were the same—they haunted his dreams, they were burned in his memory for all eternity.

How could he not have known? His father, Sophie's Uncle Daniel, had a house in Kinrie. That was the lure that had taken him there. That was where he had found Fenella.

That was where he had found Sophie de Milvery.

Chapter 11

CAPTAIN JOHN SOMERSET DREW A BREATH AND STRUGGLED to make his voice heard over the barking dogs. "I don't understand, Sir James. I would have thought you'd lock the man up."

"Couldn't very well do that to a guest, could I?" Sir James rocked on his heels. "Highland hospitality and all that."

"But the man's a murderer." Captain Somerset pushed down a dog who was pawing at his leg.

"We don't know that for a certainty, do we? We don't even know he's the man you're looking for. Awkward situation all around. I haven't told him I sent for you, of course. I hope you'll be discreet."

Captain Somerset stared at the muddy pawprints on his white breeches, then raised his eyes to Sir James's face. "I don't think you understand the gravity of the situation, Sir James. This man could be dangerous. We should learn the truth about him without delay."

"Then you'd best have a word with him, hadn't you? I believe he's in the library. He has a fondness for poetry. Never could stomach the stuff myself."

Somerset's jaw clenched. "Thank you, Sir James." He turned to his men. "Lewis, Carter, you stay here. See that no one leaves the house. The rest of you come with me."

Something sharp pinched his foot. Another of the dogs was chewing on his boot. He shook the animal off. The dog growled.

"Perseus," Sir James said. "Sorry about that, Somerset. Can't tell you how many boots I go through in a year. But what would a house be without animals?"

"Quite." Somerset swallowed, hard. "The library?"

"Of course. Only waiting for you."

Sir James moved through an archway into a cool, dimly lit corridor. Somerset followed. So did his men. So did two of the dogs. Somerset kept his gaze fixed straight ahead and ignored the sound of paws padding on the stone floor and the feel of a tail swishing against his leg. If he lived to be a hundred he would never understand the Scots. He had been stationed in the Highlands for over a year now, but he felt less at home than he had as part of the Army of Occupation in Paris. In some ways keeping the peace in the conquered French capital had been easier than enforcing His Majesty's laws in this remote backwater. At least with the Parisians one knew where one stood.

Sir James *looked* like an Englishman. He spoke with only a trace of a Scots burr. But he was plainly a breed apart. Still, whatever else he was, he was a gentleman and should be treated as such. It was a ticklish situation. It wasn't often that Somerset had a chance to do anything as important as arrest a fugitive murderer. But he knew it would not sit well with his commanding officer if he alienated one of the most important landowners in the district in the process.

"Here we are." Sir James pushed open a door. "Captain Somerset wants to have a word with you, Lester. Lester?"

Somerset followed Sir James into a dark-paneled room that smelled of leather and dog hair. Sofas, tables, wing chairs, and a pair of writing desks were arranged haphazardly about the room. Books, periodicals, and newspapers were piled on tables, stacked on the floor, draped over chair and sofa arms. But there was no sign of another person, let alone a fugitive with an injured hand.

One of the dogs jumped up on a sofa covered in burgundy leather and lay down with her head on her paws. Somerset looked at Sir James. "Dod," Sir James said. "I could have sworn he was in the library."

"Could he have left the house?"

"Shouldn't think so. He'd already taken a walk this morning."

"I mean, could he have run off?"

"Why should he? He didn't know I'd sent for you. Let's have a look in the music room."

There was no one in the music room, nor the breakfast parlor, nor a sitting room done up in bright yellow. In the dining room a footman was polishing the silver. He stammered, as though overawed by the presence of authority, but insisted he had been at the task for over an hour and hadn't seen Mr. Lester in that time. A maidservant dusting the porcelain in a small parlor hung with rose-patterned silk said she thought Mr. Lester had gone to the library. Had they looked there?

"Hmm." Sir James stepped back into the corridor. "Perhaps he went to the kitchen for a wee bite."

"I'll send two of my men to search the kitchen. Then perhaps you'd be so good as to take me to Mr. Lester's room."

"Shouldn't think he'd be there. Not the sort to rest during the day."

"Nonetheless." Somerset started down the corridor, not waiting for Sir James to lead the way.

A high-pitched shriek sounded from the hall.

"Oh, the devil. My wife." Sir James pushed past Somerset. Somerset followed him to the hall in time to see a fair-haired woman dressed in a swirl of white muslin and coral ribbons fling herself upon Sir James while the dogs jumped around them.

The woman clutched Sir James's coat. "Dearest, why didn't you tell me there was a dangerous man in the house?"

"Now, now, Meg." Sir James gave her a hearty pat on the back. "I didn't want to alarm you."

"Alarm me!" The woman pulled away from him. Her eye fell on Somerset. "Have you caught him?"

Somerset felt as if he were back in the schoolroom answering a question from his governess. "No, ma'am. Not yet. But we have every intention—"

"Not yet!" Her Dresden-blue eyes darkened with anger. "What are you soldiers good for if you can't protect innocent women and their bairns? I insist you search the house at once, Lieutenant—"

"Captain. Haven't you learned to read insignias yet, Meg?" Sir James put a restraining arm around his wife. "Captain Somerset. My wife, Lady Margaret."

"My lady." Somerset sketched a bow. One couldn't let standards slip, whatever the circumstances. He knew that Sir James's wife was a daughter of the Earl of Traquair.

"I insist you search the house, Captain Somerset. Oh, I knew we shouldn't have taken that man in."

"Did he seem dangerous to you, Lady Margaret?"

"Well." Lady Margaret hesitated. One of the dogs rested its head on her feet. Another made a grab for a knot of ribbon on her skirt. "He was certainly odd."

"Odd?" Perhaps they were getting somewhere. Lady Margaret might be highly strung, but at least she understood the dangers of the situation. "Odd how?"

"Different." She tugged her skirt away from the dog. "Very English."

Somerset heard one of his men make a choking sound. He would have to speak to them again about the gravity of their position as representatives of His Majesty's Government. "Where did you last see Mr. Lester, Lady Margaret?"

"Oh, I haven't seen him since breakfast. I've been quite distracted with my poor cousin Fenella, who's just had a baby. A dear little lassie, but I'm afraid she's not doing at all well. Fenella, I mean, not the bairn. The shock will be terrible for her. She has a nervous complaint, you know."

"I'm very sorry to hear it. Lady Margaret—"

"We've sent for a doctor from Edinburgh. He teaches at the university. An Englishman, but they do say he's clever. We're expecting him any moment now. You will be careful not to alarm Fenella, won't you?"

"Yes, for the love of heaven." Sir James looked up from scratching one of the dogs behind the ears. "I tell you frankly,

Somerset, if you leave me with a pack of hysterical females on my hands, I'll lodge a complaint with your commanding officer."

"It isn't our practice to terrorize women and children, Sir James."

"Isn't it?" Sir James straightened up to his full height. "How do you account for that incident at Loch Awe?"

"James." Lady Margaret frowned at her husband. "Don't start an argument now. Shouldn't you continue with the search, Captain Somerset?"

Somerset had intended to continue with the search for the last quarter hour. He wasn't sure how he had got sidetracked. He straightened his coat. "Mulgrave, Hagley, see to the kitchens and secure the back entrances. Carter, go along and help them. Lewis, continue on here. Sir James, if you could take the rest of us upstairs?"

Lady Margaret hurried to the stairs ahead of them. "Your men will be careful, won't they? Oh, goodness, look at the mess on the floor. You'd all best wipe your boots before you come up."

Somerset looked at his men. They looked back at him in disbelief. Somerset inclined his head, walked to the mat by the door, and scraped his boots against it.

"Bloody hell," Carter muttered under his breath. But the soldiers lined up and one by one wiped their boots clean while Lady Margaret looked on with gimlet-sharp eyes. Sir James had dropped down on the bottom step with the dogs clustered around him. His own boots were liberally caked with mud. The footman stood by with a wooden face.

"There." Lady Margaret beamed with approval. "Splendid." Again Somerset was reminded of his governess. She had spoken in just that tone when she inspected his hands before a meal. "Now—"

Her words were drowned out by banging on the door. Somerset found himself engulfed in a tangle of men and animals as the dogs rushed to the door and his men tried to move to the side. Lewis skidded on the stone and landed on his backside. Two dogs started licking his face.

"Dear me, it must be the doctor." Lady Margaret patted her hair. "I must say, I didn't expect him to make such a dreadful racket. Do see, Ronald."

"Excuse me, sir." The footman picked his way through the chaos of dogs and soldiers and opened the heavy oak door.

"Is it your practice to keep callers idling for a quarter hour?" A man dressed in a long black traveling cloak and a tall black top hat strode into the hall, ignoring the dogs, who leapt at him and tried to bite the black bag clutched in his right hand. "I am Dr. Farquarson. Where is my patient?"

"Oh, Dr. Farquarson, thank goodness." Lady Margaret hurried forward. "I am Lady Margaret. My cousin is upstairs. I'm so worried about her."

"From your letter it sounds as if you have cause. There's no telling where a nervous complaint may lead. Especially so soon after the birth of a child." Dr. Farquarson handed his hat to the footman, but showed no sign of removing his cloak or his thick black leather gloves. His hair was tinged with gold, a surprising contrast to the unrelieved black. He was younger than Somerset had at first thought, probably in his mid-thirties, but he looked as if he took little enjoyment from life. There was something fierce about his face. His brows seemed to be drawn into a permanent scowl.

Dr. Farquarson glanced about the hall. "Are these all family members?"

"Oh, goodness no." Lady Margaret made a vague gesture. "Captain Somerset and his men have come to arrest one of our guests. That is, they have if he is who they think he is, and I really am most afraid he is, but my husband would insist that we take him in. The guest, I mean, not Captain Somerset."

Somerset stepped forward. "We have reason to believe the man in question is a fugitive who committed a most brutal murder. We are in the process of searching the house to apprehend him."

"Well, don't let me stop you." Dr. Farquarson looked at Somerset. Or through him. Somerset had the feeling that the doctor regarded him as a troubling nuisance, like the dogs. "I only ask that you not disturb my patient. Any upset at such a critical time could bring on nervous spasms."

Somerset drew himself up. He was tired of conceding ground. "We have no desire to trouble any member of the household. But we have a duty to perform."

"Then you'd best get about it." Dr. Farquarson pulled a gold watch from beneath his cloak and flicked it open. "My time is valuable, Lady Margaret. I didn't come here to discuss deficiencies in our system of justice. Where is my patient?"

"Upstairs." Lady Margaret took the doctor's arm and drew him to the stairs. "James, you'll help Captain Somerset, won't you? And do see that everything is put back in its proper place. It's bad enough you brought that man into the house. I'll never forgive you if any of the china is broken."

"Weans." Sir James crossed to Somerset with a grimace of distaste. "Nasty business. Mind you, I don't blame Fenella for feeling poorly after all that. But what's a man to do when women start wailing and carrying on? Time to go after some salmon, if you ask me. Do you have children, Somerset?"

"No. I'm not so fortunate as to be married yet."

Sir James clapped him on the back. "No need for that to stop you."

Somerset coughed. "Sir James—"

"I know, you want to see the first floor. Just wanted to give my wife and that doctor fellow a wide berth. Ronald, take two of these fellows down to the kitchen and see if Mr. Lester's there."

Somerset's senses quickened as he climbed the stairs. The talk was done. Lester might be in his room, oblivious to impending discovery. Would he struggle? Was he armed? The murder had been committed with a knife, not a gun, yet it wouldn't do to underestimate the man.

But Lester was not in his room. It had a musty smell, as

though it had not been properly aired. Surprising from a hostess as fastidious as Lady Margaret. But the shaving things on the dresser and the dressing gown draped across the bed testified that Lester had indeed occupied the room. He must be hiding. Perhaps he had heard their arrival. Damn those dogs. Somerset glared at the four who had followed them into Lester's room. The other two had gone with Lady Margaret and the doctor. "We'd best see the rest of the rooms. All of them." He looked at his men. "Check everywhere. In the wardrobes, under the beds."

Sir James raised his brows. "Oh, surely—"

"Everywhere." There was a limit to accommodating the locals.

He half expected Sir James to protest, but Sir James took them through each room on the first floor, including the now-empty nursery his sons had once occupied and the bedchamber he shared with Lady Margaret. There was no sign of the fugitive, though the men searched meticulously, even going through the two wardrobes and three cedar chests that contained Lady Margaret's clothes.

"That's the lot on this floor, I'm afraid," Sir James said. "Save for Fenella's room."

Somerset met Sir James's gaze. Searching the chamber of a new mother for a fugitive murderer was not the sort of peril he'd envisioned when he bought his commission, but he had vowed never to flinch from any task required of him in the service of his country. "Then you'd best take us there."

Sir James shook his head. "You're a brave man, Somerset. Remember what I said about hysterical females."

The room had lavender-sprigged walls and smelled of milk and dusting powder and another scent, sharp and sweet. The baby was crying. A fair-haired girl was bending over the child, doing up the tapes on a napkin. "Oh, dear," she said, looking up as the door opened. "I just be changin' her, Sir James."

"Carry on, Beth." Sir James waved a careless hand.

"Quiet." Dr. Farquarson's voice cut through the room, sharp

as a rifle report. "I am attempting to examine the patient." He was standing beside the chintz-draped four-poster. The bed-curtains were partially drawn so all that was visible of the patient was a white hand and the ruffled cuff of a nightdress.

Somerset heard his men shifting their weight from one foot to the other behind him. The dogs padded over to the hearth rug to join the two already in the room. The nurse put the baby's dirty napkin in a laundry bag. Lady Margaret, who was standing beside Dr. Farquarson, came toward her husband and Somerset, a finger to her lips. "You didn't find him?"

"I'm afraid not. We must search this room, Lady Margaret."

"But surely you don't believe he could be here?"

"He must have hidden himself somewhere in the house."

"Meg!" A shriek sounded from the bed. Lady Margaret's cousin pushed back the bed-curtain. "Who are those men?"

"Oh, dear, Fenella. I did so hope we wouldn't have to tell you."

"Tell me what?"

"What a coil. Perhaps you'd better explain, Captain Somerset. Captain Somerset?"

It was a moment before Somerset could find his voice. Those frightened, fiery blue eyes, deeper and darker than Lady Margaret's, held him rooted to the floor. But it was something elusive about her face that made his throat go tight and his breath come unevenly. She looked at once as fragile as etched glass and as strong as steel.

Dr. Farquarson snapped open his bag. "The captain has some notion about finding a murderer hidden behind the curtains."

"A murderer?" Fenella's voice rose.

Somerset swallowed. "We're looking for Mr. Lester."

"Well, he certainly isn't here." She shivered and wrinkled her nose. "You know I can't abide the man, Meg."

Lady Margaret moved back to the bed. "Yes, dearest, but—"

"Then why are they here?" Fenella's eyes darkened with realization. "Have they been sent to spy on me?" She seized Lady Margaret's hands. "My husband sent them, didn't he?

Will the man give me no peace?" She looked at Somerset. "Were you sent by my husband?"

"No, ma'am, certainly not." Somerset suppressed the impulse to draw back. Fenella was a beautiful woman, but there was a wildness in her eyes that chilled him. "We—"

"It's no good trying to reason with her." Dr. Farquarson reached across the bed and took Fenella by the shoulders. "No more screaming, do you hear me?"

"Leave me alone!" She flung off Dr. Farquarson, her eyes trained on Somerset. "I still don't know who sent you."

"Here, dear, drink some nice tea." Lady Margaret took a pink-flowered cup and saucer from the bedside table.

"I loathe tea." Fenella pushed her cousin away. The tea sloshed over the counterpane. Lady Margaret rescued the cup and saucer before they smashed to the floor. The baby started to scream.

Sir James pushed Somerset forward. "Now's your chance. Search the bloody room and have done with it."

FENELLA'S HEART SLAMMED INTO HER THROAT AT THE knock on the door. She had felt a wild exhilaration while Captain Somerset was in the room, but then he and his men had left to continue searching the house and there had been nothing to do but wait. She hadn't been able to draw a breath properly since.

"All clear." Sir James stepped into the room, a broad smile on his face. "Captain Somerset has decided Lester managed to slip out of the house. Somerset thinks I'm a bumbling fool, but he couldn't very well say so to my face. He and his men are searching the grounds now."

"Thank God." Fenella felt the air rush into her lungs. She looked down at the baby, who had fallen asleep in her arms, impervious to the tension in the room. Then she looked at Paul. As soon as the soldiers had left the room, he'd retreated to one of the chairs by the fireplace. He sat staring at the flames, his back to her.

Paul raised his head, but he looked at Sir James. "Will Somerset come back to the house?"

"I shouldn't think Somerset ever wants to set foot in the house again."

"James." Lady Margaret sprang up from the bed, where she had been sitting beside Fenella. "What did you do with Mr. Hagerty?"

Sir James grinned. "I gave him an apron and put him in the dining room to polish the silver. Somerset took him for a footman. Hagerty was a bit rattled, but he stuck to the story that he hadn't seen Lester."

"Oh, dear, James, I hope you didn't threaten the poor man too badly."

Despite his size Sir James looked like a mischievous schoolboy. "I just pointed out the consequences if he caused us any more trouble. I want to have another talk with him before he leaves. I expect you do as well, Lester." Sir James gave an appreciative chuckle. "I must say Dr. Farquarson's arrival took me by surprise. You should be at Drury Lane."

"My aunt had a passion for theatricals. She trained us all. I'm a mere amateur compared to my cousin Robert." Paul was on his feet, unfastening the black cloak. "Lady Margaret helped with the costume. I'm afraid we had to raid your wardrobe."

"Wasn't he splendid?" Lady Margaret clasped her hands together. "I would have been quite taken in myself if I hadn't known the truth. And you were positively frightening, Fenella. Sophie. Lady Rutledge, that is."

The sound of her real name was like a gust of Highland wind, shattering her momentary cocoon of relief. "Fenella," she said. "I haven't yet grown used to my new name. I mean, my old one." She looked at Paul again. Confronted with returning to her old life, she wanted an affirmation of the life she had shared with him. A life that was half necessity, half illusion. A life that seemed tenfold more real than the one she had lived as Sophie Rutledge.

Paul was pulling off the heavy leather gloves. The fingers of his right hand were white with the effort he had made to hold them straight. Her own fingers tingled at the pain he must be feeling. She had an impulse to take his hand between her own and rub the warmth and life back into it. But she knew he would not allow her to do so.

Paul set the gloves down and looked at her for the first time since the soldiers had left the room. His face was shuttered, as if the man she had begun to know in the last few days had retreated behind an invisible barrier. "How much do you remember?" he asked.

His voice was quiet and neutral. She would have preferred his sharpness. When he flayed her with his tongue at least she knew she had stirred some emotion in him.

Lady Margaret and Sir James were watching her like anxious parents. Fenella rocked the baby in her arms, trying to soothe herself as much as the child with the gentle rhythm. Her memories were a jumble of images, not a coherent narrative. Candlelight, perfumed air, the strains of a waltz. Crashing waves, the taste of salt on her tongue, a paved promenade. A gray sky, damp air, dark earth being flung on the polished wood of a casket. A house of dusty-pink sandstone, its windows glittering coldly in the afternoon sun. "Tom has—Tom had a house in Lancashire . . . in the Lake District," she said, not sure where the knowledge came from.

Sir James nodded. "So he did. I've heard of your late husband. Sir Thomas Rutledge was a Member of Parliament. He represented a borough just outside of Lancaster. He was considered to have a very promising career. The papers made much of—" Sir James swallowed.

"Of his suicide." Fenella waited for remembered grief to flood over her. It didn't. She must be done with her grieving. Or else she hadn't grieved at all.

Paul was still watching her, his gaze steady and dispassionate. "The Rutledge house will belong to Ned now. You can't go back there."

"No." The mention of Ned's name brought a lightning-sharp jolt of fear. But she knew all at once where she could go. The answer came without thought. "My uncle and aunt live in Lancashire as well. At Rossmere, near the Rutledge house. My uncle will protect me." The word gave her pause. She had resisted the need to be protected by anyone. She had been forced to admit that she needed Paul's protection. It was strange to think of anyone else in that role.

For a moment she thought she saw the feeling echoed in Paul's eyes, but the flicker of emotion was gone before she could grasp hold of it. She had already asked far too much of him. It was her kin she should turn to now. But she needed his help for a short time longer. Once she had hated to ask for his help. Now she was relieved she did not yet have to let him go. "I'd be grateful if you could go with me to my uncle's. My Uncle Daniel. He's the Marquis de Ribard."

"LANCASHIRE?" DUGAL STUMBLED OVER THE UNFAMILIAR name. It might as well have been Paris or Lisbon or St. Petersburg for all it meant to the boy.

"Fenella's family are there." Paul dropped down on the top step of the service stairs and leaned against the wall so he faced Dugal. They were outside the bedroom Dugal shared with the footmen. Nighttime quiet had descended over the house, broken only by their voices, just as the small circle of light cast by Paul's candle was all that disturbed the shadows. "I'm going to take Fenella home," Paul said. "Sir James and Lady Margaret say you can stay here as long as you like."

"Work i' the kitchen and miss all the excitement? No' bleedin' likely." Dugal slid down the wall and sprawled on the step across from Paul. "Ye wouldna' ha' got this far without me. How d'ye expect to take Fenella all the way to England on yer own?"

Paul smiled despite the weight in his chest. "I think Fenella would object to the idea of being taken anywhere." He chose his words with care. The kind of trouble that awaited him at the

Ribard house was beyond Dugal's powers of assistance, but he couldn't very well say so. "We certainly wouldn't have made it this far without your help, but we should have an easier time from now on. Sir James is loaning us a carriage and coachman and sending Beth along to help with the baby."

Dugal scowled. "What i' ye meet the soldiers?"

"No one will think to find an escaped fugitive in a carriage with the McClaren crest." And if they did, Fenella would be able to continue on to Lancashire alone, but Paul had no intention of entering into that debate with Dugal.

"What about Rutledge? What'll Hagerty tell him?"

"Nothing until tomorrow. Sir James has insisted he stay the night." In truth Hagerty had seemed relieved at the excuse to put off facing Ned Rutledge. Over dinner they had questioned Hagerty again about Rutledge, but had failed to learn anything more. Hagerty was clearly Rutledge's dupe, not his accomplice. Their questions had rattled him to the point where he wasn't sure what to believe. "Hagerty knows we're leaving tomorrow, but he thinks we're going to Edinburgh. If Rutledge wants to intercept us he'll head east. By that time we'll be well on our way south."

Dugal considered a moment, then shook his head. "I'd best come wi' ye."

"Have you ever been to England?"

"What's that to say to anythin'? I was goin' to Edinburgh and I've never been there afore."

Paul rested his head against the cool, rough stone of the wall. His temples had begun to throb. No, they had been throbbing for some time. Probably since the moment the soldiers burst into the house and Fenella whispered *Papa*. "I don't know how welcome we'll be with Fenella's family."

"After ye saved her life? And delivered the bairn? They bloody well ought to make ye a knight."

"They're not royalty, Dugal. Not quite."

"I dinna care i' they thank us or no'. I want to see her home safe." Dugal glared at Paul, his chin jutting out.

"You're as stubborn as Fenella."

"Ye're no' so sweet-tempered yerself."

"It's a wonder the three of us haven't come to blows." Paul studied Dugal. His face seemed less pinched than it had when they met. He looked more his age, slumped against the wall with the easy abandon of youth. But in the past few days he had proved himself more than most men did in a lifetime. "All right, Dugal. You can come to Lancashire if you insist on it. You've a right to see this through to the end. Once I'm sure Fenella's safe with her family I'm going back to Edinburgh. I don't know what tangle I'll find myself in with the law, but I daresay my cousin can find you work in his print shop."

The candle flame caught the flare of indignation in Dugal's eyes. "Ye're just goin' to leave Fenella i' Lancashire? Wi' Rutledge still on the loose? Ye canna."

"I can. I will." Paul picked up the candle. The flame wavered, but did not go out.

"How d'ye ken ye can trust this uncle o' hers?"

Paul bit back a shout of laughter. "People of that sort look after their own." Which perhaps was why Daniel de Ribard had never claimed Paul as his own and never would.

"They havena been doin' a verra good job o' lookin' after her."

"They haven't known where she is. Her uncle is a marquis. If he goes to the law about Rutledge he'll be believed. If I do I'll be arrested."

"I say we think good and hard afore we leave Fenella with a lot o' strangers."

"They're not strangers, Dugal. They're her family. And her name is Sophie." Paul got to his feet, shielding the candle flame with his hand. "You'd best get to sleep if you're coming with us in the morning."

"I'll be ready." Dugal rose, but stood looking at Paul. "Here now, ye willna be tryin' to give me the slip?"

"No, I won't do that."

Dugal flashed a quick grin and went into his room. Paul

started down the stairs. They were narrow and winding, the treads worn smooth. There was a smell of beeswax and linseed oil and the strong, unscented soap used by the servants. Paul gripped the banister, assaulted by memories of another set of service stairs, small hands clawing at his back, a voice screaming his name. He walked quickly down the rest of the stairs, tasting vomit in his throat. Christ, he wasn't going to be sick. That would be too damned much.

He swallowed, forcing down the past. He knew what he was and what he had done. He hadn't lost control then and he wasn't going to now.

He drew a breath and then another, gripped the candle more tightly, and made his way down the corridor to his room. He had a bedchamber all to himself now. Distressed at the impropriety of having lodged an unmarried couple together, Lady Margaret had moved his things into the room she had pretended was his for Somerset's benefit.

But as he passed the room he had shared with Fenella, Paul hesitated. He stared at the reflection of the candle flame in the polished wood of the door for a moment. Then he turned the handle and pushed open the door.

Fenella was in bed. She did not stir at the opening of the door. Paul crossed to the cradle. The baby's face was relaxed with contentment. Less than a week into her young life she seemed remarkably even-tempered, though she could be stubborn when she wanted something. Like her mother.

The babe looked so small, scrunched up beneath the bedding. He could see the curve of bone where her eyebrows would grow in and tiny, spiky eyelashes veiling her closed eyes. There was a small blister on her upper lip. It had worried him, but Lady Margaret said it was from sucking. Most children got them.

The blanket was twisted. He straightened the soft wool, then quickly drew his hand back. He didn't want to wake her. And he didn't want to care more than he already did.

He moved to the bed. Fenella's eyes were closed. The resemblance was so plain, now that he knew who she was. Her face had lost the soft roundness of childhood, but the determined line of her jaw was the same, the straight nose, the high forehead, the full, wide mouth. She had been blond like her mother as a child, but her hair had darkened to the rich brown of her father. Paul looked down at the cropped curls clustered about her face and saw the blood pooling from the hole in the Comte de Milvery's head.

"Paul?" She stirred and opened her eyes, the dark-blue eyes that had once asked him to make sense of an insane world. "Did you talk to Dugal? Is he going to stay here?"

"No." At least he had his voice under control. "He insists on coming with us."

"I thought he would." Her mouth curved in a half smile that made something clench deep in his gut. "I'm glad. I wouldn't want to lose . . . I wouldn't want to lose him." She rolled onto her side. "I told Beth to wake us at seven. You'd better get to sleep."

"I'm just going to my room."

"I forgot." Her brows drew together. "I'll miss you."

His fingers ached with the impulse to touch her. He forced a smile to his lips. "As wives go, you were remarkably easy to live with."

"Except when I was giving you a black eye. Paul . . ." Her fingers curled against the sheet. "My uncle will be very grateful to you. Perhaps he can help you fight the charges over McAlpin's death."

The image of Daniel de Ribard being grateful to him almost made him smile. Ribard was more likely to throw him from the house. "I'll have to come back to Scotland and confront the charges eventually."

"But you'll stay at Rossmere for a while?"

She wanted him to stay. The knowledge was at once sweet and wounding. He looked down at Fenella. Sophie. He forced himself to use her true name. He was going to have to get used to it.

"Paul?" Her voice sharpened with anxiety.

He had told Dugal he would leave her with her family. He had thought he meant it. But he was too tightly ensnared to walk away so easily. "After all the trouble I've been through on your account, do you think I'd risk anything happening to you now? I'll stay until I'm sure you're safe."

It was a vow to himself as much as to her. He would remain in Lancashire until he was certain Sophie was no longer in danger. Whether his father liked it or not.

Chapter 12

"I REMEMBER THAT WALL." SOPHIE'S BONNET SLIPPED back from her head as she pressed her face to the carriage window. "Jemmy dared me to walk along the top of it."

"We must be near the house then." Paul glanced out the window. A rough moss-covered stone wall ran along the side of the road. It was easy to imagine a younger Sophie picking her way along the top, skirt bunched up in her hands. Even at four she'd had a reckless daring that set her apart from her cousins.

The countryside she had grown up in suited her. The road curved between sweeps of mountain. Lavender-gray clouds were massed in the sky, as wild and dangerous as the landscape. Though not as steep and rocky as the Highlands, this part of Lancashire was anything but tame.

"Who's Jemmy?" Dugal voiced the question Paul hadn't wanted to ask.

"The lodgekeeper's son." Sophie rubbed at the condensation her breath had left on the glass. "I hadn't remembered him until I saw the wall."

"Did ye do it?" Dugal asked. "Walk along the wall, I mean."

Sophie turned from the window and adjusted her bonnet. She smiled. "I made it nearly twenty feet before I fell off and scraped both my knees. *Maman* and Aunt Louisa were furious." She looked down at the basket on the seat beside her and touched the baby's cheek. "I won't object to your climbing walls, love. I promise."

In the four days since they'd left Scotland Sophie had recovered more and more of her past. Since they had crossed into Lancashire earlier in the afternoon, the memories had come thick and fast. Throughout the journey Paul had forced himself to listen as though he had no connection to her former life. He had learned that after she came to England she and her mother had made their home with Daniel and his wife and that her mother had died when she was fifteen. She had said nothing further about Tom, save that her last coherent memory was of standing at his grave. The recent past remained a blank to her.

She had mentioned that her father was dead, but she merely said he had died in the Terror and she thought he had given her the lapis lazuli brooch she wore. Perhaps that was all she would remember even when her full memory returned. She had been very young.

Paul's fingers dug into the silk upholstery. The world was a harsh and brutal place, but no child of four should have to go through what Sophie had gone through. What he had put her through.

He studied her profile as she turned back to the window. Her mouth was parted, her eyes open wide. The apprehension she felt about returning to her old life seemed to give way to eagerness as they neared her home.

Daniel de Ribard's home. Paul shifted his position on the well-sprung seat. His muscles screamed with a tension that had nothing to do with the hours of travel.

The carriage made an abrupt turn and came to a halt. Paul was thrown against Dugal. Sophie steadied the baby. Beth, who was sitting beside her, clutched the strap to keep her balance.

"Are we there?" Dugal asked.

Sophie's eyes flew to Paul's face. The eagerness was gone, replaced by fear of the not-quite-known. "We must be at the lodge." She controlled her voice with an obvious effort. "We'll have to wait while William talks to the lodgekeeper."

Dugal leaned in front of Paul to see the lodge. "Ye ha' to ask permission to go i'to yer own house? That's daft."

Sophie smiled, though her lips were trembling. "They don't know it's me."

Footsteps sounded on the gravel outside the carriage. Sophie drew a breath, turned to the window, and lowered the sash.

"Miss Sophie." A man with a weathered face and gray-blond hair appeared outside the window. "I had to see you for myself. Back with a little one, the coachman says."

"Yes, a little girl. I'd show her to you, but she's asleep." Sophie was in command of herself. She spoke with an easy combination of distance and warmth, an aristocrat addressing a valued retainer. "It's good to see you, Mr. Craymere. I hope Jemmy is well."

"Aye, though it's difficult to pry him away from his desk in Lancaster. Hard to think of my son as a solicitor. He'll be right glad to hear your news. So will Mrs. Craymere." Mr. Craymere touched his fingers to his forehead. "You'll be wanting to see your uncle and aunt. They'll be that excited."

The carriage rolled forward. Sophie leaned back against the cream silk squabs and closed her eyes.

Dugal looked out the window. "Dod, what a lot o' trees. Did ye ever climb them?"

"Whenever I could get away with it." Sophie opened her eyes and turned back to the window. "There's a stream beyond that hedge. We'll cross it later. And you can just see the Temple of Hermes beyond that rise of ground."

She kept up a steady flow of talk, as though reassuring herself with the familiar landmarks. The drive wound through an avenue of leafy, well-spaced oaks, curving and twisting to give glimpses of the white pillars of a folly, the shimmering surface of a lake, the lush lavender and pink and rose of flowering plants. There was a natural beauty to the whole that could only be the result of careful design.

For it was beautiful. Much as he wanted to loathe everything associated with the Ribard name, Paul could not deny the rich, verdant appeal of the park. It was typical of Daniel to have chosen such a corner of England. He had always taken what was best from life.

Paul tugged at his neckcloth. The air in the carriage seemed to grow more stifling as they moved deeper into Ribard land. He had known visiting his father's estate would be hard. But he hadn't known how his skin would crawl and his fists would tense with the urge to strike out.

Dugal's elbow caught Paul in the ribs as he peered through the window. "They may no' be royalty, but that fair looks like a palace."

Paul got his first glimpse of his father's house over Dugal's tousled head. The white walls shone brilliantly against the vibrant color of the garden and the blue-gray of the mountains that rose behind. The sun outlined Doric columns and glinted off diamond-bright windows. The house seemed to stretch endlessly from side to side, coolly graceful, elegantly austere.

This was not the life to which Paul had thought he was delivering his father when he'd sat crouched on the stairs in Paris twenty-three years ago. He remembered the surge of power he had felt then. How laughably pathetic. All he had done was destroy the lives of those he hadn't wanted to hurt. Then, as now, the real power had remained with his father. It emanated from the house before him, as clear and brilliant as the sunlight.

But this time he was going to harness Daniel's power to his own ends. He was going to see to it that every corrupt, decadent, amoral scrap of authority Daniel de Ribard possessed was used to protect Sophie. Paul forced down the bile in his throat. To achieve his goal he would have to swallow his pride and persuade Daniel to allow him to stay at Rossmere until Ned Rutledge had been dealt with.

They clattered over a stone bridge. "We're crossing the stream now." Sophie's voice was bright. Then the animation drained from her face. She gripped her hands together. Lady Margaret's white kid gloves, a little small for Sophie's hands, pulled taut across her knuckles.

Again she looked at Paul. Beneath the moss-green silk and peach-colored ribbons of Lady Margaret's bonnet, her face looked drawn, her eyes enormous. They held a plea that was unmistakable. She had refused his help in so many moments of danger. Now, when she was about to return to her own family, she turned to him with an unabashed appeal.

"You'll remember them when you see them." Paul forced the words past the tightness in his chest.

Sophie's eyes were trained on his face, as though he could protect her from what lay ahead. Christ, the bloody irony of it. It hadn't been safe to tell her of their past history on the journey. He couldn't risk having her turn against him before he had seen her safe with her family. But at Rossmere she would have to know the truth. He would not attempt to lie to his father. Careless as Daniel de Ribard had been of his mistress and her son, he would know the name Lescaut. Paul was prepared for Daniel to denounce him. If not, he would tell Sophie himself.

The carriage came to a stop. Sophie tugged at her gloves and smoothed the shiny green skirt of her pelisse. Dugal pushed open the door, letting in a rush of clear, fresh air. "It looks even bigger close up."

"Don't fall out." Paul grasped the back of the boy's breeches to steady him.

William let down the steps with a smooth, well-oiled *click*. Dugal sprang to the ground. Sophie drew a breath, a quick, sharp intake of air. Then she lifted the baby into her arms, took William's proferred hand, and descended from the carriage. It seemed to Paul that she and the child were passing into another world. He wanted to drag them back into the carriage and drive them away from the treacherous beauty of Daniel de Ribard's estate.

Madness. Paul waited until William had helped Beth to alight, then followed the others from the carriage.

Dugal was right. The house looked bigger close up. The limestone walls reared up before them, smooth and impenetrable. The pillars in the colonnade that linked the central block to the two wings towered above any mere mortal.

Two footmen hurried out the front door, dressed in the same green-and-black livery Paul had last seen the night he brought the soldiers to his father's house.

"Miss Sophie," the taller footman said, his eyes widening. It was a jolt to hear the man speak not in French, but in English with a trace of a north-country accent. "We didn't—"

"You didn't expect to see me with a baby. Hullo"—Sophie hesitated for a fraction of a second as though searching for the name—"Ralph. Stephen. This is Mr. Lescaut, who was kind enough to escort me home. He'll be staying with us. Show our coachman where to stable the horses."

Ralph went to help William with the luggage. Stephen hurried back to the house and held open the front door. Sophie looked at Paul. A breeze came up, stirring peach-colored ribbons and tendrils of nut-brown hair against her face. Don't make me go through this alone, her gaze said.

He couldn't deny her this last request. He put a supportive hand beneath her elbow, aware that part of him was all too glad of the excuse to touch her.

She smiled with a warmth and gratitude that made him wince. He could feel the tautness in her body. He could swear he heard her quickened heartbeat. Though he was only holding her arm the contact ran through his whole body. Not desire—though that was there too—but a reminder of the bond between them. A bond that was about to be broken.

Together they moved beneath the shadow of the colonnade and into the Ribard house, Dugal and Beth following. Paul was braced for something like the marble and gilt of the house in Paris. Instead, he found himself surrounded by golden-oak wainscoting, a cool stone floor, and the stillness of age. The facade of the house might be modern, but the hall looked to have stood unchanged for generations.

Sophie's gaze skimmed over the mellowed bronze wall sconces, the long walnut table, the heraldic frieze above the fireplace, as though seeking familiar touchstones. Then she turned to Stephen. "Please order a room made up for Mr. Lescaut. The boy can sleep in his dressing room. And have Beth taken up to my room. Are—"

"Sophie!" The cry came from the stone staircase in the shadows at the back of the hall. A girl in a lemon-yellow dress ran forward, then came to a skidding halt midway down the hall. She was younger than Sophie and shorter, with a full, rounded figure, a serious, heart-shaped face, and thick, honey-brown hair coming loose from its pins. She couldn't be much more than twenty, born after the family had come to England, but there was something familiar about her high, wide cheekbones, her deep-set brown eyes, her full-lipped mouth. An echo not of Sophie, but of someone else. With a shock of surprise Paul realized he was looking at his sister.

"Hullo, Charlie." Sophie's voice held a warmth Paul had heard only when she spoke to the baby. "I haven't come back quite as I left."

"You've had the baby. But you weren't—"

"She came early. Don't you want to see her?"

Charlie picked up her skirt and ran to Sophie's side. "You'd think I'd have got used to nieces and nephews, but I can't get over how small they are." She raised puzzled eyes to Sophie. "What happened? Are you all right?"

"Yes, but neither I nor the baby would be, without Mr. Lescaut. We both owe him our lives." Sophie turned to Paul. "Paul Lescaut. My cousin, Charlotte de Ribard."

"I'm very pleased to meet you, Mr. Lescaut. Thank you for taking care of Sophie." Charlotte held out her hand.

Paul took it, trying to make sense of the introduction. The last thing he had expected was that this child of his father's, born after his own act of betrayal, would have been given his mother's name.

Charlotte glanced at his hand, but did not question his injury. "I still can't believe it," she said, turning back to Sophie. "Did you see Ned? Does he know about the baby? You must tell me—No, I suppose I'd better wait until you can tell us all at once. *Maman* is in the sitting room with Céline."

Ralph returned with the luggage, and a maid appeared. While Charlotte spoke to the servants Sophie drew Paul to one side. "Don't say anything about Ned until we can speak to my uncle alone."

"I didn't intend to." Paul searched her face. Her eyes had darkened with a new worry.

Sophie looked across the hall at Charlotte. "I didn't remember until she asked about him." Her voice was low, taut with anxiety. "He and Charlotte are betrothed."

Paul followed the direction of Sophie's gaze. Charlotte looked even smaller standing between the two footmen. He knew nothing about her save that she had a direct manner, she hadn't flinched at the sight of his hand, and Sophie was fond of her. That she was his sister was a mere biological accident. He had never felt a particular bond with her elder sisters when he lived in the Ribard house in Paris. Yet at the thought of her giving herself over to Ned Rutledge, he was gripped by the same fear he saw on Sophie's face.

"That's that then." Charlotte walked over to them. "I told them to fetch the cradle from the nursery and set it up in your room, Sophie. You'll want the baby with you, won't you?"

"Absolutely."

The maid took Dugal and Beth upstairs, and Charlotte led Sophie and Paul down a corridor lined with watercolors and marble-topped tables. Paul felt the weight of the Ribard wealth pressing in upon him. He would have preferred to seek out Daniel directly and have matters out between them, but he was still playing the role of Sophie's rescuer, innocently caught up in the affairs of the family.

Charlotte ran ahead and flung open a door. "*Maman*, you'll never guess who's here."

Paul had a brief impression of blue-and-white-striped satin, gilt moldings, white-painted woodwork. The scent of hyacinth swept him into a vortex of memories. For a moment he was a boy of nine, stepping into an unfamiliar room in the unfamiliar house to which his father had brought him, the grief of his mother's death still raw in his throat.

The memory was broken by a stir of movement, a rustle of

fabric, and two echoing cries of "Sophie!" Sophie and Charlotte moved forward, and Paul had a clear view of the two women who had sprung to their feet at Sophie's entrance. One was Sophie's age, with golden hair arranged in glossy ringlets around a pretty, well-groomed face. Her lips, rosy pink with rouge, were open in surprise. Her china-blue eyes were fixed on Sophie as though she could not take in what she saw. An embroidery hoop dangled forgotten from one beringed hand.

The other woman was some twenty years older. Her face was fuller than Paul remembered and her fair hair streaked with gray. But the shrewd, worldly eyes and the thin, strong mouth were just as he remembered.

So was her self-command. Louisa de Ribard looked at Sophie, glanced down at the baby, then looked back at her niece's face. "So that's what you've been doing with yourself for the past three weeks. I told you it was a mistake to go haring about the countryside in your eighth month."

Sophie smiled, as though the familiarity of the words and tone put her at ease. "Don't make me admit you were right, Aunt Louisa. You know how I detest it."

"Thank heaven you're in health." There was genuine relief in Louisa's well-modulated voice. "But what in God's name—"

"Don't scold, *Maman*. Only think of what Sophie must have been through." The golden-haired young woman threw down her embroidery hoop, ran across the room, and flung her arms around Sophie. "Goodness, you can't do anything like the rest of us, can you? What a sweet little baby. Is it a boy or a girl?"

"A girl." Sophie lifted the baby so the other woman could see her face.

The golden-haired woman glanced at the baby with a vague smile. "They *are* quiet at this age, aren't they? Not a bit like my two. I must say I like that hat enormously, Sophie."

"Bother the hat, Céline." Charlotte moved closer to Sophie. "I want to hear what happened."

Louisa walked forward and looked down at the baby. Paul

remained in the shelter of the doorway, watching Sophie be enveloped by her family. He felt as if an invisible curtain had been dropped between them.

"She looks healthy." Louisa glanced up from the baby. Her gaze went past Sophie to the doorway. Her strongly marked brows rose in inquiry.

Sophie turned to the doorway and smiled as though the curtain did not exist. "This is Paul Lescaut, who rescued me. My aunt, the Marquise de Ribard, and my cousin Céline—Lady Silverton."

In the hyacinth-scented room twenty-four years ago, Louisa had looked at him with disdain and cold, long-banked rage. Now her gaze took in his cravat, his tan kid gloves, his polished Hessian boots. The unmistakable marks of a gentleman. Her face relaxed into a smile. "Mr. Lescaut." The name would mean nothing to her. In the Ribard household he had been too lowly to be distinguished by a surname. "I'm very grateful for any help you rendered my niece."

Céline ran her gaze over Paul, then turned back to her cousin. "Did you say he rescued you, Sophie? Rescued you from what?"

Sophie drew a breath. "Perhaps we should sit down."

"Yes, I think that would be best. Mr. Lescaut." Louisa waved him to a straight-backed chair covered in pale blue damask.

"Of course, how thoughtless we've been." Céline drew Sophie to the sofa, sweeping aside her sewing box and embroidery silks and pushing the tapestry cushions into order.

Sophie adjusted the baby's blanket. She looked at Paul, as though reminding him to follow her story. He gave a slight nod.

"I was attacked by thieves at a fair in Kinrie," Sophie said, looking from her aunt to her cousins. "Mr. Lescaut rescued me. I was wounded—not seriously, though it felt serious enough at the time—and I had a bad blow to the head."

Céline gasped.

Louisa stared at her niece with the look of a woman thieves would not dare approach. "Why didn't you send word to us?"

"Does Ned know? Did you go to him?" Charlotte asked.

Sophie's fingers clenched the folds of the blanket. "I couldn't. I'd lost my memory. I couldn't remember my name or where I lived or to whom I was related."

The room went still. Charlotte's brows drew together. Louisa opened her mouth and then shut it. She was not a woman, Paul remembered, who took kindly to anything out of the ordinary.

"But—" Céline fingered her coral beads. "You didn't remember anything at all?"

"Nothing. I didn't know my own name for over a week."

"Good heavens, it's like something out of a novel." Céline sounded as if she wasn't sure whether to be horrified or envious.

"You mean you forgot about us?" Charlotte asked. "Do you know who we are now?"

"Yes and yes, Charlie. Mr. Lescaut says blows to the head frequently affect people this way. Fortunately some very kind people named McClaren took us in."

"I've heard of the McClarens. An old Argyllshire family." Louisa seemed reassured by this piece of information. "You were with them when the baby was born?"

"Yes." Sophie neglected to add that the baby had been born in a crofter's hut on the McClaren estate.

"And you didn't know who you were when she was born?" Céline shuddered, her ringlets stirring about her face. "How beastly. As if being confined isn't horrid enough."

Louisa regarded Paul. "My niece was fortunate you were there to come to her aid, Mr. Lescaut." She adjusted her embroidered shawl, smoothing the heavy gold silk. "I don't believe we are acquainted with any Lescauts. The name is French, is it not?"

"It is and so am I. I recently came to Scotland to visit relatives."

"Ah." Louisa inclined her head. "So that is what took you to Kinrie?"

Paul smiled at his father's wife. "No, I was collecting information about the Clearances. I'm a journalist."

"I see." Louisa drew back in her chair.

The baby squirmed in Sophie's arms. Charlotte looked down at her. "Does she have a name yet?"

Sophie had always evaded questions about her daughter's name. Now she looked across the room at Paul. Something in her gaze sent a brief charge through him. For a moment it was as if they were still Paul and Fenella Lester, cut off from the rest of the world.

"Yes," Sophie said. "Her name is Fenella."

The name had never sounded sweeter to Paul than it did in that moment. The link to their recent past struck a chord of warmth within him. He looked away, lest he be singed by the brightness in Sophie's eyes.

"How pretty," Charlotte said.

Louisa raised her brows. "Are you sure? She hasn't been christened yet. There's no need to burden her with a Scots name."

The newly named Fenella stirred again and announced she was awake by giving a loud cry. "She's hungry." Sophie put the baby against her shoulder and rubbed her back. "I should take her upstairs."

Céline drew back as though afraid the baby might be sick on her gown. "Oh, heavens, you don't have a wet nurse, do you? You poor thing. We'll arrange for one right away."

Sophie pressed a kiss against the baby's head. "There's no need. I quite enjoy nursing her myself."

Céline wrinkled her nose. "You've more stomach than I. It's such a nasty business. But you'll at least need a nurse to look after her."

"Eventually. For now I have a girl the McClarens sent along to help." Sophie looked at her aunt. "There's also a coachman and a boy named Dugal who helped us in Kinrie. Mr. Lescaut has taken him into service."

Louisa inclined her head. "They'll all be accommodated. But Céline is right. You should—"

"Well." She was interrupted by a deep baritone voice from the doorway. "You don't do anything by halves, do you, Sophie?"

Even were he not in the Ribard house, Paul would have known that voice anywhere. It was like a punch straight to the gut. He scarcely heard the flurry of exclamations from the women. For a moment he was unable to move. Then he got to his feet and turned to the doorway, prepared to be introduced to his father.

Chapter 13

❧❦

DANIEL DE RIBARD WAS THE SAME. THE BROAD SHOULDERS, the dark heavy brows, the hooded eyes, the full-lipped mouth. His chestnut hair was now streaked with gray. The younger Daniel had worn a powdered wig. Paul remembered watching through a crack in the door as his mother's visitor replaced that wig with exquisite care after he had risen from her bed.

A wave of revulsion swept through him, as swift and sharp as a flight of kestrels. But the unwilling fascination remained. The Marquis de Ribard exuded power, as clearly as the citrus scent of his shaving soap. Paul had recognized it as a child. It was even more evident today.

"Ma chère." Daniel moved swiftly across the room and took Sophie by the arms. The arms were full of Sophie's baby, who was making small noises of distress. Daniel had to lean forward to kiss her.

A smile of recognition crossed Sophie's face. "Uncle Daniel." She stepped back and held up the baby. "My daughter. I didn't intend to have her quite so early."

"She's beautiful."

"Gammon. You've never liked them at the red, squalling stage. Only a mother can see the beauty that's there." She looked down at the squirming infant, who was growing redder and more agitated by the moment.

Daniel smiled. "Outspoken as ever." His English had always been fluent, but there was still a hint of France in his pronunciation. "Are you well?"

"As well as can be expected after a carriage journey from the

Highlands. Uncle Daniel, this is Paul Lescaut, who brought me home from Scotland. He can tell you everything that's happened. We'll talk later."

Paul looked into the dark eyes that were the twin of his own. His body tensed, braced for confrontation. For a moment he thought his father went still. Then Daniel inclined his head. "Mr. Lescaut." There was nothing in his voice or demeanor to indicate recognition.

The baby howled and turned her face toward Sophie's breast. Sophie shifted her daughter to her shoulder. "I must get her upstairs."

Charlotte had been hovering near Sophie. *"Papa,"* she said, her eyes bright with excitement, "Sophie has the most extraordinary story to tell."

"Does she, *ma petite*? I'll be eager to hear it."

Sophie and Charlotte left the room. Louisa rose with a brisk and purposeful motion. "I'm sure you want to talk to Mr. Lescaut, Daniel. I have a thousand things to see to. Céline?"

"Yes, *Maman.*"

"Daniel, we shall speak later." Louisa tapped her husband lightly on the chest. There was no doubt about her meaning. She was not satisfied with Sophie's story, she had misgivings about Paul, and she expected her husband to give her a full account of their conversation.

Daniel watched the door close behind the women. Then he turned to Paul. "I'm indebted to you, sir."

The cool voice cut like glass. Better if Daniel had thrown him from the house. At least that would acknowledge some past relationship between them. Paul was powerless to control the rapid beating of his heart, the involuntary clenching of his hands. He spoke abruptly, hoping the signs of his distress would not be visible to the man before him, knowing full well that they were. "Do you know who I am?"

Daniel took a moment to reply. His gaze was dark and unreadable. "I do," he said at last. Then, in a lighter tone, "But I'm in a forgiving mood, and that was a long time ago. You were only ten." He regarded Paul for a moment. "I wouldn't have recognized you."

"I would have known you anywhere," Paul said, once more master of his body. "Though I would have sworn you were taller."

Daniel laughed and moved to a chair. "Sit down, Paul."

It was deliberate, the use of his given name. It marked the differences between them, both in age and station. Paul sat and leaned forward in his chair, his hands clasped between his knees. The bitterness that had clouded his life for nearly as long as he could remember welled up inside him. He could taste it on his tongue. "We can dispense with the courtesies, Ribard. I don't expect you to pretend you're glad to see me. I won't pretend I'm glad to see you. Were it not for Sophie, this is the last house in England where I'd show my face."

Daniel crossed one leg over the other. He wore immaculate biscuit-colored pantaloons instead of the satin knee breeches Paul remembered. "I'm eager to hear your story."

Frustration closed Paul's throat. He was thirsting for a confrontation and Daniel wasn't going to give it to him.

"For me it begins in Kinrie." Paul matched his father's level tone. "I don't know where it begins for Sophie. It was in Kinrie that our paths first crossed." He related the events as they had occurred, taking his time, wanting to make Daniel feel Sophie's fear and frustration, her courage and determination. He spoke of their encounters with the soldiers, the refuge they had found in Granny Doon's hut when Sophie's time had come, the birth of her daughter and their discovery by Lady Margaret. He described their masquerade as husband and wife, Sir James's suspicions, his summoning of the soldiers, and the arrival of Hagerty claiming to be Sophie's husband.

Daniel listened in silence, like a cautious judge weighing the evidence. But at the mention of Ned Rutledge's name, he drew in his breath. Paul had rarely seen his father give so great a sign of discomposure.

"Hagerty was an imposter," Paul said. "Sophie knew it at

once. She was frantic to learn what was happening, who she was. Hagerty couldn't withstand her. He gave her her name. He told her it was Ned Rutledge who had set up the masquerade. Hagerty was to bring Sophie to him."

Paul fixed Daniel with a hard stare. "Sophie couldn't trust Rutledge. Not after her encounters with him." It was a question, a challenge. He waited for Daniel to meet it.

"I can understand her fear." Daniel got to his feet. "I could do with a drink. I imagine you could as well." He went to a black-lacquered Chinese cabinet, took out a decanter of brandy, and poured two glasses. "I've known Ned Rutledge since he was a boy. The Rutledges are neighbors of ours. Did you know?"

"Sophie told me."

Daniel crossed to Paul and held out one of the glasses. "So you brought her home."

"Where she would be safe." Paul looked at his father over the glass. "Can you keep her safe, Ribard? With Rutledge nearby?"

Daniel returned to his chair and took a long drink of brandy. "I've cared for Sophie since her father died. I have no intention of letting her come to harm. But I won't say I'm not shocked at what you've told me. I find it hard to imagine Ned Rutledge attacking any woman, let alone Sophie."

"And you know him far better than you do me."

"So I do."

The subtle aroma of the brandy wafted from the glass. It occurred to Paul that he was sharing a drink with his father for the first and possibly the last time. Yet another irony on a day full of them. "You think I'm lying?"

"No." Daniel cradled his brandy glass between his hands, warming it, but his voice remained cool and controlled. "I suppose you might have concocted the story in some misguided effort at revenge, but Sophie would hardly go along with it."

"Then how do you explain Rutledge's behavior?"

"I suspect he thought he was protecting Sophie from you."

"It wasn't protection that he had in mind."

"You're very certain. I'd have thought by now you'd have learned that events are open to more than one interpretation." Daniel took another sip of brandy. "Where is Rutledge now? Still in Scotland?"

"I have no idea."

"He's bound to return here. I'll lay the story before him. Until then I prefer to say nothing of the matter to my wife and daughters."

"That's your affair." Paul leaned forward, gathering his forces for the most crucial test of wills. "I won't leave Lancashire till I'm convinced Sophie is out of danger."

Daniel raised his brows. "I said I'd keep her safe. You don't trust me?"

"I don't trust anyone with Rutledge at large."

Daniel set down his glass. "She's my responsibility."

"And she's become mine." Paul's gaze met his father's. For a long moment they took each other's measure. Paul was not sure if the other man was adversary or colleague. He suspected Daniel was wondering the same.

It was Daniel who broke the silence. He smiled and inclined his head. "It will probably be best if you speak to Rutledge directly. But you must stay here, at Rossmere."

It was exactly what Paul had hoped for. Yet it was a hollow victory. He was sure Daniel hadn't conceded anything he wasn't perfectly willing to give from the beginning.

Daniel picked up his glass. "There's just one more question. What in the name of God took you to Kinrie?"

"I learned that I was born there."

"The devil." Surprise flared in Daniel's eyes. Paul felt a burst of triumph. "Who told you that fairy tale?"

"My aunt. My mother told her brother and his wife that she was going to Scotland with her lover. Her brother was furious, his wife sympathetic. Several months later she returned to Paris with a baby." Paul waited, studying Daniel's face. "I learned this only a few weeks ago."

Daniel took another swallow of brandy. His hand was steady, but he seemed to be gripping the glass tightly. "Yes, I took Charlotte to Scotland," he said, his voice even and deliberate. "When it was time to return to France I learned she was pregnant. I was fond of her and arranged for her care. After her child was born I returned to Scotland and brought Charlotte and the baby back to Paris."

He had not admitted it. They stared at each other for a long moment. Move and countermove. Paul considered himself a good chess player, but Daniel was a master. Paul wouldn't put the question directly. He wouldn't give Daniel the satisfaction of letting him see that it mattered. It didn't matter. Or shouldn't.

The moment passed, the chance for confidences gone. Paul leaned back in his chair. "I hadn't expected to find your youngest daughter named Charlotte."

A smile warmed Daniel's wintry face. "Let's say it was a sentimental whim. Charlotte was born late and unexpectedly. I was pleased. My elder daughters are beautiful and clever and, I regret to say, inclined to be shallow. This one I thought might turn out differently. I called her Charlotte as a belated tribute to a woman who once meant a great deal to me."

The civilized tones were too much. Paul pushed himself to his feet, rage bubbling up inside him. "Where were you when she needed you? Where were you when she died, still calling your name?"

A spasm that might have been pain crossed Daniel's face. Paul watched him steadily, willing his father to acknowledge some measure of guilt.

Daniel picked up his glass and raised it to his lips with great care.

Paul strode to the windows. The fingers of his good hand clenched. He longed to smash his fist through the plate glass. Memories he thought he had sealed off engulfed him. When his mother lay coughing blood he had defied her wishes and made his way to the Rue de Grammont to find the man who was her lover and make him return to her. The footman who answered the door told him the marquis and his wife and children had gone to Italy. When he protested, the footman struck him and threw him bodily into the street, warning him that he would be given into custody if he ever approached the front door of the Ribard house again.

Paul would never forgive his father for that final betrayal. It might have been Louisa who insisted on leaving Paris. She was a powerful woman, but Daniel was a powerful man, not one to run in fear of his wife. He had known Charlotte's health was worsening. He would not have left Paris unless it had suited him to do so.

Daniel's voice came from behind him. "Does Sophie know who you are, Paul?"

Paul turned from the window. Anger gave way to a sick weight in the pit of his stomach. Daniel wasn't the only one with past sins to account for. "I couldn't very well have confessed in the carriage. She might have refused to travel with me. I'll tell her as soon as she's had a chance to settle in."

"You don't need to tell her at all."

"But I do. We've shared too much to part on a lie." Paul moved across the room. He felt drained and weary, as if his body had been pummeled in a bruising fight. Yet his opponent had refused to fight back. "We've said what needs to be said. There's no need to prolong the conversation."

"Of course. You must be tired." Daniel rose and held out his hand. Paul hesitated, then put out his own to grasp it, wincing under the unexpectedly firm pressure. Daniel kept his gaze on Paul's face, as though the deformity was not worth noticing.

Paul left the sitting room quickly, suffocated by the emotions that had swirled about him, the words both said and unsaid. A footman in the great hall gave him directions to his bedchamber. He climbed the stairs and paused on the landing to get his bearings. The faint sound of women's laughter came from the corridor on his right. Sophie's room? He paused in front of the door, hoping to hear her voice. He longed for a glimpse of her and the child as a parched man longs for water. He could feel the warm weight of the baby as he held her in his arms or laid her in her cradle. At least her name would remind Sophie of the bond they had shared for a few momentous days.

Idiot. Sophie would never remember him at all save with disgust. Paul turned from the door and walked quickly down the corridor.

SOPHIE OPENED HER DRESS AND GUIDED THE BABY TO HER nipple. The small eager mouth tugged and pulled, but her breasts were tight and swollen and she welcomed the discomfort. These were the moments when she became one with her child. Her daughter. Fenella. She voiced the name, speaking quietly because the baby heard her gentlest whisper. Fenella. Yes, it felt right. It fit.

She glanced at Charlotte, who was kneeling on the floor beside her, looking on with avid curiosity. "Does it hurt?"

"Not now. My breasts have toughened. Though I'm not sure I'll withstand the onslaught of teeth."

"Sophie . . . your breasts . . . I mean . . . they're different. More like Céline's."

Sophie looked down at her breasts. They might be a match for Céline's now, but she knew they would soon return to their normal size—well-formed but not in the least impressive. It had been her despair during the years of her growing up. She laughed. "It's the milk, I'm like a cow that must have her udders pulled every day. After Fenella is weaned they'll go back to their normal size. Nothing will give me Céline's figure. Nor yours," she added, glancing at her younger cousin.

Charlotte's face reddened. "I thought maybe mine were too . . . obvious."

Sophie reached down and stroked Charlotte's hair. "You're a beautiful girl, puss. Be proud of what you have."

"I wish I could. When I look at Céline or Georgine or Marie-Louise or even *Maman*, I don't feel beautiful at all. They seem so sure of themselves."

"That's called 'town bronze.' You're better off without it."

"But Ned will expect . . . Oh, I don't know why he ever offered for me."

Alarm quickened Sophie's pulse. "You love him very much, don't you?"

"I do. I feel positively dizzy when he's with me." Charlotte dashed away the welling tears in her eyes. "What's the matter with me?"

"Oh Charlie, you're in love. The dizziness won't last. It turns into something different. More comfortable, but just as deep." It was a lie, but lies were all Sophie had to offer her.

Fenella released the nipple and made a fretful noise. "Hand me that blanket, will you, Charlie?" Sophie said, feeling a craven relief at the distraction from Ned. She settled Fenella against her shoulder and patted her back.

Before she and Charlotte could resume their conversation, there was a scratching at the door. "Come in," Sophie called.

Céline entered the room. "At last. Free from *Maman*. Charlotte, she wants you. It's my turn to have some time with Sophie."

Céline started across the room, but stopped short as Fenella let out a loud belch.

"Good girl." Sophie kissed her daughter. "Feel better now?"

"Oh Sophie, how can you?" Céline said. "You absolutely must have a wet nurse. What were the McClarens thinking of? Don't worry. We'll find one tomorrow."

Charlotte got to her feet. In the Ribard household none of the women kept Aunt Louisa waiting. Charlotte made a face behind her sister's back, grinned at Sophie, and left the room.

"Don't you dare, Céline," Sophie said. "If you do I'll send the woman packing." She looked down at her daughter, relaxed in her arms now. "I don't want a wet nurse. I enjoy nursing too much."

"You'll be a slave to the child."

"I don't mind."

"And you'll lose your figure."

"I can't think of that now." Fenella had fallen asleep. Sophie put her down in her cradle, adjusted the blankets, then set her own dress to rights.

"You're hopeless." Céline threw herself across the bed. Sophie climbed beside her and clasped her hands around her knees. For years they had shared confidences this way, whispering and giggling when they were young, having intense conversations about eye blacking, rouge, clothes, and men when they were older. The memories came back, as clear and vivid as the watercolors on the walls of her room.

Céline sat up so she was facing Sophie. "But seriously, you must think about it. You're a young woman; you'll marry again."

"I'm through with marriage."

"You can't mean that. What do you intend to do, immure yourself in the country forever? Oh, I'm sorry, you've had a dreadful time. Marriage must be the furthest thing from your mind. But when the season starts and you come to London, you'll see. You'll be glad to get back to your own life."

"I'm not going back to London, Céline. I've thought of returning to Bath."

"Bath? That dreary place, full of gossipy old women and desiccated men suffering from the gout? I've never understood why you went there in the first place."

Sophie stared down at her wedding band. Tom was no longer just a name to her. During the journey from Scotland she had recovered enough fragments of memory to piece together a picture of her marriage. It was not pretty. "I had to get away from Tom. And the life we led." She glanced at the cradle. "And I needed to find someplace quiet to let the baby grow."

Céline shook her head. "Motherhood never took me that way." She was silent for as long as she was able. Céline abhorred a conversational vacuum. "You know, it looked very bad, your leaving your husband."

Sophie tightened her grip on her knees. "I don't care a brass farthing how it looked."

Céline twitched her skirt out from under her. "You were the handsomest, most sought-after couple in London. I know Tom wasn't the best of husbands. But if every woman with an unfaithful husband were to go to Bath, the waters there would be depleted and there wouldn't be a hostess left in London."

"And the husbands would pursue their *amours* in peace. If their light-o'-loves were still there."

Céline's face grew serious. "It was worse, wasn't it?"

Sophie nodded. "I wouldn't have minded so much if he'd kept an opera dancer or a shopgirl. But he tried to bed every friend I had, and he succeeded with most. There wasn't a soul I could confide in."

Céline sat back on her heels. "You could have come to me."

"Could I?" Sophie gave her cousin a sharp look.

It was a moment before Céline understood. Her blue eyes widened. "Oh, no. Sophie, you can't think . . . Don't tell me that's why you never confided in me. Why, we grew up with the Rutledges. I saw through Tom by the time I was ten."

Sophie laughed. The day seemed suddenly brighter. "And I didn't?"

"Of course you did. But you married him anyway."

"I had to marry someone." Sophie grimaced. "Or so I was told. Aunt Louisa reminded me twice a day—more if it rained and we were confined to the house—that three years was quite enough time to wait for a man who was very, very dead and not at all likely to return home and claim me."

"Harry."

"Harry."

"He wasn't a very good catch."

"I loved him." Images of her first betrothed flooded into her memory as though they'd been waiting patiently at a gate that Céline had inadvertently jarred open. The idea of Harry remained a vivid presence, though the outlines of his face and form had grown dim through the years. A younger son with few prospects, he had bought a commission and set out for the

Peninsula to help Wellington run Napoleon's forces out of Spain.

She had kept every one of his treasured letters, bound them in bright red ribbon, and locked them up safe from prying eyes. Where were they now? That memory, too, was dim, though she remembered that the letters had grown fewer and fewer and then there had ceased to be any letters at all. It was a year before the casualty lists included his name. Sophie had never forgiven the nameless quill-scratchers who had lost track of so precious a being. A year. A year of anxious waiting when she should have been free to mourn.

"Does it still hurt so very much?" Céline asked.

"No," Sophie said without thinking, then realized she had spoken the truth. "No, Harry is long gone from this earth and from my life, and I'm no longer twenty."

Céline threw herself back against the pillows and indulged in a long, catlike stretch. "Thank heaven we're no longer young." She sat up abruptly. "But why Tom? I still don't understand why you married him."

"Why not Tom? I thought I knew the worst he had to offer, and he could sometimes make me laugh. He was ambitious. I liked that in a man, though not when it went hand in hand with such blatant self-regard. And I would become Lady Rutledge."

Céline laughed. "A marriage made in heaven."

"A marriage forged in hell. Don't speak to me of acquiring another husband, Céline. I couldn't bear to travel that road again."

"It's not as if you'd have to spend all your time with a husband. Silverton and I are frequently in different places. I've been here with the children for over a month while he makes a duty visit to his parents. I almost begin to miss him."

"You're saying I should take another husband so I can enjoy my privacy?"

"You're hopeless. I never could persuade you to do anything you didn't want to do." Céline stretched out a hand. "Come, let's stay friends. If you'll visit us in London, I'll even promise to come to Bath."

Sophie grasped her hand and exploded in laughter.

"What is it? That's not one of my cleverer sallies."

"I don't know," Sophie said, gasping for breath. "Being here at Rossmere. Being with you. I'm beginning to feel like Sophie de Milvery again." She saw Céline's lifted brows and quickly said, "Sophie Rutledge." But a part of her she had not acknowledged for several hours said that she was still Fenella.

"And who," Céline said in a manner that was not wholly teasing, "is Mr. Lescaut?"

"Truly I don't know. Our paths crossed in Kinrie and he saved my life."

"A guardian angel. He seems a trifle harsh for the part."

Sophie withdrew her hand from her cousin's clasp. "At least not a demon. A decent man with an unwilling sense of responsibility for his fellow creatures."

"An intriguing demon then. Don't let yourself be possessed."

"Possessed? Never." Sophie pulled the pins from her hair and shook it loose so that it fell free about her shoulders. "I belong to no one but myself."

Chapter 14

>⊱⊰<

SOPHIE WOKE FROM A DEEP SLEEP TO FIND THAT SHE HAD slept the rest of the afternoon away. Charlotte, who was seated on her bed, informed her that dinner would be served within the hour, and though allowances might be made on this occasion she knew *Maman*'s views on punctuality.

Charlotte's announcement was followed by Fenella's scream. "Aunt Louisa," Sophie said, "will have to wait." Aunt Louisa be damned, she said to herself as she left the bed and took the squalling infant from Beth. Beth was a treasure. Her daughter was mercifully dry, and Beth was already on her way to the boudoir to deal with the soiled napkin.

"Lady Rutledge."

Sophie looked up into a face she could not immediately put a name to.

"Wentworth," Charlotte whispered behind her back.

Wentworth, of course. Fenella's cries had drowned out the discreet scratching that always preceded her maid's entrance into her room.

"What will your ladyship wear tonight?" Wentworth kept her hands clasped loosely at her waist. Her eyes were focused on a point just above Sophie's head, avoiding the unseemly sight of her mistress's naked breast.

Sophie bit back a laugh. "Whatever you think best." She had a strong desire to be rid of the woman. "Lay it on the chaise longue. Then you can retire for the evening. Charlotte will help me dress."

Only the slightest thinning of Wentworth's lips indicated her disapproval of this arrangement. She went immediately about

her task, laying out a gray-blue dress of conservative cut along
with stockings and shoes and gloves and fan. Then without a
word she made a brief curtsy and left the room.

"You've offended her," Charlotte said.

Sophie shifted Fenella to her other breast. "It's not the first
time. I remember now. Wentworth never forgave me for leaving the London house and retreating to Bath with no more staff
than a cook and a parlormaid. She was forced to eat alone to
preserve her place."

Charlotte laughed. "At least she's in a proper establishment
at Rossmere. Taking tea with the housekeeper as is her due.
However do you manage with the servants, Sophie? I know I
shall make a proper hash of it when Ned and I are married."

"I don't suppose I think about the servants at all. Not unless
they fail to give satisfaction. Then they have to be dismissed."
It was a harsh judgment, worthy of Céline or even Aunt
Louisa. It was a shock to find the words coming from her own
mouth. In the last few days she had not only grown fond of
Beth, she had talked with her, woman to woman, and it had
seemed natural to do so. And she thought of Dugal, whom she
would scarce have regarded in her old life, as a friend. "I don't
mean to sound like Aunt Louisa. One must be kind, of course."

"You were always kind. You pensioned Roger when he was
too old to manage the horses, and you gave a handsome gift to
Jane Ebbersly when she left to get married."

Jane Ebbersly had been her first lady's maid, Sophie remembered. Wentworth had been in her service less than a year.
"That's only money, Charlie, welcome as it may be. I fear I
was often thoughtless."

"To Wentworth? You don't much like her, do you?"

"No," Sophie said with a vehemence that surprised her. She
took Fenella into the boudoir and gave her into Beth's care.
"I'm not sure why," she said as she reentered the room. "She's
very efficient. I suppose it's my wretched memory. Too much
is happening at once."

"What on earth are you two talking about?" Céline had entered the room. She had changed into a gown of silver gauze over satin and was fastening a diamond bracelet.

"Servants," said Charlotte with mock gravity. "And whether or not they have souls like the rest of us."

Céline raised her brows, then burst into laughter. "I've never given the matter a moment's thought, and I advise you to do the same." She moved to the chaise longue and fingered the gray-blue dress. "Where's Wentworth?"

"Taking a hard-earned rest, I trust." Sophie undid the remaining buttons on her dress and let it fall to the floor. "What do I need with Wentworth when I have my cousins to help me?" She sat on the chaise longue and pulled off the serviceable stockings she had worn on the journey to Rossmere. The gray stockings Wentworth had laid out seemed impossibly fine, though she knew she was accustomed to such luxury.

Her wound was healing, but she still moved with care. She managed the stockings and thin kid slippers by herself, then stood so that Charlotte could drop the evening gown over her upraised arms and fasten the innumerable buttons that ran up the back of the dress. She was forced to suck in her breath. The gown had been made when her breasts were their normal size. If she wasn't careful, the buttons would pop off at the dinner table. "No wonder we need maids," she said. "Look at the way our clothes are made."

"If we could do things for ourselves, the servants wouldn't have anything to do." Céline walked to the dressing table and picked up a silver-backed brush. "Come, let me do your hair."

Sophie put on her earrings and brooch and surrendered to the pleasure of her cousin's deft fingers turning her into the fashionable woman she once had been. "You're pale," Céline said when she was finished. She picked up the rouge pot. "May I?"

Sophie nodded her agreement. It was a game they'd often played when they were young, but its practice had served them well when they were old enough to go into society. "Speaking of servants," Céline said as she brushed a delicate wash of color over her cousin's cheeks, "where did you find the scruffy dark-haired boy you brought with you?"

"Dugal? He's not a servant. He's my friend."

Céline set down the rouge pot and brush with unusual care. "One isn't friends with children."

Sophie swung round to look up at her cousin, aware of a warm flush in her face that had nothing to do with rouge. "Why not? If it weren't for Dugal I might have died. He gave me a name when I had none. He was our guide, our interpreter. He was with me when my time came and all through the baby's birth."

"But you were at the McClarens'," Charlotte said.

"We were in an abandoned hut on the outskirts of the Mc-Claren estate. Lady Margaret didn't appear until the next day."

Céline stared at her. "You delivered the child yourself? With no one but an ignorant boy to help you?"

"Mr. Lescaut helped me," Sophie said, remembering just in time not to refer to him as Paul. "He delivered my daughter." She stood up, surveyed herself in the dressing-table mirror, picked up her gloves and fan, and turned to the others. "There. Am I presentable?"

Charlotte was laughing. "Oh, Sophie, you're a marvel."

"You're the most outrageous woman I know. To allow a man—a man you scarcely know, and not even a doctor—" Céline shook her head. "If *Maman* only knew."

"That's precisely why I didn't tell her."

The three cousins left the room amidst a burst of hilarity, and arm-in-arm they descended the stairs to join the family in the drawing room before dinner. They had, Sophie was pleased to see from a small porcelain clock on the half-landing, exactly seven minutes to spare.

SOPHIE'S HIGH SPIRITS WITHERED DURING THE COURSE OF what seemed an interminable dinner. She had expected no one but the family and Frank Storbridge, her Uncle Daniel's private secretary, a clever young man she remembered having always liked. But Aunt Louisa had previously invited guests, and Sophie's arrival was too late, she told her niece in a quiet voice, for her to put them off. They included the Longstreets and the Sunderlands, both neighboring families, and Father Anselm, a frequent visitor, especially when Aunt Louisa needed to balance her table. Sophie had known them most of her life, but now they stood at the periphery of her memory. It was an effort to bring them into proper focus.

She was conscious always of Paul's presence. He was an attentive listener, but said little himself. His behavior could not be faulted in any particular, but everything about him screamed out that he did not belong. Or so it seemed to Sophie, who looked on the group gathered around the extravagantly laden table through his eyes. I could be myself if he weren't here, she thought. I could accept who I am. I could take up my old life.

Céline glanced at Paul, then looked at Sophie, a speculative gleam in her eyes. Sophie knew she had gone too far with her impulsive confession in her bedchamber. She turned to Father Anselm, who had taken her in to dinner, and answered his question about her journey. From that point on she was careful to keep her gaze from Paul.

She had thought that Lady Margaret set an elaborate table, but it was nothing compared to the richness of Aunt Louisa's offerings. She picked up her spoon and dipped it into her soup, savoring the rich, clear broth. By the end of the fish course the edge was gone from her hunger. After the joint was served she was surfeited, and there were still birds to follow. She had never regarded the extravagance and waste of her usual mode of dining. Now she felt shamed by it.

The truth was, she'd been spoiled by her few days in the Highlands. The danger, the hunger, the rain, and the cold had been real. She would not willingly embrace them again, but there had been a perverse kind of pleasure in facing and surmounting these obstacles to survival. How far removed from the carriage races and moonlight masquerades and other reckless behavior for which she was noted in London. She had told herself she was courting danger, but it was sensation she had sought, an affirmation that she was still alive.

The dinner was over at last and the ladies were free to return to the drawing room. Sophie's jaws ached with smiling and her head throbbed with the effort to remember faces and events. With one accord her family had agreed to say nothing to their guests of her errant memory.

The gentlemen joined them after a time, and Aunt Louisa poured tea. Céline's children were brought in by their nurse. At Céline's prompting Lydia and Charles dutifully kissed Sophie. Then they ran to Charlotte, who pulled them onto her lap. Céline turned to speak to Mrs. Sunderland, apparently feeling her maternal duty was done.

Sophie felt the pressure of Paul's gaze upon her. Her face grew warm. Surely he knew she wasn't like Céline. But until Fenella she'd had little interest in babies. She hadn't been much of an aunt. It wasn't a side of her she cared for Paul to see.

Suddenly she ached to hold Fenella. She got to her feet and pleaded the fatigue of the journey.

"I'll go with you if I may." Her uncle took her arm. "I'd like to talk to you," he added when they were in the hall. "If you're not too tired."

Much as she wanted to be with Fenella, Sophie knew she should talk to her uncle alone. She did not yet know what had passed between him and Paul. "Of course," she said, telling herself her daughter would be all right for a few more minutes. She followed Daniel into his study. "You've talked with Mr. Lescaut?"

He motioned her to a leather-covered settee and sat down beside her. "He was most thorough. What an ordeal, *ma chère*. I can scarcely credit it."

"I can show you the wound," Sophie said. "It's healing well."

Daniel covered her hands with his own. "I have no doubt you were attacked. What I wonder about is the identity of your attacker. Are you certain it was Ned Rutledge? You understand my concern. Charlotte . . ."

Sophie withdrew her hands and moved a little apart. "Do you think I find it easy to believe? Do you think I can possibly understand it?" Her fingers tightened around her fan. "Ned, Tom's brother. I've known him forever. Don't you think I look at Charlotte and see her love and trust in him and grow cold at the thought of what may lie ahead? But there's the evidence of my own eyes, my own ears."

"Ah, but that's just it." Daniel leaned back against the settee. "Your eyes. What do they tell you but what your mind instructs? You went to Kinrie to find Ned, I don't know why. You expected him to be there, and what you expected you saw."

"No!"

"Think, Sophie. The happiness of more than one person may depend upon it. Tell me in your own words everything that has to do with Ned."

He took her through the story several times. Ned's appearance at the foot of the hill, his chasing her through the mist-shrouded land near the streambed, Hagerty's appearance and Hagerty's story.

But to each of these events Daniel raised a question. Had she truly seen a knife in Ned's hand? Was Ned trying to separate her from Lescaut without leaving a blot on her reputation? Did Ned resort to the stupid trick of sending Hagerty to find her because he feared Lescaut had turned her against him? It may not have been that way, but it was possible, was it not?

Sophie's head began to throb again. "I know what I saw," she said. But the doubt had been sown. Those first few hours after the attack in the alley had been filled with terror and pain. How could she trust her memory of that time when her other memories were so erratic?

"I'm sorry," Daniel said. "You've been under a tremendous strain, even before this business in Scotland. You and Tom may not have had an ideal marriage, but I know how disturbed you were by his death. I wish I'd been able to be more of a comfort to you at the time. It couldn't help but stir memories of your father."

Sophie's heart gave a lurch. Something tugged at the blackness in her memory, something she didn't want to look at. "What about my father?"

Daniel regarded her for a moment, as though seeking answers to questions she didn't understand. "I see. You don't remember your childhood?"

"I remember bits and pieces. But there are still gaps in all my memories. I have an image of my father's face." She touched the lapis lazuli brooch she had pinned to her evening gown. "I remember being told that he died a hero."

"Which he did."

Sophie searched her uncle's face. Her heart was pounding, though she could not have said why. "What did you mean about Tom's death and my father?"

Daniel was silent for a fraction of a second too long. "Merely that you lost your father at a young age and then lost your husband. The rest is unimportant." He touched her hand. "Go up to your child, Sophie. Try to think about the future instead of the past."

Sophie kissed her uncle good night and made her way upstairs, mulling over the questions he had raised. Her consciousness prickled with images that were just out of reach. Perhaps if she talked to Paul she could order the tumult of her thoughts. But Paul was still in the drawing room in the midst of a crowd. When he left it he would go upstairs to his solitary room. She could not go to him there. At the McClarens' he had been her husband. Now he was simply a guest in her uncle's house.

Sophie paused on the stairs, feeling the mantle of propriety settle on her shoulders. For the first time it occurred to her that in coming home she had lost some of her freedom.

PAUL ENTERED THE BREAKFAST PARLOR AT AN EARLY HOUR the next morning and found it empty. The ladies, the footman on duty told him, were never up at this hour. The marquis was closeted with Mr. Storbridge. What would Mr. Lescaut take to break his fast? He began to enumerate the dishes the kitchen could provide. Paul, glutted with the abundant rich fare he had consumed at dinner the night before, raised a hand to stop him. He swallowed a cup of coffee, pocketed a roll, and made his way out of the house, grateful that he was not obliged to make conversation.

A morning mist was rising, revealing lawns of an intense green, gray-green wooded hills in the distance, and the dark movement of waters on the lake in between. He caught a glimpse of white columns and a cupola on a rise of ground some half mile distant. A folly, or at least a retreat done in the Grecian style. He made for it for want of another goal.

It was a circular building of green-veined marble, open at the sides, with a bench running the complete circumference save for the entrance. Paul stepped inside. The mist had lifted and the sun, now visible above the eastern hills, sprinkled the lake with gold. He saw why the architect had chosen this particular spot. It commanded an unimpeded view of the lake, which meandered snakelike as far as he could see in either direction. The house and its outbuildings were scarcely visible. One would come here to be alone.

Paul pulled the roll from his pocket and shared it with an inquisitive squirrel who appeared on the back of the bench. When the squirrel had left him, despairing of further food, he sat down, stretched out his arms and legs, and lifted his face to the morning sun. His eyes closed to better savor the moment, he was aware of nothing but the breeze with its welcome hint of warmth, the calling of birds, and the lapping of water against the shores.

He wasn't sure when he was first aware of another presence. He opened his eyes to see Sophie standing at the entrance of the folly. "I might have known you'd find my favorite spot," she said, stepping inside and turning to look at the view of the lake. "It's glorious, isn't it?"

Paul quickly got to his feet. "Shall I leave you alone?"

"Don't be an idiot." She turned to him with the hint of a smile that made his heart turn over. She wore a pale-gray dress with a high-standing lace collar, like in an Elizabethan portrait. He studied her, trying to separate Sophie Rutledge from the terrified nameless woman he had found in Kinrie. It was impossible. They were one.

Sophie knelt on the bench, clasping its back. "I used to come here when I wanted to get away," she said, watching the lake below. "I thought if I made a raft I could sail away until the morning of all mornings."

Paul suppressed an impulse to move to her side. "It's been hard, hasn't it, coming home?"

"It's been a peculiar form of purgatory. Not just the effort of remembering. Trying to remember myself. I feel as though I'm hovering above Rossmere and the people in it, watching myself as though I were a stranger. It's only with Fenella that I feel truly anchored." She swung round to sit on the bench, her legs curled under her. "And with Dugal and with you. How's Dugal faring? I haven't seen him since we arrived."

"Friends with everyone and a favorite with the cook. How do you suppose he manages to look malnourished every time he steps into the kitchen?"

"Because he is, I suppose. I doubt he's had more than a half dozen proper meals in his life."

He watched her for a moment. She was poised between two worlds, fearful of embracing either. The temptation to pull her into his world was as overwhelming as his sudden desire to take her in his arms. "It will pass, you know, this feeling of not belonging," he said. "Too much has happened too fast. You may still be in danger. When we know more, when we can be sure you're safe, you'll find it easier to slip into your own life."

"Perhaps." She reached up to touch the cameo that hung from a black velvet ribbon around her throat. It was carved on onyx, as delicate and unyielding as Sophie herself. "Paul, Uncle Daniel is dreadfully disturbed about your accusations against Ned. Could I have been wrong? Perhaps Ned was trying to help me when I ran away from the barn. Perhaps I only imagined the knife in his hand. I was out of my head with terror. How can I trust my memory?"

Damn Daniel for raising doubts in her mind. But Paul did not want to contradict him directly. "Can you trust my memory? Ned Rutledge attacked me in the alley in Kinrie."

"He might have thought you attacked McAlpin and me."

Paul wanted to shake Sophie and tell her not to be a fool. But it was only to be expected that she would listen to the questions Daniel had raised. Ned Rutledge was her brother-in-law, while she had known Paul less than a month. He controlled his voice with an effort. "We know Ned lied through Hagerty."

Sophie looked down at her hands. "It's possible he attempted the charade with Hagerty because he didn't trust you and thought it was the safest way to get me away."

"It's possible."

She looked up at him. "But you don't really believe it."

"I find it hard to credit. But I'm willing to listen to his story. Your uncle thinks he'll return to Lancashire soon."

She struck her fist on the marble bench. "And then? Whom shall I believe? Is this a farce of misperceptions? Or will it all be lies?"

"Sophie . . ." It was time. He could put it off no longer. He moved to the bench, some distance from her, and sat with his hands clasped loosely between his legs. "Sophie, there's something you should know about me."

"Yes?" she said when he did not go on.

His guts were twisted into a hard mass. He took a slow, deep breath. "Do you remember your father?"

She drew back against the bench. "My father is dead. He died before we left France."

"Do you remember how he died?"

"I was four years old. What do you expect of me? I know he was killed by revolutionary soldiers."

"He died by his own hand, but there were soldiers there. They'd come to arrest him."

Her body went taut, her eyes wide with surprise. "How do you know? Why are you telling me this?"

"Do you remember when the soldiers came to the Mc-Clarens'? You ran up the stairs. You were terrified. You whispered *Papa*."

She seemed to shrink within herself. "No."

"Soldiers came to your uncle's home in Paris. They shouted and pounded at the door. You came out on the landing to see what was happening. You saw a servant boy kneeling on the floor, peering through the balustrade at the foyer beneath."

"Paul." It was a bare whisper of sound. He knew she was looking into the past, not addressing him.

"You knelt by the boy's side. You asked him what was happening. Your father pulled out a gun and turned it on himself. Your mother screamed and threw herself upon him. There was a lot of blood."

Her fingers gripped the marble of the bench. She looked at him as though he were a stranger.

"You clung to the boy and asked him what was happening, when would your father get up. The boy ran away and you ran after him, clinging to him, pleading for an answer. He shook you off and ran out into the night, your screams filling his ears. He's heard those screams every day of his life."

"Holy Mother defend me." She jumped from the bench and moved as far away from him as the folly would allow. He saw the horror of that night burst upon her as though illumined by an explosion of fireworks. "It was you. The boy, Paul. You informed on my father and brought the soldiers there. You killed my father."

Paul got to his feet. "Your father was plotting murder. I didn't want him to die. I wanted him stopped."

She wrapped her arms around herself. "You didn't tell me. Why didn't you tell me?"

"Tell you what? How was I to know who you were? You

had no name, and when you were called Sophie it meant nothing. There are many Sophies in the world. I didn't lie to you. My name is Paul Lescaut. Even if you'd had your memory you wouldn't have recognized it. In your world servants didn't have surnames."

She flinched, as though he had slapped her. "When did you know?"

"When the soldiers came to the McClarens' house I suspected. I didn't know for certain until you named your uncle."

"You waited five days to tell me?" Her voice cut like a blow of retaliation.

"What did you expect me to do, blurt it out in the carriage? With Beth and Dugal and the baby?"

She shook her head. "I trusted you with my life. You gave me my daughter. You became my friend."

"I am still your friend, Sophie Rutledge."

"No." Her eyes grew dark with fury. "No, it can never be the same. Stay here if you must till Ned's return. Your safety as well as mine is at stake. But stay out of my way, Paul Lescaut."

She turned on her heel and strode away, too proud to run, too proud to admit the hurt he had done her. Paul watched her as her figure grew smaller, then vanished altogether. There was a great hollow in his chest, as though she had wrenched his heart from his body and flung it into the blue and uncaring lake.

Chapter 15

PAUL WALKED DOWN THE STEPS OF THE FOLLY AND STRUCK out along the lake. The blood pounded in his head, propelling him forward. He turned onto the lawns, heedless of his direction, conscious only of the need to keep moving.

At last he checked his rapid stride. As a boy he had run from the consequences of his actions, but he could not outdistance this pain. He felt it settle within him, twisting and tearing, battering him with the inevitability of his loss.

He stared at the mountains in the distance. Cloaked in the morning mist they held a rough mystery, a welcome escape from the too-perfect world of the Ribard estate. Sophie's world. A world he never should have entered.

He tugged at his cravat. He felt as if it were choking him. He pulled the linen loose and breathed in the lavender-scented air. The pain would pass. Scars would close the gnawing hole she had torn in his defenses. He would learn—relearn, *sacrebleu* he was slow—to relish the freedom of being alone.

The bonds he had in the world—his aunt, his cousin, his cousin's wife and children—were safe ones. They belonged more to one another than to him. He'd nearly lost even those ties, thanks to his more recent transgressions. But it was on the night he ran out of the Ribard house that he had damned himself to a solitary fate. He had long since given up expecting or wanting anyone of his own. Except for these past days when he had let himself be seduced by the fantasy of a family life that he had lived with Sophie and the baby.

"Are you all right, Mr. Lescaut?"

It was a woman's voice, warm and friendly. Paul turned to see Charlotte emerge from a beech coppice, accompanied by Daniel's secretary, Frank Storbridge. Paul had no desire for company, but it was just as well that he be rescued from the ravages of self-pity. Even if he had lost Sophie's trust he was still determined to see her safe. There was much he might learn from Charlotte and Storbridge.

"Just stopping to admire the view," he said, knotting his cravat and tucking the ends beneath his waistcoat. It might lack style, but at least it gave a nod to propriety.

"Oh, good. I thought perhaps your wound was troubling you." Warmth showed in Charlotte's eyes as well as her voice. Unlike her mother and sister, she seemed unaffected by the realization that he was not quite the gentleman he had at first appeared.

Paul found himself smiling back despite his bitter mood. "Believe me, after four days in a carriage there's no medicine better than a brisk walk."

"Yes, I suppose so. I know Sophie hates being cooped up." Charlotte glanced about the lawn. "Where is she? I thought she went to look for you."

"She found me by the lake." Paul kept his voice level. "Then she went back to see to the baby. I wanted to explore more of the grounds."

"I'm cutting flowers for the drawing room." Charlotte wrinkled her nose. "*Maman*'s orders, but at least it gets me out of the house. Frank's being splendid and helping." She smiled at Storbridge, who carried a basket filled with cut flowers and pruning shears. "Come with us, Mr. Lescaut. We'll show you the view from the rose knoll. It's the nicest on the estate."

She picked up the slightly muddy skirt of her white muslin gown and started forward with an easy assumption of camaraderie. Storbridge nodded at Paul, and they fell into step on either side of her.

"I've seen few parks this lovely," Paul said. His cousin

Robert, a former intelligence officer, had once told him that rank flattery was the most effective tool for loosening tongues.

"*Papa*'s terribly proud of it. Rossmere wasn't nearly this grand when he bought it, so I think he sees it as his creation."

"Your father bought the estate after he came to England?" Paul knew the hunting box in Kinrie had come to Daniel as part of his wife's dowry, but he wasn't sure about Rossmere. He was aware of a curiosity about his father's life that had nothing to do with exposing the threat to Sophie. Aware and ashamed.

Charlotte nodded. "It was built in the time of Henry the Eighth. The original owner's wife was Henry's mistress—oh, don't look at me like that, Frank, everyone knows about it."

Paul studied the girl who was his sister, as fresh and young as the new grass and the summer air, still innocent enough to find scandal in the tale of a long-dead king's love affair. He had mocked at innocence often enough in the past, but he found himself wishing Charlotte's would last. He wondered if Sophie had had that air of bright naïveté at Charlotte's age. But perhaps Sophie had become hardened to the world at four, when she saw her father blow his brains out and the boy she thought was her friend abandon her.

They left the lawn for a path that twisted uphill, bordered by ferns and small clusters of white flowers that spilled onto the flagstones. Charlotte kept up her cheerful stream of information. "It must have been all over by the time Henry divorced Catherine of Aragon—Henry's affair with the lady of Rossmere, I mean—because the family didn't join the Church of England. They stayed Catholic. That's why Rossmere has a secret chapel and an underground passage. So they could hold Mass and smuggle the priest in and out. Did Sophie tell you?"

"She mentioned something about a chapel."

"Oh, that's the new one *Papa* built." Charlotte pushed aside a frond of fern. "The secret one's much more interesting. One of the daughters of the house met her lover there during a ball and eloped."

"Not one of your sisters?" Paul kept his voice light. It was strange to remember that Charlotte's sisters were also his sisters. God knew how many nieces and nephews he had by now.

"No, it was the family who used to own Rossmere." Storbridge spoke up for the first time. "Don't tease him, Charlie."

"You can't blame me for wanting to borrow excitement. Here we are. You'd better give me the basket, Frank."

The path ended on a rise of ground massed with rosebushes—pure white, bloodred, soft pink. Their scent slammed Paul in the gut, an echo of Sophie's perfume. He told himself not to be a fool. He'd be damned if he'd let a bunch of bloody flowers unsettle him.

Charlotte led them along a well-kept walkway to a clearing at the center of the knoll, stopping every so often to add roses to her basket. "I once devised a formula to calculate how many rose bushes there are on the knoll. That was a much more interesting use of the flowers than decorating the drawing room. There." She set the basket down on a table of white-painted wrought iron. "Even if I've seen it a hundred times I have to admit the view is lovely."

Rossmere was spread below them. The brilliant green of the terraced lawns, splashed with bright flowers, the leafy branches of the beech coppice, the smooth surface of the lake, the twin serpentine curves of the drive and stream. At the center of it all, connecting the disparate elements into a unified whole, stood the house itself, shining in the morning sunlight.

Charlotte plucked a stray rose leaf from her sleeve. "The people who built Rossmere didn't do very well over the years. Kept picking the losing side. By the time *Papa* bought the estate a lot of the land had been sold off. *Papa* bought it back and turned the park into—" She gestured below her with an ungloved hand. "And he built a new facade for the house and added the two side wings. So in some ways it seems as if it's more ours than that original family's, even if Henry the Eighth did give them the land. Oh, dear, I hope that doesn't sound horridly priggish."

"Not in the least." To his surprise Paul meant it. For all he mocked at family pride it was impossible to find that sort of arrogance in Charlotte. "You have a right to be proud of what your family has accomplished."

Charlotte tugged at the brim of her bonnet, a plain plaited straw. "I don't appreciate it as much as I'm supposed to. As much as my sisters do. Perhaps it's because I'm the only one who was born in England. Or because of my name."

"Your name?" Paul's pulse quickened.

"Charlie." Storbridge's voice was low with warning.

"Don't be stuffy, Frank, I don't care who knows about it." Charlotte looked up at Paul, her eyes wide and candid. "I overheard my nurse telling one of the footmen the story when I was barely out of leading strings. *Papa* named me after one of his mistresses. *Maman* didn't realize until after I'd been christened and it was too late to change it. I think perhaps that's why she's never quite liked me."

There was no censure in her voice, only a statement of fact. The repercussions of the past spread through the years like ripples in a lake, touching even this girl who had been born after all that insanity. Whatever sins had been committed, she should not have to pay for them.

"You know that's not true, Charlie." Storbridge put his hand out, then let it fall to his side. Paul was sure he would have touched Charlotte had they been alone. "The marquise is just—"

"Difficult," Charlotte finished for him. "But then, I'm a great trial to her. I'm not at all like my sisters. They always know the right thing to say and do. So does Sophie, but most of the time she doesn't do it."

She turned away and fumbled with the strings on her bonnet. "I must get these flowers in water or *Maman* will be cross. Thank you for your help, Frank. I know you have to get to the lodge. It was nice to see you, Mr. Lescaut. Perhaps you can walk to the lodge with Frank if you want to see more of the park."

She picked up her basket and set off down the walkway with a determined, slightly awkward gait. Storbridge looked after her, his sharp gray eyes gone soft and misty. Young fool. If they were better acquainted Paul would have warned him of the dangers of reaching for the moon. "Now that Miss Ribard has volunteered you, do you mind the company?" he said instead.

It was a moment before Storbridge responded. "Not in the least." He pushed his unruly shock of dark-brown hair back from his forehead. "I have an errand with Craymere. I was on my way there when I met Miss Ribard."

Storbridge led the way down the knoll. Paul was tempted to ask about Charlotte's moment of distress, but such a question would probably put Storbridge on the defensive. Better to stick to neutral territory. "It must have cost a fortune to do everything Miss Ribard was describing," Paul said as they reached the bottom of the knoll. "I take it the marquis didn't come to this country destitute like so many *émigrés.*"

Storbridge started across the open parkland in the direction of the stream. "He managed to sell off his property and get the money out of France before he was forced to leave. Then he was very clever with what he had."

Paul hadn't expected this last. He knew his father was intelligent, but he had never thought of Daniel as clever about anything as practical as money. "Investments?"

Storbridge nodded. "He has an eye for what's profitable. He bought a share in a Jamaican plantation soon after he came to England. It's now one of the most successful on the island. He bought a tin mine in Cornwall just when the demand for tin was increasing. He owns a share of a bank in Lancaster and another in Bristol."

They had reached an unpaved path that wound along the stream. The air was cooler here, cleaner. Paul listened to the rush of the stream while his image of his father broke apart like the water striking the rocks in the streambed. He remembered a worldly, hedonistic aristo, with velvet coats and lace-trimmed cuffs and white, unsoiled hands. Hands that caressed Paul's mother and occasionally ruffled Paul's hair, but never did work more serious than taking snuff or drinking a glass of brandy.

Paul looked at Storbridge, who knew his father better than he did himself. "You've described a successful bourgeois."

Storbridge grinned. "In some ways that's exactly what Ribard is. He's begun to invest in voyages to India now that the trade is opening up. He made a handsome profit on the Exchange after Waterloo when everyone panicked at the reports that Napoleon had won. I sometimes think he's more proud of what he's accomplished in England than of his heritage in France."

"He's been very fortunate." Paul could not quite keep the irony from his voice. No one accumulated so much wealth and influence and kept his hands clean. "You've worked for him long?"

"Three years. Since I left university."

"An interesting life, I would think."

"That's what I keep trying to explain to my father. He still can't understand my choice of profession."

Paul kicked aside a stick that had fallen across the path. "Fathers and sons. Always a difficult relationship. He had other plans for you?"

"He wanted me to follow him into the church."

"And you didn't have a taste for it?"

Storbridge grimaced, his eyes on a yew hedge on the opposite side of the stream. "My father's a clergyman in an impoverished parish. He works himself to the bone trying to better life for his parishioners. The truth is, he has only slightly more power than they do. It's difficult to make much of a difference in the world without power."

"You have political ambitions? It sounds as if Ribard could be a useful patron."

Storbridge met Paul's gaze squarely. "He's on intimate terms with half the Government. Not that I necessarily—"

"Agree with him?"

Storbridge regarded Paul, as if taking his measure. "Ribard worries revolution could come to England as it did to France. The machine breaking by the Luddites and the rioting at Spa Fields last year made him very nervous."

"Ribard doesn't strike me as the nervous sort."

Storbridge smiled. "Perhaps 'wary' is more accurate."

"It hasn't occurred to him that change may be the only way to prevent revolution?"

"In a word—no."

"So he sees repression as the best antidote to poverty and lack of employment?" Paul was almost relieved that in this at least his father conformed to his expectations. Daniel was aware enough of the forces reshaping the country to invest his money shrewdly, but not to realize that political change had to go along with economic.

Storbridge stared at the leaf-strewn ground. "I wouldn't put it quite that way."

"Of course not." Paul clasped his hands behind his back. "He's your employer and you're much too diplomatic."

Storbridge gave a reluctant grin. "You can't really blame Ribard. What he saw in France must have been horrific. Lady Rutledge's father was killed in the Terror."

"I'd heard." Paul gripped his hands together, so tightly he could feel the scrape of bone on bone. "Wasn't Lady Rutledge's husband in Parliament? Did he favor Ribard's views?"

"In general. Tom Rutledge's patron, Lord Harrowgate, is considered one of the ultra-Tories. He's an ally of Lord Sidmouth." Storbridge glanced at Paul. "Our Home Secretary, that is. I keep forgetting you're not an Englishman. Sidmouth was the one responsible for putting down the rioting last year."

Paul had heard of Sidmouth. A monster to hear his cousin Robert tell it. Sidmouth was rumored to have a network of agents who infiltrated radical groups and stirred them to violent action in the hopes of provoking popular outrage. It was even said that it was Sidmouth's people who had provoked the rioting at Spa Fields in London the previous December. So that was the company Sophie's husband had been keeping. Paul was aware of an unworthy surge of satisfaction. He didn't want to like Tom Rutledge. "Do you think Tom Rutledge's brother—Sir Edward, isn't it—will follow in his footsteps?"

Storbridge's mouth tightened. The breeze from the stream blew his hair off his face, making him look older and harder. "I don't know," he said. "I don't really know Edward Rutledge at all."

"I saw Mr. Lescaut when I was out walking today." Charlotte flopped down on the window seat in Sophie's bedroom and stretched her arms above her head, heedless of the pull on the seams of her dress. "He's nice. Not a bit stuffy."

"Not in the least." Sophie smiled. Then her mouth went stiff, because smiling was the last thing she felt like doing when it came to Paul.

Charlotte bent over to unlace her half boots. "I don't think *Maman* quite approves of him. He's not at all the sort of man we usually have to stay at Rossmere. But she can hardly deny him hospitality. If it weren't for him—"

"I'd be dead. And Fenella would never have been born." That was still true. But Sophie now knew that the man to whom she owed her life was the man responsible for her father's death. She looked down at Fenella, who was consuming her late-morning feeding. The weight of the baby in her arms was reassuring, as was the insistent pull at her nipple. Whatever else she had lost she still had Fenella. But she no longer had Paul, not the Paul she had learned to trust without question, had come to depend on in a cravenly weak manner.

It shouldn't matter so much now that she was in the midst of her own family. She looked around the bedchamber that had been hers since childhood. The French-blue wallpaper that Aunt Louisa had let her choose herself when she was fourteen. The stack of cream-colored paper on the writing desk that was embossed with her name. The silver brush and comb on the dressing table that were engraved with her initials. The pots of rouge and powder and blacking in carefully chosen colors. The crystal bottle that held the rose scent she had specially blended at Floris.

She could see herself sitting at that same dressing table on the night of her first grown-up party, while Céline put her hair up and Charlotte sprawled on the bed watching them. Yet for a mad moment it seemed to her that she had never belonged in this room the way she belonged in that lavender-sprigged bedchamber at the McClarens', pretending to be Paul's wife.

Charlotte dropped her half boots on the Wilton carpet with a thud and curled her feet up on the blue-flowered chintz of the window seat. "Sophie? Can you stand to talk about something that'll probably seem trivial after what you've been through?"

"Of course, Charlie." In truth, Sophie was eager for distraction. Anything that would ease the ache of loneliness she had felt since she left Paul in the folly. "What?"

Charlotte picked up a petit point cushion and hugged it to her chest. "*Maman* is being beastly. She insists Ned and I wait until he's out of mourning so we can have a big wedding in London. It'll be ghastly. Lots of people I barely know and I'll probably trip going down the aisle. Besides"—Charlotte plucked a loose thread off the cushion—"I don't want to wait."

In the sunlight streaming through the window at her back, Charlotte's eyes were bright with love. Young, adoring, whole-hearted love. Love for the man who had probably tried to take Sophie's life.

Sophie transferred Fenella from her left breast to her right. "I know it's hard to wait, but I think it's always as well not to rush into marriage."

"But we've been betrothed for months." Charlotte made this sound an eternity. "What I'd really like is a quiet wedding in the chapel here. Or better yet in the secret chapel."

"It would have to be a very small wedding to be in the secret chapel." Sophie kept her voice light, with an effort. Even in the security of her childhood bedroom, the mention of Ned Rutledge's name made her throat go dry and her body tense as though in anticipation of a blow.

"I wouldn't mind that." Charlotte grinned. "Perhaps I should convince Ned to elope."

Fear shot up Sophie's spine. "Charlie—"

"Well, it would save a lot of fuss. But I wouldn't like to get married without you there. Ned will want you there too." Charlotte leaned back into a corner of the window seat, her face soft with longing. "He says if you hadn't had me to stay with you in London last year, he might never have realized I'd grown up. Do you remember the night he took us both to Vauxhall? I think that's when I fell in love with him." She sat up. "Oh, I'm sorry, Sophie. I forgot you still don't remember everything."

"No. No, I do remember that night." Sophie was braced for another onslaught of panic. Yet the memory that came to her was not of knives and threats and mist-shrouded Highland landscapes. It was of a warm spring evening, colored lights, a smiling fair-haired man leaning over to whisper something to Charlotte. It was a moment before Sophie realized the man was Ned. "Ned"—the name stuck oddly in her throat—"was very charming that evening."

"Ned's always charming. He's a terrible flirt. I used to think I could never be sure he was sincere, until—" Charlotte buried her face in the pillow, lost in a memory that was apparently too private to voice.

Sophie stroked her fingers against Fenella's cheek. Now that she had opened the gates to a memory of Ned before the attack, other recollections crowded in upon her—Ned tossing her up onto her horse, bringing her a glass of champagne at a crowded ball, saying quietly, "Is Tom being a beast again? Shall I thrash him for you?"

If she hadn't been holding Fenella Sophie would have rubbed her eyes. Those memories had nothing to do with the knife-wielding attacker she had been certain meant to take her life. But they were the same person.

Unless her uncle had been right to question her memory. She forced herself to think back to the morning she had met Ned by the stream outside Kinrie. He had been smiling, friendly, concerned. Then she had seen the knife in his hand. At least she thought she had seen it. She had been so sure. Yet she had no clear image of it now, only a memory of heart-pounding terror, the hard, rocky ground, Paul's arms closing around her.

She closed her eyes, trying to blot out the memory. Little as she wanted to think about Ned Rutledge, she wanted to think about Paul even less.

"Is something wrong, Sophie?"

Her distress had pierced Charlotte's daydreams. Sophie opened her eyes and smiled at her cousin. "Just memories. They still take me by surprise."

"You don't remember the last months at all, do you?"

"Not yet." And it was a weakness she hated. It had been a mistake to let herself depend so much on Paul. She would have to learn again to rely on no one but herself.

"Sophie." Charlotte put down the cushion and leaned forward. "I know I'm selfish to think of myself, with Tom just dead and you having been through such a horrible ordeal. But I love Ned so much it frightens me sometimes. When he's away from me I can't quite believe our betrothal is real. And now there've been these delays and he's been gone nearly a month. Sometimes I lie awake at night worrying about the silliest things. You'll be on my side, won't you? You'll be sure nothing gets in the way of the wedding?"

Sophie looked into her cousin's wide, intent eyes. She

wanted to wrap Charlotte in her arms as she did Fenella. But Charlotte could not be so easily protected. If Ned was the man Sophie feared he was, she would move heaven and earth to see he did not marry Charlotte. But she would have to be very sure. Because if by any chance she was wrong she would be breaking Charlotte's heart for nothing.

"I'll do everything possible to be sure you're happy, Charlie," Sophie said. "I swear it."

Chapter 16

>%<

PAUL STARED AT THE ROAN MARE STANDING OBEDIENTLY on the hard-packed ground of the stable yard. She raised her head and regarded him with calm brown eyes. He would swear she could see right through his mask of confidence. He turned to Daniel, who had already swung up onto a chestnut stallion. "This is the first time I've ridden."

Paul could count on his good hand the number of times he had seen Daniel de Ribard taken by surprise. This made another one. The strong brows rose. The words *Everyone knows how to ride* hung in the air between them.

But Daniel was not fool enough to speak them. "Shall we take one of the carriages?" To be fair, there was no hint of condescension in his voice.

"No, I got up early and had Timothy give me lessons. I think I can manage." Paul walked forward with an assumption of ease. *Whatever you do, don't let the horse see you're nervous,* Timothy had told him.

Timothy, one of the grooms, was holding the horse's reins, pretending to be invisible, as servants did. But as he handed Paul the reins he smiled with encouragement. Paul swung into the saddle. The roan mare didn't rear up or bolt or otherwise express the belief that he was an impostor. So far so good.

Paul gripped the reins, forcing the fingers of his right hand to close around them. "Ready when you are, Ribard."

Daniel had business with the steward at Tiverton Park, the Rutledge estate. Paul had invited himself along. He wanted to talk to Burghley, the head gardener at Tiverton. Thanks to judicious questioning of the staff at Rossmere, Paul had learned that Burghley knew more than anyone about the Rutledge family.

Daniel had been startled when Paul asked to accompany him, but he hadn't protested. The trip had been twice delayed, for it had rained for the past week—the week since Paul's confession to Sophie. But today the sky was clear and the air had the clean freshness that follows a storm. The same could not be said of the storm between Sophie and him. He could feel the weight of his revelations between them whenever they met. He tried to avoid her as much as possible.

He and Daniel rode out of the stable yard in silence. The movement of the horse was jarring—he did not quite have the trick of sitting in the saddle—but the roan mare trotted along in the appropriate direction. Either he was doing a better job of guiding her than he thought or she was simply following Daniel's horse. They went a little way down the drive, then cut off through the fields. Daniel held the reins easily in his kid-gloved hands. He sat in the saddle as if he had been born to it. Were he alone, no doubt he would be cantering over the fields, not moving at this sedate pace. It was a degree of consideration Paul could not remember his father ever showing him in the past.

"Bearing up all right?" Daniel asked as they entered a coppice of sycamore.

Paul shifted his weight in the saddle, trying to find a more comfortable position. "It's all relative. This is nothing compared to a forced march."

"I hadn't realized you were in the army. Did you fight at Waterloo?"

"I didn't last that long. I was invalided out after Austerlitz."

"Of course. Your hand. I'm sorry."

There was no horror or pity in Daniel's voice, but Paul caught a hint of curiosity. It occurred to him that, thanks to Frank Storbridge, he knew more about Daniel's life in the last twenty-three years than Daniel knew about his. For once the balance of power between them had shifted in his direction.

"You went back to your uncle and aunt in Paris after you were wounded?" Daniel asked.

Paul turned to look at his father. He had said nothing about living with Gerard and Anne Lescaut.

Daniel met his gaze, his own impassive as usual in the shadows cast by the sycamore branches. "I made some inquiries about you after I reached England. I wasn't entirely without interest in your fate."

Paul gripped the reins, his fingers unsteady. Those dispassionate words acknowledged a responsibility Daniel had never before admitted toward him. Paul wasn't sure whether he was glad or sorry. It was far too late for the cool waters of their relationship to be muddied by sentiment.

They rode in silence for a few moments, the only sound the soft clop of the horses' hooves on the damp ground and the stirring of the breeze in the branches. "Your uncle ran a newspaper, didn't he?" Daniel said.

They emerged from under the trees. Clear, bright sunlight assaulted Paul, leaving him no refuge. He chose his words with care. "That's how I found him. My mother had told me the name of the newspaper. I'd only met my uncle a half dozen times." He skipped over the weeks he had spent on the Paris streets before hunger and desperation drove him to his mother's estranged brother.

"Charlotte mentioned that she had a brother, but we never met."

"That's hardly surprising. The only thing you have in common is that you both married Englishwomen." It was strange to be speaking of the past this way with Daniel, as two adults. "Gerard Lescaut and his wife took me in without question."

"They had children of their own?"

"Two sons. Robert's a year older than I am, and Edouard was a year younger."

"Was?"

The roan mare shied as Paul clenched the reins. He forced his fingers to relax. It had been a mistake to say anything at all.

Now he was trapped. "We all joined the army together. Robert and I had just finished at the University of Paris. Edouard hadn't even started. We were filled with Republican fervor."

He flung this last out as a challenge. Daniel ignored it. "What happened to them?"

"Robert went on to become a colonel. Edouard was blown to pieces at Austerlitz, like me. Only he didn't survive."

There was a brief silence. A thrush rose from a nearby bush and flapped its wings, agitated by their passing. "The youngest," Daniel said. "You must have felt responsible."

Paul fixed his gaze on a box hedge to the right. The tough, dark-green leaves weren't enough to blot out the sight of Edouard's guts spilling onto the ground, the feel of his last shuddering breaths, the overpowering stench of death. "Robert felt responsible. I was too mangled to feel anything for weeks."

"And then?"

"I went to work on the newspaper with my uncle. When he died I took it over."

"Trying to change the world with the pen rather than the sword?"

Paul looked his father directly in the face. "Hardly. Robert's always been the idealist, not me. But I liked being able to voice my rage."

Daniel raised one brow, a trick Paul remembered envying in childhood. "I understand voicing rage at the Government isn't popular in France just now."

"That's why I left. Robert married a Scotswoman two years ago and settled in Edinburgh. He runs a newspaper, the *Edinburgh Leader*. Aunt Anne went to live with them. I decided to pay them a visit."

"And your aunt told you you'd been born in Kinrie."

"Yes. But that isn't the reason I went to the Highlands. I was collecting information for a story on the Clearances."

Another challenge. Again Daniel did not respond. "But of course," he said. "I shouldn't imagine you like being idle."

They crossed a ha-ha, a cleverly disguised ditch separating

the park from the farmland. Smoke curled above the larches and fir, breaking in on the pastoral solitude. They rode further and passed a cottage garden, bright with late-blooming flowers. Two boys of about Dugal's age stood amid the flowers and vegetable beds. One was tossing a ball to the other, who held a flattened stick that Paul recognized, thanks to Robert's son, as a cricket bat. As they rode by the boy with the bat sent the ball sailing into the air. It crashed against the whitewashed wall of the house, perilously close to one of the sash windows.

Daniel reined in his horse. "A good hit, Crispin, but if I hear your parents need a new window, I'll know whom to blame."

The boys tugged off their caps. "I'm sorry, my lord," said the boy with the bat.

"Steer your aim toward the fields instead of the house."

"Yes, my lord," the boys said, almost in unison. They stood watching, caps clutched in their hands, as Paul and Daniel rode on. Paul winced at the servility. And yet the boys had treated Daniel with respect rather than fear. The cottage looked well-kept, with a neat stone wall around the garden and new-looking slates on the roof. As landlords went, Daniel did not seem to be among the worst.

"Charlotte told me a lot of the Rossmere land had been sold off and you bought it back." Paul was glad at the excuse to turn the conversation back on Daniel. He still felt raw from his father's inquisition.

"Yes." Daniel accepted the shift in the conversation without argument. "The estate had been badly mismanaged, but it turns a handsome profit now. It will make quite an inheritance for Charlotte."

"She inherits the whole estate?" Ned Rutledge was a greedy man indeed. His fiancée would inherit all of Rossmere, and he was still willing to commit murder for the Rutledge lands.

"I had to choose one of the girls. I don't want to see the estate broken up. Charlotte's the most sensible of the four and she has quite a head for figures." Daniel's face softened, belying his ironic tone. He was silent for a moment, then added, "If I'd had a son, of course, it all would have gone to him."

"You mean if you and the marquise had had a son."

"Of course." Daniel guided his horse around a fallen branch. "Legitimate children are the only offspring men in my position are allowed to count. Surely you realized that long ago."

Paul was not sure if the words were a warning or an apology. He wasn't sure he wanted to know. "And Ned Rutledge? Are you satisfied giving Rossmere—and Charlotte—into his keeping?"

"Ned's a bit feckless, but he shows signs of growing out of it. I might have chosen a more brilliant match for Charlotte, but it's Ned she wants."

"And if my accusations against him prove true?"

Daniel looked Paul full in the face, his eyes hardened to steel. "I still believe there must be another explanation. It's difficult for me to imagine a man I've known since he was a boy behaving so monstrously. But if Ned's done what you accused him of, I'll kill him before I let him so much as touch Charlotte."

"I see." Paul smiled, though he was not quite sure why. "Then it seems, sir, that for once in our lives we are in agreement."

They said little more for the remainder of the ride. Perhaps they had both revealed more than they intended and were retreating to nurse their wounds. It was a novel idea. Paul was not used to thinking of Daniel as being vulnerable.

Rossmere merged effortlessly into Tiverton Park. Paul would not have known they had crossed to the other estate had Daniel not pointed out the hedge that marked the boundary. The tenants they encountered were respectful, but the cottages did not look as well-kept as those at Rossmere. Perhaps Tom Rutledge had been too busy with his political career to pay much attention to his tenants. Or perhaps, Paul admitted, he was all too ready to think ill of the man who had been Sophie's husband.

"There's the house," Daniel said as they rode down a slope of ground.

Paul looked at the place where Sophie had gone as a bride. The mellowed pink sandstone blended into the landscape, where Rossmere's stark white called attention to itself. It was smaller than Rossmere, but still imposing by any standard. Sophie had run that house. Paul counted eight chimneys and thought of the cramped two stories above the print shop in his uncle and aunt's house in Paris.

They left their horses with a groom in the stable yard. Daniel went into the house. Paul struck up a conversation with the groom. In five minutes he'd learned that Burghley, the man he wanted to talk to, was working on the north lawn.

Paul walked around to the back of the house, where a flag-stone terrace stretched to the grass. A man was kneeling to weed a bed of primroses on the far side of the lawn, a barrow drawn up beside him. As Paul approached, the man looked up and tipped his broad-brimmed hat, but did not pause in his task.

"Good morning." Paul fell back on his cousin's advice about rank flattery. "I take it you're responsible for these beautiful gardens?"

The man set down his spade, wiped his dirt-smeared hands on his linen breeches, and got to his feet. His hair and beard were gray, but his face was surprisingly youthful. "It takes more than one man to keep the gardens in order, sir. But I'm head gardener at Tiverton Park. I have been for nigh on thirty years. Joseph Burghley's the name."

"My name's Paul Lescaut. I'm a guest at Rossmere. I rode over with the marquis."

"Ah, you're the man who rescued Miss Sophie." Burghley smiled, seaming his face with laugh lines. Paul had the impression he had moved into a circle of trust. "Half the staff here have relatives in service at Rossmere," Burghley explained. "Anything happens at one house we're sure to hear of it at t'other. We were all glad to learn the babe was safe delivered and Miss Sophie was well."

"You must have known her for a long time." Paul dropped down on a stone bench. It was a profound relief to be on solid ground again. His right hand throbbed from the effort of holding the reins, and his half-healed wound smarted. "Please don't let me keep you from your work, Mr. Burghley."

"Thank you, sir. Truth is, I'm not quite comfortable when I don't have my hands in the dirt. Mrs. Burghley's never been able to understand it." Burghley knelt again and tugged at a narrow green shoot that was forcing its way up between two yellow-eyed purple flowering plants. "Aye, I've known Miss Sophie since she was a girl. There was always a lot of visiting between Tiverton and Rossmere. Never could learn to call her Lady Rutledge after she married the young master, God rest his soul."

"Sir Thomas." Paul forced regret for Sophie's erstwhile husband into his voice. "A sad business that."

"An odd business." Burghley tossed the plucked weed into his barrow, but did not volunteer more. "Miss Sophie's planning to stay at Rossmere with the baby then, is she? Or to go back south?"

"I don't know." Paul leaned back and rested his hands on the sun-warmed stone of the bench. Sophie had told him nothing of her plans, and he had no right to ask her. "She may return to Bath. I understand she'd been living there."

"Aye, in recent months, though it's not the place I'd picture her. Always liked town, did Miss Sophie. She's a good-hearted lass, but country life was too slow for her. And for Master Tom. Even Master Ned spends most of his time in London or Lancaster." Burghley tipped his hat back and wiped his hand across his forehead. "Tiverton may look quiet now, Mr. Lescaut, but it was fair bursting with life when the old master was alive."

"Perhaps that will change. I heard Mr. Rutledge—Sir Edward—is soon to marry."

Burghley smiled. "Most sensible thing Master Ned ever did, proposing to Miss Charlotte, if you'll permit me to say so, sir. She's a good girl. Settled, like."

Sophie, Paul gathered, had not been settled. But perhaps Tom Rutledge had given her little enough reason to want to settle.

Burghley looked up at Paul, his hands momentarily idle. "See here, Mr. Lescaut. Is Miss Sophie all right?"

Paul hesitated. "She suffered no lasting harm from the attack, and she's recovering from the birth of the child."

"I'm glad to hear it." Burghley looked down at his hands. "I . . . I'm glad to hear it."

"But perhaps you had other concerns about her?"

Burghley picked up his spade, then set it down again. "She was very quiet at the funeral. Cold, some said, but to my mind it was shock. Hard enough for a woman to lose her husband at all, but to lose him like that—"

Especially when her father had also taken his own life. Paul gripped the stone of the bench. "Did Sir Thomas leave any letter to explain his actions?"

Burghley shook his head. " 'Tweren't like him to give way to the dismals. Besides, he hadn't anything to be dismal about."

"I understand Lady Rutledge had gone to live in Bath."

Burghley snorted. "He wasn't the sort to be overly disturbed by a disagreement with his wife, if you take my meaning, sir. Mind you, I think he'd have preferred she come back under his roof. But he was looking forward to the birth of his heir. And everyone was saying he'd be in the Cabinet before long, especially with his speech after the fire."

It was a moment before Paul caught the significance of this last. He straightened up, Sophie's nightmare screams echoing in his ears. "Fire?"

"You hadn't heard of it? Ah, I forgot. From foreign parts, aren't you? Wouldn't know it to hear you speak. Got myself into a tangle of explanations, haven't I?"

Paul hesitated, weighing his words. "I'd like to hear anything that may concern Lady Rutledge."

Burghley shot him a speculative glance. Paul shifted his weight on the bench. For a moment he had the distinct feeling the older man saw things he had not even admitted to himself.

Burghley picked up his spade and turned back to the primroses. "Old Lady Rutledge was the daughter of a merchant from Lancaster. Quite an heiress. It's thanks to her the house and gardens look as fine as they do. She was an only child, so she inherited her father's cotton mill. She left it to Master Tom and Master Ned."

"Equally?"

"Aye, though Master Ned saw to the managing of the mill, since Master Tom was busy in Parliament." Burghley dug up another weed. Paul waited. "These are unsettled times, Mr. Lescaut. Protests and such."

"Many are lacking food or work or both."

Burghley regarded Paul for a moment. "True enough, Mr. Lescaut. My grandfather was a weaver, but he worked out of his cottage, with his wife and children beside him. Now whole families go off to the factories, especially the women and children. The managers like them because their hands be small." A shadow of distaste crossed Burghley's face. "The new weaving machines have made jobs scarce. And now that the war's over, the factories don't have Government contracts to keep them going."

"Yet people keep leaving the countryside for the cities." Paul knew that enclosures had driven tenants off their land in England as well as Scotland.

"Aye, that's the right of it." Burghley relaxed into a confiding posture. "There'd been grumbling, especially among the Rutledge millworkers. Their housing wasn't fit for animals, they said. Then last March someone set fire to the mill. Burned it out to naught but a shell. Three of the millworkers were arrested for it. Master Tom talked of the incident in a speech in

Parliament. It helped him pass a bill increasing the penalties for the destruction of property. Made the Government very happy, I understand."

"And the millworkers who were arrested?"

Burghley jabbed his spade into the ground. "They were hanged, all three."

There was a man. He was being hung. I was trying to cut him down, but the knife kept slipping from my hand. The connection to Sophie's dream could not be coincidence. Sophie was a generous woman; she would have been concerned about the men. But by Burghley's account she had little interest in life in the country. In recent months she had also had little interest in her husband. Why had it been the plight of her husband's workers that had haunted her dreams?

"Miss Sophie was in Bath when it happened," Burghley continued. "But after the funeral she kept asking questions."

"About the fire in the mill? Or about Sir Thomas's death?"

"About all of it. She was staying at Rossmere, but she drove over to Tiverton near every day and went through all Master Tom's papers. Then she went to Lancaster to talk to the millworkers' families. Make sure they were all right."

"How long was that before she went to Scotland?"

"She never came back. Just sent her uncle and aunt word that she was going on to Scotland to see Master Ned. It was as if she couldn't sit still. Grief takes some that way. When my oldest girl got word her husband had fallen at Vitoria, she stayed up night and day cleaning the house." Burghley shook his head. "I hope Miss Sophie's feeling more herself now. Do you think she is, Mr. Lescaut?"

"I hope so." Paul smiled. There was no need for Burghley to know that he was now turning over possibilities that had more to do with Sophie's safety than her state of mind. "She's got the baby to keep her occupied."

"Aye, that's good. Take her mind off the other."

Paul remained with Burghley a while longer, learning more about the history of the estate, the long-standing friendship between the Rutledges and the Ribards, and the escapades Tom and Ned had got up to as children. He could not press Burghley more about the fire and the hanged men without making the gardener suspicious. Other than Sophie, the one person with whom he could discuss his ideas was Daniel. Paul actually found himself eager to rejoin his father.

At last Daniel emerged from the house. Paul waited until they had left Tiverton and were riding down a hedged lane overhung by a tangle of oak. Then he went straight to the heart of the matter. "Was the Rutledge Mill heavily insured at the time of the fire?"

Daniel raised his brows. "It seems you had a busier afternoon than I did."

"I had a long talk with the head gardener. Was it insured?"

"Ned may be imprudent, but he's not a fool in business matters. It was insured."

"Handsomely?"

Daniel hesitated. "Well."

"So the fire gave the Rutledge brothers the insurance money and helped Tom Rutledge pass a bill that advanced his career." Paul adjusted his hold on the reins. He was coming to feel more comfortable on the roan mare. "I understand Tom Rutledge was an ally of Lord Sidmouth. Sidmouth is said to employ *agents provocateurs* to incite violence among the discontented."

Daniel shot him a quick glance. "As a journalist you should know better than to listen to rumors."

"As a journalist I've learned to smell the truth. The Rutledge brothers didn't do badly out of the fire."

"Your point?"

Paul turned his head to look at his father. "Oh, come, sir. Surely you saw my point from the first."

Daniel met his gaze. A breeze stirred in the branches overhead. "It's a grave allegation."

"I've already accused Ned of trying to murder Sophie. You can hardly expect me to cavil here. Did the millworkers ever confess to starting the fire?"

Daniel stared down at the spotless tan kid of his riding gloves. "No."

"So three men went to their deaths protesting their innocence. And two months later Tom Rutledge put a bullet through his head for reasons no one understands."

Daniel gave a twisted smile. "Aye, there's the rub in your theory, boy. If—*if*, mind you—Tom had done as you say, he wasn't the man to take his own life in a fit of remorse."

"*That's* a grave allegation."

"That's a statement of my late nephew-in-law's character."

Paul fingered the reins. "You didn't tell me Sophie began asking questions about the fire after Tom's death."

"No, I didn't." There was no hint of defensiveness in Daniel's voice. "I didn't see any point in stirring more speculation until we heard Ned's side of the story. And I didn't see the need to reawaken troubling memories for Sophie until we had to. After Tom died she was desperate to latch on to any explanation for his suicide."

"Whatever the reasons for Tom's suicide, if Tom and Ned—or Ned alone—were behind the fire, and Sophie had begun to suspect it, that could be the reason Ned wants her dead."

Daniel's eyes narrowed. "A lot of ifs. But yes, it's possible—assuming Ned does want her dead."

Paul stared at the ground ahead, dappled with shadow by the overhanging trees. Sophie's life could depend on their ability to distinguish truth from the shadows of suspicion. "If Ned wanted to get rid of Sophie because of the inheritance, he no longer has a motive now that the baby is a girl. But if he wanted to get rid of her because of what she knows, she's still in danger."

"I had considered that." Daniel's voice took on the same edge it had held when he spoke of Charlotte's safety. "Just because I'm hesitant to accuse Ned doesn't mean I'm careless of my niece's safety. I have no intention of letting Sophie come to harm."

Paul looked at his father and saw an echo of his own determination in Daniel's eyes. "Neither do I."

Chapter 17

"If I'd known there was so much to be learned at Tiverton Park, I'd have gone there myself." Sophie avoided looking at Paul and kept her mind on little things. The ghostly early-morning mist veiling the garden. The cool, damp air on her face. The weight of the baby carriage as she pushed it. If she concentrated on such details she could almost forget that she was walking alone with Paul for the first time since he had told her he was the man who had betrayed her father.

The story of his trip to Tiverton yesterday echoed in her mind, stirring a jumble of frightening images. She could not be sure if they were real or conjured by Paul's words, but she shied away from them instinctively. "You're suggesting Tom and Ned set fire to their own mill, possibly with the blessing of the Home Secretary, and I went to Kinrie to confront Ned because I'd learned the truth?"

"What do you think?" Paul's eyes were dark and opaque, revealing nothing, forcing the question back on her.

She gripped the handle of the baby carriage. The damp ground felt treacherous beneath the soles of her half boots. The disturbing chaos in her mind settled into a single, clear image. A young girl's face, round and determined, framed by bright red hair. "Amy Caxton." She looked at Paul. "Amy went to Bath with me. I was training her to be a lady's maid. Before I took her into service she worked in the Rutledge Mill. She was an orphan who lived with her uncle and aunt like I did. Her uncle was one of the men hung."

"That was what started your concern about the fire?"

Cold, unexpected shame washed over her. "Yes, I suppose

so. If it wasn't for Amy I probably wouldn't have paid much attention. The mill always seemed very distant. And I was pre-occupied with my own worries at the time."

"You'd left your husband."

She tugged at her shawl. There were areas of her life too in-timate for Paul's probing. "Not officially, but yes, I had. Then the fire happened and Amy's uncle was arrested. Amy had to go home." She pieced together the fragments as they came back to her. She had remembered Bath, but the fire and Amy had been a blank until now. There were still barriers in her mind, blocking off memories that were painful. "I wrote let-ters—to Tom, to the local magistrate. It did little good."

"You thought the men were innocent?"

She could feel the barriers crumbling, like the mist breaking up over the mountains. She forced down the panic that rose in her throat. "I can't be sure of what I thought. I think I had doubts even then. Amy was so certain her uncle couldn't have been involved. At the very least I thought the men should be shown clemency. I'd visited the mill with Tom. I knew food was expensive and wages low and their housing deplorable. I'm not entirely blind to such concerns, you know."

"I didn't say you were."

Sophie stared at her white net gloves. She had been more blind than she liked to admit. "I should have gone to Lancaster myself for the trial, but I didn't. I read about the hangings in the newspaper." Somehow that admission seemed worst of all. She could see herself, holding the newspaper over the rose-and-cream Staffordshire breakfast dishes. She was afraid to look at Paul, sure she would see censure in his eyes. He might have his faults, but he would have gone to Lancaster and fought to see justice was done.

She looked at Fenella, asleep in the baby carriage, her small hands curled against her pink blanket. "Amy had lost the man who was like a father to her. I thought about the baby I was go-ing to have. Fenella changed a lot of things for me."

"Did you think Tom and Ned might have had anything to do with the fire?"

Something flinched inside her. She wanted to strike out at Paul for breaking down the barriers in her mind. Yet she knew those barriers were not a haven but a house of cards. "I'm not sure. I know I was furious with Tom for making political capital out of human misery. I don't think it was until after he died that I began to wonder—"

"So you did wonder?" Paul's voice was razor-sharp.

She hesitated, teetering on the verge of an ugly abyss. "Yes. I had to understand how he could have . . . done that. Taken his own life. Whatever we had together was finished, but I didn't want my baby to grow up wondering why her father had left her. Like—"

She broke off. Paul's gaze met her own. Echoes of shots and screams and feet scrambling on wooden stairs tightened the air between them.

"Like you wondered." Paul's voice was flat and expressionless.

Sophie swallowed. Her mouth was dry, thirsting for something she couldn't name. "Yes."

"So." Paul turned away, hands clasped behind his back, eyes on the lawn. "You went through his papers. You thought he might have killed himself out of guilt?"

"Tom wasn't the sort to be troubled by guilt. But he wasn't wholly devoid of honor." She looked at Fenella again. *Dear God, my baby's father. I should mind more than I do.*

"Did you find anything in his papers?"

"I don't think so." She willed herself to look into the shadows that still lurked in the recesses of her mind. "This part is hazy. I do remember deciding to go to Lancaster. I wanted to see Amy and talk to the families of the other men who had been hung. I don't remember anything after that. Truly." She stopped, holding tightly to the baby carriage, looking at the glossy leaves of the beech that bordered the lawn. Her chest hurt and her breath came in quick, painful gasps. She felt as she had when she'd raced horses against her cousins and pushed herself farther than she thought she could go.

"I know this isn't easy for you." Paul's voice was strangely soothing, like the warmth of a well-worn cloak on a cold day. A trick of memory. She didn't want to be soothed by Paul anymore.

"I'm all right." She forced herself to look him full in the face. He was bareheaded, his hair damp from the mist and falling over his forehead. It made him look too approachable. "I remember being angry with Tom. Suspecting he had something to do with the fire. I don't remember suspecting Ned. Perhaps I thought Tom was in it alone. Perhaps I went to Kinrie to tell Ned of my suspicions, not to confront him."

"But Ned tried to kill you."

"Yes." Her promise to Charlotte echoed in her ears. "So it seems."

"*Seems?*" Paul gripped her arm. She tensed at the feel of his fingers digging into her flesh. He released her, but held her with his gaze. "Sophie, the man's a killer. You can't doubt what you saw."

She gave a laugh that was meant to be brittle, but came out sounding shaky. "These days I doubt everything."

SOPHIE EASED FENELLA INTO THE CRADLE AND DREW THE blankets around her. Fenella made a small gurgling sound, but didn't open her eyes. She had fallen asleep at Sophie's breast. With luck it would be another four hours before she woke. Violet, the Ribard maid who had taken Beth's place upon her return to the McClarens, was asleep in the boudoir. Sophie and Fenella were alone in their small world. Warmth welled up in Sophie's chest. What a fool she had been not to want a child. Not since her father was alive had she felt she belonged so completely to another human being.

She looked down at her daughter a moment longer. Then, relishing the thought of blankets and sleep, she picked up her candle and turned to go back to the bed.

A rap sounded on the door. Her heartbeat quickened. Idiotic. She was in her own house. Perhaps it was Charlotte. She sometimes came to Sophie's room late, though rarely as late as this. Sophie moved to the door and pulled it open.

Paul stood outside, in his shirtsleeves, his hair tousled, the candle he held casting flickering shadows over his face. She tensed with surprise. He had not sought her out since their discussion about Ned over a week ago.

"Dugal has some news you'd best hear," he said.

She hadn't realized that Dugal stood beside him. She smiled at the boy. Thank God she did not have to admit Paul to her bedchamber alone. "Of course." She stepped back into the room, not so far that they would disturb Fenella, but far enough to keep her distance from Paul. "What is it, Dugal?" she asked when Paul had shut the door.

Dugal's body was tense, as though he could scarcely contain his news. "I saw him. Mr. Rutledge."

Sophie stared into Dugal's bright eyes. Her hands and brain went numb. Hot wax fell against her fingers, jerking her out of her paralysis. She righted the candle. "Where? When?"

"Just now." Dugal drew a breath, gathering wind for his story. "Dickon and I were goin' to go to the folly, see. Dickon works i' the stable. He says the folly's haunted and the ghosts come out at midnight when the moon be full, but he got scared and wouldna come, so I went by myself. I didna see any ghosts. But I saw Mr. Rutledge. Walkin' through the trees near the folly he was, furtive like. I tried to follow him, but he disappeared behind some bracken and I didna see him come out the other side."

"The secret passage?" Paul's gaze was fixed upon her.

"On the edge of the beech coppice, where the ground starts to slope up?"

Dugal nodded.

Sophie clenched her hands. Her questions about Ned's guilt had fled in the face of the remembered fear she carried in her body. "Yes."

"So Rutledge could be in the house by now." Paul's voice was taut.

"No." Now that the first shock had worn off, her brain worked quickly. "There's a lock on the panel between the secret chapel and the library. So the King's men couldn't trip the spring and expose the hidden priest. The lock can be opened only from inside the house. Someone would have had to let Ned in. Oh, dear God." Sophie's throat constricted. "Charlotte."

"You think Rutledge sent word to her?" Paul asked.

"She told me she'd like to elope. She even mentioned the secret passage. Perhaps Ned thinks that once they're actually married Uncle Daniel won't dare turn on him. Why didn't I— Stay with Fenella. I'll check Charlotte's room."

Charlotte's bedchamber was two doors down from Sophie's. Sophie tapped at the door, but was too anxious to wait more than ten seconds. She stepped into the room. The bed-curtains were drawn, the covers pushed back. Moonlight seeped through the window curtains and shone against an empty expanse of white sheet.

There was no time to panic or curse. Sophie returned to her own room. "She's gone. We'd better check the library. No, let me get a cloak. We may have to look outside." She went to the wardrobe, wrapped a blue velvet cloak over her dressing gown, and reached for a pair of shoes.

"What about Fenella?" Dugal asked.

Sophie tugged on the second shoe and moved to the cradle. Fenella's face was relaxed with well-fed contentment. "She should sleep for another two hours at least. Violet's in the boudoir. If Fenella does wake she'll come in."

The house was still and quiet, the lamps turned down, the doors and windows carefully bolted by attentive servants. The carpeted corridor and the cool stone of the staircase felt familiar and safe, yet Sophie's heart beat as quickly as it had in the Highland mountains. She led the way down the stairs, but when they reached the library Paul moved ahead of her. "I don't want you walking in on Rutledge."

He pulled open the door. The room was in darkness, the heavy velvet curtains drawn. No sound disturbed the tobacco-scented quiet. She brushed past him and walked to the fireplace. The memory ingrained in her fingers, she felt for the Tudor rose of inlaid bog oak on one of the pilasters flanking the fireplace. A clever conceit. King Henry's device concealed the chapel that defied him.

The panel was locked, as she expected. She turned back to Paul and Dugal. "The keyhole is behind the books. My uncle keeps the key in his study. Unless Charlotte's taken it."

Daniel's study adjoined the library. Sophie had seen him take the key from his desk many times. In childhood she had borrowed it herself on more than one occasion. She set her candle down on the ink blotter, tugged open the left-hand drawer, and felt at the back where the key was kept, fastened to a nail by a bit of black satin ribbon. Her fingers found the nail, but no key hung from it. She pushed the drawer shut with the force of her frustration. "It's gone. Charlotte must have taken it."

She moved toward the door to the corridor. Paul caught her arm as she walked past. "Where are you going?"

"Outside and through the other end of the passage. They may still be in the chapel. Perhaps Ned merely asked her to meet him, not elope tonight. It's the only chance of catching them."

"I'll go. Wake your uncle."

She pulled away from his grip. "There's no time. You can take on Ned. I'll deal with Charlotte."

"Go back to bed, Sophie." Paul moved to the door ahead of her. "It's not safe."

Sophie reached past him for the door handle. "Charlotte's my cousin."

"She's my sister."

Dugal sucked in his breath. Sophie stilled, her fingers gripping the brass handle. She had heard the servants' whispers in Paris years ago. But it was different to hear Paul so baldly state his relationship to her uncle.

The candle flame danced in Paul's eyes, bright with reckless defiance. They told her how much it had cost him to admit his link to the Ribard family. "All the more reason for you to come with me," she said.

She twisted the door handle and pushed past Paul. His footsteps sounded in the corridor behind her. She half expected him to try to physically prevent her from leaving the house, but he made no attempt to do so. Dugal ran after them.

They left the house by a side door. A quarter moon shone from a cloudy, purple-black sky. The cool wash of moonlight drained the park of color. A chill breeze tugged at her cloak and the unwieldy layers of nightdress and dressing gown beneath.

The moonlight played treacherous games with the dips and rises in the landscape. She stumbled over the skirt of her dressing gown as they descended the stone steps from the upper terrace of lawn. Her candle went out. Paul relit it with his. An owl called to their right. The beech coppice. They were nearly there.

It was cool and dark beneath the trees, but the curtain of bracken shielded by a beech trunk was instantly familiar. The bracken was disturbed, as though someone had recently pushed it aside. She tugged at it, felt the open space beneath, drew a breath of relief. "This is it."

The passage was narrow and low. The dirt ceiling grazed the top of her head. Paul had to walk stooped. He made his way slowly, with a silent economy of movement. Each second stretched her nerves tighter, yet a part of her brain acknowledged the need for caution. The light of their candles flickered against the close walls. The air was damp and musty. The rocks underfoot cut through the thin soles of her shoes. She had been dressed more appropriately when she explored the passage as a child.

Paul stopped abruptly, flattened himself against the wall, and motioned for them to do likewise. As she drew back against the moist earth Sophie became aware of voices. One voice at least.

The door from the passage to the chapel must be ajar. She could see a faint glimmer of light up ahead. But she couldn't make out the words.

Paul inched forward, keeping close to the wall. She and Dugal moved after him.

"It's too late for caution, I tell you." Ned's voice rang out with sudden clarity, sending a chill along her nerves. "If we delay any longer she'll remember. We have to get rid of her. And Lescaut."

There was a mumbled reply, as though the speaker was at the far end of the room. Sophie, prepared to rush in and rescue Charlotte, stared at the crack in the door, trying to make sense of the situation.

"You must agree with me." Ned's voice was sharp with desperation. "You were the one who said we couldn't afford to let her live. She's twice as much of a danger now. And if anything happens to her that bloody bastard Lescaut won't let matters rest."

Silence. Then footsteps, as though Ned's companion had crossed to the near end of the chapel. Sophie felt sweat break out on her forehead. Paul reached back and gripped her arm. Dugal was absolutely still beside her.

"There's no need to insult the boy's parentage, Ned. But I must admit that for once you're right. It's too dangerous to let them go."

Sophie felt the tremor of shock that ran through Paul. Only then did she realize to whom the second voice belonged. The man who was her uncle and Paul's father had just agreed that they should both be killed.

Chapter 18

⇥⇤

PAUL'S FINGERS BIT INTO HER WRIST. HE PULLED HER DOWN the passage, away from the chapel. She stumbled over the rocky ground. She seemed to have lost control of her body. Her brain felt thick and heavy, as though her thoughts were filtered through a gauze of disbelief. She was vaguely aware that Dugal was running along beside them.

The cool air as they emerged from the passage jerked her back to reality. She looked up at Paul. "We don't even know—"

"We know enough." He drew her through the tangle of beech. There was a rustling in the underbrush. She started, heart slamming against her ribs. Paul went still. "An animal," he said after a moment. They moved on.

When they reached the upper terrace of lawn, Paul stopped. "The servants' entrance?"

"This way." Dugal started forward before Sophie could answer. At the back of the house Paul gestured for them to wait, inched open the door, then turned and nodded. "Shoes," he said, bending down to remove his own.

They slipped inside and climbed the plain wooden stairs she and her cousins had often run up and down in childhood. The smell of lemon oil and the whitewashed walls were as familiar as family portraits. So was the thick carpet in the first-floor corridor, its soft cream warmed by the candlelight. She could catch a trace of hyacinth from Aunt Louisa's favorite potpourri. But the familiar marks of home now seemed beset by traps.

Paul opened a door and pushed her and Dugal inside. It was

only when she saw Sir James's burgundy brocade dressing gown flung over a chair back that Sophie realized they were in Paul's room. Safe for the moment. A shudder tore through her. She was cold, a bitter cold that cut to the bone.

"Are you all right?" Paul searched her face.

She gripped her arms, trying to still the shudders that racked her body. A trickle of perspiration ran between her breasts. Beneath her cloak and dressing gown, her nightdress was plastered to her skin. Strange, when she felt so cold. "I can't believe it." She tugged at the high collar of her nightdress, longing for the feel of clean air. The ugliness at the heart of her family seemed to cling to her skin. She looked at Paul's face, obscured by the shadows. "But I have to believe it, don't I?"

"Yes." His voice was stripped of emotion. He set down his candle and lit the lamp on the bedside table.

Dugal dropped down on the bench at the foot of the bed. "They're goin' to try and kill ye. They said it plain enough. We ha' to get out o' here."

"So we do. Tonight." Paul looked at Sophie, as though expecting an argument. She nodded, not trusting her voice. He turned back to Dugal. "Could your friend Dickon get us a carriage and horses?"

"One of the older carriages." Sophie spoke without thinking. "And the grays. They're reliable, but they aren't the fastest horses in the stable, so they may not be missed as quickly as some of the others. Tell Dickon to say he was acting on my orders if anyone questions him later. I'll leave a note for my—I'll leave a note."

"Right ye are." Dugal started for the door.

"No." Paul gripped the boy's shoulder. "None of us leaves the room until Ribard is safely back in his own."

"Fenella," Sophie said.

"She's not the one at risk." Paul's voice left no room for question.

"Where are we goin' to go?" Dugal asked. "Back to Scotland?"

"No." Again Sophie spoke without thinking. "I want to go to

Lancaster, to talk to the families of the men who were hanged. That's what I did before, and whatever I found sent me to Scotland to see Ned."

Dugal returned to the bench. "It was askin' questions that got ye i' trouble i' the first place. Ye should be goin' somewhere safe."

"We won't be safe until we know the truth."

Paul nodded. "We can't protect ourselves against Ribard until we know why he wants us dead."

"Dod." Dugal stared at Paul, as though trying to make sense of the inexplicable. "Is he really yer father?"

A muscle twitched beside Paul's mouth. "He's never admitted it."

"But—"

Paul held up his hand for silence. He moved to the door and eased it open a crack. Then Sophie heard it as well. The thud of a man's shoes on the stone stairs. Daniel. Her insides cramped with fear.

"My dear girl, what on earth are you doing up at this hour?"

For a numbing moment Sophie thought her uncle was speaking to her. But the door was open only a fraction of an inch. Daniel could not know where she was.

"Lydia's come down with a cold and Charles seems to be getting it as well." Charlotte's voice spoke in reply, softer than Daniel's and edged with weariness. "Their nurse woke me. You know Céline's never much use in the nursery in the middle of the night."

"Or at any other time. You're a good aunt, Charlie." Daniel's deep tones were unmistakable, as they had been in the chapel. Yet now they were transformed by warmth.

"You're working late, *Papa*."

"Some correspondence with the plantation in Jamaica. I must have it in the post tomorrow. Tedious business. Best get some sleep, *chérie*. You may be summoned to the sickroom in the morning."

"Very likely. Good night, *Papa*."

"Good night, *ma petite*."

There was a brief pause. Sophie could imagine her uncle kissing Charlotte on the brow as he had often kissed her. Her skin crawled at the memory.

Charlotte's door clicked shut. Daniel's footsteps faded into the distance. Paul eased his own door closed. "Give them a few minutes to settle. Then go and pack what you need for yourself and Fenella. Bring any money you have and whatever jewelry you can carry easily. Can you manage not to wake Violet?"

"I think so," she said. Paul's crisp voice steadied her nerves. "If she does wake she'll know better than to question me."

A faint smile tugged at the corners of Paul's mouth. "*Noblesse* has its uses, doesn't it?" His face hardened. "You understand that we can't trust anyone in the house. Not even your personal maid."

"Especially not Wentworth. She—" Sophie broke off as another memory fell into place. "Just before I left for Lancaster I surprised Wentworth by my writing desk. I could tell my letters had been disarranged. That's why I didn't take her with me. I was going to confront her when I got back. I suppose—" Unease prickled the back of her neck. "I suppose Ned or Uncle Daniel paid her to spy on me."

"Probably." Paul seemed to take the additional betrayal for granted. He couldn't understand what an invasion it was to have the person who helped select one's clothes and tend one's complexion and dress one's hair subverted by the enemy. Sophie might not have been as fond of Wentworth as of her previous maid, but it had never occurred to her that she couldn't trust the woman.

"I'll come to your door in an hour and knock three times," Paul continued. "By then the house should be quiet. Dugal, you go to the stables and arrange with Dickon about the carriage. I'll pack for you."

"I dinna need anythin'."

"Sophie and I would prefer it if you had a change of

clothes." Paul cracked the door open again. "All quiet. One hour."

Sophie and Dugal walked down the corridor in silence, carrying candles and shoes. At the head of the stairs Dugal gave her a quick grin and darted down the stairs. Sophie moved past the stairs to her own door. Her room was as quiet and dark as she had left it. She went at once to the cradle. Fenella had pushed off the blanket, but she was still asleep. Relief flooded through Sophie.

She lit the lamp, stripped off her cloak, dressing gown, and sweat-soaked nightdress, and pulled on a clean, cool chemise and drawers. Fortunately she kept most of her clothing in the bedroom and used her boudoir more as a sitting room. She put on a walking dress of indigo sarcenet, innocuous enough to blend into a crowd, and a spencer in a lighter shade. The hat she normally wore with the dress and spencer was too elaborate. Instead, she chose a plain, close-fitting straw bonnet.

Most of her luggage must have been left in Kinrie, but she found a valise on a shelf in her wardrobe and began to fill it with necessities. Fenella's things first. Napkins, gowns, caps, spare blankets. Then clothes for herself, her brush and comb, her toothbrush and tooth powder. As an afterthought she reached for her rouge and powder and blacking and scent. She might be running for her life, but she wasn't going to let herself crumble completely.

Her jewel case was too heavy to take. She pulled out a few items with sentimental value—her mother's pearls, the lapis lazuli brooch, the amethyst betrothal ring Harry had given her—and some of the more expensive pieces that had been gifts from Tom. Those could be sold for traveling funds. As she picked up a pair of sapphire-and-diamond earrings, her eye fell on an amber cross. Her hand clenched, pressing the earrings into her palm. Daniel had given her the cross when she was confirmed. She remembered the feel of his fingers clasping it around her neck while he told her how proud he was and her mother and Aunt Louisa looked on, smiling.

She resisted the urge to hurl the cross through the window and forced her fingers to uncurl. There was a smear of blood on her palm where the earrings had broken the skin. If the wound left a scar it would be a fitting reminder of the folly of trust. She wound a handkerchief around her hand, pinned the brooch to her dress, clasped the pearls round her throat, and tucked the other jewels she had chosen into the corners of the valise.

Done. She had managed to cram a surprising amount into the valise, and without any help from Wentworth. Absurdly satisfied by having achieved this small goal, she carried the candle to her writing table and reached for a clean sheet of paper. After a moment of thought she dipped her pen into the inkpot and began to write.

> *Charlie,*
>
> *I thought it would be a relief to be home, but though everyone has been so kind, the memories are too painful. After all that has happened these past months, I need to be alone to try to sort my life out. Mr. Lescaut has kindly offered to escort me to Bath. Please try to make Aunt Louisa and Uncle Daniel understand (a Herculean task, I know, especially in Aunt Louisa's case) and tell them I will send the carriage and horses back as soon as possible.*
>
> *Love to Céline and the children.*
>
> *Love and thanks to you,*
>
> *Sophie*

She hesitated, the pen dripping black dots on the cream paper.

> *P.S.*
>
> *Please, dearest, promise you won't get married without me. I couldn't bear to miss it.*

Sophie dusted the letter with sand and left it on her writing table where the servants would find it in the morning. There were a few pound notes at the back of one of the drawers. She stuffed them into a blue-net reticule just as three raps sounded on the door.

Paul slipped into the room carrying a valise and a lamp. "Not a sound," he said in a conversational tone. "Ready?"

"I just have to get Fenella."

Fenella stirred, pushing her head against Sophie's arm as Sophie lifted her from the cradle. "Shush, love, it's all right." Sophie wrapped Fenella in two extra blankets and settled her in the basket in which she had traveled from Scotland. Fenella made a fretful noise, but didn't open her eyes.

Paul had tucked her valise under his arm and was holding the door open. It was only as she stepped through the doorway that Sophie realized she might never again set foot in the room that had been hers since she left the nursery. She started to turn back, then lifted her head and walked into the corridor. She would rather remember her life at Rossmere as it had been before tonight.

Despite the carpet, their footfalls seemed to echo through the house. The light of the lamp seemed dangerously bright. And the distance to the service stairs seemed to have grown longer. But at last they reached the baize-covered door and started down the stairs, slowly so Fenella would not be jostled and the boards would not creak. When they reached the bottom Sophie was breathing hard. She gripped the stair rail to steady herself. Fenella let out a yowl.

Sophie lifted her daughter from the basket and murmured to her. Fenella cried again. Sophie tugged off a glove and held out her finger. Fenella's mouth rooted about and closed over her knuckle. Paul opened the door to the outside.

They were nearly there. As they rounded the side of the house Sophie saw a carriage drawn up in front of the stable. She recognized the outline of one of the older traveling carriages. The moonlight fell on the crested panel and the slick coats of the matched grays in the harness. Two small figures stood beside the carriage. Dugal and Dickon.

When they reached the carriage Sophie drew a pound note from her reticule and gave it to Dickon. "I can't tell you how much you've helped us. We'll send the horses and carriage back tomorrow."

"It's all right, Miss Sophie. Dugal said it was a matter of life and death."

Dickon's eyes shone, as though this was an adventure like looking for the ghosts in the folly at midnight. He couldn't possibly know how true Dugal's words were.

Sophie settled Fenella in her basket on the carriage seat and turned to Paul. "Should I drive?"

Paul stowed the second valise at the back of the carriage. "You need to be with Fenella."

"Have you ever driven a carriage?"

"I've driven a cart. It's the same principle." He offered her his hand.

She should have learned long since that it was no good arguing his abilities. She took his hand and climbed in beside Fenella. Paul leaned inside the carriage and spoke in a lowered voice. "Where did you say we were going in your note?"

"Bath."

He nodded. "We'll drive south for a few miles and find a posting house where we can hire a carriage and horses and send these home. Then we'll double back to Lancaster. It may not deceive Ribard, but it's worth a try." He drew back and turned to the boys. "Dugal, you ride inside with Sophie."

Dugal sprang into the carriage. Fenella began to cry again. Her schedule had been disturbed and she was hungry. Sophie pushed back her cloak and began to undo the buttons on her dress.

Fenella was already suckling when the carriage rolled forward. The tug on her breast was somehow reassuring. Sophie closed her eyes as they turned down the drive. She should feel relief or fear, anger or sorrow. But she was too numb to feel anything at all.

THE SCENT OF COAL SMOKE SEEPED THROUGH THE WIN-dows of the Rose and Crown's best private parlor. Sophie set her teacup down on the windowsill. A weight settled over her that had nothing to do with the events of the past night. Lancaster always depressed her. Through the window she could see the curve of river and the dark mass of the castle beyond. The view might have been dramatic but for the gray smoke that hung over the city.

A red-brick building with white-framed windows and a graceful cupola stood across the river. It could have passed for a country squire's house, but she knew the interior was nothing like Rossmere. The brick facade housed a cotton mill, and the pretty cupola contained a bell for summoning workers.

"Dinna ye want somethin' to eat?" Dugal said from the table.

Sophie picked up her cup and turned back to the inside of the room. She was light-headed with fatigue, but too tightly wound to sit still. The joint of beef, loaf of bread, and fruit and cheese on the table turned her stomach. She took a sip of tea, relishing the clean, astringent taste. Then she looked at Paul and asked the question that had been echoing in her mind since she had been able to think at all. "Why?"

Paul set down his makeshift sandwich. "Because of what you know. What you knew in Kinrie and still haven't remembered. Whatever it is threatens Ribard as well as Rutledge. How far would Ribard go to protect Ned for Charlotte's sake?"

"Not this far." Sophie moved to the table. She had been still too long. "He could have withdrawn his consent to the marriage."

Dugal spread mustard on a fresh piece of bread. "Below-stairs they say he's a canny one. But he's no' pleasant to cross swords wi'. He fair puts the screws to people who rub him the wrong way."

"People?" Paul reached out to rock Fenella's basket, which was on a chair beside him.

Dugal cut a slice of double Gloucester cheese. "When he first came to England some folk looked down their noses at him because he was a Froggy and a Papist."

"It's true." Sophie stirred more milk into her tea, seeking to keep her hands busy. "There was one man who tried to black-ball him at White's and another who snubbed him at court. Uncle Daniel bought up their debts and forced them into bankruptcy." She took a sip of the lukewarm tea. "I knew he could be ruthless. But I never thought—"

"I know." Paul's hand moved toward hers, then stilled, as though the touch might be unwelcome. "I've hated him most of my life, but I never thought he'd be capable of this either."

Sophie set down her cup. She wished Paul had touched her. Daniel's treachery had cut her off from her family. Save for Fenella she was once again alone in the world. "We won't get anywhere speculating. As soon as you're finished, I want to call on Amy. Perhaps she can shed some light on the mystery of the fire."

PAUL LOOKED AT THE COTTAGE SOPHIE HAD LED HIM TO, a narrow, two-story box. One of the ground-floor windows was cracked, the other boarded up. The door hung drunkenly from a single hinge. The other cottages that lined the street looked little better. "I see why the millworkers were protesting their living conditions," he said.

Sophie stepped around a pile of rotting vegetables near the door. "None of the mills provide commodious housing, but I fear Tom and Ned were among the most negligent millowners."

She rapped at the door. A few moments later it was opened by a thin woman with straggling fair hair. The woman's tired eyes widened with pleasure as she took in the sight of Sophie standing on her doorstep. "Lady Rutledge."

"Hullo, Mrs. Caxton." Sophie's smile was as warm as her voice. One would never guess what she had been through in the past twelve hours. "I was hoping to see Amy. Is she at home?"

"Oh, yes." Mrs. Caxton wiped her hands on her apron and patted her hair. She was little older than Sophie, Paul realized, but her face was drawn with lines that owed more to exhaustion than age. "Please come in. Amy be upstairs putting the little ones down for a nap. I'll get her."

Paul ducked beneath the lintel and followed Sophie into the cottage. There were patches of damp on the peeling whitewash that covered the walls. The air was heavy with mildew, overlaying the smell of the coal burning in the stove and the greasy scent of the rushlights stuck in tin brackets on either side of the room.

There were two rush-seated chairs that Mrs. Caxton waved them toward before vanishing up a sagging wooden staircase. Paul watched Sophie settle the gauzy fabric of her skirt with a gloved hand. She looked as incongruous in the cottage as Sèvres porcelain among the earthenware crockery set out on Mrs. Caxton's scarred dresser.

Footsteps clattered on the stairs, then slowed to a more sedate pace. A girl appeared at the base of the stairs, smoothing the skirt of a cotton print dress that exposed several inches of growing legs and strained across a developing chest. As she walked forward, the rushlights turned her braided hair a fiery red-gold.

"Lady Rutledge." Amy curtsied with care. "We heard—" She hesitated, as though unsure how much to admit she'd heard. "We heard you had the baby. I'm so glad."

"Thank you, Amy." Sophie got to her feet with a smile. "If you've heard that much, you must also have heard about Mr. Lescaut, who came to my rescue."

"Miss Caxton." Paul inclined his head.

"I'm pleased to meet you, sir." Amy curtsied again, but for all her careful manners her gaze was frank and direct. Apparently, he made a favorable impression, for she smiled. A dimple appeared in one cheek, giving a hint of mischief to her round, serious face.

Sophie went to Amy's side and took her by the shoulders. "I'm glad to see you, love. I know you must have been having a beastly time of it."

Amy swallowed, but her gaze remained matter-of-fact. "Times are hard for everyone, especially with the mill closed and the price of corn so high. They've cut back at the other mills as well, and there are all the men home from the war looking for work. Oh, I'm sorry, my lady, I don't mean to be rattling on. Please sit down. I daresay you aren't feeling strong."

"I've had a month to recover," Sophie said, but she moved back to her chair. Paul gestured for Amy to take the other chair. She hesitated, then seated herself, adjusting her skirt exactly as Sophie had done.

"Have a lot of the Rutledge workers moved away?" Sophie asked.

"Quite a few. The Tanners and the Norrises went to Manchester, and Bill and Mary Talbot went to their cousins in London. No one can feed a family on the Poor Rate. Aunt Abigail's even had to stop paying a funeral society for the children." Amy hesitated. "Of course, Mrs. Burden's doing all right. I think her nephew sent her some more money." The girl's voice was sharp with a bitterness that seemed out of character.

"Mrs. Burden?" Sophie's eyes narrowed. Paul recognized the look she got when more of her memory returned. "It was Mrs. Burden's nephew who testified against your uncle and the other millworkers." Sophie made it not quite a question. "Jack Burden. He went away after the trial, didn't he? I'm afraid I still don't remember everything clearly."

"Aye, he went away. Quick as he could. No one's sure where. But left money with his aunt. Which is odd, because he never had any money to speak of."

"I talked to her on my last visit to Lancaster." The memory

filled Sophie's eyes. "She claimed she didn't know where Jack had gone or how he had got the money, but—"

"What?" Paul asked.

"She admitted she'd seen Jack talking with Ned. That's what sent me to Kinrie." Sophie was silent for a moment, as though letting the memory settle in her mind. "Amy, when I was here before, how much did I tell you about my suspicions?"

"Not too much." Amy's hazel eyes were wide, her gaze steady. "But I've suspicions of my own." She fiddled with the end of her braid. "Aunt Abigail's planning to leave Lancaster too. She's taking the little ones and going to live with her sister in Durham. But there's no room for me there. I was wondering . . ." She pushed the braid back over her shoulder and folded her hands in her lap. "Lady Rutledge, could I have my place back? I could help the baby's nurse. I've had lots of practice with my cousins."

Guilt flooded Sophie's face. "I'd be glad to have you back, Amy. And I know you'd be splendid with Fenella. But I'm not going back to Rossmere or to Bath just yet."

"I don't care where—"

"And traveling with Mr. Lescaut and me may be dangerous."

Amy was brought up short. She looked from Sophie to Paul and nodded slowly. "If you're in trouble all the more reason you'll need my help, my lady. Especially with the baby." Something in the way she lifted her chin made her face look less round and youthful. "And if the danger's anything to do with the fire, I'm as much concerned as you."

Sophie was silent for a moment. She glanced at Paul. He nodded. "Come to dinner with us at the Rose and Crown tonight," Sophie said. "We'll tell you the story. Then you can decide for yourself."

They stayed at the Caxtons' for another quarter hour, drinking cups of strong tea, which Mrs. Caxton pressed on them when she came back downstairs. She was obviously delighted at the prospect of Amy finding employment. Sophie said nothing further about danger in front of Amy's aunt, but when they left the cottage she turned to Paul. "Is it utterly mad to think of taking Amy with us?"

"There's more than one kind of danger. I wouldn't call it safe to leave her in Lancaster with no family and no employment."

Sophie grimaced. "Did you hear what she said about her aunt not being able to pay the funeral society? They have to scrape pennies to ensure their children have a decent burial if they die." Her hand went to her mouth. "I should have thought . . . I should have done something for Amy sooner. I knew her aunt needed her during the trial, but I should have realized they might not stay in Lancaster forever. I shouldn't have been so preoccupied with my own problems."

"Don't start wallowing in regrets now," Paul said. He knew how fruitless the ravages of guilt were. "We haven't got time for it. Do you want to see Mrs. Burden?"

"Yes, though it may be a fool's errand. I don't know if she'll admit anything more about Jack."

"Your last visit to her sent you to Kinrie. Anything we can learn about why you went to see Ned will be useful. Do you remember the way to her cottage?"

"I think so. Two streets over and to the right."

Paul took her arm to help her over the gutter that ran down the center of the street. He was tempted to retain hold of it. Instead, he quickly released her. They walked in silence down narrow streets lined with rows of cramped two-story buildings. The Rutledge Mill cottages were built so nearly on the same pattern that Paul wondered how a man could tell his own, particularly at night when he was deep in drink.

Mrs. Burden's cottage was identical to the Caxtons, save that there were shiny new hinges on the door and clear, unbroken glass in the windows. Sophie knocked at the door. Except for a striped cat that was sniffing around some slops outside one of the cottages, the street was quiet.

"Perhaps she's out," Sophie said when a minute had gone by with no response.

"I doubt it. There's a light inside." Paul could see a yellow glow through one of the windows. "Is she hard of hearing?"

"I don't think so." Sophie rapped on the door again, more loudly. "Mrs. Burden?"

The striped cat skittered off down the street. There was no other response. Sophie looked at Paul. "Do you think we should . . ."

Paul felt a prickle of unease. He reached for the door handle. The door was unlatched. "Mrs. Burden?" he said, pushing it open.

He knew the smell the moment he stepped over the threshold, sharp and sweet, branded on his mind from his first battle. He put back a hand. "Stay outside, Sophie."

Her footsteps sounded behind him. "Don't be ridiculous, I've—Mother of God."

The light he had seen came from an oil lamp on a small round table at the center of the room. A woman sat in a chair beside the table. She had gray-brown hair, and a flowered shawl was wrapped around her shoulders. The front of her skull had been beaten in and her face was obscured by a stream of blood.

Chapter 19

➤⬥

VOMIT ROSE UP IN SOPHIE'S THROAT. SHE TURNED FROM the pathetic bloody figure sprawled in the chair. Paul's arm went round her, but she pushed him away. "No, I'm all right."

She wasn't all right, but she could not acknowledge the horror in the small fetid room. She stumbled to the window and clung to the sill, breathing in the fresh air that seeped round the glass. Then she forced herself to turn and look at the details of the room. It was sparsely furnished but immaculately clean, just as it had been on her earlier visit.

"Agatha Burden." She walked forward, not letting herself look away. "I didn't like her. But she didn't deserve to die."

Paul put his hand against Mrs. Burden's face. "She's still warm. I'd judge she was killed within the hour." He drew his hand away. "It was a monstrously vicious attack."

Sophie crossed herself, a gesture she had used little of late. Her mother and Aunt Louisa were Catholic, but their religion was of a pragmatic sort, neither a moral guide nor a source of consolation, but a part of who they were. Sophie was less sure of her own response, but in the face of death she had nothing else to fall back upon.

She stared at what remained of Agatha Burden's face. Beneath the blood she could still make out gaunt, lined features. Mrs. Burden's hair, more gray than brown, was pulled tightly back from her forehead, emphasizing her long beaky nose. "Paul," Sophie said, "she was little more than a dozen years my senior."

He met her gaze. "It's a harsh life for people like this. She worked in the Rutledge Mill?"

What would you know of harshness, his tone implied. She bristled, sought a retort, and in the end said nothing. "Yes, she worked in the mill. She was a widow. Her husband worked in the mines and died in an accident there. She bore seven children and buried five of them. Two boys survived. They turned their backs on Lancaster. One went to Liverpool, where he works unloading the ships. The other went to sea."

She turned back to the dead woman. "She was proud, and she didn't like prying. She only agreed to talk to me because I was Tom's wife. Her mouth was pinched. She grudged every word she uttered. She kept her arms wrapped tightly about her body, as though to ward off any intrusive thought."

Mrs. Burden's arms were now thrown wide, her mouth was open, her eyes staring. Her legs were splayed and her feet twisted. One worn shoe had come off in whatever struggle had taken her to her Maker. "This isn't Agatha Burden." Sophie's voice shook with a burst of passion. "This is a woman *in extremis*."

"Sophie." Paul reached out his arm toward her.

She stepped back. "No." She was shivering with cold and fear. "I've seen death, but not like this, by a violent hand. Save for my father," she added after a moment, "and the hand was his own." Now that she had recovered her past it was her strongest memory, and one of her earliest. *Papa*'s familiar face, obliterated by blood. She had not been frightened at the time, only puzzled. She had not known her father was dead.

But Paul had, and he had run away. Worse yet, he had known why her father had died and who was responsible. She had lost a friend that night, and she had lost a parent. No, two parents, for from that moment her mother had turned her back on her daughter to give herself up to her grief.

Paul moved away from the dead woman, stepping carefully around the blood spattered on the floor. He opened the inner door and disappeared inside. Sophie remained immobile, teetering on a line between rage and pity, a past she could scarce recall and a present she could not understand.

"Kitchen and pantry." Paul emerged from the other room.

"Spare but neat. I don't think anything's been disturbed. I doubt it was someone looking for money."

Sophie voiced the fear that had haunted her since she entered the house. "It's because of me, isn't it? It's because I sought her out and asked questions. It's her blood I have on my hands." She held them out so he could see that she meant this literally. Her pale-gray gloves were disfigured by a bright red smear. "I killed her. I didn't mean to."

Paul's gaze met her own. For one agonizing moment she wondered if he had lived with these words since he was ten years old. But his face was shut against her.

"If she was killed for what she had, Sophie, it's not your doing. If she was killed for what she knew, it matters little who questioned her. She was a threat to someone. Let's look upstairs." He preceded her up the crude staircase at the back of the house. She might have taken his hand now, but he did not offer it.

There were two rooms, one on either side of the small landing. The doors were open, showing a narrow bedstead in one room, a larger, quilt-covered bed in the other. This was where Agatha Burden had slept. Sophie was reluctant to intrude on the poor woman's refuge. "I'll take the other," she said. "It must be where Jack slept when he stayed with her."

The anonymous room held no terrors. Coarse sheets, a thin blanket, and a feather-filled pillow on the bed. She looked underneath. It was swept clean. There was not a scrap of paper in the room, no clothes hanging on the pegs. A basin and ewer stood on a small dresser near the single window, but the drawers were empty. She moved to the window and looked out on the street below. A woman with a familiar hurrying gait was approaching the house.

Sophie ran to the landing. "Paul."

He appeared on the landing, the light of discovery in his eyes. "Sophie, come here, you have to see this."

"There's no time." She was already halfway down the stairs. "Mrs. Burden has a visitor."

She heard Paul's muffled curse, then the sound of his footsteps behind her. She ran to the door, skirting the horror in the chair without thinking. "Agatha?" an anxious voice called from outside. "Agatha, is anything the matter?"

Sophie tugged at the latch and opened the door. The other woman had moved away from the door and was trying to peer through the window. At the sound of the door she swung around. "Aga—Heaven preserve me, it's Lady Rutledge."

Sophie thanked the providence that had brought the woman's name to her memory. "It's Grace Elliott, isn't it? You'd better come in. Something terrible has happened."

She put her arm around the visitor and closed the door behind them, hoping to forestall a scream or a fit of hysterics. Mrs. Elliott gasped as she took in first the stench and then the sight of the bloodied woman. "Oh, poor Agatha." Throwing off Sophie's arm, she moved to the murdered woman and lifted her hand. "Cold she's growing." She set the hand down carefully and passed her own over Mrs. Burden's face, closing the staring eyes. "It's not decent else."

"I was afraid to touch her," Sophie said.

"You needn't be. She's naught but dead now. We all come to it in the end."

Grace Elliott looked up and caught a glimpse of Paul, standing in the shadows by the stairs. She gave a small squeak of dismay and hurried back to Sophie, as though to protect her from a dangerous intruder. "This is Mr. Lescaut," Sophie said quickly. "He came with me. We found her like this."

"I didn't mean to frighten you." Paul came toward the women, but did not step too close. "Lady Rutledge wanted to speak to Mrs. Burden again about the men who were hanged. I understand they were convicted on the word of her nephew Jack. If that was all the evidence the magistrates had, it seems a monstrous miscarriage of justice."

"It was that." Mrs. Elliott ran her gaze over Paul. Her posture relaxed slightly. Sophie suspected it was his sympathy for the hanged men, more than his clothes and fair speech, that had allayed her suspicions. "He was bribed, I would swear to it, but who would listen to a millworker like me? Agatha wouldn't hear a word against Jack. And I had no evidence, save the rightness of my heart." She tapped her chest vigorously. "As God is my judge, he's a wrong one."

"There *is* evidence, Mrs. Elliott." Paul opened his crippled hand to reveal a small cloth bag. "Where would Agatha Burden come by such wealth?" He flung the bag on the table Mrs. Elliott was standing near. There was no mistaking the clink of coins as it landed.

"Jack Burden," Sophie said. "He gave it to her."

Mrs. Elliott spilled the coins out on the table. "Aye, he was fond of his aunt if he was fond of anyone. He always said he'd take care of her." She put the coins back in the bag and drew the drawstring tight. "It won't seem much to you, Lady Rutledge, but it's a fortune to folk like us. I knew Jack gave Agatha money, but not this much. No wonder she would never take help after he left." She laid the bag carefully on the table, her gaze fixed upon it. "Do you suppose this is why she was killed? For the money?"

"I doubt it," Paul said. "There's no evidence of a search, and the money was not hard to find. We think she may have been killed because of something she knew about her nephew."

Mrs. Elliott looked up at Sophie. "That's why you came, isn't it? Because you're after the truth of the fire."

It was there again, that gnawing stab of guilt. Sophie kept her voice firm. "Because I'm after the truth of my husband's death."

"And because Lady Rutledge is in danger," Paul added. "She went to Scotland in her search, and it nearly cost her her life."

"Dear God." Mrs. Elliott looked from Paul to Sophie. "And you fear for your life still."

"Mine and Mr. Lescaut's. He saved me from death by killing my attacker. He's wanted in Scotland, and for all we know he may be wanted here as well. I'm a danger to anyone who tries to help me, Mrs. Elliott. I killed Agatha Burden with my questions. No, don't make it easy for me," she said as Mrs. Elliott put out a hand in protest. "You must run and find a constable and tell him what has happened here."

Mrs. Elliott pursed her lips, then shook her head. "No, Lady Rutledge. I've no love for constables and even less for the magistrates. Their justice is not for the likes of us. I'll tell the constable in due time, but I'll say not a word about you or Mr. Lescaut. I came calling on Agatha because I hadn't seen her of late, and I found her like this and I closed her eyes. That's all they need to know."

"It's dangerous."

"Life's dangerous. I can look after myself, Lady Rutledge. Poor Agatha couldn't. She had a secret and it made her weak."

"We're grateful to you." Paul picked up the bag of coins and held it out to her. "Say nothing of this. Who knows whose pocket it will line if you give it to the authorities."

Mrs. Elliott recoiled. "Oh no, I couldn't take it. It's Agatha's."

"Strictly speaking, it's Jack's. Do you want to return it to him?"

"Not for the world."

"Then take it. Not for yourself, if that gives you trouble. But for the people who lost their livelihoods in the fire. You'll know who they are." Paul placed the bag in her hand and closed her other hand over it. "Be very careful in the spending of it. Money breeds suspicion."

The hint of a smile crossed her face. "Aye, that's how we suspected Jack. He talked money and spent money, and not a soul believed he'd come by it honestly." She tucked the bag inside her bodice. "Now come with me." She led them into the kitchen and pointed to the pantry. "There's a door there leads to the back. I live two houses down. No one else is at home this time of day. Make for the Lune. Even gentlefolk walk along the river. You'll not be noted."

Sophie smoothed her skirt. "What will *you* do, Mrs. Elliott?"

"Why, sit a spell. It gave me such a turn, seeing Agatha like that, I was fit for nothing. I may have to make a cup of tea to settle my stomach. When I'm feeling more myself I'll go find the constable." Mrs. Elliott pulled out a chair from the table that filled the center of the room and sat down firmly. "Go on, my dears."

It was a familiarity Grace Elliott would never have taken in the ordinary way of things. Sophie hesitated, fighting off an urge to put her arms around the woman, then followed Paul out the back door.

The day was muggy with a sky gray with clouds, but to Sophie the air smelled fresh and sweet. The bit of dirt at the back of the house had been cultivated, though the closeness of the other cottages kept the sun away. Little grew besides a few straggly cabbages and some of the hardier herbs. A change in the wind brought the scent of the privy. Sophie hurried after Paul, who was making his way down the lane that separated two rows of the Rutledge Mill cottages.

Paul stopped near the end of the lane and put out his arm to hold her back. "Wait," he whispered, glancing to either side. After a moment he took her arm and led her into the street that crossed the lane.

The street was empty. Even should they meet someone, they were merely a couple walking companionably toward the river, hurrying a bit perhaps because the surroundings were not to their taste. But they would not be taken for fugitives, nor would anyone suppose they had just witnessed the aftermath of a murder.

The solidity of Paul's arm gave Sophie strength. When the river was in sight she risked a glance at him. "The man who attacked her, he wouldn't stay in the neighborhood?"

"He'd be a fool if he did. I'd venture he was a paid assassin."

"Not Ned then?"

"Could Ned have done what was done to Agatha Burden?"

"I don't know anymore. He was ready enough to stick a knife in my ribs." She pressed Paul's arm and felt an answering pressure in return. "Why should Mrs. Burden be attacked at all? Uncle Daniel and Ned don't know we overheard them in the chapel. It will be hours before they know we've run off from Rossmere. That's the moment we become a threat."

"Agatha Burden was a threat before we came to Lancaster. She knew something that made her dangerous to her killer. Or he thought she knew something. Whether or not she talked to us had nothing to do with her death. She could have talked to anyone."

Paul was offering a way to lift the guilt from her shoulders, but Sophie could not absolve herself. She knew at some level of her being that she was culpable. "Paul, I want Fenella. I need to hold her."

It was only when the words were out that she realized how odd they must sound. Paul did not seem to find them odd at all. "We'll find a hackney further on," he said. "We'll go back to the inn. Then we should leave Lancaster. I don't know where you'll be safe, but you'll be safer in Edinburgh than here."

"We have to see Amy first. It's too dangerous to take her with us now."

"It may be more dangerous if we don't. If Mrs. Burden was vulnerable, Amy may be as well. And her family."

Sophie stopped and clutched Paul's arm as though it were a lifeline to sanity. "Dear God. What have I set in motion?"

"Not you, Sophie. Ned Rutledge. There's little doubt Jack Burden was bribed to give evidence. Who else would it be but Ned?"

"You're forgetting Tom." Sophie let go of Paul's arm. She had known her husband might be as guilty as his brother, but naming him now steadied her nerves. Despite the events of the morning she was less afraid. She was able to take note of her surroundings. Trees grew along the riverbank; had there been any sun in view they would have provided welcome shade. The moisture from the river rose to meet the slight dampness of the air. Solitary men bent on business passed them by. They met couples, strollers like themselves, walking at a slower pace, and even a family with four children in tow, their natural exuberance held in check by a stern-visaged father and a wife who echoed feebly his every word.

Beyond the path rose the red-brick cotton mills that hired the men not already employed in the nearby coal mines and most of their wives and children. "There," Sophie said, pointing to a spot where the rooflines were broken into jagged spars. "That's the Rutledge Mill, what's left of it. It was a fine building once. It towered over the others when it was built, four stories. In its time it was the largest cotton mill in Lancaster."

"The damage is mostly inside?"

"Anything of wood. The roof is gone, and most of the beams and the interior walls and the ceilings. The machinery was smashed when the floors went. As far as I know it's been left much as it was. There was nothing worth salvaging."

They had drawn closer to the ruin. Sophie stopped. "Would you like to see it? It will take only a moment."

"I would." Paul's face was grim. He would know nothing of the days when the mill had been a source of family pride. He would think only of the lives it had wasted and the lives it had taken. Sophie had an impulse to take his arm again, but that would be a sign of her weakness, of her failure to stop the horror she had learned of too late. She thought incongruously of the Doons, carrying their few belongings out of the Highlands where they had been born. They were resolute people. She would be resolute too. She walked on, keeping her step firm and her back very straight.

They left the river path and turned toward the mill. She was aware first of the quiet. The hum of machines had followed them all along the river, a sound so familiar she had not heeded it. The gaping soot-edged hole where the double doors had once stood loomed before her. She stopped to adjust her sight to the blackness within.

Raised voices came out of the mill, breaking the stillness. Her heart gave a great jolt. Paul pulled her to one side, out of sight of anyone in the building. He looked down at her, not voicing the obvious question.

"It could be anyone," she said, keeping her voice low. "There's nothing in the mill worth stealing. Someone looking for refuge or a shelter."

"Or a meeting place." Paul's face was drawn tight. He seemed to be listening for something. He pulled her away, back toward the river path. "I'll put you in a hackney. Go straight to the inn and stay there."

But it was too late. Sophie had heard it too. She broke free of Paul's grasp. "That was Ned's voice."

Chapter 20

PAUL CAUGHT HER HAND. "THIS IS NO PLACE FOR YOU."

"Nor you. If you won't run, neither will I."

He looked at her for a long moment. "Very well. We'll listen and learn what we can. Don't interfere with what I may do. Keep your lines of escape clear. If anyone comes near you, run to the river, to the nearest person you can find."

She nodded, vowing to be sensible, hating the need for her inaction. Paul was right. He had fought off two men in the alley in Kinrie. She would not help by distracting him now.

They moved back to the mill, keeping out of sight of the door. They slipped inside and waited, searching through the dark piles of twisted machines and blackened wood to locate the men, straining to make sense of their words. One voice was sharp and angry, the other quiet and impatient. The second voice was Ned's. He was trying to hide his annoyance, but Sophie could tell he was close to losing control.

Ned was answered by a whining voice with a heavy Yorkshire accent that Sophie had difficulty following. There were three of them, then.

It was not as dark as she had supposed when she first approached the mill. The holes where the windowpanes had been let in a feeble light. The light grew brighter as she raised her eyes to the point where the roofless building opened itself to the gray sky above. She was distracted by the flutter of pigeon wings, followed the swoop of their flight, saw them settle, cooing, on the open windowsills.

The men were visible now, standing near the south wall, which had escaped the worst of the fire. A staircase rose to the floor above and continued partway to the next floor. Pieces of flooring clung to what was left of the interior walls, but a great jagged hole gaped where the second-floor machines had dropped through to the ground floor, destroying everything in their path. The insurance investigators had said the remains of the flooring were unsafe. One had nearly fallen when an edge of the irregular floor gave way beneath him.

Ned had taken refuge on the staircase. He was a tall man, but the stairs gave him an added advantage of height over the thick-girthed men who moved restlessly before him.

"The job's worth a guinea, that's what you told me, Rutledge." The speaker was the angry man. Sophie could see little of him save his coat, which was split up the back seam, and his hair, a dark curly mop that covered his neck.

"A guinea it is. But I hired one man for the old woman, not two."

"The job took two, if you cared to have it done right and no word get back that Sir Edward Rutledge was plotting murder."

Ned drew himself up. "That wouldn't be wise, Gant."

Gant muttered words Sophie could not hear.

"Did it right, did you?" Apparently Ned had decided to be conciliatory.

"As pretty a gash as you're like to see. And blood on my sleeve to prove it." Gant thrust his arm in front of Ned's face. "If you don't believe me, go see for yourself."

Ned retreated a step, putting himself well above Gant. He reached into his waistcoat pocket and drew out an object that glittered in the light streaming through a broken window on the second floor. "Here's a guinea. Share or not, as you like. There'll be six more to follow, if you're still for the game."

The men went quiet. "Here now," Gant said, "I don't fancy being strung up."

"That's your problem, isn't it?"

Gant was silent for a moment. "Who's the cove?"

"No one who'll be missed."

"Save by you. And he's worth six guineas for the pleasure

it will bring you. What's he know to your disadvantage, Rutledge?"

"No questions, or I'll take my custom elsewhere." Ned's voice turned cold.

Gant raised his hands in a gesture of surrender. "No questions. And six guineas it is." He glanced at his companion. "Donner and I agree to it."

"Four. That's for the man. Another two for the woman who affects his company. That's the lot. Whether it takes one man or two or twenty."

Six guineas. Sophie stifled a laugh that was dangerously close to hysteria. Six guineas would keep a mill family alive for a year, but she had spent that much on a ball gown or a particularly outrageous hat.

Ned leaned over the railing and held out the single guinea, the price of Agatha Burden's death. Gant pocketed it with a motion almost too quick to follow. The Yorkshire man, who must be Donner, clawed his arm.

Gant shook off his companion. "When?"

"I don't know." Ned brushed his hand against his breeches, as though it had been soiled by the contact with the assassin. "But the thing must be done soon."

"Here? In Lancaster?"

"Or on the road from the south. I'll find a means to bring them here."

"And how will we know them?"

Sophie knew the answer. She was surprised only by the precision of Ned's description. Ned's assertion that she was no more than a piece of game to be flushed had lost the power of surprise.

Paul tightened the pressure of his hand. "Now," he mouthed. Sophie nodded, the barest hint of movement. She turned to the door and ran, praying that Paul was running with her. Only a few feet to the door and light and safety.

Something crunched beneath her foot. A stick, a bit of

fire-blackened wood. The sound seemed to echo in the cavernous building.

"Who's there?" Ned shouted.

Paul caught up with her and gripped her hand. They ran through the doorway into cloudy daylight that now seemed mercilessly stark and revealing.

"Christ, that's them." Ned's voice shook with disbelief. The men uttered a joyous yell, two hunters freed to pursue their quarry. Sophie could hear the pounding of their feet.

Paul tightened his grip on her hand. His chest burning with effort, Sophie fixed her gaze on the river and the path that held their only hope for safety.

"Six guineas!" Ned called, urging his pack on. But he would not risk running with his hounds, not here in Lancaster, where the Rutledge Mill and Rutledge faces were all too well-known.

Sophie and Paul raced through the outer gate of the mill onto the tree-lined path that followed the Lune on its course to the sea. There was no one in sight now. The Rutledge Mill stood a little apart from the others that fronted on the Lune, and the fire had heightened its isolation.

They stopped a dozen yards down the path from the mill. Sophie looked at Paul. He hesitated, his swift glance sweeping the river in both directions. The sounds of pursuit grew louder. "Can you swim?" he asked.

She nodded, breathless from the run. All hesitation gone, hands clasped, they raced to the river, stumbled down its bank, and leaped into its clammy waters.

IN THEIR RAPID DESCENT PAUL LOST SOPHIE, HER HAND torn from his grasp. A moment later he found her, a goddess rising from the center of a foaming spray, the blue satin ribbons of her bonnet shimmering in the light of an unexpected afternoon sun. Paul felt a welling of joy. He would have shouted aloud had it not been for the splash as Gant flung himself into the water some forty feet upstream.

So Gant could swim. Paul had prayed that he could not.

"Make for the opposite bank," he told Sophie. The current would carry them downstream, back toward Mrs. Burden's cottage, toward the people they had been trying to avoid. But safety now lay in numbers. Gant knew this too. He uttered a heartfelt curse, but his powerful stroke did not falter.

Paul and Sophie cut across the river at a diagonal. Paul kept himself between Gant and Sophie. Sophie was swimming competently, but he feared she would soon tire. He urged her toward the opposite bank. "I'm all right," she insisted.

"We may have to make for land."

She looked away and lengthened her stroke. The stubborn set of her chin had grown familiar to Paul. So must she have looked to Jemmy, who had challenged her to walk the length of the stone wall when she was—how old?—probably not much more than four.

Apparently Donner could not swim. He was racing along the river path, his gaze moving between Gant and Paul. Of course. It was Paul who was the valuable target. What had Ned told them? Four guineas for the man, two for the woman. Donner was waiting for Paul to emerge from the water, when, weakened by his swim, Gant would no longer have the advantage.

But Gant showed no sign of failing. He continued to cleave the water with powerful strokes, drawing closer and closer to Paul as they neared the bank. His aim was clear enough. He would take Paul in the water while his friend Donner was forced to remain on land. So much for honor among thieves.

They had reached the shallows. Gant was so close Paul could hear his panting breaths. Sophie was a few feet ahead, gripping the rocky bank. An anger cut through Paul that was deeper than anything he had ever known. By all the gods above, he would not let this woman be taken from him. He swung on Gant.

The unexpected movement gave Paul a momentary advantage. Gant drew back, then launched his heavy body at Paul's. Paul slipped from his grasp. Gant flailed about in the water, seeking some purchase on the slimy stones that covered the river bottom.

Paul raised his arms, his left hand grasping the wrist of his right. Gant laughed at the sight of Paul's useless claw. Paul laughed too, a laugh bitter with rage and despair. He brought his arms crashing down on the back of Gant's hairy neck.

Gant went under. He came up sputtering for air. Paul pushed him down again. And again. And again. He heard a gasp from Sophie, looked up, and caught her gaze upon him. He had seen that horror on her face when they entered Mrs. Burden's cottage. He knew that he had gone too far.

With a self-disgust he had known once as a child, Paul lifted Gant's heavy body under the arms and pushed and pulled the lumpy mass onto the bank. "Live," Paul said under his breath. "Damn you for a bastardly gullion, but live, for her sake. Then be squashed like a flea and die with the knowledge of your sins in your gullet."

He pushed down on Gant's back. A trickle of water came from his mouth. The man was retching, moaning, but he was alive.

Paul stumbled back into the water and stretched out a hand to Sophie. Gant would not threaten them now, but Donner was still on the opposite bank and there was a bridge downstream. Ned had disappeared, but he was capable of anything. Even now he might be setting watchers in either direction.

"Can you swim some more?" Paul asked.

Sophie nodded, though her arms were quivering with exertion. Paul led her away from the bank, helping her over the slippery stones. The bottom gave way and they began to swim again, Paul pacing himself to match her diminishing strength. She was breathing hard, but she was determined.

"I know," Paul said, meeting her gaze. "You're all right." He turned his attention again to the course of the river. It was then that he realized Donner was no longer on the path.

There was a quiet splash behind them. Paul whirled around in the water, hoping that it was no more than an otter. But the sound was all too human. Donner was in the water, swimming with quiet strength. But swimming toward Sophie, not Paul.

With Sophie in danger, Donner would have them both. Sophie was no threat, and Paul would go at once to her aid.

"Paul," Sophie called in dismay. She, too, had seen Donner's intent.

"Go back to the bank," Paul answered in French. "When I tell you to, climb out of the river and run as fast as you can in the opposite direction."

Sophie nodded and struck out toward the bank.

Paul cut in front of Donner, blocking his access to Sophie. Donner drew back, as though he wanted Paul to take the lead.

"Oh, no," Paul said. "I think not, my friend." He turned on his back, swimming with a broad backstroke that let him keep Donner well in sight.

They played this game till Sophie had nearly reached the bank. Donner gave Paul a kind of salute, grinned, and dove deep, lost from sight. *"Run,"* Paul yelled to Sophie. "He'll surface soon."

Sophie was pulling herself onto the bank. "Here." She pointed to a bubbling in the water a few yards upstream.

"A fair, good maiden." Paul had turned on his stomach and was swimming toward Sophie with all the strength he could command. He could only guess how much she longed to rest on the cool, hard dirt beneath her. "No time to rest now. Run downstream, turn between the two brick buildings. Whatever you do, keep out of his sight. I'll find you."

Sophie was on her feet. She stood up, her arms trembling with cold as she wrung the water from her dripping dress. Then without a word or a look back she began to run. In a moment she had disappeared from sight.

Donner surfaced. "Sophie," Paul called, putting the panic he truly felt in his cries. "Sophie!"

He looked around in desperation, a man demented by losing his beloved to the river. He dragged himself onto the bank and covered his head with his arms, rocking wildly in his feigned grief.

Donner was scrabbling out of the river. A rock caught Paul on the back of the head. Paul gave a sharp leap, as though the blow was worse than it was. Then he collapsed, rolled down the bank, and slipped into the water.

Entering the damp cold of the river when his body yearned for warmth and quiet was one of the hardest things he'd ever had to do. The next step was even harder. He forced himself to slide under the water, floating with the tide, a piece of flotsam abandoned by the elements. He kept his eyes open, a macabre touch he quite enjoyed. It would keep watchers at a distance, but attract their attention.

He bobbed with the rise and fall of the water, taking a breath and letting his face submerge, releasing it when the pressure to breathe was too great and he was forced to come up for air. In this way he kept track of Donner, who was watching from the bank, no doubt reluctant to return to the cold of the river. Paul waited till Donner glanced aside, then forced himself under water and tugged his cravat loose. A hat would have been better, but he had long since lost his in his fight with Gant.

He felt the cravat slip from his neck and float down the river before him. Donner gave a cry of triumph and ran after it, breaking off a large tree branch to reach his trophy. He would present it to Ned as proof of Lescaut's death. Ned might hesitate, but Paul suspected Donner would earn his four guineas today.

Donner watched Paul a moment longer, perhaps debating the wisdom of carrying a drowned man along the banks of the Lune. He decided against it and pocketed the dripping cravat. He made a quick reconnaissance, then headed upstream without a backward glance at his friend Gant, who still lay unconscious on the bank.

Paul waited till his would-be assassin turned down a street and disappeared from view. He had grown quite comfortable with his watery bed, but he was infernally cold. He turned and swam to the bank. He climbed it carefully and looked up the river path. There was no sign of Donner. Crouching, running low, Paul made for the opening he had pointed out to Sophie and collapsed on the ground between the two brick buildings.

Chapter 21

❯❮

SOPHIE BENT OVER PAUL AND CHAFED HIS HANDS. THEY felt like ice. "You said you would find me, but there's not a man I can trust. No time to rest now. Can you walk?"

For answer he pushed himself to his feet, using the side of one of the buildings for support. She could hear water sloshing in his boots. "Of course I can walk." His voice was harsh and not quite steady. "Where's my coat? How did you get it off me?"

"With great difficulty." She forced herself to stand as straight as Paul. Her fingers were numb and her legs had turned to jelly some time ago. "You weren't the least bit cooperative. It's ruined, but it's wearable. I wrung out all the water I could and hung it up to dry." She pointed to an iron stanchion, which supported a now-illegible sign. "You'll have to carry it or wear it. I don't think I can carry anything besides you, and I'm not even sure of you. Oh, Paul, I've never waited so long for anyone."

"Easy. We've a mile and more to walk." Paul shrugged into the coat. "Come. Donner's about. We need to lose ourselves in the town."

"And Gant?"

He took her hand. "Who knows?"

"He's not—"

"No, Sophie, he is not."

He pulled her around a corner, then another and another until the cobblestones swam dizzily before her eyes. The people they passed took in their disreputable appearance with suspicious eyes.

"Are we lost?" Sophie asked, pausing to draw a breath.

"Deliberately lost. It's as good a means of escape as any. We were lost in the Highlands and we found the McClarens. Sooner or later we'll come across a Doon, someone we can trust."

They rounded yet another corner. Donner was trudging along a cross street up ahead.

Paul pushed Sophie into a deep-set doorway and covered her mouth with his own. Her heart beat fast with panic, but his lips warmed her. It was the first time she had been warm since they jumped into the river.

After an interval she couldn't measure, Paul drew back and glanced into the street. "He didn't see us. I doubt he saw anyone at all. If he's as tired as I am he'll sleep for a week and to the devil with the four guineas."

She gave the ghost of a laugh, but her legs were buckling under her. The sodden folds of her dress weighed her down. She was so cold it was difficult to breathe.

Paul searched her face. "We'll find shelter, but we need something safer than a doorway. Come, we'll follow the path Donner took. He's explored it already."

It wasn't as bad as trudging into the hills outside Kinrie. If she had managed that she could manage this. Just a step and then another. If only her body would stop shaking.

"There." Paul gestured to a squat brick building with a pierced window. The glass would shed a green and gold light over the altar on the rare days when sunlight bathed the nave in glory.

"A Saint Sebastian's, I think," Sophie said. It was difficult to focus.

Paul pulled her toward the church steps. "I don't care which bloody saint it is. It's sanctuary."

The entrance hall was empty, but she could hear the murmur of the clergyman in the midst of a service. An open door gave a glimpse of mostly unoccupied pews.

"Not there," Paul said. "We don't want to face questions."

He half drew, half carried her down a flight of narrow stone stairs. The air was cool and damp. A single lamp set in the wall revealed raised oblongs of stone. Tombs. They had escaped death and were hiding in the crypt of a church.

It occurred to Sophie that this ought to be funny, but she couldn't muster a laugh or a smile. All she knew was that she no longer had to move. She collapsed against Paul and let the shivering take her.

Paul's arms came round her. His warm breath fluttered against her face. His skin smelled of river water and street grime. She could feel the rapid beat of his heart. She was not alone in her fear. She pressed her face into the damp cloth of his coat.

His hands moved over her back. Her trembling eased with his touch. She lifted her head and looked at him. His face was in shadow, but his eyes caught the lamplight. There was an unexpected flare of gold in their dark depths. She wanted to draw strength from that brightness, to feel the solidness of life in the midst of all this death. She pulled his head down and pressed her lips against his own.

He went very still. She clung closer, sucking at his mouth, tracing his lips with her tongue. He dragged her against him. His mouth softened and parted. Heat flowed into her. His tongue met her own, washing away the taste of fear.

But even this wasn't enough. A burning need swept away her exhaustion. She had to reaffirm that they were both alive. She pushed back his coat, impatient with the layers of fabric that kept them apart.

"Sophie." He held her by the shoulders. His voice was rough. "You don't want this."

The shadows pressed in on her. The cold air bit her skin. "You can't know what I want." She flung herself on him, pulling at the buttons on his waistcoat, tugging his shirt free of his trousers.

"*Sacrebleu*, Sophie." His arms were around her again. His lips were against her hair, her cheek, her throat. Where she had been numb with cold and fear, her body came alive with sensation. She tugged off her gloves, cursing the slippery damp leather, ran her bare fingers over his chest, reached down for the flap on his trousers. She felt the hardness of a need that answered her own.

"Paul—"

"Yes." He pressed her backward, his mouth moving across hers, until she was braced against something rough and solid. Stone. One of the tombs. It didn't matter. It was enough to support her weight. It and Paul's hands, sure, compelling, anchoring her in the darkness. She wrapped her legs around him. He bunched up her skirts, found the slit in her drawers, stroked her, reached inside her.

The shock of the contact tore a sob from her throat. Need hummed through her, driving out the demons. She closed her hand around his arousal. He shuddered and lifted her, gripping her bottom. His hands were shaking. So were hers. She pulled him closer and then he was inside her, filling her emptiness. Her inner muscles clenched around him, even as her hands gripped his shoulders.

The joining still wasn't enough. She moved against him and he thrust into her, pushing deeper, his breath warm and ragged on her face, his mouth finding hers again.

Her hands twisted in the folds of his shirt, drenched with sweat and river water. She wanted to be closer, to take him deeper into her, to lose herself more completely. She didn't want it to end.

But it was going to, too soon. Release tore through her. For one pure moment she was fused with him, freed from all but the present.

He gasped something that sounded like her name. She felt the tremors that racked his body. She slumped against him, her head pressed into the hollow of his shoulder. Her body pulsed with the aftermath of climax. She could taste the salt on his skin, feel the roughness of his breath, hear the thudding of his heart.

Slowly, other sensations intruded on her peace. The gritty feel of the stone. The smell of mildew in the air. The numbing chill. She was in the crypt of a church, propped up against a tomb, with her legs wrapped around Paul and Paul still inside her. She had let him take her—she had taken him—like a rutting animal.

She lifted her head and looked at Paul. He was watching her, his gaze intent and strangely soft. She drew a breath of the musty air, trying to calm her frayed nerves. "I don't know—"

He shook his head and laid his fingers over her mouth. Without speaking, he withdrew from her body and helped her to stand, smoothing her skirts, steadying her when she swayed.

"I'm all right." She didn't like being helpless now any more than she had when she'd been injured. She bent to retrieve her fallen gloves and the hairpins that had survived the river. She twisted up her hair and pushed the pins into it, armoring herself.

By the time she was done Paul had fastened his trousers and buttoned his coat and waistcoat. No reminder of their frantic coupling remained, save the damp warmth between her legs and the taut awareness that lingered in the air.

Footsteps sounded on the stone stairs. Her pulse leaped. Paul put himself between her and the door.

"Is anyone there?" The footsteps stopped. Over Paul's shoulder she saw a man with the dark coat and clerical collar of a clergyman.

"Forgive us, sir." Paul drew her to his side. "My wife needed a few moments to compose herself, so we came down here."

"Of course." The clergyman hesitated, then stepped forward. He looked little older than Paul, and though his face was serious the lines about his eyes hinted at a sense of humor. He squinted against the dark, taking in their disheveled appearance. "Good God. I didn't realize it was raining."

"It isn't." Paul's fingers moved against Sophie's arm, in reassurance and warning. "We took a brief swim in the river."

"I—I see." The clergyman regarded Paul for a moment. "My dear sir, may I ask if you are in need of help? I don't mean the spiritual variety. Shall I summon the constable?"

"This isn't a matter for the police." Paul pulled Sophie closer. "We were being pursued by an unpleasant man, who was employed by the brother of my wife's late husband. Her brother-in-law objects to her remarriage and is attempting to gain custody of her children."

The clergyman nodded. "I see. Not an uncommon problem, I'm afraid."

"Someone may come to the church and ask questions about us. We would prefer that you make no mention of our visit."

The clergyman's mouth curved slightly and the lines about his eyes crinkled up. "I can't possibly remember the faces of all those who pass in and out of the church." His face grew serious. "There's nothing else I can do?"

"You could summon a hackney."

"I'll send someone to the George directly. One or two hackneys always hang about in the yard. A carriage should be here in ten minutes. I'll have the driver go round to the back of the church. If you wish to wait upstairs—"

"Thank you, I think we'll do better down here."

The clergyman inclined his head. "As you wish." He turned to Sophie. "Madam. I trust you and your children will have a more tranquil future. It's clear your new husband cares deeply for them."

Sophie's face grew warm at the memory of the act she and Paul had performed on sanctified ground. She knew a mad impulse to kneel and say, Bless me, for I have sinned. But it was a long time since she had taken the tenets of her religion so seriously. Instead, she smiled. "Thank you. My husband and I are most grateful."

"It's the least I can do. It's not often we get such excitement at Saint Sebastian's."

They waited in silence until the clergyman's footsteps faded upstairs. Sophie moved away from Paul and leaned against one of the tombs. She could still feel Paul's hands on her skin. She could swear the scent of their coupling lingered in the air, though the clergyman had not seemed to notice it. "Will Ned believe we're dead?" she said when the clergyman was out of earshot.

"I don't know." Paul's voice was cool and level. It was difficult to believe this was the same man who had gasped her name in passion a short time ago. "He may want greater proof."

"If so, he'll start looking for us. He'll ask questions—" Fear shot through her. "What a bloody fool I've been. He'll ask questions at the inns. I've got to get back to Fenella."

She started for the stairs. Paul grasped her arm. "It's not safe, Sophie."

She jerked away from him. "You think I care for my safety beside Fenella's?"

"We'll neither of us be much good to her dead." He gripped her by the shoulders. "It's little more than an hour since Ned saw us. As far as he's concerned, the odds are that we're dead by now. Donner will try to convince him that we are. Even if Ned has doubts he won't start looking for us until he hears from Donner. He won't start at the Rose and Crown. And we've paid the inn staff well to deny our presence."

"Ned might offer them more."

He brushed his fingers against her cheek. "Ten minutes, Sophie. If you left now and ran all the way, you couldn't get there any sooner than we can in the hackney."

His touch softened something inside her. She turned her

head away. The last thing she wanted to be now was soft. "You're right. Damn you, you always are."

Paul dropped his hands. "That sounds more like my—the Sophie I'm used to."

She moved a little away from him. "It won't take long to pack our things and hire a carriage. We can be out of Lancaster within the hour. Oh, dear God, Amy." The image of Agatha Burden's bloody corpse danced before Sophie's eyes. "Ned will guess I'd visit her. Even if we take Amy with us, Ned may try to wring the truth out of Mrs. Caxton."

"Not if she's out of Lancaster. We can hire a carriage to take her and her children to Durham. Tonight if possible. But we'll need time to make the arrangements, and it won't be safe to stay at the Rose and Crown. Do you have any friend in Lancaster who can give us shelter for a few hours?"

Sophie put a hand to her head, trying to find her balance in the dizzying swirl of events. Then she realized that though she had been cut loose from her former life, she was not entirely without friends. "Jemmy. Jeremy Craymere, my solicitor."

"You're sure he's to be trusted?"

She felt a smile break across her face. "Implicitly. He's the one who dared me to walk along the wall."

JEREMY CRAYMERE RAN HIS FINGER AROUND THE MODER-ately starched points of his shirt. His eyes had been sharp and intelligent when Sophie introduced him to Paul. Now they were glazed with shock.

"I can understand if you don't believe me," Sophie said.

"Oh, no, I believe you. When have I ever doubted you, So— Lady Rutledge? You'd have no earthly reason to tell such a story if it wasn't the truth." Craymere shook his head as though to clear it. He looked from Sophie and Paul, who were seated in chairs in front of his desk, to the leather sofa against the wall, where Dugal perched with Fenella in her basket beside

him. "Good God. Ribard. Your own uncle." Craymere's regu-
lar features twisted with revulsion.

Paul could understand Craymere's reaction. He could understand a number of things about the solicitor. The respectable
order of Craymere's office—the polished oak desk, the leather-
bound law books arranged in precise rows—was a far cry from
the raffish world of the Latin Quarter that Paul called home.
But the careful formality with which Craymere treated Sophie
struck a chord of familiarity. Had Paul grown up in the Ribard
household, he and Sophie would now be on similar terms.

Craymere drummed his fingers on the desk top. "If you write
out a letter for the Caxtons, I'll send my clerk round with it. He
can bring young Amy back here. Meanwhile, I'll make
arrangements for a carriage to take Mrs. Caxton and her children to Durham and another to take you . . . Where?"

"Edinburgh," Paul said. "I have family there."

Craymere gave up his desk to Sophie and went to summon
his clerk. Paul looked over at Dugal. "How's Fenella?"

"Her eyes be open, but she doesna seem troubled."

Paul turned back to Sophie, who was bent over a sheet of
writing paper. She had spent only a few minutes preparing to
leave the Rose and Crown, but she had managed to change her
dress and repin her hair. He would swear she had scrubbed
every inch of her body. She smelled of roses again, not fear and
river water and sex.

Within a quarter hour the letter was written and Craymere's
clerk, a sensible-looking young man, had been dispatched to
the Caxtons. An errand boy had been sent to a livery stable to
see about the carriages. There was nothing to do for the present
but wait, Craymere said, returning to the room with a tray of
tea and biscuits. They'd best take some refreshment while they
could.

Paul settled back in his chair and sipped the delicately
scented tea, very different from the strong brew Mrs. Caxton
had served them. His muscles tensed at the inactivity. Perhaps he didn't relish having the reins of control removed

from his hands. Or perhaps he was bothered by the way Sophie was smiling at Craymere. Despite the gulf of social station, she was clearly very fond of him. And Craymere was a well-favored man, with dark hair and finely drawn features. Not to mention the use of all his limbs. Paul's stomach churned. Christ, he was jealous. Over a woman he had no right to call his own.

Craymere returned to his desk. "There's something you should know. Strictly speaking, it violates my professional code to speak of it, but under the circumstances . . ." He spread his hands before him in a helpless gesture. "You must be aware that the mill had not been profitable in recent years, Lady Rutledge."

Sophie stirred milk into her tea. "Tom didn't talk about it a great deal, but I heard him complain that the mill was as much a burden as an asset. And please call me Sophie, Jemmy. You're practically my oldest friend. Besides, I don't feel much like claiming the Rutledge name at present."

Craymere's intent expression relaxed into a smile. Paul's chest constricted another notch. Perhaps he was jealous not because Sophie was fond of an attractive man, but because Craymere was Sophie's friend, while Paul had forfeited all right to her friendship twenty-three years ago. A few heated moments in the crypt of Saint Sebastian's couldn't change that.

"Recently, your husband and Mr. Edward Rutledge received a much-needed infusion of capital," Craymere continued. "I drew up the papers, but the name of the man who loaned them the money was to be kept secret. He said the business could appear weak if word of the loan got out."

"Uncle Daniel," Sophie said.

Craymere nodded. "In essence he owns a twenty percent share in the mill."

"So the insurance settlement from the fire benefited Uncle Daniel as well as Tom and Ned." Sophie turned to Paul.

Paul shook his head. "It would have been a paltry sum for a

man of Ribard's wealth. Unless his fortune isn't as secure as it appears?" Paul quirked a brow at Craymere.

"I don't handle Ribard's affairs, but I know his solicitor," Craymere said. "By all reports his loan to the Rutledge brothers would have barely made a dent in his pockets. Despite the paperwork I had the impression it was more in the nature of a gift to his niece's husband and his daughter's fiancé."

"It might not have been money Uncle Daniel wanted from the fire." Sophie leaned forward. "The fire helped Tom pass the bill increasing the penalties for destruction of property. Uncle Daniel was very happy about it. Riots are one of the few things that truly frighten him."

"You think Ribard instigated the fire to provoke repressive measures?" Paul asked.

"Why not? You said that might have been Tom's motivation. You even suggested the Home Secretary might have tacitly given his blessing."

Craymere's eyes widened. "I suppose it's possible. It's not the worst thing I've heard Lord Sidmouth accused of."

"It's entirely possible," Paul said. "But even if Ribard was involved in the fire—even if he put the Rutledges up to it—he'd have made sure his hands were clean. If he feared exposure he'd lay the blame on Ned, not resort to murder. Morality aside, he's putting himself at risk by attacking us."

"You seem very sure of him," Craymere said.

"You could say that." Paul hesitated. Craymere had been honest with them and was going to considerable risk for their sake. The least Paul could do in return was be equally honest. "Ribard was my mother's lover. He's probably my father."

Surprise and something that might have been sympathy flickered in Craymere's eyes. "I see. His niece and his son. He is truly without conscience."

"He's decided we're expendable. But I don't think even Ribard would come to such a decision lightly. That's why I'm convinced he's motivated by more than any role he played in the mill fire."

Sophie sipped her tea. "This all started when I began asking questions about Tom's death. Did Tom ever say anything to you about the fire, Jemmy? Did he ever seem remorseful in any way?"

Craymere shook his head. "I can't say he did. In truth, the last time I saw Tom he was looking very pleased with himself. It was at the Blue Dragon. Lord Harrowgate had come up from London to see Tom. Tom asked me to stop and have a drink with them. He wasn't usually so sociable with me, but he said he was in a mood to celebrate. He was about to make his fortune."

"His fortune?" Sophie set down her teacup. "Did he mean the insurance settlement? Or his success in the House?"

"It was well after the insurance settlement. And it didn't sound like he was talking of politics."

Sophie's brows drew together. "Do you think Harrowgate knew what Tom was talking about?"

"I can't swear to it, but I had that impression."

Paul stared into the dregs of his tea. "Harrowgate was Tom's patron, wasn't he? Where's he now?"

"Visiting his Irish estates," Craymere said. "Near Drogheda, I believe."

"And you'd say he was in Tom's confidence?"

Sophie nodded. "Other than Ned, if Tom confided in anyone it would have been Harrowgate."

"Drogheda's on the east coast, isn't it? Just across the Irish Sea." Paul was silent for a moment, remembering the map in the schoolroom at his cousin's house.

"Bloody hell." Dugal's voice came from the sofa, where he was devouring a plate of biscuits. "He wants us to go to Ireland."

Paul looked at Sophie. "What do you think? Ribard knows I have family in Edinburgh, but he won't think to look for us in Ireland. We'd have to question Harrowgate carefully. We don't know how much he knows about the fire. But if we can discover the reason for Tom's death, we may be able to get to the bottom of this."

Sophie turned to Craymere. "Do you think you could get us a boat, Jemmy?"

Chapter 22

Dugal leaned against the rail and glared at the small cabin into which Sophie and Amy had vanished. "I dinna see why we need her."

"Sophie needs help with the baby." Paul ran his eye over the placid green bank. They were moving down the river toward Morecambe Bay. Only when they reached the Irish Sea would he feel they were safe from pursuit. But thanks to Craymere's ingenuity they had traveled from the solicitor's office to the dock without incident.

Dugal turned to look at the water. "I help her wi' Fenella. So d'ye."

"Another pair of hands won't come amiss. Or are you that attached to changing nappies?"

"It's no' worse than muckin' out a stable." Dugal's brows drew together. "Her dress be too tight."

"Fenella's?"

"Dinna be daft. Yon Amy's."

Paul bit back a laugh. "I don't imagine she's had a new dress for some time. You could do with a new pair of trousers yourself. I think you've grown a half inch since Kinrie."

"Gettin' taller's one thing. Amy's growin' out. It's no' decent." Dugal was silent for a moment. "Besides, she's bossy."

"I have no doubt you'll hold your own."

The rigging creaked as a young sailor climbed up to adjust the sails. There was only a small crew, and Craymere had vouched for their trustworthiness. The captain had gone below to check the cargo, which Paul suspected was not entirely legal. All the better. The captain would have as much wish to avoid pursuit as they did.

The cabin door opened. Sophie picked her way around the coils of rope and patches of tar on the deck and joined them at the rail. "Fenella's gone down. Amy's sitting with her."

Dugal looked up. "I could ha' watched Fenella."

"I thought you'd enjoy being on deck."

Dugal squared his shoulders. "I'd better go sit wi' them. Fenella might wake and Amy willna ken what to do."

"Oh, dear." Sophie watched Dugal go into the cabin. "He's jealous."

Paul grinned. "I'd say it's one part jealousy, two parts attraction."

Sophie stared at him. "They're children."

"Growing children. Dugal thinks Amy's dress is too tight."

Sophie laughed. It was so long since he'd heard her laugh, he'd forgotten how much he liked the sound of it. "I should have remembered how it feels to be eleven years old," she said. "One can't stop thinking about such things. Though I'd have thought today's events would turn Dugal's thoughts in a different direction."

Yet the events had had quite the opposite effect on Paul and her. Paul saw Sophie come to this realization a fraction of a second after he did himself. The laughter faded from her eyes. She tugged at the brim of her bonnet, as though to shield her face.

Paul moved a little way down the rail. Their interlude in the church should have slaked his desire. Instead, he felt stripped raw in her presence, as though every nerve had been exposed and the merest touch or look could shatter his control. The memory of her was branded on his senses. The texture of her skin, the feel of her hands, the taste of her mouth.

Sophie looked up at him. The pleated lavender silk that lined her bonnet cast a wash of color over her face. How could so much heat exist beneath such a cool surface?

"Paul." Her fingers moved against the rail, as though seeking the right words. "In the church—"

"A brush with danger can take people that way." His voice sounded strained to his own ears. "It's natural to turn to a fellow creature for comfort." He paused. "Even the man responsible for your father's death."

She looked away. "You weren't . . . I know what I owe you, Paul."

"I don't want your gratitude." His voice turned as rough as the churning water. He forced the feeling from it. "Nothing that's happened in recent weeks changes the past." He ran his fingers through his hair. "There's no sense in pretending. Or in dwelling on actions taken under duress."

The words came out more harshly than he intended. Sophie drew a breath. He couldn't tell whether she was glad or sorry. "Very well. We'll talk about something mundane, like my husband's suicide." She rested her arms on the rail. "It makes less and less sense. Why Tom would have killed himself."

"Perhaps the fortune he expected didn't materialize."

"But what was the fortune?" She looked down at the water, greasy from the refuse of the mills. "I knew him even less than I thought."

Paul leaned his shoulder against the rail, still a careful distance away, and looked sideways at her. "Are you sure he killed himself?"

Her eyes widened. The lace at her throat stirred as she drew in her breath.

"No one seems to understand why he would have taken his own life," Paul continued. "When you tried to learn the truth, you uncovered something that threatened Ribard and Ned Rutledge so much they were determined to kill you."

"You think Uncle Daniel and Ned killed Tom?" Sophie shook her head. "I don't believe I'm even saying this."

"Where was Tom when he died?"

"At Tiverton Park. In his study. Most of the servants had been given the night off to go to a village fete. One of the footmen found him in the morning. He'd shot himself in the head." She hesitated a moment. Her father's shattered body was like a physical force between them. "The gun was in his hand."

"But he left no note?" Paul shut his mind to images of the Comte de Milvery. "Suicides usually do."

"He left nothing." Her brows drew together. "Tom and Ned were fond of each other, as much as they were capable of caring for anyone but themselves. It's true Tom's death gave Ned the title. But only if my baby was a girl. Surely he couldn't have planned to be rid of all of us from the first."

"I wouldn't put it past him. But that doesn't explain Ribard's involvement."

Sophie fingered the pearls she had worn since they left Rossmere. "What if it was only Ned who was behind the fire?"

"And Tom threatened to expose him?"

"Yes. No. What loyalties Tom had were to his brother, not the workers in his mill. Besides, you said the fire wasn't enough to explain Uncle Daniel's involvement."

"It isn't. But I'm at a loss to see what is."

"You? At a loss? What an admission." The familiar lilt of mockery was back in her voice. Their eyes met and suddenly the air was charged with all they had agreed to leave unspoken. Paul drew a breath of the salty air, trying to force desire from his lungs. Tom Rutledge must have been murdered. Or mad. No sane man would have left Sophie.

The breeze tugged at the collar of Sophie's dress and the ribbons on her bonnet. Paul realized the air had turned cooler and the salt tang had grown stronger. "We're nearing Morecambe Bay," he said in as normal a voice as he could manage. "Without a sign of pursuit."

Sophie smiled, though her lips were trembling. "Safety. As much of it as we can hope for."

"Yes." But the words echoed hollowly in his head. There

was danger on all sides. From Daniel, from Ned. From themselves.

LORD HARROWGATE RELAXED INTO HIS FAVORITE WING chair and swirled the Irish whisky in his glass. "So, my dear. Tell me what was so urgent it sent you off to Ireland at this difficult time."

The question had been puzzling Harrowgate ever since Sophie had turned up on his doorstep an awkward half hour before he was to sit down to dinner with a house party of guests. She wasn't wearing mourning, and she was accompanied by a Mr. Lester, who was now seated beside her. She described Lester as a family friend, but Harrowgate had never heard mention of him before. In addition, she'd brought along a squalling baby, a maid who was little more than a child, and a servant boy who looked like a street urchin.

Ah, well. Tom's wife had always been given to mad freaks. And women who had just given birth should be handled with care. So Harrowgate's wife had murmured to him after dinner, when she suggested he take Sophie and Lester off to the library while she entertained their other guests.

Sophie leaned forward. She always put Harrowgate in mind of a prize racehorse—lovely but skittish. "I need to understand why Tom took his life. You must appreciate that, Lord Harrowgate. You were as puzzled by his suicide as I was."

Harrowgate took another swallow of whisky. Damned fine stuff, the best thing to come out of Ireland. He hoped he wasn't in for a scene. Talking about Tom's suicide made him uncomfortable. It was an ugly business. Besides, it had followed too close on the fire for comfort. Harrowgate wasn't sure how much Tom had to do with the fire. He didn't want to know. It was one thing to employ *agents provocateurs* in the service of the Government as his friend Lord Sidmouth did. It was another for a gentleman to soil his own hands with such matters.

"Tom's death was a great tragedy, Sophie, a great tragedy." Harrowgate tapped his fingers against his glass. "For the country as well as his family. Tom knew how to put Jacobins and rabble-rousers in their place. England needs strong men in these troubled times. By God, even my Irish tenants keep muttering about tenant-right and Catholic Emancipation." He coughed, remembering that Sophie was Catholic. Another of the awkward things about her. "But we can't hope to understand—"

"I spoke with our solicitor, Jeremy Craymere, a few days ago. He said he'd seen Tom with you in Lancaster not long before his death. He said Tom was in capital spirits."

"He had good reason to be. Worried about the state of the country, of course, but even that seems to be looking up now that the Government has had the courage to take the right steps."

For some reason Harrowgate found himself looking at Lester as he said this last. "Quite," Lester murmured, but there was a glitter in his eyes that Harrowgate didn't care for.

Sophie shot Lester a quick glance. "Mr. Craymere said Tom talked of making his fortune."

"Ah, yes." Harrowgate let out a small sigh. Thank God she hadn't brought up the fire. "Nothing mysterious about that. Is that why you came? For his papers?"

There was a brief silence. "Papers?" Sophie asked.

"Yes, there was no need to travel all this way, my dear. I was going to send them to you as soon as you'd had time to recover your equilibrium. I wasn't quite sure where you were staying."

Sophie sat back in her chair. "Tom gave you these papers when you visited him in Lancashire?"

"No, he sent them to me later. He wanted me to keep them for him while he was in France."

There was another pause. Harrowgate could swear his words echoed through the room with a meaning he hadn't intended and couldn't begin to fathom. "France?" Sophie asked.

"Yes, surely you knew—" Harrowgate took refuge behind his glass. Confound it, it wasn't natural, a wife setting up her own household. Far better if she'd been discreetly unfaithful, like half the political hostesses in London. Harrowgate glanced at Lester. He treated Sophie with almost painstaking formality. But when he looked at her . . .

"You must know Tom and I weren't close enough for confidences in the last months of his life." Sophie didn't look away or give any sign of embarrassment as she spoke. That was the trouble with her. A politician needed a wife with a decent respect for the look of things. "Why was Tom planning to go to France, Lord Harrowgate? On political business?"

"Good God, no. It was purely on your account, my dear. That's why I assumed you knew."

"My account?"

"Yours and the child's you were carrying. I understand your father was a very wealthy man."

"Was. His estates were confiscated after his death."

Harrowgate shook his head. "Barbaric, what happened to private property in France. But now that the monarchy has been restored, Tom hoped your father's estates could be returned to you."

"I see." Sophie adjusted the folds of her skirt. Harrowgate admired the way the lavender silk clung to her bosom. Still, she really ought to be wearing black. Odd, too, that she hadn't changed for dinner. Neither had Lester. "Tom was planning to travel to France to learn about my father's estates?" Sophie asked.

"He'd written to make inquiries, but he was having trouble getting a straight answer. Everything's in a fearful tangle over there. Trust the French to make a muddle of things. Tom thought he'd have better luck if he went himself. He sent me some notes on what he'd managed to learn just a fortnight or so before his death. He said he wanted to be sure the information was in safe hands. Frankly, I'm not sure why he was making such a fuss. I fear it's a sign that his mind was already disturbed."

"You still have the papers?" Sophie's gaze was intent in the candlelight.

"Oh, yes, they're about here somewhere." Harrowgate

rummaged through the clutter on his desk. He found the papers at last, sandwiched between a copy of the *Parliamentary Register* and some notes for a speech on the suspension of habeas corpus. "Here we are, my dear. Perhaps you'll find them of use when you feel up to renewing the inquiries yourself. It should be a comfort to know he was thinking of you in his last days."

"Yes, of course." Sophie folded her hands in her lap. "Thank you, Lord Harrowgate."

But Harrowgate had the feeling that it wasn't a comfort at all. Worse, he suspected comfort was the last thing Sophie Rutledge wanted when it came to her late husband.

Sophie and Lester said they'd go straight up instead of joining the others in the drawing room. They had a long day of travel ahead of them. Harrowgate remained in his study after they left, frowning into his whisky. Deuced odd, Sophie running about with this Lester fellow, asking questions about Tom's death. Who knew what she might uncover. It wouldn't do to have her stumble across information that would tarnish Tom's memory and all the things he had stood for. It wouldn't do at all.

There must be some way to rein her in. Harrowgate poured himself another glass of whisky. By the time he finished it, the answer came to him. Of course. He would write to Sophie's uncle and drop a friendly word about her visit and the questions she'd been asking.

Harrowgate reached for a sheet of writing paper and dipped a pen in ink. Daniel de Ribard would know how to handle Sophie.

PAUL DIDN'T RISK SO MUCH AS MEETING SOPHIE'S EYES AS they climbed the mahogany-railed stairs to the first floor. The papers Harrowgate had given her rustled slightly in her hand, as though she was gripping them tightly. When they stood in the shelter of the scagliola columns on the landing, she at last turned to look at him. "Come to my room. Dugal and Amy will be waiting up for a report."

Paul hesitated, conscious of the light from the chandelier in the hall below.

"Everyone will be in the drawing room for another two hours," Sophie said. "Besides, I think Harrowgate already suspects the worst about us as it is."

Dugal's voice greeted them almost the moment Sophie opened the door of her room. "Well? Did ye learn anythin'?"

He was sitting cross-legged on the hearth rug bouncing Fenella on his lap. Amy stood by the wardrobe, brushing out the folds of Sophie's cloak.

"Perhaps," Sophie said. "We—"

At the sound of her mother's voice Fenella let out a cry. "She's been fussin' for near half an hour," Dugal said.

Sophie gave the papers to Paul. "I'll have to feed her. Here, lambkin, I didn't mean to be so long."

While Sophie took the baby from Dugal and settled her at her breast, Paul spread the two sheets of paper out on a satinwood work table. Dugal and Amy crowded around him. "What does it say?" Dugal peered at the dark writing as though he could make sense of it if he stared hard enough.

"It's French, isn't it?" Amy said.

"How d'ye ken?" Dugal looked at her from beneath lowered brows. "Can ye read?"

"A little. Lady Rutledge was teaching me."

"You're right, Amy," Paul said. "It's a list of the property Lady Rutledge's father owned in France, the dates it was sold, and the names of those who bought it."

"Then Harrowgate was right. It's nothing out of the ordinary." Sophie spoke from the chair where she was nursing Fenella. Her voice was weary with disappointment.

"Not on the surface. But there must be something—" Paul stared down at the list. *Bourgmont, principal estate in Normandy. Sold to M. Philippe Clerville, 27 February, 1794. "Sacrebleu."* Paul turned to Sophie. "Do you remember when you left France? The exact date?"

"It was spring—"

"April. It was the eleventh of April when—"

Understanding flashed in her eyes. "When my father died."

"Yes." But for the moment the excitement of discovery was stronger than the pain of the past. He crossed to her side and held out the list. "Look at this. The latest date of sale is March nineteenth."

Sophie stared at the writing as though it was as incomprehensible to her as to Dugal. "I don't understand. *Papa*'s estates wouldn't have been confiscated until after he died."

"Whose word do you have for it that they were confiscated? Ribard's?"

"Everyone's. My mother, Aunt Louisa. My father was considered a traitor. Everything he owned was forfeited to the Government."

"Unless he'd sold it already. And moved the money out of the country, as Ribard had."

"But—" Sophie shook her head so vehemently that Fenella made a protesting noise. "My mother would have known."

"Would she?" Paul conjured up his memories of Isabella de Milvery, a soft woman from her blond ringlets to her full, pretty face. "I doubt your father confided to her about such matters. I doubt Ribard told the marquise about his plans."

Sophie settled Fenella back at her breast. "You're suggesting *Papa* sold everything he owned—"

"Quietly, bit by bit, and sent the money to a foreign bank. It's what Ribard did. Your father was his brother-in-law and closest friend. They were both involved in a treasonous plot. It would be only natural for them to make plans to flee the country. Your father was a wealthy man. Wealthier than Ribard, as I recall."

"I suppose so." Sophie straightened Fenella's blanket. "*Maman* was always telling me that we once had more money than Uncle Daniel and Aunt Louisa. She hated having to live off their charity."

"And Ribard was deep in debt before he left France, despite his lavish manner of living. I remember the tradesmen who hung about the doors with their bills." Paul moved to the fire-place and leaned his arm on the pedimented mantel. "It would have been very tempting for Ribard. If he realized he had access to your father's money and no one else knew it—"

"Here now." Dugal ran across the room and perched on the arm of Sophie's chair. "Ye're sayin' the marquis stole Sophie's father's money and then killed Sophie's husband because he was askin' questions about it?"

Paul looked at Sophie. "What do you think?"

Sophie's brows drew together. "If it's true about the property . . . I've had to face that Uncle Daniel could be capable of anything." She put Fenella against her shoulder for a burp. "Tom must have received letters from France that he used to put this list together. What happened to them?"

"I expect he meant to take them to France with him," Paul said. "But in case they were lost or destroyed he sent a copy of his discoveries to Harrowgate for safekeeping."

"Why did he need to go to France i' he already kenned about the property?" Dugal asked.

"He knew the property had been sold before Milvery's death," Paul said, "but I suspect he was looking for proof that Ribard had taken the money."

"I don't understand." Amy walked across the room, twisting her braid around her finger. "What does this have to do with Mr. Rutledge and the fire?"

"Nothing," Paul said. "Yet. But this is the closest we've come to a motive for Ribard to want to get rid of Sophie. Not to mention Tom Rutledge."

Dugal slumped back against the chair. "We're goin' to France."

"Sophie?" Paul asked.

"It's as good a place to run to as any. And if you're right . . ." She put a hand behind Fenella's head, as though to anchor herself. "We should find out, one way or another. But is it safe for you to go back?"

Paul gave a whoop of laughter. "It's not safe for us to go anywhere."

"You know what I mean. You came to Scotland because you were about to be accused of sedition."

"No formal charges were made against me. And tempting as it may be, I don't plan to reopen my newspaper and accuse the Bourbon Government of trampling on the rights of its citizens."

Sophie settled Fenella at her other breast. "So we lay low and make discreet inquiries about my father's estates?"

"That's the idea. I have a number of contacts in Paris."

Her brows rose. "You have contacts in the Bourbon Government?"

He smiled. It was amazing how his spirits had lifted now that a course of action was clear to them. "A good journalist has contacts everywhere. I have a friend on the British Ambassador's staff. Adam Durward. He used to be an English spy. He and my cousin Robert saved each other's lives during the Peninsular War and became inseparable friends. He and his wife Caroline will give us shelter, and Adam will help with the inquiries."

"France." Dugal bounced on the chair arm. "We're goin' to see the Froggies."

Amy folded her hands primly. "You won't like it there. You won't understand what people are saying."

"I dinna understand what they're sayin' in England half the time. We'll ha' to go in another boat, willna we?"

"We'll take a ship to Greenock," Paul said, "and travel overland to Edinburgh. My cousin will help us find passage to France."

He looked down at Sophie, struck by the fact that she was finally going to meet his family. He could not be sure what she would make of life in Old Fishmarket Close. Of his aunt, Anne Lescaut, a Devon clergyman's daughter, who had married a French journalist with radical views. Of his cousin Robert, who had fought and spied for Napoleon and turned journalist in his turn when the war was over. Of Robert's Scots wife Emma, a miracle of a woman who had taught Robert to love and be human. Of the children, who spent as much time in the print shop as in the schoolroom.

Paul told himself it didn't matter what Sophie thought of them, just as it didn't matter what she thought of him and the life he lived. But as he watched her bend over Fenella and felt his heart contract, he knew he was lying.

Chapter 23

><

ANNE LESCAUT TOOK A BUNCH OF LEEKS FROM THE gnarled hand of the herb woman and dug into her reticule for the correct change. A stout matron wearing a hat that had to be a foot across jostled against her. Anne maintained her ground. Years of living in Paris had been good training for Edinburgh's herb market.

"Leeks, celery, carrots." Anne rejoined her daughter-in-law, raising her voice to make it heard over the lusty cries of the herb women, the babble of customers haggling over purchases, the shouts of the children running through the market. "That takes care of tonight. What do you think of onion soup tomorrow?"

"Splendid." Emma Lescaut pulled up her daughter's baby carriage as a head of lettuce sailed across the High Street in front of them to be neatly caught by a woman in a stall on the opposite side. "It's Robert's favorite."

"Paul's too." Anne pushed down a prickle of worry. They'd had only one brief letter from her errant nephew since he left for the Highlands.

Emma laid a hand on Anne's arm. "Paul will turn up. He always does. Probably the night we serve the onion soup."

The two women moved back toward the center of the street clogged with sturdily gowned tradesmen's wives, maidservants in print dresses, and a number of fashionably dressed women who had left the elegant environs of New Town to do the marketing themselves, servants following a step behind to carry their packages.

A woman brushed by them wearing a filmy lavender dress and a net-covered bonnet in defiance of the morning drizzle.

"The rain's going to ruin that silk," Emma said. "Not that I've anything against frivolous bonnets, mind." She tucked a strand of auburn hair beneath the brim of her own yellow chip. "But they seem a bit excessive at market at nine in the morning. Oh, look, that stall has onions."

They fought their way through the crowd to the other side of the street. Emma stopped to adjust her daughter's blankets. Anne turned toward the onion stall. The pungent smell carried her back to Paris and the early days of her marriage. Robert and Paul got their love of onion soup from her husband. It was the first receipt she had mastered as a bride.

"Mrs. Lescaut?"

Anne looked round, not sure if the speaker was addressing Emma or her. She was used to hearing her name mangled by the Scots, not pronounced without effort as it was now.

The speaker was the woman in the impractical lavender dress. Her gown and bonnet stood out, even in the color and variety of the market. It was something about the cut and style. Or perhaps it was the way the woman wore them. The net that draped her bonnet lent her an air of mystery. Anne was sure they had never met before. She would not have forgotten those deep-blue eyes or that distinctive, finely boned face.

"You are Mrs. Lescaut?" the young woman repeated.

"I am. My daughter-in-law is Mrs. Lescaut as well." Anne indicated Emma, who had straightened up from the baby carriage.

"Robert's wife." The woman smiled.

Emma started and cast a questioning look at Anne.

"Forgive me," the woman said. "I feel I know you already. My name is Sophie Rutledge. I'm a friend of Paul's."

Emma drew in her breath. Anne felt a shock of surprise, followed by the tightness of anxiety. She resisted the urge to ask a dozen different questions. Knowing Paul, the explanations were too complicated for the herb market. "I might have known my nephew couldn't do anything as simple as send us a note. I hope he hasn't embroiled you in something dreadfully complicated, my dear."

"I'm afraid it's more the other way round." Sophie Rutledge glanced from side to side, then stepped closer. "We thought it would be safer for me to approach you. Paul's waiting by Saint Giles's with my baby and my maid and a young boy who's been helping us."

"I see." Anne glanced toward Saint Giles's Cathedral. But with the crowd it was impossible to see much more than the top of the crown spire. And Paul would know better than to stand anywhere too obvious.

"I take it you're being followed?" Emma said.

"We may be," Sophie Rutledge returned as calmly as if she were discussing the price of carrots.

Emma nodded. "You were quite right not to come straight to the house." Two young girls hurried by, intent on gossip. "Yes, there are some splendid onions just over here." Emma moved toward a bin that was temporarily free of customers. The proprietor was engaged in a noisy transaction at the far end of the stall. "There's a man watching our house," Emma continued. "Robert noticed him two days ago. We thought it might be something to do with Paul. Robert says the man is a bit obvious. Fortunately, he follows Robert, and Robert's out this morning, so he won't be watching the house now."

"But you'd best not all come in at once. The neighbors would notice so large a group." Anne picked up an onion and pretended to study the thickness of its skin. It didn't matter how old your children grew. You never stopped worrying. "You and your baby and maid can come with us, Mrs. Rutledge. No one will think it odd for Emma to bring a friend home for luncheon after the market. Paul can go round the back with our parcels as if he's making a delivery."

Edinburgh's chill northern wind whipped up, blowing the rain against them. Emma pushed the baby carriage farther under the stall's awning. "My older daughter and stepson can collect the young boy. They're running about the market somewhere."

Sophie Rutledge smiled. "You're both very good at this."

Anne returned the smile. "Self-preservation. You have to learn to be a conspirator when you marry a Lescaut."

PAUL TOUCHED HIS FINGER TO ONE OF THE NEWSPAPER sheets strung from clothesline across his cousin's print shop. The ink was nearly dry.

"Miss it?" Robert's voice came from the desk.

Paul forced a grin to his face. The smell of ink kindled a warmth within him. If it weren't absurd he would have described it as comfort. But he wasn't about to admit those feelings to anyone, not even the cousin who had been his closest friend since boyhood. "When have you known me to go sentimental about anything, let alone paper and ink?"

"People change. I haven't known you to pick up dependents either." Robert unstoppered a flask and poured more whisky into the two tumblers on his desk.

Paul moved to a stool, away from the circle of warmth cast by the desk lamp. "Dugal can take care of himself. And God knows Sophie can. She'd flay you alive for implying otherwise."

"But she admits you saved her life on more than one occasion." Robert held out one of the glasses. "*Nom de Dieu,* Paul. I thought I'd seen the face of hell in battle. But the story you told us—" He shook his head.

Paul sipped the pungent whisky. He couldn't afford to get drunk, but he could afford to grow a little numb. "It's bad for Sophie. Ribard raised her."

"Your father." Robert looked hard at Paul. His eyes were the same blue-gray as Anne's and just as adept at seeing past defenses. "Don't tell me that doesn't hurt."

Paul held firmly to the tumbler, using it as a shield. "It's hardly the first wound I've received at Ribard's hands."

"It's one thing to be ignored. It's another to learn that the man who fathered you considers you so insignificant he'll squash you like an ant."

Paul lowered the tumbler. He should have known Robert would understand. It would have been easier if Daniel had wanted him dead out of rage. What cut deepest was the dispassionate tone in which his father had admitted the need to have him put to death. "Damn you," Paul said. "No wonder you drove the British Army mad. You see far too much."

"A trick of the trade. It's as handy in journalism as it is in espionage." Robert flung himself into his chair and propped his feet on his desk. "Sit down. Stop wasting energy pretending you don't have feelings and tell me how the devil you mean to get out of this mess."

Paul grinned in spite of himself and dropped down on the stool. It had been after dinner before he and Sophie had been able to relate the events of the five weeks since their meeting in Kinrie to Robert, Emma, and Anne. Then the babies had awakened and prevented any detailed discussion of their plans. "We can't hope to stop Ribard or Rutledge until we learn their motives."

"And if you find the answers in Paris? Will you stay there?"

Paul shook his head. "I don't fancy a life spent in hiding. And Ribard's a difficult man to hide from. Our only hope is to expose whatever he's afraid of. Then we'll cease to be a threat to him."

Robert settled back in his chair. "I never thought to hear the word *we* pass your lips with such ease."

Paul stared down at the pale-gold liquid in his glass. The tumbler was fine crystal. It would never have been found in their house in Paris. Emma was gentrifying his cousin. He took a sip of whisky and called on his reserves of irony. "I should have known it. Just because you and Emma still stare at each other like idiots after two years, you want to tie everyone else's life up in neat little packages."

"Neat is the last word I'd use to describe you. And I didn't say anything about marriage."

No. It was his own mind that had made that dangerous jump. Paul set down the tumbler. He was growing careless.

Robert folded his arms behind his head. "She strikes me as a remarkable woman."

Paul resisted the urge to reach for the tumbler. His throat

ached, but it wasn't whisky he craved. "She's everything I despise."

"Courageous? Loyal? Beautiful?"

"Wealthy. Titled. A creature of society. No, that's not fair. She's got a surprising conscience. It's the world she comes from I despise. But any alliance between us is strictly a matter of necessity." He shut his mind to memories of damp, naked flesh pressed against his own and hot breath caressing his skin.

"I've seen the way you look at her. That isn't necessity."

"You said yourself she's beautiful. I'm not blind."

"And I watched you holding the baby. I always thought you'd make a good father. God knows you were more of a parent to David than I was those years I was in the army."

"It's impossible." The words were torn from Paul's throat with a roar of passion and longing that surprised him as much as it did Robert. He swallowed, trying to quench a fire inside him that had nothing to do with the whisky.

Robert watched him, saying nothing.

Paul studied his cousin in the light of the desk lamp. It was like looking into a warped glass. As boys they had often been taken for brothers. Paul knew their features were similar—sturdy, rough, blunt, the legacy of their Breton ancestors. But he also knew they were as different as light and shadow, a difference that went deeper than the contrast between russet hair and gold, blue-gray eyes and brown.

People liked Robert. More important, Robert liked them back. It had been a blessing and a curse in his years of espionage. For all Robert might claim to despair about the state of the world, there was a part of him that was untouched by war and death and disillusionment. Deep down he still believed in honor and loyalty and justice. He still believed in the future.

Paul rubbed the fingers of his right hand. His uncle and aunt had never pressed him about the events that had driven him from the Ribard house. The foiled plot against Robespierre had been the talk of Paris, but Paul had never told anyone of his own role in exposing it. Through the years he had shared many confidences with Robert, from his first woman to the first man he had killed in battle. But the blackest corner of his soul had remained locked away.

Now he looked down at his twisted fingers and sought the right words. "Sophie and I knew each other as children, that year I lived in the Ribard house. Her parents stayed with the Ribards when they were in Paris. The Ribard children ignored me, but Sophie took a liking to me for some reason."

"Remarkable the ideas children get into their heads."

"Quite." Paul forced a smile to his lips. "I was a sort of errand boy, but Sophie would follow me around when she could." He gripped his hands together, as though he could still the pain. "Sophie's father, the Comte de Milvery, was one of the conspirators in the plot against Robespierre. When the soldiers came to the Ribard house, he was home and Ribard wasn't. Milvery shot himself. Sophie and I both saw it."

Robert released his breath. "*Sacrebleu.* No wonder you were so quiet when you first came to live with us. It was a month before you'd talk to me, let alone look at any of my toys."

Paul stared at a knothole in Robert's desk. "I was watching because I wanted to see the soldiers arrest Ribard. I'd overheard him and his friends one night in the library." He looked up and met Robert's gaze. "I was the one who betrayed them."

Robert was silent for a long moment. "How careless of Ribard to let you overhear. You couldn't have done anything else, of course. God knows I had little love for Robespierre, but assassination is assassination."

"I wasn't thinking of saving anyone's life. I wanted to destroy my father."

"Very natural under the circumstances." Robert scanned Paul's face, as though searching out the extent of a wound. "Does Sophie know?"

Pain shot through Paul's damaged hand. "She knows."

"Yet she trusts you."

"She has no one else. But she'll never forget."

"It's clear you never will."

Paul's fingers curled inward. "It was my first act of betrayal. Though hardly my last, as you well know."

Robert's gaze did not waver at this reference to more recent events. "Lucie's in the past, Paul."

"Past sins have a strange way of sticking in the memory." Paul pushed himself to his feet and strode to the counter, where dry sheets of newspaper were laid out for assembly. "Shall I help you with this?"

Paul felt his cousin's gaze upon him. At last Robert stood and began to take sheets down from the line. "Add these to the ones on the counter, will you? They should be in order. When will you leave for Paris?"

"As soon as can be safely arranged." Paul put the sheets in the appropriate piles. "The man watching your house must have been sent by Ribard or Rutledge. That means they've realized we didn't drown in the Lune River."

"We've outwitted cleverer men than your father's spy. Damn, the ink ran on this one." Robert crumpled the sheet and tossed it into a wastebasket. "Emma's Uncle Gavin has many clients with links to France. He's bound to know someone with access to a boat."

Paul nodded. Gavin Blair was one of the most prominent advocates in Edinburgh.

There was a clatter of feet and the sound of barking in the corridor. The door to the print shop burst open. Robert's son David and Emma's daughter Kirsty ran into the room, followed by Dugal and Amy and the family dog.

"Uncle Paul." Kirsty went straight to Paul and hitched herself up on the counter. "Dugal's been telling us how you delivered Sophie's baby all by yourself."

"Hardly that. Sophie did most of the work." Paul ruffled Kirsty's hair. She seemed to have grown in the weeks he'd been away. She reached the middle of his chest now. At nine years old she looked more and more like Emma, with her gray-green eyes and riot of auburn hair.

"And Dugal says you killed a man and outwitted a troop of

soldiers." David, a dark-haired, serious boy of twelve, cleared a stack of papers off a chair.

"*Several* troops o' soldiers." Dugal watched David hand Amy into the chair, his face a mask of conflicting emotions.

"Several soldiers would be more accurate," Paul said. The dog thunked her tail against his leg. He bent down to scratch her behind the ears. Pauline, Kirsty had named her. Paul took it as a compliment.

"I may have a job for you two tomorrow," Robert told David and Kirsty. "Can you walk round to Uncle Gavin's with a message?"

David's eyes narrowed. He suddenly looked older. "You mean so the man watching the house won't be suspicious?"

Robert nodded. "Exactly."

"I'll help." Dugal moved a little closer to Amy's chair without looking directly at her.

"I'm afraid that would defeat the purpose," Paul said. "We don't want Ribard's spy to know any of us are in the house."

Kirsty slipped her hand through Paul's arm. "Don't worry, Uncle Paul. David and I know how to look very innocent when we put our minds to it."

SOPHIE SETTLED FENELLA IN HER BASKET, WHICH WAS resting on the bed in Robert and Emma's bedchamber. Emma Lescaut was in an armchair by the fireplace, nursing her own daughter Alison. Alison was pushing against Emma's breast with a coordination Fenella did not yet possess. Four months old last week, Alison was not only larger than Fenella, but seemed far more solid and sturdy.

"You seem so comfortable." Sophie crossed the room to join Emma. "Half the time I still feel as if Fenella's like the porcelain doll I broke when I was seven."

Emma smiled. "Babies are much sturdier than dolls. I think you're always more at ease with the second one. I worried Kirsty had stopped breathing if she went an hour without crying. Of course my life was very different then. I lived in the country, in an enormous pile of a house. If I left Kirsty in the nursery, it took her nurse a half hour to find me."

Sophie dropped down in a chair covered in a simple, unfussy pattern of burgundy and sage green. The upholstery was a little worn and there were nicks in the wood, but the chair was surprisingly comfortable. She reached behind her to adjust the cushion and saw that it was embroidered with a picture of a brown-and-white puppy rather like the Lescauts' dog, Pauline.

"Kirsty made that for Robert and me when we got married," Emma said.

Sophie smiled, thinking of the Italian tapestry cushions strewn about Rossmere. She settled back and felt some of the tension drain from her body. The fireplace was unlit, but the brass lamp cast a cozy glow. In its light she studied Paul's cousin's wife. Emma's dark-green dress was stylish yet practical, her auburn hair uncropped and pinned up simply, her brows thick and unplucked. There were traces of ink about her nails. Sophie had the impression that she spent as much time in the print shop as her husband did.

Emma seemed completely at home in the two stories the Lescauts occupied above the print shop. Yet this was her second marriage, and her life before must have been very different. At dinner she had mentioned that she'd been born a Blair. Sophie had heard of the Blairs. They were one of the largest landowners in Midlothian.

"It must have been difficult." Sophie smoothed the lavender silk of her gown, not sure of the right words. "Moving from your old home to Edinburgh."

"Coming down in the world?" Emma had a quick, ready smile.

Sophie's face grew warm. "I didn't mean—"

"It's all right." Emma put her daughter against the towel she had draped over her shoulder and patted Alison's back. "I always wanted to live in Edinburgh. I felt terribly cut off from the world at Blair House. It's different for you. You're used to London."

Sophie felt her mouth curl. "I don't miss it as much as I would have thought. No, that's not quite true. I miss the theater, and the shops, and the excitement. I grow bored easily. Not that that's been a problem lately."

Emma carried Alison to her cradle. "You're very like Paul. Not many people could laugh at your situation."

"At this point it's difficult to do anything else." Sophie fidgeted with her mother's pearls, discomfited by this turn in the conversation. She forced her mind back to the Lescauts. Emma was tucking the blankets around Alison. She had mentioned having a nurse for Kirsty, but now she had only one servant. Sophie sought a tactful way to broach her question and decided Emma would prefer directness. "You don't find it difficult, not having as many servants as you were used to?"

Emma turned from the cradle, wrinkling her nose. "I must admit I'm not overly fond of housework. But I have a much smaller house to see to now. I used to spend hours settling disputes among the staff. I don't miss that. And I quite like the privacy. It's taken work to adjust, of course. But then, marriage always does."

Hot, betraying color flooded back into Sophie's face. She realized how her questions must seem to Emma. That was ridiculous, of course. Whatever her future held, it was not a life with Paul.

"The babies have both gone down?" Anne appeared in the doorway, a tea tray in her hands. "Robert and Paul are working on the newspaper. Kirsty and David took Amy and Dugal down to help, so I brought tea upstairs." She set the tray down on a small round table by the fireplace and began to pour tea. "It's good to see Paul back in the print shop. He's always happiest when he can mess about with words and ink and type."

Sophie accepted a cup from Anne. "He seldom talks about the newspaper in Paris, but it must have been hard for him to close it."

Anne smiled. There was something very English about her long, narrow face. Her father had been a vicar in Devon, but like Emma she seemed to belong in the life she had married into. "Paul seldom talks about his feelings." Anne passed a cup to Emma. "When he first came to live with us it was weeks before he even mentioned his mother's name."

"Had you seen a lot of him before? When he lived with his mother, I mean." Sophie realized she knew as little of Paul's life before he had come to the Ribard house as after he had left it.

"Not a great deal." Anne settled herself in a chair. "Charlotte—Paul's mother—quarreled with her family when she went off with the marquis. To tell the truth, I don't think my husband disapproved of her being a kept woman as much as her being kept by an aristocrat."

The words were spoken lightly, but they sent a shock of memory through Sophie. She studied Anne over the rim of her cup. It was impossible to associate this kindly gray-haired woman bent over the blue-and-white tea service with the menacing revolutionaries of her childhood. Yet to her family, the Lescauts would have been the enemy.

"I remember calling on Charlotte once," Anne continued. "She had at least a dozen people in her *salon*. I found Paul alone in his room reading a book. He was six years old."

Sophie glanced at Fenella's basket. Paul's mother may have belonged to the demimonde, but her life sounded not unlike the one Sophie had lived in London.

Emma handed round a plate of biscuits. "Yet I've always had the impression that Paul loved his mother very much."

"He adored her. Difficult as it is to imagine Paul adoring anyone. And Charlotte loved Paul. She just had other interests." Anne took a biscuit and broke off a piece, but didn't eat it. "It was his father who hurt him the most. Never acknowledging him."

Sophie's fingers trembled, making the tea slosh in her cup. She had been lulled into tranquillity. Anne's words threw her back into the tumult of her life as swiftly as their plunge into the Lune River.

Anne laid a hand over hers. "Oh, my dear, I'm sorry. I shouldn't have mentioned him."

Sophie shook her head. She could feel the pressure of tears behind her eyes. Why should she cry now, of all times? "There's no forgetting Uncle Daniel or what he's done." She set down her cup and rubbed her arms. A chill had stolen over her. "I keep thinking I should be angrier or more devastated. Instead, I feel numb."

Emma's gray-green eyes warmed with sympathy. "It must seem unreal. He was like a father to you."

Sophie stared at the spilled tea in her saucer. Neither of the women knew the manner of her father's death or Paul's role in it. "No, not really. I remember my own father vividly. No one could take his place. I was well cared for in the Ribard household, but I always knew I was an outsider."

Anne squeezed her hand. It was a long time since anyone had shown her such simple comfort. Aunt Louisa was not given to affectionate gestures. "It was the same for Paul, I think," Anne said. "He's always seen himself as a little apart from the rest of us." She shook her head. "He once apologized to me because he'd come back from the war and my younger son Edouard hadn't. He didn't understand that hard as it was to lose Edouard, it would have been just as hard on Gerard and me if we'd lost Paul."

Emma added more tea to Sophie's cup. "Paul and Robert have never forgiven themselves for not protecting Edouard better. But I think perhaps it's worse for Paul. He and Edouard were fighting together at Austerlitz. The same shell that killed Edouard smashed Paul's hand. Robert found them on the battlefield. Paul had flung himself over Edouard's body. I suspect Paul thinks that if he'd moved more quickly Edouard would still be alive and he'd have been the one to die."

Sophie looked from Emma to Anne. "He was very badly wounded, wasn't he?" she said, voicing the question she knew she would never be able to ask Paul.

Anne sipped her tea. "The doctors said it was a miracle he

survived. His hand was the least of it. He was covered in bandages when he came home. There were weeks when we weren't sure if he'd recover or what sort of shape he'd be in if he did. Sometimes I think he healed only because he thought dying would be too easy a way out."

"Out of what?" Sophie asked.

"Life." Anne settled back in her chair with a sigh. "At best, Paul sees life as a challenge. I don't think he's ever expected it to bring him happiness."

"It's worse than that." Emma swirled the tea in her cup. "He doesn't think he deserves to be happy."

Chapter 24

><

"STILL NO SIGN O' THEM." DUGAL PRESSED HIMSELF against the paneling between the parlor windows, craning his neck to see out the window without being seen from the street below. "Ye'd think they'd be back by now."

"Kirsty and David know enough not to rush home from Uncle Gavin's," Emma said from the gateleg table where she and Paul sat, a chessboard between them. "It would look suspicious."

Sophie stuck a pin through the sprigged muslin skirt in her lap. She and Anne were helping Amy alter one of Emma's dresses. "Is that man still watching the house?"

"Oh, aye." Dugal nodded, eyes on the street. "He be leanin' against a streetlamp, plain as daylight. He must think we're fair witless no' to ken he's there."

Sophie reached for more pins. It was absurd, but her nerves were drawn more taut in this cheerful room with its green paisley wallpaper and jumble of toys and books than they had been in Kinrie or Lancaster. Waiting was always the hardest.

"Checkmate." Emma moved a gleaming ebony bishop. "I'd be prodigiously proud of myself if I didn't know the game was the last thing on your mind, Paul."

Paul smiled and touched her hand.

"Sophie." Robert turned from the writing desk where he sat with a pile of newspapers spread before him. A packet had arrived from France that morning. Well out of date, he said, but there were still interesting bits of news to be gleaned for his paper. "Weren't there two others involved in the plot to kill Robespierre, besides your father and Ribard?"

"The Vicomte d'Epigny and the Baron de Mouffetard." Sophie had no memory of them, though they had been her father's close friends. "They were arrested and guillotined."

"That's what I thought." Robert held up a sheet of newspaper. "There's a d'Epigny mentioned here who has the title now. A younger brother, I think. He's one of the lucky aristos who's already managed to get his estates restored. He's married to a daughter of the Minister of the Interior."

Emma pushed some loose strands of hair into the knot at the nape of her neck. "Hasn't the name de Mouffetard been in the French papers in recent months as well? Something about him being appointed to a Government post."

Robert nodded. "It seems they were rewarded for their relatives dying heroes' deaths. Judging by their success, your husband would have had good luck pressing your father's claim, had there been a claim to press."

Sophie jabbed another pin into the muslin. "All those years. All those years *Maman* and I believed we were living on Uncle Daniel's charity. And if we're right, all the time—"

"He was living on yours." Paul picked up the white king from the chessboard and turned it over in his hands. "It should all have been yours, Sophie. The money he bought Rossmere with. The money he invested so cleverly and used to make more money. His whole fortune is built on deceit."

Fenella made a small noise. Sophie rocked her daughter's basket with her foot. "Is that what Uncle Daniel's afraid of? That I'll try to take it all away from him?"

"That you'll tarnish his image." Paul's gaze was clear and steady. "That you'll hurt Charlotte's future prospects."

"But I love Charlie. I'd never hurt her."

Robert folded the newspaper. "English society has a way of tainting children with the sins of the parents. And Ribard has committed a cardinal sin as far as the English upper class is concerned. He betrayed one of his own."

Amy looked up from the bodice she and Anne were pinning. "It still doesn't explain about the fire."

"No." Paul set down the chess piece. "There are a lot of unanswered questions."

Dugal let out a cry. "I see them. Actin' as i' they're just out for a stroll. The spy barely looked at them."

Paul grinned across the room at Anne. "You see how all your theatricals have paid off. You never guessed you were raising a family of spies, did you?"

Anne took a needle from her sewing case. "I'm glad to see you all putting your talents to use."

A few moments later Kirsty and David came running into the room, Pauline at their heels. David pulled a paper from inside his jacket and handed it to his father. "Uncle Gavin says he can arrange for a ship if you give him three days."

"I think he was glad to be asked to help." Kirsty tugged at the strings on her bonnet and tossed it onto a chair, then bent down to unfasten Pauline's lead. "He says he can always count on us to bring excitement into the house."

Robert scanned Gavin Blair's letter. "If we can't keep you safe for three days, we're sadly lacking in ingenuity. I've already written to my friend Adam Durward. He'll have started making inquiries by the time you reach Paris."

Sophie patted Pauline, who had run over to sniff Fenella's basket. "We're very grateful. I hope we won't be too much in your way while we wait."

"Nonsense," Anne said. "That's what family are for."

Paul looked at his aunt for a moment, as though letting the word *family* settle in his mind. "Anne's always been good about taking in strays."

Anne bit off a thread. "You're not a stray, Paul. You never have been."

Paul smiled, but said nothing.

SOPHIE LOOKED FROM THE RACKS OF TYPE TO THE CURTAIN of drying newspaper. "Is this what your print shop in Paris is like?"

"Believe it or not, it's smaller." Paul was in his shirtsleeves, his neckcloth loose, his tan cotton waistcoat unbuttoned. She had seen him in many guises, but she suspected this was the closest she'd come to the real Paul. "Not that the house in Paris is really mine," he added. "It belonged to my uncle. Properly speaking it's Robert's now."

Sophie studied him, remembering Anne's words the night before. "You were the one who worked on the newspaper with your uncle and kept it going after he died."

"I wasn't fit for much else after I was wounded."

"And you thought it was the least you could do considering they'd lost their younger son?"

Paul swung his head round to look at her, his gaze sharp as a lance. Sophie knew she had crossed some unspoken boundary, but it was too late to go back and she was tired of having her life laid bare while she knew nothing of his. "Anne told me about your cousin Edouard last night," she said. "I'm sorry."

"Yes, so am I. Robert joined the Republican Army because he wanted to change the world. I joined because I wanted to go out and smash things. Edouard joined just because he was following our lead. It was criminally unfair that he was the one to die, but if you're suggesting my choice of profession was an attempt to make up for it, you're wrong. I'm not so bloody self-sacrificing."

"No." Sophie rested her hands against the counter behind her. "I think you became a journalist because you couldn't bear to keep silent in the face of injustice."

He gave a self-derisive, bone-dry smile. "You're beginning to sound like Anne."

"Is that so bad?"

"Only when your critical faculties are turned on me."

She thought he had let his guard down a little, but it was difficult to read his expression. The print shop was filled with late-afternoon shadows. "Had you spent a lot of time in the print shop before you came to live with your aunt and uncle?" she asked.

"Hardly any. *Maman* hated it. Afraid she'd get ink on her

gown. Metaphorically as well as literally. She didn't like being reminded of her origins. But I remember Robert showing me how to work the press on one visit. I was fascinated. There's a lot of power in being able to manufacture words."

Sophie looked at the heavy printing press. "You must have been younger than Dugal and David."

"Nine. Or perhaps eight." He turned and began to straighten a stack of papers on Robert's desk. "It was before my mother's health worsened."

Sophie had an urge to stroke his face as she would Fenella's. "It must have been hard for you when she fell ill. I know it was for me with my mother." Though she had been older and had Aunt Louisa and her cousins.

For a moment she thought Paul wasn't going to answer. Then he spoke without looking at her. "All her friends stopped coming to the house. And then Ribard did as well."

Sophie put out her hand, but checked herself, knowing the touch would be unwelcome. "No wonder you hated him."

Paul stared down at the papers. "I'm not sure which of them I was angrier with in the end. Ribard for not coming, or my mother because it was Ribard's name she called when she was dying and not mine."

He said it in a flat voice, but she had a feeling it was something he'd never admitted before. He hadn't moved, yet it was as though he had extended his hand to her. "I remember coming into my mother's room once when she was reading over my father's letters," she said. "I'd scraped my knee. She'd been crying. She told me never to interrupt her again."

Paul turned to look at her. She felt a bond stretching between them, as fragile and shimmering as silk thread. Yet she knew that if she probed deeper the bond would snap. "Anne said you and Robert practically haunted the print shop when you were boys."

Paul's posture relaxed. "And all the way through university. Writing an article always seemed much more immediate than defending a thesis."

"You were at the University of Paris before you joined the army?" This was a new side of Paul. "What did you read?"

"Classics." He grinned. "Don't I strike you as a classical scholar?"

"Well, yes, rather. There's nothing so straightforwardly bloodthirsty as the Greeks and Romans. They don't waste time on sentiment."

His mouth twisted. "I liked reading about family histories even more tangled than my own."

Sophie adjusted the shawl Emma had lent her. "Kirsty told me you're the cleverest man in the world except possibly for Robert."

"Kirsty took an unaccountable liking to me when we first met. I can't think why. I wasn't very gracious to her or to Emma, as I recall. Robert's first marriage was a disaster. I didn't want to see him hurt again."

"You were wrong."

"Completely. Surprised I can admit it?"

"I long ago ceased to be surprised by anything you do." She smoothed the soft, claret-colored wool of the shawl. "You're a far better uncle than I've been an aunt. When I see you with Kirsty I remember the way I used to follow you about when I was a child."

The words came out easily, without thought, but they opened an unintended floodgate. The room went still. Her chest constricted. She tried to draw a breath and found she was shaking.

"Sophie." Paul moved toward her.

She put out a hand to stop him. Perhaps a part of her had wanted to force the issue. At some point they had to have it out between them. "Why did you do it?" She fought to get the words out, past an ache that was too painful to bear. Hot tears were streaming down her face. "You were my friend. Why did you run away from me?"

Paul's face was drained of color. His eyes were black with torment. He looked at once very young and unutterably weary.

"Why?" She stepped toward him and grasped hold of his waistcoat.

"I was frightened." The words seemed to be wrung from him. "Frightened and ashamed."

Whatever she had expected, it was not this. She was the one who had been frightened that night, more frightened than she had ever been in her life. She drew back.

"It was my father I wanted to hurt, not yours," Paul continued, the words coming in a torrent. "You trusted me. Even with your father lying dead before us. I couldn't bear it." He swallowed. She was aware of the pulse beating beneath his jaw. "I couldn't bear to see your face."

A carriage clattered by in the street outside. Somewhere upstairs a door opened and closed. Pauline started to bark.

Sophie stared into Paul's eyes. The pain they held was a mirror of her own. She again saw the boy hurtling down the service stairs ahead of her, refusing to look back. Running from her. Or perhaps from his own demons. "You seemed so grown up." The knot of pain had eased and her voice was steadier. "But you were younger than Dugal."

"I hurt you." The hatred in his voice was like a lash.

How could she be angry with him when he was so angry with himself? "You were frightened. You were confused. You were a child." She moved toward him. "It was too great a burden for any child to bear."

"Child or no, I was responsible. I have to live with that."

She had offered absolution, and he would not accept it. "We can't live in the past."

"No." He moved toward the door, his habitual ironic mask closing over the pain. "But neither can we forget it."

PAUL MADE HIS WAY UPSTAIRS, HIS CANDLE CASTING FLICKering shadows on the white-painted woodwork and the polished stair rail. It had been a strange evening. Robert, Emma, Anne, and the children had kept up a flow of innocuous conversation. He had listened and even joined in occasionally, though he could not now remember a word he had said. He suspected it was the same for Sophie. They had scarcely looked at each other. Yet the echoes of the afternoon reverberated in the air between them.

Sophie had gone up early to nurse Fenella and had not come back downstairs. Paul had lingered in the parlor and volunteered to lock up. He felt edgy, unable to sit still. Something had shifted between Sophie and him this afternoon. Strained as their old relationship had been, at least it had been familiar. Paul was wary of the unknown.

"Paul." Sophie's voice stopped him as he reached the top of the stairs. She was standing in the doorway of her room. Her eyes looked black and enormous, her face thin and fragile.

Paul crossed to her side at once, but resisted the impulse to take her hands. "What is it?"

"I haven't been able to sleep. I heard you come up." She drew back a little, fingered a fold of her dressing gown. It was a deep-red silk, far more vibrant than the clothes she been wearing in semimourning for her husband. The fabric clung to her full breasts. Her hair tumbled over the silk with tempting abandon. "Paul—"

"Yes?" His throat had gone tight. He knew his hands were shaking, because the candlelight leapt and danced over her face. The few inches of air between them felt heavy, charged with feelings he would not dare voice.

Sophie swallowed. The pink ribbons on her nightdress fluttered over her pulse at the base of her neck. "I don't want to be alone tonight."

Paul heard the breath rush from his lungs. Longing choked him. He could taste it, hot and forbidden. "I can't, Sophie." His voice was thick and unsteady. "I can't do what I did at the McClarens. I can't lie beside you and not touch you. I'm sorry."

"I don't want you to." Her eyes were sapphire-bright in the candle flame. "I don't want you not to touch me." She reached out, hesitated, then gripped his shattered right hand. His fingers tensed and throbbed, but for once not with pain.

The familiar, ironic smile played about her mouth. "If we're going to suffer, at least we needn't do it alone." She drew him into her room and pushed the door shut behind them.

They stood facing each other, hands linked. There was a table near the door. He set his candle down, his gaze not leaving her face. Need raced through him, but he waited for her to move first.

She lifted his hand and pressed her lips against his twisted fingers.

Sharp, sweet, unbearable sensation shot through him. His self-control shattered to bits. He pulled her close and kissed her without hesitation or apology. Her mouth parted, her tongue met his, eager, unashamed of her need. Her fingers twisted in his hair. He bunched the silk of her dressing gown up in his hands. At this rate they wouldn't make it to the bed.

"No." He lifted his head, still holding her. "Not like last time. Let me make love to you."

The words were a common-enough phrase, more graceful than the usual crude terms for the act. Yet they echoed through the room with an unexpected resonance. Sophie went still in his arms. "I thought that was exactly what you did last time."

"Oh, no." He cradled her face between his hands. "We coupled. It's not the same at all." He kissed her again, softly, lightly. She melted against him with a small, surprised intake of breath, as if tenderness was not something to which she was accustomed.

He brushed his lips against the corner of her mouth, the line of her jaw, the pulse beating at the base of her throat. The fragrance of roses teased his senses. He tugged loose the ribbon that held her nightdress closed. The muslin fell open, revealing the shadowy cleft between her breasts. The sight was more potent than the most blatant display of nakedness. He grazed his trembling fingers against the exposed curves.

She made a strangled sound in the back of her throat.

His fingers stilled. "Sophie?"

"It's all right." Her voice was unsteady. "Don't stop. You're much gentler than Fenella."

At the reminder of the baby he drew his hand away and looked at the cradle in the shadows beyond the bed.

Sophie put up her hand and turned his face back to her own. "She's sound asleep. She'll sleep for hours yet."

She pulled his head down and leaned into him, giving without restraint. He drew her closer. Then, because they had to get to the bed and he couldn't bear to let go of her, he swept her up in his arms.

She turned her face into his shoulder and gave an unsteady laugh, which vibrated against his skin. "You've done this before."

"On occasion. I'm not usually given to such gestures."

Her arm tightened around his neck. "I mean you've carried me."

"So I have. Through the streets of Kinrie. Don't tell me you remember. You were unconscious."

"I was thinking of when we were younger."

The memory returned, swift as a blow in the back. He'd carried Sophie up the stairs in the Ribard house, when he was ten and she was four and her father was still alive.

"I didn't mean it like that." Sophie pressed her lips against his cheek. "It's a happy memory. We have to take happiness where we can find it."

He set her down on the blue and red quilt Anne had made when he was a child and leaned over her, his gaze holding her own in the light of the single lamp. "Is that what this is?"

"Oh, yes." She tugged his loosened neckcloth free and pressed her lips against his chest while her fingers sought the buttons on his waistcoat.

He flung off his coat. His waistcoat soon followed. Her dressing gown slithered off her shoulders and pooled around her, wanton red against the pristine white sheet. She lifted her arms and pulled her nightdress over her head.

He had tended her wounds and helped pull a child from her body. He had touched her, known her in the brutally carnal sense. But he hadn't realized the way her skin could shimmer with the flush of desire. Or the tantalizing mystery the shadows could create out of the curve of shoulders and breasts and waist and hips. He hadn't realized that the sight of the rich dark hair curling between her thighs could nearly turn him back into the animal he'd been in the church.

He pushed her back against the pillows, but held himself away, his fingers clenching on the coverlet. "Tell me." His voice shook as though he was some callow stripling with his first woman. "Tell me what you want me to do."

She tugged his shirt free of his trousers. "Take your clothes off. I want to see you too."

He pulled the shirt over his head and dropped it to the floor. She was sitting up and fumbling with the buttons on his trousers. Her touch tore a groan from his throat. "*Sacrebleu*, Sophie. You've already driven me mad."

"It doesn't matter, my hands are shaking too much. Oh, God, Paul, hurry up."

The childlike plea had him laughing and breathless at once. Trousers, shoes, and stockings quickly joined his shirt on the floor.

"Oh, Paul."

The softness in her voice took him by surprise. He looked up, a stocking clutched in one hand. She was staring at his chest. He had no illusions that it was his manly beauty that had drawn her attention. Caught up in the urgency of the moment, he hadn't been thinking of his battle-scarred body. He forced his mouth into a smile. "I'm not as pretty as you."

"I think you're beautiful." She traced the network of scars that crisscrossed his chest, the long, puckered welt that had nearly made him lose his right arm. "It must have hurt terribly."

"I was too delirious to notice. It healed."

Unlike other wounds. She met his gaze and he was sure she understood. For a moment he thought the press of feelings would suffocate them both. Then she pushed herself up on her knees and drew him to her. She ran her lips over his shoulder and down his arm, as though her kisses could erase the scars.

His hands twisted in her hair. Need quickened his blood. He pressed her back among the pillows. She looked up at him. The sympathy was gone from her eyes. Her gaze had turned at once smoky and playful. She laced her fingers through his own, drew his hand down between her breasts, over her rib cage and stomach, into the soft tangle of hair between her thighs.

"There?" His voice was hoarse.

"There." She pulled his hand against her.

He stroked her and felt her muscles quiver and jump in response. When he reached into her warm cleft she turned her face into the pillow with a strangled cry. Then she snatched his hand away. "I want you inside me, Paul. Now."

Her hand closed around him, making him gasp with a need he had not thought could grow sharper. She guided him into her, with a small cry that maddened him as much as her touch. He began to move within her, slowly, deliberately, raw passion leashed by tenderness and care.

She wrapped her legs around him and pulled him deeper, urging him to a faster rhythm. Her hands roamed over his back, tangled in his hair, pulled his head down to her own. Her kiss held an edge that went beyond desire. "Please, Paul." The words were torn from her throat as she strained against him.

He reached between them and stroked her at the place of their joining. Her eyes went wide and dark, drawing him in. Her body tensed and throbbed around him. Pleasure broke across her face. For once, for this moment, he had given her joy instead of pain.

The thought was a potent aphrodisiac. She pulled him against her warm skin. He covered her mouth with his own and tumbled after her over the edge.

SOPHIE RAN HER FINGERS THROUGH PAUL'S HAIR. SHE felt light, weightless, free. Delight lingered in her body, holding at bay the fears that still hovered at the edge of her consciousness.

Paul pushed himself up on his elbows. Cool night air rushed in where the warmth of his body had covered her.

"Don't leave." She gripped him by the shoulders.

"I won't. But I don't want us both to freeze." He rolled to his side, drew the covers over them, and propped himself on one elbow. With his other hand he pushed the hair back from her face and stroked his fingers against her cheek. "No regrets?"

Tom would never have touched her like that, as though she were something precious that might break. She covered his fingers with her own. "None. Before, I used to—I often despised myself afterward."

He said nothing, but his gaze was questioning.

"I'd swear I'd never let someone as undiscriminating as Tom touch me again. We'd be in the midst of a blazing row and then before I knew it we'd be in bed. That's how we made Fenella."

"Then it can't be said to have been entirely a waste."

She felt a smile break across her face. "I was furious with him when I learned I was pregnant. That was before I realized how much I wanted the baby."

His fingers played with her hair. "We all need release. There's no need to despise yourself for taking it."

She searched his face, seeking clues to his own past. "You've never felt self-disgust afterward?"

His hand stilled and his eyes went dark.

"I'm sorry," she said. "I didn't mean—"

"No." He lifted his hand from her hair. "It's as well you know." He shifted his position, drawing a little away from her. "I told you Robert's first marriage was a disaster. I didn't tell you I contributed to the disaster."

She drew in her breath. Paul's mouth twisted in bitter acknowledgment. "Yes, I know. My own cousin. My best friend. But Robert was off fighting in the Peninsula. Anne had taken

David to visit relatives. Lucie and I were alone in the house. Lucie was bored. I was a rutting fool."

Sophie swallowed, trying to make sense of the revelation. "Does Robert know?"

"I made a drunken confession when he came home. Robert had already guessed the truth."

"You weren't her first lover." It wasn't a question.

"Hardly." Paul's eyes glinted with self-mockery. "Does that make it any less of a betrayal?"

She studied the lines of bitterness etched in his face. "Robert's still your best friend."

The fingers of Paul's clawed hand tightened. "Robert's capacity for forgiveness is almost as great as his head for drink."

Paul's honesty had brought a lump to her throat. "I once suspected Tom had bedded Céline. I was furious. But even if he had, our marriage was irretrievably damaged long before. Perhaps that's how Robert felt."

Paul made no response. Sophie knew nothing she could say would heal his self-hatred. Instead, she reached for his hand. "In the church I thought I'd given way to my baser instincts again, but what happened between us tonight was different. Wasn't it?"

He was silent for a moment. She feared he wasn't going to answer. Then he pulled her to him and rested his face against her hair. "You were right. At least we needn't suffer alone."

"THIS IS A *D*, LIKE YOUR NAME STARTS WITH. AND THIS IS A *U*, the second letter." Kirsty and Dugal sat side by side on the parlor sofa, a horn primer between them.

Dugal peered down, then scowled. "I dinna need to ken how to read."

"But you can't set type if you can't read," Kirsty said, as if that should be reason enough for anyone.

"She's right, you know. You don't like being at a disadvantage." Paul glanced over his shoulder at the children. He was at the parlor writing desk, scouring the French papers for any other news that might relate to the Milvery estates.

Sophie kept her head bowed over the book she was pretending to read. She had scarcely met Paul's gaze all day, yet she was aware of him at every moment. The awareness warmed her body, tingled in her nerve endings, played havoc with her thoughts. She stole a glance at Emma, who was at the table with David, correcting a Latin exercise. Surely so great a change in her relationship with Paul must be visible to everyone, but Emma and the others behaved as if everything was the same as it had been yesterday.

The door opened to admit Anne, followed by Amy, wearing the altered sprigged muslin dress. They had added a light-blue sash and unbraided Amy's hair and tied it back with a matching ribbon.

David scrambled to his feet. "You look pretty. I'd never guess that was Emma's dress."

Dugal stared hard at Amy. "Well," he said at last, "at least it fits ye better." He turned back to Kirsty. "Show me the next letter."

Sophie got to her feet. "You look lovely, Amy."

"Very grown up." Paul spared her a smile, then looked away before he could meet Sophie's eyes.

There was a step on the stairs. Bessie, the Lescauts' maid, came into the room, breathless, as though she had hurried up the stairs. Sophie felt the blood drain from her face and her hands go numb. She moved toward Fenella's basket.

"There's a caller below, Mrs. Lescaut." Bessie twitched her apron into place. "A Lady Margaret McClaren."

For the first time that day, Paul looked directly at Sophie. Sophie felt a laugh of relief and surprise well up in her throat and saw it echoed in Paul's eyes. "You'd best show her up, Bessie," Paul said.

A few moments later Lady Margaret swept into the room, the pink ostrich plumes on her bonnet bobbing with her haste. "Oh, my dears, I am so glad to have found you. I simply couldn't rest after you left us, for I told Sir James I was sure we hadn't heard the end of it. We just took the boys back to school after their holidays—which were much too short, they always are—and I insisted we pay a visit to our house in Edinburgh, and bother if there is still good fishing to be had. What are such considerations when one's friends are in trouble?"

Paul was smiling, in spite of himself it seemed. "We're delighted to see you." He pressed Lady Margaret's hand, then turned to Emma. "My cousin's wife, Mrs. Lescaut," he said and proceeded to introduce Anne and the children.

"Oh, how terribly rude you must think me." Lady Margaret shook Emma's hand and automatically patted Pauline, who was sniffing her skirts. "I was so excited to see my dear friends that I quite forgot my manners."

"Not at all," Emma said. "We've heard everything you did for Paul and Sophie, and we're most grateful. My husband is below in the print shop or he would thank you as well. Bessie, could you send up some tea?"

Lady Margaret's eye fell on Alison, asleep on the ottoman. "Merciful heavens, Sophie, that can't be your wee bairn."

"No," Emma said, "that's my very sturdy four month old."

"Her name be Alison." Dugal approached Lady Margaret. "She can hold her head up and make sounds and she kens how to hold a rattle."

"Two little lassies." Lady Margaret darted from the ottoman to Fenella's basket, entranced. Houses above print shops could not be what she was used to, but she was soon sitting on the sofa, Fenella in her lap, drinking tea as if she was in one of her friend's drawing rooms. Even Paul, with his low opinion of aristocrats, would have to admit there was very little of the snob about Lady Margaret.

Footsteps sounded on the stairs again. Sophie glanced up, expecting that Robert had come to join them, but it was Bessie again. "Oh, ma'am." This time Bessie's round face was pale. "There be—That is—"

Two men brushed past her and stepped into the parlor. Two

men in the scarlet coats of soldiers. Sophie's tea splashed into her lap. She looked at Paul. Run, she wanted to scream. But there was no escape from the parlor.

One of the men sketched a quick bow at Emma. "Your pardon, ma'am. We're looking for a Paul Lescaut."

Paul got to his feet before Emma could answer. "I'm Paul Lescaut. What do you want with me?"

The soldier pulled a paper from inside his coat. "We have a warrant for your arrest for the murder of Matthew McAlpin."

Chapter 25

❖❖

SIR JAMES SET DOWN HIS NEWSPAPER AND PUSHED HIMSELF to his feet. "Lady Rutledge. How pleasant to see you again."

Sophie Rutledge entered the room behind Margaret and walked forward quickly, her hands outstretched. "I cannot tell you how grateful I am for your help, Sir James."

"My help. Yes. Quite." Sir James took her hands, aware that her skin had lost its softness and there were lines of strain around her eyes, but aware, too, that she was a stunning woman whose beauty was undimmed by her single strand of pearls and simple dark-red dress. "Help you, yes, of course. Come sit down. Will you take some sherry?"

"I've ordered tea." Margaret waved Lady Rutledge to a petit point settee by the fireplace. "Though I have no objection to sherry in its place. James has a splendid palate, my dear. You can certainly trust his taste in wines. Ours is an informal household, I'm sure you remember that. We prefer it that way. Don't we, James?"

"I fear there isn't much time." Lady Rutledge's voice was taut. "I scarcely know where else to turn. Sir Nathaniel McAlpin, the magistrate, is our only hope, and he's not inclined to listen to anything that reflects badly on his son Matt. But he might listen to Mr. Hagerty."

Sir James grasped hold of this last. "By God, no one should listen to Hagerty. The fellow lied to me in my own parlor. An out-and-out barefaced lie. I've been lied to in my time, I won't pretend I haven't, but not by one of us. Turns things around, it does. A fellow doesn't know where to stand when that sort of thing happens."

"No, no, of course not." Lady Rutledge leaned forward. Her blue eyes were luminous with her plea. "That's why I was sure you'd know where to find him—and how to persuade him to talk to Sir Nathaniel."

"I would? Persuade whom?"

"Mr. Hagerty, my love." Margaret shifted her knitting and sat on the settee beside Sophie.

"Hagerty? What the devil does he have to do with this?"

"Sir James." There was a quaver in Lady Rutledge's voice that gave Sir James the unnerving feeling this splendid woman was about to give way to tears.

"Not that he doesn't deserve to be hauled before the baillie, mind you," he said quickly, hoping to forestall this catastrophe. He dropped into an armchair. "But I haven't the foggiest idea where the man is to be found. Or what we're to do with him when he is."

Lady Rutledge turned to Margaret. There was no doubt now about the tears. "You told me . . . You were so sure—"

"Of course I'm sure. It's September and it's the Highlands. James, you know where Mr. Hagerty can be found."

"I do?"

"You do."

"Then in God's name, where?"

A note of exasperation crept into his wife's voice. "Fishing."

"It's Paul," Lady Rutledge said simply, turning to Sir James. "He's been arrested for the murder of Matt McAlpin. That's why we must bring Sir Nathaniel McAlpin together with Hagerty. We have to find a way to convince Sir Nathaniel that his son was bent on murder when Paul killed him. Hagerty is an old friend of Ned's. It's possible he knew Matt McAlpin as well. It's possible—I pray it's possible—that Hagerty knows something about why Matt was involved in the attack."

Her voice trembled, a note more evocative than tears. "I saw Matt McAlpin, Sir James. I know what he tried to do to me. God help me, *someone* must believe what I say is true."

Sir James sprang to his feet and paced back and forth across the hearth rug, glancing now and then at the divine Lady Rutledge. Oh blessed woman, voice of sanity. He was quite ready to help now that someone had explained the situation to him. "Why," he asked of the world in general, "wasn't I informed?"

Margaret rolled up a ball of soft, fuzzy yarn. "I could have sworn we've done nothing but repeat the story to you since we returned home. I'd best see about dinner, and you and Sophie can plan what should be done." She tucked the yarn in a corner of the settee and left the room in a flurry of violet scent.

Sir James hooked his thumbs in his waistcoat pockets and looked down at the glossy-haired creature on the settee. "Well," he said. "Yes, well indeed. Can you tell me what's happened? What's being done?"

Lady Rutledge folded her hands in her lap, as though to still their trembling. "Paul is in the Tolbooth Prison. Robert—that's Paul's cousin, he prints the *Edinburgh Leader*—has gone to see him. Emma—Robert's wife—has gone to seek help from her uncle, Gavin Blair. He's an advocate. Lady Margaret brought me here."

Sir James resumed pacing and gnawed his thumb. "How would the authorities know whom to arrest? We never used Paul's name. We were careful to keep it a secret from everyone on the estate. I swore I'd send Hagerty to hell on a string if he breathed so much as a word."

"Oh, no, Sir James, I'm sure it wasn't you. Or even poor Mr. Hagerty. He wouldn't dare go against your command. It was my uncle who alerted the authorities, I'm sure of it."

"Your uncle?" Sir James shook his head, hoping to clear it. "The Marquis de Ribard?"

"Yes. It's a long story, but never mind about that now." Suddenly, Lady Rutledge seemed brisker, more a creature of iron than spun glass. "The point is, they know who Paul is."

"Aye, that's the devil of it." Sir James let loose a long sigh. "Paul Lescaut. A Frenchman, a foreigner. Worse still, a journalist, like his cousin, who's already established himself as a man of strong opinions." He made a wry face. "I've read the *Leader*. Paul is everything the Scots could have hoped for when they went looking for McAlpin's killer."

"And everything McAlpin's father could have hoped for. Robert says Sir Nathaniel has no great love for the French." Lady Rutledge ran her hand through the folds of her dress, as though she could not bear its weight in the heat of the room. "We would have run if we could, Sir James. I would have insisted on it. We didn't have a chance."

Sir James thought back to the incident with Captain Somerset. "Lescaut's not the running kind."

"No, he's not, is he?" She refastened the pearl buttons at her neck, as though this small act would justify her failure to save Lescaut from prison. "Apparently someone sent Sir Nathaniel word of Paul's name and where Paul could be found. Sir Nathaniel came to Edinburgh to see to the arrest personally. He's the magistrate in the case, isn't he? I mean the baillie. He wants to question Paul himself."

"And you want me to persuade Sir Nathaniel to speak with Hagerty." The situation began to settle clearly in Sir James's head. "Why couldn't Meg have said so from the first?"

Over an early and informal dinner Lady Rutledge told them everything that had happened in the five weeks since she and Lescaut left Argyllshire, from the barbarous revelation that Ned Rutledge and her uncle were behind the attack on her in Kinrie to their flight to Lancaster and their further journeys to Ireland and Edinburgh.

Now that he understood what was required of him, Sir James began to feel the thrill of the adventure. At least it would be a change from cooling his heels in Meg's drawing room. He had quite enjoyed foiling Captain Somerset. And Lescaut was a very good fellow, even if his opinions were a bit extreme. Couldn't leave him to rot in prison for a crime he hadn't committed. "I'll leave early," he told his wife when they were gathered around the tea table. "I'll collect Lady Rutledge and we'll set off for the Brideswells. That's where Hagerty said he was staying. I won't disturb you."

"Oh, you won't in any case." Margaret picked up a pink-flowered cup and moved to the tea urn. "The Brideswells always rise early. Don't you remember? They spent the Christmas holidays with us last year. It's their boys—adorable children, but they will insist on seeing their father first thing in the morning, and the man has no notion of discipline. Not at all like you, my love."

Sir James leaned back in his chair. The devil take it, there she went again, moving ahead of him. A fellow couldn't get his bearings in this house. "You've already sent the Brideswells a note."

Margaret handed a cup of tea to Sophie. "Yes, dear, explaining the problem and what they are to do."

"What they are to do." Sir James smiled in spite of himself. "Exactly. I don't suppose it would occur to Brideswell to do anything other than what he is told?"

"Why of course not, love. He's not that kind of man at all. Not like my dear, dear husband." Margaret squeezed his hand and began to pour a second cup of tea. "If they send him off at a reasonable hour, Mr. Hagerty should be here sometime tomorrow afternoon. You can take him to see Sophie. I'm sure between the two of you you can persuade him to talk sense."

"Sense? Hagerty?" Sir James sipped the tea she had given him. "I wouldn't count on it."

"I have every faith in you, James." Meg's voice was as soothing as the hot, sweet tea. "And then you can take Mr. Hagerty to see Sir Nathaniel, if he has something to tell Sir Nathaniel, which I'm sure he will because we're all depending on it and really it is the best way out of this predicament."

"Not the best way." Lady Rutledge set down her cup. She had seemed desperate before, but now there was a new edge to her desperation, as though for the first time her real fear had broken through. Sir James did not consider himself a fanciful person, but he would have said her eyes were haunted. "The only way."

"ROBERT." PAUL HELD OUT HIS HANDS AND CLASPED HIS cousin's. They stood in silence, the two of them, surrounded by mildew and close stone walls and the shadows cast by a single, smelly rushlight. They had never been wont to waste words on sentiment, but Robert's crushing grip conveyed a feeling that stretched back to boyhood. It occurred to Paul that perhaps he had been less alone all his life than he had realized.

Robert grimaced. "How did it come to this? And all I did was send you off to the Highlands with ink and paper and a pair of eyes and ears to make use of. My agents in Spain never got in near so much trouble, and half their attention was on the prettier of the local women."

"You haven't seen the Highland girls."

"I've been Sophie." Robert glanced around the small cell. "How are they treating you? What do you need? What do we do next?"

"Paper. Ink. A decent lamp. Robert, listen. I have an idea."

Paul pulled his cousin to a cot covered with a scanty pillow and a thin wool blanket. They sat hunched side by side, their voices low. Paul did not ask how his cousin had managed to secure him privacy and the crude light. At the moment it scarcely mattered. He had to communicate his plan to Robert at once.

"I'm going to write the story, Robert. Everything that's happened to Sophie, everything Ribard and Rutledge have done, everything we've guessed about the Milvery estates. It's the only weapon left to me."

Robert was silent for a long moment. Then he asked the crucial question. "Is it enough?"

"To bring Ribard down? I'm not sure."

"To stir up a hornet's nest?"

"Ah, that I can guarantee."

Robert nodded. "Then that may be enough. If you can do it without bringing harm to Sophie. Or putting her in further danger. Ribard hasn't balked at hired killers. Can you stop him now?"

Paul clenched his hands. Damnation, he was shaking with the effort to control his fear. To keep Sophie safe. Above all, he must keep her safe. Anything more could not be hoped for.

Anything more. The thought was audacious beyond belief. Christ, he was a fool. Sophie de Milvery had no room in her life for Paul Lescaut. What would she do with him? What could she make of him? How long could a love born of fear and panic last?

Paul thrust himself from the narrow bed and paced the tiny width of the room. Had Robert not been there, a quiet, shadowy presence, he would have beaten his arms on the ancient gray stone of the walls until they were bloody.

"Love can destroy you, *mon ami*." Robert's voice was soft and even. "Keep your head clear. The rest will come later."

"Later?" Paul gave a laugh that grated against the rough walls. "Nothing will come later. There's nothing to come, cousin."

"There won't be if you take that attitude." Robert leaned back and regarded him, hands braced on the cot. "Have you even admitted what it is you want from her?"

"What the hell do you think I want?" The words tumbled from Paul's lips with a certainty that surprised him as much as it did Robert. "A wife, a child, a light burning in my life that never ends. What you and your Emma have, that's what I want. How did you find it? What magic did you make? What is it that you did?"

Robert's smile glinted with self-mockery in the dim, flickering light. "I nearly lost it, that's what I did. I nearly let it slip through my fingers. I had too much pride, too much fear—fear of the past, fear of the future. Fear that Emma wouldn't want me. Fear that she would and we'd only hurt each other. The time isn't now, Paul, but when it comes, don't let it go. Seize it."

Paul shook his head. "You always were a blind idealist."

"And you always were a stubborn cynic."

"Clear-sighted, not stubborn." Paul watched a trickle of damp run down the stone above Robert's head, then dwindle to nothingness. "Some hurts don't heal, Robert. Some gulfs are too wide to be bridged." He pushed himself away from the wall and strode back to the cot. "I didn't mean to turn maudlin. It must be the air in this place. I have a long night's work ahead of me."

"You write the story, I'll print it." Robert's eyes shone with a light Paul remembered from the battlefield. "I'll plaster it on every house and storefront in Edinburgh. No one will talk of anything else. They may not believe it, but they won't forget it. Let Ribard make a move against you or Sophie and they'll remember. 'Ribard—wasn't there something about him and Lady Rutledge?' 'Ribard—wasn't there something between him and that journalist Lescaut?' "

Paul dropped down on the scratchy blanket and studied his cousin. When they were boys Robert had accepted Paul's intrusion in the household without jealousy. He was being no less generous now. "You may find yourself sued for slander," Paul warned.

"Let them try. Controversy is the spice of journalism. Besides, I don't think Ribard will want the truth of the story debated in open court. Paul?"

"Yes?"

"You *can* still write, can't you?"

Paul grinned. "Don't insult me, cousin. I was running a newspaper while you were still playing hero on the battlefield. How will you get the story out of the Tolbooth?"

Robert raised his brows. "You think I ran an espionage network for nothing? I'll find a way. There'll be a messenger here tomorrow morning. Is that enough time?"

Paul got to his feet. "Is there enough ink? Enough light?"

Robert stood and put his arms round Paul, a taut, desperate

embrace that said everything that had not already passed between them. *"À demain, mon ami."*

"I HAVE JUST THE MESSENGER," SOPHIE SAID.

"Who?" Robert and Emma asked at once.

"Lady Margaret."

They exploded into laughter.

Robert looked across the parlor at Emma with a wry grin. "Paul won't be the first man to put his head in a noose for a woman."

Sophie lifted Fenella from her basket and gave her a thorough hug. "It's dangerous, isn't it?" Robert had returned from his visit to Paul, exhilarated by the scope and audacity of Paul's plan. It would work, Robert had insisted, and they needed nothing but a messenger and a great deal of hard work and inky fingers.

"It's always dangerous," Emma said, her voice gone quiet. She put down the shirt she was mending. "Men like it that way."

Robert got up with a lazy stride and planted a long, tender kiss on Emma's cheek. "You like to see us that way."

Sophie felt a jealous warmth coiling in the pit of her stomach. She knew it now. She had known it the moment the soldiers took Paul away. She loved Paul, as simply and easily as Emma loved his cousin. It was a wondrous discovery, yet strangely unsurprising, as when a sculptor chips away at marble to reveal a figure that seems to have been buried in the stone all along, waiting to be freed. Paul was the man she loved, the man she would love all her life. It mattered not at all that he was unsuitable, that he hated the world she came from, that he had destroyed her father. They were bound together in ways she could not explain, even to herself.

Robert turned from Emma and gave Sophie a hard, frank look. "Paul can take care of himself. He's been doing it for thirty-three years." He crossed to Sophie's side and ruffled her hair. "He wouldn't thank you for worrying."

"Don't you dare do that, Robert Lescaut," Emma said through lowered brows. "She's much too distractingly pretty." She turned to Sophie. "The truth is, we can't win. If we worry about the brutes they accuse us of fussing. If we don't worry they think we don't love them enough. And if we say nothing at all they mope because we don't appreciate their manly exploits."

"I," said Robert, "have never moped in my life, and usually you're too busy running risks yourself to waste time worrying about me."

"That's exactly what I mean." Emma knotted off a thread and put the shirt in her mending basket. "Uncle Gavin's pulled what strings he can to ensure Paul isn't treated too badly in the Tolbooth. He says there's little else he can do until the case comes to trial. We'll have to pin our hopes on Mr. Hagerty and Sir Nathaniel." She stood, glanced at the ottoman to be sure Alison was still asleep, then turned to Sophie. "Come, love, give me Fenella, you look ready to drop."

Sophie struggled to sit straighter in her chair. "Fenella." She looked down at the baby, curled against her breast. "What will I do with her when we go to see Sir Nathaniel? I may be gone all day."

"Leave her with me." Emma lifted Fenella from Sophie's arms. "There we are, my pet, I'm glad someone in this house is able to relax. We'll do very well together. She took my breast, did I tell you? This evening when you were at the McClarens and the wee mite was desperate with hunger. Alison didn't mind; there was enough for both of them. Fenella will be well looked after for as long as you need to be gone, and she'll be with you as soon as you return home."

Sophie could not object. Indeed, she could scarcely move, but it did feel good to relinquish her child and for once be cosseted and nourished. She had played the fragile female this evening to rouse Sir James's chivalrous instincts, but in truth she felt she could shatter as easily as the crystals on Emma's girandole candlesticks. She closed her eyes and lay back in the chair, listening to her daughter make soft cooing noises against Emma's breast.

Tears seeped through Sophie's eyelids, though she would have sworn she slept. The room had grown quiet, with no sound save the loud ticking of the clock on the mantel. Her child was in the room, and Robert and Emma and Alison. Dugal and Amy and Kirsty and David were upstairs with Anne. She was surrounded by people she cared for, trusted, even loved. Yet there was a raw, gaping hole inside her. She felt as alone as she had at four years old with her father dead on the floor of the foyer and her mother locked in grief.

"Don't leave me, Paul." Sophie did not know if she spoke aloud or to herself, but she framed the words she had sworn she would never speak to anyone. "I need you."

Chapter 26

SIR JAMES STEPPED OUT OF THE BREAKFAST PARLOR AND found his wife in the hall, lavishly dressed in sprigged muslin sashed with salmon-colored silk. An enormous poke bonnet framed her face. He had thought they were to spend the morning waiting for Hagerty, but he had woken to find that Meg had gone out on an early errand with Lady Rutledge. He saw Sophie Rutledge now through the open door to the front parlor, rummaging through a sturdy wicker basket trimmed with salmon-colored ribbon.

"I tell you, Meg, it isn't seemly, spending all your time fussing over other people's children," he said in a low voice.

"I needed to take Sophie's mind off Paul and Mr. Hagerty and that dreary Sir Nathaniel whose name I never can remember." Margaret pulled him into the front parlor. "Besides, I needed an excuse to visit the Tolbooth."

"The Tolbooth?" Sir James's voice rose despite himself. "What in the name of God were you doing visiting the Tolbooth? Or any other prison for that matter? You're a respectable woman. What will people think of your running in and out with that confounded ribboned basket on your arm? What is it today?" He peered at the large container, which Lady Rutledge had just dumped unceremoniously on the chaise longue. "Peaches? Lavender?"

"We couldn't find peaches that were ripe enough," Lady Rutledge said. "The apricots have gone all squishy. And the berries, Meg, the berries." She peered more closely at what remained of the fruit. "They've made a positive fright of the cotton blanket in the bottom of the basket."

"All the better, my dear. Who would ever suspect two such muddle-headed creatures as ourselves of any kind of rational act?"

Sir James pushed his hand in among the sticky mess, thought better of it, and wiped his hand carefully on his handkerchief. Something red-stained and papery fluttered to the ground.

"Oh, dear." Lady Rutledge dropped to her knees and began to wipe his boots. "I am so sorry, Sir James. I wouldn't want your man to be faulted for leaving a berry stain on the tongue."

"Here, what's this?" Sir James bent over and snatched up the deep-red strip of paper that Lady Rutledge had peeled from his boot. " 'The Comte de Milvery . . . Robespierre . . . Rossmere.' God in heaven, madam."

"Oh, Sir James. We were trying so hard not to trouble you." Lady Rutledge sprang to her feet, took the paper from his nerveless fingers, unfolded it, refolded it into a neat square, and placed it carefully in her reticule. "There, that's quite enough red and lavender and apricot for two foolish women for one morning."

Sir James stared down at his boots. Hardly damp and without a trace of strawberry red. His wife, if he read her correctly, had been calmly passing seditious literature out of the Tolbooth Prison. "Lady Rutledge," he said quietly, "would you wait for us in the breakfast parlor? There should be a fresh pot of coffee on the sideboard. Meg, you'll oblige me by remaining here."

"Why, of course, James. You know I'm always happy to oblige you."

Lady Rutledge gathered up the basket and left the room. Meg occupied herself with her knitting—a shift, Sir James concluded, intended expressly to annoy him. "Margaret," he said firmly. He had to ask her a second time. "Margaret, do you have any idea of what you have done?"

Meg frowned and put down her knitting. "Not precisely, my love." Her brow wrinkled in a cluster of becoming lines. It occurred to her husband that in some things women have the advantage. No one would be so unkind as to place this utterly charming woman in custody. "You won't get into trouble, will you? Robert assured me you would not. It's not that I've done anything beyond bringing Paul a basket of fruit and a half dozen rolls. Compassion, James. You've told me often enough that we must not forget our compassion."

"Nor our good sense."

"What's that, my dear? You really must speak up. In the last few months my hearing's grown uncomfortably dim."

"Margaret, what is it that you brought back from the Tolbooth?"

"Brought back? Oh, odds and ends, my dear. Men's work. You know how it is. They never want to tell us what they're up to. And no wonder," she added with sudden vigor. "It's so impossibly dreary. It would never occur to me to ask what my husband was thinking about. I'm sure my husband is wise enough for both of us. That's what I shall tell the baillie, my dear, if there's any question of a baillie, which perhaps there won't be at all." She rolled up her knitting as though it was prepared to bite her. "Yes, wise enough for both of us. I always rely on you to keep me quite safe. Is there anything else, James? Sophie is returning to the Lescauts. I've assured her you'll bring Mr. Hagerty there as soon as he arrives."

"Yes," Sir James said faintly, forgetting why he had wanted to speak to his wife.

Meg walked toward him, bent over his chair, and planted a firm, sweet kiss on the center of his brow.

Sir James felt himself enveloped in a great welling of comfort and care. Sweet Meg. What would he do without her? He was so used to her being about that he was scarcely aware when she had left the room.

Not that he had quite got over his anger. It wasn't so much that Meg had disobeyed him or even that she had involved herself in God-knew-what danger in this crazy, audacious plan of Lescaut's. No, Sir James acknowledged, what really rankled was that Meg had allowed him no part in this piece of the adventure.

LEWIS HAGERTY LOOKED ABOUT THE UNTIDY PARLOR WITH curiosity. The chairs were covered in a sturdy black fabric that he thought was haircloth, though he'd never actually seen haircloth outside the housekeeper's room. There was a spot on the carpet that was not quite concealed by the tea table. A china doll and a set of lead soldiers were strewn on the hearth rug. Something that looked suspiciously like a baby's rattle peeped out from under the sofa.

In Hagerty's circle people did not live in Old Fishmarket Close. Nor did they live above a print shop. But he was not immune to Anne Lescaut's good humor and Emma Lescaut's disarming smile, nor the high spirits of Emma's daughter and Robert Lescaut's son, nor the arrogant behavior of the pair called Dugal and Amy, who seemed to be not quite servants and not quite anything else.

"We hope to see Sir Nathaniel McAlpin in the next day or two," Sir James told him when the children had disappeared and they were seated in the parlor with Lady Rutledge and Emma and Anne Lescaut. "Matt McAlpin's father, the baillie. You appreciate that it will be a delicate interview."

"Oh, quite."

"As I have been telling Lady Rutledge, I fear Sir Nathaniel is not inclined to listen to a woman's opinion."

"Woman or not," Lady Rutledge said, "I was the one Matt McAlpin came after with a knife, and my opinions in the matter are very strong, Sir James. He's bound to listen to them. Isn't that reasonable, Mr. Hagerty?"

Hagerty stared at Ned's sister-in-law. "Oh, yes, I daresay. Oh, yes. Not that I think old Ned actually intended to do his worst with the knife—one doesn't like to think that of one's friends, especially one that's just pulled in a twenty-incher. Twenty inches. Imagine that. Never got above sixteen myself, though I have an uncle who claims to have once brought in seventeen. Still, his memory isn't of the best, and he's getting on in years." Hagerty shook his head. "Never know about a man, do you? What sets him off, and all that. Poor old Ned."

The awkwardness of the moment was broken by the Lescaut children, who ran into the room, a brown-and-white dog frisking about their heels, and demanded refreshment in the print shop below. They wore inky aprons, and their hands, faces, and stockings were liberally smudged as well. They were skilled typesetters, Emma Lescaut informed him with evident pride, and what they were doing was not to be construed as play.

"I see. You're making a newspaper," Hagerty said, pleased to have found some means of communication with this odd group of strangers.

The girl, whose name was Kirsty, seemed ready enough to talk, but the boy suddenly became withdrawn. They were doing very well, he said. Amy and Dugal were ready to work as soon as they had finished, but his father still needed help and they would appreciate some toast and cocoa as soon as it could be arranged.

They left the room with Anne Lescaut and promises of food and the distinct feeling of secrets in the air. Lady Rutledge leaned forward. Hagerty could feel the pressure of her gaze upon him like a weight, pinning him to the simple straight-backed chair. "Tell us what you know about Matt McAlpin, Mr. Hagerty," she said.

"McAlpin?" Hagerty straightened his cravat. "Hardly anything at all."

"But you've met." Her gaze was unwavering.

"Once or twice. Perhaps a bit more. Ned's known him for years. Didn't go to Cambridge though. Didn't even go to Oxford."

"You met him with Ned."

"Well, yes, he was Ned's friend. Hadn't seen McAlpin in an age though. Not since that time last March."

"Last March?" Lady Rutledge's voice quickened.

"Yes. That is—" Hagerty uncrossed his legs, then recrossed

them. Deuce take it, now he had put his foot in it. The last thing he wanted to talk about was his visit to Ned the previous March.

"Where did you see McAlpin last March, Mr. Hagerty?" Lady Rutledge's eyes bored into him.

"Uh . . ." Hagerty swallowed. "At Ned's. That is, not Tiverton, the house in Lancaster, but—"

"Lancaster?" Lady Rutledge's voice was suddenly as sharp as a newly polished razor. Sir James gave a grunt of satisfaction. Emma Lescaut drew in her breath.

Hagerty looked from one of them to the other. After his visit to the McClarens it had occurred to him that perhaps he was hovering on the edge of something decidedly nasty. He had done his best to ignore the unpleasantness, hoping it would go away. But it clung to him like coal smoke staining clean linen.

"Always thought it was a bit rum," he said. "Ned was deuced insistent that I come stay. McAlpin was the only other one there. Dash it, I never did care for Lancaster."

There was a long silence. Hagerty stared at his boots, noting a rare smudge near the left toe. He was afraid to meet Lady Rutledge's gaze again.

"Perhaps," said Sir James, "you had better start at the beginning."

Deciding there was no help for it, Hagerty did so.

Dugal, who seemed able to slip in and out of the smallest of holes without detection, had distributed most of Paul's flyers by nightfall. Amy entered into the game with unexpected zest and proved resourceful beyond expectation. The gaudy handbills were everywhere, on tenements and shops, tucked onto the points of railings, slipped into unsuspecting market baskets, adorning the finer borders of the houses in New Town, appearing without comment in neat piles in the Registry Office, decorating the muskets of the castle guards.

"A pretty sight," Dugal concluded at dinner that evening. "Livens the town up a bit, that it does." He had returned to Old

Fishmarket Close as directed, the remaining handbills with him for further distribution the next morning.

One of these had already been delivered to the McClarens in Queen Street. Sir James read the document through with pleasure, then scrawled across the front *I think we should talk about this. What time would be convenient?* and addressed it to Sir Nathaniel McAlpin.

Sir James received an answer later that evening, appointing one o'clock the following afternoon for their meeting. Much pleased, he set the missive in a place of honor on the mantel, where he trusted it would inspire Lewis Hagerty to remember everything he could about Lancaster, Ned Rutledge, and Matt McAlpin.

"THAT DAMNABLE TISSUE OF LIES—FORGIVE ME, LADY Rutledge—is all over Edinburgh." Sir Nathaniel McAlpin, an elderly man with a shock of fine white hair, glared from Sophie to Sir James to Hagerty. "There's not a tavern or a shop in the town that isn't holding public readings of the handbill. There's not a man to stand up for my poor Matt. What is the world coming to, I ask you, when any felon can put about any lies he pleases?"

Sophie sat forward on the edge of her chair, white-gloved hands clasped demurely in her lap, heart hammering against her ribs. Sir Nathaniel had been raging about Paul's story ever since they were shown into his rooms in the Queen Charlotte Hotel. Yet his anger had kindled a spark of hope within her. There was something too insistent about it, as though Paul's accusations had touched a nerve that was already raw. As though he feared that if he ceased to rage he would find himself staring at the truth.

Sir Nathaniel pushed himself to his feet with his cane and tottered about the room like a wounded bird uncertain of where to light. "And in our courts of law no less. The Old Tolbooth. Is nothing sacred? I ask you, is nothing to be sacred in this vale of tears? I weep for our land, Sir James. I weep for our land,

Lady Rutledge, Mr. Hagerty." Sir Nathaniel pulled out an enormous square of clean lawn and wiped his head. Sir James helped the baillie back to his chair.

"And the fascinating thing," Hagerty said, putting down the remains of a cup of strong coffee, "is that it was done right under our noses as it were." Sophie longed to tell him to be quiet. "How the devil do you suppose it happened?"

"If I ever learn, Mr. Hagerty, there'll be heads to roll. The press have too much freedom entirely." Sir Nathaniel gave Sir James a fierce look. He must have heard that the McClarens were visitors in Old Fishmarket Close.

Sophie gripped her hands together. "The Tolbooth Story is a true one, Sir Nathaniel. I was there." She went on to tell her story in a quiet voice, not allowing any interruptions. Sir James said that his wife could vouch for the depth and severity of Lady Rutledge's wounds. The hardest point came, as Robert had warned her, when Sir Nathaniel insisted that women were prone to be not quite right in the head when it came to a man for whom they had some tender feelings. The long and the short of it was that they didn't hesitate a moment to tell any barefaced lie they pleased for the man they loved. He did not doubt that Lady Rutledge believed the taradiddle Paul Lescaut had told her, but murder was a serious matter and she had been in no condition to understand what was happening to her. Wasn't that so, Mr. Hagerty?

"What? Oh, yes, can't say I understand it myself. I've known Ned Rutledge for years, and he's always seemed a proper-enough fellow. We were at Cambridge together. And he knows the Brideswells. They're a distant connection of the McClarens." Hagerty nodded sagely at Sir James. "You know how it is, one's friends know one's friends. Man has a devilish good cast. Counts for something, one would think."

"Hmm." Sir Nathaniel frowned. "My son and Ned Rutledge had known each other since they were children. The Rutledges used to visit the Ribards' box in Kinrie. I must say, Ned always struck me as a feckless sort, but he's well-connected."

"Oh, the best. It's a damnable turn of the cards, isn't it?" Hagerty went on. "Printing the story of Ribard and the mill fire and the men who were hanged, let alone Ned's attempt on Lady Rutledge's life. If that's what happened."

Sir Nathaniel stared at him. "You have some doubt about what happened, Mr. Hagerty?"

"Doubt? Well, no, not exactly. One doesn't know quite what to believe, does one? Here I'd known Ned forever. Well, since university. When you get right down to it I didn't know him all that well, but one behaves as though one does, don't you know?"

"I have no doubts at all, Mr. Hagerty." Sir Nathaniel pounded his cane on the floor for emphasis.

Sophie swallowed, trying to force down the knot of anxiety in her chest. "Ned Rutledge was in Lancaster the night of the mill fire, wasn't he, Mr. Hagerty?" she said, steering Lewis Hagerty toward what he had been induced to tell them the day before. "You were in Lancaster visiting Ned at the time, you told us. Matt McAlpin was in Lancaster too. In March of this year."

"Matt? In Lancaster? I doubt that Matt has been in Lancaster in his life." Sir Nathaniel shook his head with undue emphasis.

The denial was too vehement. Sophie's pulse quickened with the first stirrings of triumph. "Oh, but I'm sure he has." She leaned forward. This was it, the crucial test of wills. "There were just the three of them staying at Ned's house. Ned and Matt and Mr. Hagerty. Ned had most particularly asked Matt and Mr. Hagerty to be there." Matt to help set the fire. Hagerty, Sophie suspected, because Ned thought he could be duped into supplying them with an alibi should it be necessary.

Sir Nathaniel got to his feet and moved across the room. "I never heard anything about it."

Sophie followed him with her eyes. "I'm surprised your son didn't tell you. It was a fortunate night for him. He told Mr. Hagerty he'd come into a lot of money. Up in the boughs about it. Some business to do with Ned."

Sir Nathaniel gave Hagerty a sharp look.

Hagerty shrank within himself. "No, sorry, sorry, I don't know what it was about. Hole in the corner kind of thing, not my style at all." He ran a finger round his collar, which was damp with sweat. "Wish I'd never accepted the invitation. Dreary sort of place, Lancaster."

There was a long silence. "Is it possible, Sir Nathaniel," Sophie said in a quiet voice, "that Mr. Lescaut's story is true?"

The baillie turned away and stared out the windows.

"Sir Nathaniel," she said again. "Matt did go to Lancaster, didn't he? You know he did. You knew something was wrong about the visit. That's why you didn't want to admit it to us."

For a moment the room was very still. Sir Nathaniel stood silhouetted against the afternoon light. His shoulders were set in a solid, uncompromising line. Slowly they seemed to wilt. At last he turned. His pale blue eyes were rheumy. "I fear," he said in a quavering voice, "that I have not always been proud of my son."

The story, when it came, was simple enough, and the baillie, to his credit, was an honest man. Matt was constantly in debt, and his father had bailed him out on more than one occasion, but had refused to do so again. "We had a fierce argument," the old man said. "In the end he found the money he needed. It was mine."

Sir Nathaniel put his hands over his eyes as though to shut out the light. "I knew something had happened in Lancaster. Yes, Matt was there in March. He'd visited Rutledge more than once. He was too ebullient when he returned from this particular trip. He paid back the money he had taken from me, and our quarrel was as though it had never been."

Sophie reached out her hand and clasped his own. "It was Ned's doing, Sir Nathaniel, not your son's. Ned planned and set the fire and hired Matt to help him. There was a large insurance settlement, and Ned knew how to be grateful."

She rubbed Sir Nathaniel's hand with a soft, gentle motion, as she might with Dugal or Amy. "It was a dreadful temptation.

It was even more dreadful, what happened later in the alley in Kinrie. They had been trapped by their own actions by that time. They feared they would be taken up for what they had done."

Sir James got to his feet and clapped a hand on the baillie's shoulder. "I think, Sir Nathaniel," he said, "that it's time you had a talk with Paul Lescaut."

Sir Nathaniel spent the best part of the afternoon with Paul and later with Sophie. At the end of it the warrant for Paul's arrest was withdrawn and a warrant issued in its place to hold Ned Rutledge for questioning about the attack on Sophie Rutledge and the events that led to the death of Matt McAlpin.

NED FLUNG HIMSELF BACK IN THE BRONZE DAMASK CHAIR. "The story can't stand. No one will believe it. Lescaut's stalemated. He's ruined himself with you, with the marquise, with Charlotte. Sophie will run back to Rossmere like a whipped puppy."

"Go home, Ned," Daniel said for perhaps the dozenth time that evening. His gaze moved to the copy of Paul's handbill that lay between them on the polished rosewood of his desk. "Everyone's talking about the Tolbooth Story."

"All the better. The more it's talked of, the less it's believed." Ned tossed off the last of his glass of brandy. He'd been drinking steadily since he arrived at Rossmere an hour ago, clutching the handbill, insisting it was nothing to fear, yet refusing to stop talking about it.

Daniel took a sip from his own glass, taking the time to appreciate the subtle flavor. This bottle was one of the better years in his cellar. "The more it's talked of, the more it's wondered if there's something to believe."

Ned reached for the decanter and refilled his glass. "The Marquis de Ribard, afraid of a common scribbler? What's happened to you, Ribard?"

Ned's hand was shaking. Drops of the precious liquid spattered onto the Aubusson carpet. Daniel wondered once more what had possessed him to give his last beloved child to this arrogant, panicked puppy. Ned was a fool and a coward. Paul was neither. He had surprised Daniel at every turn. Had Paul put everything he knew into the Tolbooth Story, or were there still some cards he was holding back?

Daniel looked down at his desk. A miniature of Charlotte, Paul's mother, was hidden at the back of the center drawer. A foolish, sentimental thing to have kept, but Daniel had not been able to part with it. He could hear Charlotte's light, musical voice. *The boy's so like you.* She had been more right than either of them knew.

Daniel tapped his fingers against the handbill. Clever little bastard, his son. He could be proud to sire a man of that understanding. But it was too late for regrets. Paul would do anything for Sophie and would destroy Daniel in the process if he had to. The only solution was to destroy the pair of them first.

"Ribard?" Ned was staring into his glass.

"Hmm?"

"There's no real danger, is there? Of it all coming out?"

Daniel raised his eyes from the handbill and looked at the flushed, overheated face of his daughter's fiancé. "It *has* come out, Ned. Everyone knows the story."

"But it will blow over. Won't it?"

Daniel shrugged. "You want certainty in this life? There's none, Ned. You're man enough to know that."

A calculating look passed across Ned's face. "Because we're all involved, aren't we? Me. You. Even Charlotte."

There was no mirror in the study, so Daniel could not see his reflection, but he knew his face had turned white with rage. The whelp. Ned would drag Charlotte through his own filth to save his quivering skin. Daniel would kill him first.

"You're involved, Ned. I'm not. Nor is Charlotte. You've never learned that, have you, my boy? How to protect what's yours." Daniel pushed back his chair with deliberation. "But even in your case I daresay it won't come to that. Whose word have they got? Yours? A scruffy journalist's? Be a man, Ned.

And so help me God, take care of Charlotte or you'll have nothing worth living for." Daniel collected Ned's cloak, which had been flung over a chair back.

"Where are you going?" Ned asked.

"To bed." Daniel tossed him the cloak. "You're going home, where you shall endeavor to behave as normally as possible. You're a millowner. Get about tomorrow. Show yourself. You have nothing to hide."

Ned stood and fastened the cloak. The black folds emphasized his blond hair and lent him stature. He was a handsome devil, Daniel would give him that. No doubt that was why Charlotte was so besotted with him. He smiled broadly at his future father-in-law. "Yes. Yes, of course. Nothing to hide."

Daniel remembered now why Ned had seemed a useful partner in the past. At least his moments of panic were brief. And he was conveniently positioned to take the blame if it came to that. It was beginning to look as though it might.

Daniel walked Ned to the door of the study, but did not accompany him into the hall. He could hear Charlotte calling to Ned from the stairs. Poor Charlie. She would be terribly hurt if the marriage did not take place. Daniel hated to deny her anything. But she would recover. Daniel had no intention of being stopped by a prospective son-in-law who was proving less than satisfactory. Or by a bastard of a son who was proving all too clever.

IT WAS GROWING DARK WHEN PAUL RETURNED WITH Sophie to Old Fishmarket Close after their long interview with Sir Nathaniel. Hagerty had already set off for the Brideswells, where he would presumably dine on the story of the past two days for the rest of the month. Lady Margaret and Sir James dined with the Lescauts—and exceedingly well tŏo, as Sir James was at some pains to point out—and Paul told them all the incredible story of how a scruffy journalist had been imprisoned in the Tolbooth and had come out to tell the tale.

Sir James, Paul noted with amusement, saw it as a private triumph. In her own way Lady Margaret did as well. She forbade her husband to say one word in the future about a single one of her baskets. Paul felt as weary as he ever had in his life, but he was suffused by an inner peace. He exchanged a look with Anne and thought that perhaps she understood.

Sophie, holding Fenella, seemed blissfully happy. When Paul had stepped from the prison she had seized his hands in both her own. Her touch had been like an embrace. But there had been no chance to speak of anything but the needs of the present. There was no point, Paul reminded himself, in speaking of anything more. The present was all they shared.

"What will you do now?" Sir James asked.

Paul leaned back in his chair. They were all gathered in the parlor, the curtains drawn, the lamplight warm and bright. But Paul was under no illusions about their safety. Daniel could attack them here as easily as he could slash the paisley wallpaper and rip the chintz curtains to shreds. "Confront the Marquis de Ribard," he said.

"Oh, surely not." Lady Margaret dropped her knitting on the floor. "It would be much too dangerous, even if Sir Nathaniel has withdrawn the warrant."

"Ye canna," Dugal said at the same time. He was sitting at the foot of Paul's chair. He had scarcely left Paul's side all evening. "Ribard will kill ye for certain."

"Such touching faith you have in our abilities." Paul rested his hand on the boy's head. "I don't think Ribard will make another attempt on our lives. Anything he does to hurt Sophie or me now will only confirm the Tolbooth Story."

Robert frowned. "He's not one to collapse under pressure. Don't tell me you'd rely on his good behavior."

"Not a whit." Sophie shifted Fenella on her shoulder. "But I rely on Jeremy Craymere. We won't meet Uncle Daniel at Rossmere. We'll meet him in Jemmy's office in Lancaster, with a clerk keeping record of all that transpires. Even

Uncle Daniel will have to put the past behind him in Lancaster."

"Then what?" Amy asked from the hearth rug where she sat with Kirsty and David.

Sophie patted Fenella's back. "I offer to give up any claim on his property if the attempts on our lives cease."

"That's all?" Dugal stared at her. "Ye're givin' up?"

Paul could understand the boy's indignation. And yet, as Sophie had pointed out to him more than once this afternoon, bargaining with Ribard was the best course of action open to them. The only course of action. Save for killing Ribard with his bare hands, which was tempting but probably futile.

"We can't go on running from Uncle Daniel," Sophie said. "We don't have enough proof to go to the authorities. We have to force him to come to terms with us."

"And if he does?" Emma looked up from Alison, who was nursing industriously. "Can you trust him to abide by the agreement?"

"I don't trust Daniel de Ribard farther than my line of sight. If that." Paul realized his hands were balled into fists. He forced himself to unclench them. "I'll write another story and leave copies to be published if anything happens to either of us. Ribard will know that."

Sophie settled Fenella in the crook of her arm. "Uncle Daniel has one weak point. Charlotte. I don't think he'll risk her learning more of the past than she already knows."

"What does she know?" Anne asked. "She sounds like a clever girl. She can't have been kept entirely in ignorance."

A shadow of pain crossed Sophie's face. "I don't know. That's a demon she must face in her own way and her own time. But I have to be sure she learns the truth before she ties herself to Ned."

Robert met Paul's gaze. "Do you want me to come with you?"

"We'll both go." Sir James's voice boomed with enthusiasm. "By God, we'll show Ribard a force to be reckoned with."

Their simple readiness to help touched Paul more than he would have thought possible. It was a moment before he trusted himself to speak. "No," he said. "Thank you, but no. If it comes to sheer numbers, Ribard has far greater forces than we can hope to muster. You'll do better here, threatening to raise a ruckus if we don't return. Besides," he added, forcing a note of lightness into his voice, "Emma and Lady Margaret wouldn't forgive us if you came to harm."

"Nonsense." Lady Margaret reached into her knitting bag for more yarn. "I'm sure you wouldn't let it come to that. Not that James isn't very well able to look after himself, for of course you are, my love."

Emma sent Paul a look that was at once needle-sharp and warm as sunlight. "*I* won't forgive you if you or Sophie come to harm, Paul Lescaut."

"I'll see to that." Dugal sat back on his heels. "I'm no' stayin' behind."

"Oh, but you must," Sophie said. "For Fenella's sake. I can't take her to Lancaster, and I know she'll be more comfortable if you're with her." She looked at Emma. "I rely on you to take my daughter into your keeping."

"Always." Emma stretched out her hand to her friend.

"You'll take our carriage of course," Lady Margaret said. "William Coachman will see you safely to Lancaster."

"And we'll print any more stories that have to be printed, Uncle Paul," Kirsty said. David nodded vigorously. Pauline, lying beside them, raised her head and wagged her tail as though she understood the situation if not the words.

Sir James picked up his coffee cup and frowned into the dregs. "I don't know, Lescaut. It all sounds a bit mad."

The room fell silent. Paul knew that his family were a step ahead of Sir James. Anne's knuckles had gone white. Emma was holding Alison tightly. The children looked at Sir James with surprise, as though they were too polite to point out that he had stated the obvious.

It was Sophie who put it into words. "Oh, it is. Quite mad." She met Paul's gaze, then looked back at Sir James. "But you see, madness is our only hope."

Chapter 27

MOONLIGHT SLANTED ACROSS SOPHIE'S FACE AS THE McClarens' carriage swayed around a curve. Her lips were drawn, her eyes shadowed with worry. The same worry had gnawed at Paul since they left Edinburgh that afternoon. He resisted the impulse to take Sophie in his arms. Since his release from prison he had made no attempt to resume their physical relationship.

"She'll be all right," he said. "She has Robert and Emma and Anne and the McClarens. Not to mention Dugal and Amy."

Sophie met his gaze across the width of the carriage. "That's what I keep telling myself. But if anything goes wrong—"

"I won't let Ribard or Rutledge hurt you, Sophie. I swear it."

A smile drifted across her face. "Even you can't promise that, Paul. But I have no intention of letting them hurt me. We're both going back to Fenella."

The words were a shock at once sweet and painful. Paul looked at her, shaken by the perfect unison of their thoughts. For the first time in his life, the treacherous, seductive word *we* applied to him. If caring made a family, for this moment they were a family.

It wouldn't, couldn't last, whatever the outcome of their journey to Lancaster. But—however briefly—he had something he had never hoped to have. Something he had never let himself admit he wanted. He held out his arm.

Sophie's breath left her on a harsh sigh. Then she closed the distance between them and his arm was hard around her. She pressed her face into his shoulder. He pushed back the hood of her cloak and brushed his lips against her hair.

The carriage lurched to one side. The horses neighed in fear. They skidded to a halt and the carriage whipped across the road. The wheels grated against the dirt. Solid ground slipped from under them. Paul crashed into the silk-lined wall of the carriage. Sophie fell against him.

He ran his hand up her arm. "Are you all right?"

She nodded.

The carriage door was tugged open. William Coachman's face appeared in the drunkenly angled doorway. He had unhooked one of the exterior lamps. The light revealed the concern in his eyes. "Lady Rutledge? Mr. Lescaut? Ye're no' hurt, are ye?"

"Just shaken," Paul said. "What happened?"

"We lost a wheel. Canna think how. I checked the carriage myself first thin' this mornin'. The horses be fine, but we've landed in a ditch. Can ye get down if I lower the steps?"

Paul climbed down to the rough ground of the ditch and helped Sophie from the carriage. The front left wheel was firmly wedged in the rubble. The back left wheel had come off entirely and was lying several feet away.

William knelt to inspect the damage. "Bloody hell."

"What?" Paul asked. It had to be bad for the coachman to use such language in Sophie's presence.

"The axle's been cut."

Sophie drew in her breath.

"It wasn't an accident?" Paul asked.

"No accident would be this clean, sir. It took just one jolt to knock the wheel off."

A cloud drifted across the moon so that the only light was the glow of the carriage lamps. Wind whistled through the trees overhanging the road and made the carriage shake. Paul put his arm around Sophie. "Check the other wheels."

A few moments later William cursed again. "The left front axle's been cut as well. The wheel's only on now 'cause it be wedged i' the dirt. It's a miracle they didna both come off at once. I' they had—"

"We'd have overturned." Sophie's voice was matter-of-fact. Danger had become part of the fabric of their lives.

William straightened up. "I'm sorry, my lady, sir. I could swear no one got near the carriage. But I should ha' been more careful."

"It's not your fault, William." Paul pulled Sophie closer. He'd protect her from unseen dangers with his body if necessary. "How far to the nearest town?"

"We should be little more than a mile out o' Peebles. I'll ride one o' the horses and bring back a carriage for ye and Lady Rutledge."

Paul hesitated. It would be dangerous to wait in the carriage, but even more dangerous for Sophie to walk along the open road. He was sure Daniel's spies had sabotaged the carriage. But they couldn't have known exactly where the wheels would come off. It was unlikely they had planned an ambush.

Paul and William pushed the carriage back onto the road and unharnessed one of the horses. William set off for Peebles. Paul helped Sophie back into the carriage and reached under the seat for the brace of pistols Sir James had given him. He handed one to Sophie. "Do you know how to use it?"

Her mouth twisted in a dry smile. "Uncle Daniel taught Charlie and me. I learned to be a fair shot, though I used to be afraid of guns."

Not surprising, when she had seen her father take his life with one. Paul's stomach clenched, a familiar reflex. The past continued to intrude in every corner of their lives. He settled back, his pistol at the ready. "I'll hire a carriage in Peebles and go on to Lancaster. William can take you back to Edinburgh."

"No." The moonlight was streaming through the windows again, revealing the familiar defiance in Sophie's eyes. "We've come this far. I'm not turning back now."

Images raced through Paul's mind. Sophie thrown from the carriage and lying sprawled in the road, her body broken and twisted. Sophie bleeding from a knife in the back, felled by a bullet, bludgeoned like Agatha Burden. "I thought we had

Ribard stalemated," he said. "But he must have known there'd be rumors if we died in a carriage accident. He was willing to risk it."

"Uncle Daniel doesn't take idle risks."

"Exactly. So there must be more to the story than what I wrote. Something we haven't discovered yet. Something that's worth the risk of killing us to keep secret."

"All the more reason for us both to go to Lancaster." Sophie's gaze was as unyielding as the metal of the pistol barrel.

"Damn it, Sophie." Fear made his voice rough. "You said I couldn't protect you. You were right. I'm no bloody hero."

Something sparked in her eyes that made his heart lurch. "If you aren't a hero, I don't know who is," she said.

There was a strange tightness in his chest that did not come from fear. "Don't try to change the subject," he said. "Daniel's like a wounded tiger. He'll be ready to pounce."

"He's proved he can find us wherever we are. I'd rather go to him than have him come after me. And if he's going to attack me again, I don't want to be in Edinburgh with Fenella." Sophie settled the pistol in her lap. Her fingers did not tremble as she gripped the gleaming metal. "I set this in motion, Paul. I have to see it through to the end."

He wanted to enfold her in his arms and cover her face with kisses that would ward off danger. He wanted to sweep her off to a place where his father's machinations couldn't touch her. But such a place did not exist. And it wasn't in her nature to hide. He couldn't try to change her. He didn't want to do so. She wouldn't be the woman he loved if he did.

He nodded. "We hire a fresh carriage and continue on to Lancaster."

"Both of us," Sophie said.

"Both of us."

REFLECTED TORCHLIGHT TURNED THE LUNE RIVER TO molten fire. The road along the river was clogged with marchers, slowing Paul and Sophie's hired carriage to a stand-still. The air was thick with shouts, but Sophie could not make out the words. She turned from the window to Paul.

"Lancaster has reached the boiling point," he said.

Now she could make out one word, shouted over and over amid the jumble of sound. *Justice.* Fear bubbled up from the wellspring of childhood memory. "It's like France," she said, clenching her hands. "I was stopped by a mob once. In a carriage with my parents. I must have been about three."

"I joined a crowd of protesters at the Tuileries once. I was eight."

She looked into his dark eyes, feeling the weight of a past that at once bound them together and pulled them apart. For a moment they were comte's daughter and bastard serving boy again, aristo and revolutionary. She had thought they'd put their different backgrounds behind them, but the experiences of a lifetime could not be so easily set aside.

The shouts grew louder, swelling on a tide of anger. She heard the words *Rutledge Three.* She turned back to the window. More marchers were spilling out of a side street. They held a crude wooden gallows overhead. A straw-filled figure dangled from the noose. Like a Guy Fawkes, save that it had hair of bright yellow yarn.

"Ned," Sophie said. "They're hanging Ned in effigy. And shouting for justice for the men hanged for the fire. They must have heard about the Tolbooth Story. Mother of God, Paul, what have we let loose?"

"This has been smoldering for months. We revealed an injustice. It was Ned who did the damage."

Sophie knew he was right, but the anger on the torchlit faces sent a chill through the folds of her cloak. She feared it was an anger that could be vented on any well-dressed people in a fine carriage. Thank God Fenella was safe in Edinburgh. Yet Sophie's arms ached to hold her daughter. Her breasts ached as well. She'd had to squeeze her milk into a basin when they changed horses at the last posting house.

The main body of the procession moved by, and their carriage was able to inch forward. At last William drew up in front of Jemmy's house. The street was quiet save for a few pedestrians and a sporting phaeton, but the wind carried fragments of shouting from the river. Relief washed over Sophie as Jemmy's manservant admitted them to the candlelit security of the entrance hall. Then her insides twisted with shame, because the anger she was hiding from had been stirred by her class, her family. And she knew it was an anger that was all too well justified.

Jemmy was dining alone in a snug oak-paneled room. He pushed back his chair and sprang to his feet when the servant announced them. "Sophie. Lescaut." He adjusted his coat and brushed a crumb from the lapel, the boy Sophie remembered giving way to Craymere the solicitor. "You're just in time to join me for dinner. Two extra places, Philip."

"We're sorry to barge in on you, Jemmy," Sophie said when they were seated and the servant had withdrawn. "You're the only friend we have in Lancaster. But it looks as if word of our story has got here before us."

Jemmy nodded. "Copies of the *Edinburgh Leader* have been circulating for the past two days. The town's fair gone wild. I hope you appreciate what you've unleashed, Lescaut."

"The truth." Paul took a swallow of wine. Sophie noted the way the claret glowed in the candlelight. Bloodred, the color of revolution.

Jemmy pushed a piece of beefsteak around his plate. "In theory I'm all for reform. But I confess I have a horror of mobs."

"So do I." Paul set down his glass. "I didn't foresee this, but if I had to do it again, I wouldn't conceal Ribard and Rutledge's crimes to control the masses." He paused. "We have to learn to live with the consequences of what we set in motion."

Sophie caught the edge of bitterness in his voice. She knew

he was thinking not of the events tonight but of those twenty-three years ago.

Jemmy cut into his Yorkshire pudding. "This storm's been brewing for months. If you hadn't written the Tolbooth Story, something else would have loosed the torrent. I take it you meant to checkmate Ribard."

"We thought we had." Paul described the carriage accident.

A growing frown darkened Jemmy's face as he listened. "You still plan to confront Ribard?"

Paul nodded. "There must be something else Ribard is afraid could come out. The trick will be to bluff him into thinking we know it already."

Jemmy shook his head. "It's a bloody great risk, Lescaut."

Paul's mouth twisted in a sardonic smile. "Every move we make is a risk. We're trying to take the most calculated risks possible."

"We'll send word to Uncle Daniel asking him to come to your office tomorrow." Sophie was methodically mashing the peas on her plate. Her stomach was too tense for food. "There's a limit to what even Uncle Daniel can do in front of witnesses."

"If you're sure, I'll do anything I can to help." A smile crossed Jemmy's face. "I must admit it would be a pleasure to watch Ribard put on the defensive."

"The more we can learn before the meeting the better." Paul sat back in his chair. "That's where Ned Rutledge comes into play. Where is he? Have the protesters sent him running off to Tiverton Park?"

"No, he's at his house in Church Street. Too proud or too foolish to be afraid."

Sophie speared a piece of carrot. "Ned's both proud and foolish. But I'd lay odds he's bloody terrified."

"And angry." Paul's eyes brightened, like a hound picking up the scent. "Frightened, angry men are prone to talk."

Jemmy's brows rose. "You think Rutledge will talk to you?"

"If we can convince him Ribard is going to throw him to the wolves. Which, if I know Ribard, is exactly what he'll do. Rutledge is more a liability than an asset to him now. Our best chance of getting proof of their crimes is to break one of them, and Rutledge is infinitely more breakable than Ribard."

"So you'll summon Rutledge tomorrow as well?" Jemmy asked.

Paul shook his head. "Better to catch him in the midst of the protests, when he's at his most vulnerable. We'll call on him tonight."

Jemmy looked from Paul to Sophie. "Both of you?"

Sophie fixed Paul with a hard stare. "Both of us."

A FLARE OF ORANGE ILLUMINED THE NIGHT SKY. ACRID smoke choked the air. More fire, and this not from torches. There was a sound of splintering glass. Sophie peered into the shadows at the end of the lane. The noise had come from up ahead.

Paul's grip tightened on her arm. "It looks as if the protest has become a riot."

They were on foot. It would be difficult for a carriage to pass through the crowded streets, Paul had said. Besides, the mob was not on the side of those in carriages. Now Sophie sensed his hesitation. "We're halfway to Ned's," she said. "It's as dangerous to turn back as to go forward."

Paul glanced up and down the lane, nodded, and drew her forward.

They rounded a corner and stepped into chaos. Shop fronts on either side of the street had gone up in flames. Shards of glass littered the street, sparkling in the firelight. Silver, porcelain, and bolts of cloth were being hauled or tossed through the smashed windows. Knives slashed through fabric. Dishes and tableware crashed to the ground.

Men stripped off their coats to use as makeshift sacks. Women filled their aprons with loot and tucked knives and forks down the front of their bodices. Children younger than Dugal darted about picking up the leavings.

Sophie stared down at an evening glove trimmed with ivory ribbon that lay forgotten in a puddle of damp. "I used to shop here. This was my favorite street in Lancaster."

There was a fresh crash as a torch was flung through another window. Paul released her arm and gripped her hand. "It's no place for you tonight. Let's try the next street over."

They ran across the street, skirting two women arguing over a bolt of silk and a man stumbling along with a bulging pillow-case slung over his shoulder. A dark figure lunged at them out of the shadows.

Sophie stumbled backward, catching her heel on her cloak. Paul steadied her.

"Here now, that's mine." The flames were reflected in the glistening sweat on the man's forehead. He gestured to a silver teapot that lay a foot off, its spout bent from being hurled to the cobblestones.

"By all means." Paul pulled Sophie against him. "If you're wise you'll take it home while you can still get through the streets."

The man snatched up the teapot, one eye on Paul. "What's it to you?"

"Just some friendly advice."

"And don't forget, justice for the Rutledge Three," Sophie said.

The man's face relaxed. He laughed and lifted the teapot in a gesture of camaraderie.

A gasp of pain sounded from farther down the street. Sophie saw a man fall to the ground as she and Paul ran past. The next street over was quieter, but even the quietest parts of Lancaster bubbled with life tonight. Someone had broken the lock on a bakeshop and was throwing loaves of bread into the street. The air smelled of smoke and spilled wine and excitement. But beneath the wild glee Sophie felt anger like a physical force in the air. Small knots of people ran by, echoing the cries of "Justice" that could still be heard from the river.

She pulled Paul down a narrow lane that cut through to Ned's street. Three men loomed in front of them, seeming to come out of nowhere. A sweaty hand seized her cloak. "What have we here? You're a pretty one."

Paul's fist slammed into the man's jaw, knocking him to the ground.

"Christ, Billy, keep your hands to yourself." One of the man's companions turned to Paul. "Sorry, mate. Billy's a bit the worse for—" He stopped, staring at Sophie. Sophie realized her cloak had fallen back. She was wearing a dress of Emma's in a plain pale gray, but it was of fine twilled sarcenet and her pearls were round her throat. "Right fine dressed you be," the man said.

"The mistress's castoffs." Paul's hand went behind his back. He had put Sir James's pistol in the pocket beneath the flap of his coat before they left Jemmy's.

"Oh, Lord." The third man was also staring at Sophie. "It's Lady Rutledge."

Sophie looked back at him. The torch he carried cast a red-orange glow over his face. He had close-set eyes, a wide nose, a full-lipped mouth. It was not a face she recognized. Most of the Rutledge workers had been as faceless to her as they were nameless. "I'm sorry—" she said.

"John Turner. I worked in the mill, Lady Rutledge."

"Rutledge?" Billy scrambled to his feet.

The name was a snarl of loathing, like the lash of a whip. Sophie reached into the pocket of her cloak and felt the reassuring weight of the second pistol. The walls of the houses on either side of the lane pressed close, offering little chance of escape. "My husband and I were living apart."

"What does that matter? You're one of them." Billy's eyes narrowed. "I remember you, sweeping down the street in your fine carriage. My wife's brother died for your husband's crimes."

His eyes burned into her. For all the dangers of the past weeks she had never been face to face with such blinding hatred. He hated her because she was a Rutledge, because she shared Tom's name. She felt an hysterical desire to laugh, yet sweat prickled her forehead.

Paul moved in front of her. "If you've heard the story, you know Ned Rutledge is more of a threat to Lady Rutledge than to anyone."

Doubt flickered in Billy's eyes. "Quality don't threaten each other."

"Nay, it's true, Billy." John Turner put a hand on Billy's arm. "Lady Rutledge was asking questions. Ned Rutledge tried to have her killed to keep her quiet. I saw it in print with my own eyes."

"Didn't read it, did you?"

"You know I can't read. But I heard it read down at the Lion."

"So did I," said the third man.

"I wrote it." Paul's voice was quiet, yet strong as steel. He proceeded to quote the first paragraph of the Tolbooth Story word for word.

"Blimey, that's it. The very words." John stared at Paul with wide eyes. "We're in the presence of a bleedin' hero, Billy."

"Gullible, John, that's what you be." Billy's lower lip jutted out. "If he wrote it, why—"

"Shut up, Billy. He has more important things to do than answer your questions." The third man grabbed Billy's free arm.

John tightened his own grip on Billy. "Best be off, sir. Billy turns nasty when he takes too much to drink." He made an awkward attempt at a bow while still hanging on to Billy. "Apologies, Lady Rutledge."

"Thank you." It was all Sophie had time to say. Paul took her hand and they ran down the lane.

They emerged in a wider, treelined street of three- and four-story houses with ornate front doors and neat area railings. An eerie quiet hung in the air. Curtains were drawn, doors and windows no doubt bolted. The looters and protesters had not found their way to this part of the city. Yet.

Sophie stopped and looked up at Paul in the glow of a street-lamp. "He hated me. I'm not sure it would have made a differ-ence if you'd convinced him I wasn't on Ned's side. He hated me for what I was. Am." A chill washed over her that was part fear, part shame. "He has a right to."

Paul's fingers clenched her hand. "Hatred breeds ugliness."

The yellow gaslight fell over his face, and she knew he was seeing the ugliness he thought was within himself. "Paul—" she said, trying to break through the fog of the past.

His touch eased. "Which way to Ned's?"

The sandstone house that Tom and Ned's father had built for his wife shortly after their marriage stood in splendor on the street corner. It looked as still as the other houses, though lamplight showed through chinks in the curtains. Only as they climbed the steps to the Corinthian portico did Sophie realize she was breathing hard and there was a pain in her side. They must have run half the way from Jemmy's. She paused on the top step to smooth her cloak. Then she turned to Paul and straightened his neckcloth. "There. You'll do. Ready to face the enemy?"

He pulled her to him and gave her a quick, hard kiss. "If it comes to it, run and don't worry about me."

Sophie kissed him back. "I won't leave you, Paul," she said and rang the bell.

After a longer interval than usual the door was opened by one of the two footmen Ned employed. "Hullo, George." So-phie moved past him into the hall. "We've come to see Mr. Ned. I mean Sir Edward. Is he at home?"

"No. That is, yes, but—" George glanced about the hall. "He wasn't expecting you, Lady Rutledge."

"Of course not. Mr. Lescaut and I have come to Lancaster unexpectedly." Sophie crossed the black-and-white marble floor. "The library? Or the drawing room?"

"The study. But . . . he gave orders that he's not to be disturbed."

"Who's he with?" Paul asked.

George turned as though to give a denial. Paul's gaze stopped him. "Miss Charlotte called a half hour ago."

Sophie drew a breath of surprise and alarm. "Thank you, George," she said, moving to the study. "We'll announce ourselves."

The study was at the back of the house behind the library, a small room heavy with brass and mahogany. Sophie pulled open the door to be greeted by hot, close air and her cousin's desperate voice. "In God's name, Ned, you have to explain. Why would Mr. Lescaut write such lies?"

Charlotte was clutching the blue superfine lapels of Ned's coat. Her face was upturned, her gaze clinging to his face.

Sophie stepped into the room. "They weren't lies, Charlie."

Charlotte turned. She wore a crumpled brown velvet riding habit. A beaver hat slipped from her hair, which was even more unruly than usual. She put a hand to her head, as though to order her thoughts. Then she cried out, ran across the room, and threw her arms around Sophie. "Thank God you're all right. But—" She drew back, her face echoing her question.

Paul followed Sophie into the room. "Don't tell me you haven't told her the whole, Rutledge. Surely there should be no secrets between husband and wife."

"I don't believe I gave you leave to enter my house, Lescaut." Ned's face was a pasty white and his straw-colored hair clung damply to his forehead, but he held himself with his usual careless arrogance.

"He says he's going away." Charlotte gripped Sophie by the arms. "He says I can't come with him. He won't tell me anything else."

"Running away?" Paul leaned against a high-backed chair. "I see your point, Rutledge. But surely you realize the authorities will find you wherever you go. Ribard will see to that. He needs a scapegoat. You won't be able to cover your tracks."

Paul glanced at the fireplace, where a fire was burning despite the warmth of the evening. Sophie realized there were sheets of foolscap amid the coals.

"Sophie." Charlotte's fingers dug into Sophie's arms. "Someone sent a copy of that handbill to Rossmere today. *Papa* wouldn't talk to me about it. Why did Mr. Lescaut say such terrible things?"

"Because they're true." Sophie made each word as clear as a pistol shot. "Ned and Uncle Daniel tried to have Mr. Lescaut and me killed."

"No." Charlotte backed toward the fireplace, her gloved hand pressed to her mouth. *"No."*

"I didn't want you to find out like this, Charlie. But it's true, every word of it. Why in God's name would I tell such a story if it wasn't?"

Charlotte's gaze darted from Sophie to Ned. The anguished confusion in her eyes tore at Sophie's heart.

"Don't listen to her." Ned's voice was strained. "She'd tell any lie to save Lescaut. The blackguard seduced her."

"Actually it was more the other way around." Sophie folded her hands, conscious of the reassuring weight of the pistol in her pocket. "I wouldn't lie to you, Charlie. You have to believe that."

Paul leaned toward Charlotte, arms resting on the ruby velvet of the chair back. "Your cousin has little cause to like me, Miss Ribard. She became my ally only because we were both threatened. She wouldn't lightly turn to a stranger over her family."

Charlotte backed up another step, as though to distance herself from the revelations.

Ned moved toward her. "Charlie—"

"No." Charlotte put out a hand to stop him.

Ned's eyes went wide with astonishment. "Good God, you can't believe—"

"I don't know what I believe."

A taut silence gripped the room. The clock on the mantel struck the hour with meticulous precision, punctuating the stillness. A coal fell against the grate and sent a puff of smoke into the room. It was a moment before Sophie realized the door had opened. She turned and found herself looking at her uncle.

Chapter 28

Sophie braced herself for a surge of fear. Instead, cold anger shot through her, driving out the heat from the fire.

Daniel paused on the threshold and took in the four people in the room. Unlike Charlotte, he showed no signs of a hasty journey from Rossmere. He was dressed for dinner in a close-fitting black coat and cream-colored breeches, and his chestnut hair was smooth and unruffled. But there was a strain to the set of his face, as though it took an extra effort to maintain his customary control.

"Well." Daniel pushed the door shut behind him. "I didn't expect such a gathering. Is this why you ran off so abruptly, Charlotte? To meet Sophie?"

"No." Charlotte lifted her chin. "I came to learn the truth. You wouldn't tell me."

"I see." Daniel turned to Paul. "And you, Lescaut? Have you come to apologize for your slanders?"

"The truth requires no apology, Ribard." Paul's gaze met Daniel's. Tension tightened the air between them. "We came to see Rutledge. Just in time, as it turns out. He's on the point of leaving Lancaster. Perhaps leaving the country."

"Ned?" Daniel lifted a brow. "Surely you realize running away is the last thing a falsely accused man should do."

"It's all very well for you to talk." The words burst from Ned with the sting of venom. "No one's trying to arrest you."

"The conceit of a mad Highlander crazed with grief for the death of his son. He couldn't make the charges stick against Lescaut, so he turned on you. Go to Edinburgh and tell the truth, my boy. The charges will be dropped in no time."

"I wouldn't count on it." Paul's gaze bore into Ned. "It's no longer just your word against Sophie's and mine. There's Hagerty's evidence as well. He may be slow, but he sticks to his story. It was a mistake to involve him, Rutledge. He's not as much your dupe as you think."

"Ned—" Charlotte's voice held a plea.

Sophie moved toward her cousin. "Ned attacked Mr. Lescaut. He tried to knife me. Uncle Daniel tried to make me think I was mistaken, but I know I wasn't. I'd gone to Kinrie to confront Ned about his meeting with Jack Burden. I went to the hunting box. Ned was staying with the McAlpins. I sent word to him and he arranged to meet me at the fair." Forgotten details came back with crystal clarity as she spoke. "We were to meet in a lane away from the center of town. I was waiting for Ned when Matt McAlpin attacked me. I ran down the lane. There was a man near the far end."

She was back in Kinrie again, the cobblestones beneath her feet, her chest tight with terror, the evening sun silhouetting the man at the end of the lane. "His back was to me, but I thought if I shouted loud enough surely he'd hear. I screamed. He turned."

She broke off. The last of the veils was rent from her mind. The memory slammed into her, leaving her shaking and winded. "You." She whirled round to face Daniel. "You were there. In Kinrie."

"Sophie?" Paul's voice was sharp with inquiry.

"He was the man standing at the mouth of the lane," Sophie said, her eyes not leaving Daniel's face. "He turned and looked at me. Then he walked away."

Daniel's expression did not waver. "You're imagining things, *ma chère*."

"No. I've tried to forget it. I tried so hard I forgot everything else as well." Sophie looked at Paul. "McAlpin grabbed me and pushed me against the wall. That must have been when you and Dugal saw me." She turned back to Daniel. "I wrote you and Aunt Louisa that I was going to Kinrie to see

Ned. You must have set off for Kinrie at once yourself." She thought back to those moments in the passage outside the chapel. Ned's voice echoed in her head. *You were the one who said we couldn't afford to let her live.* "You were afraid I was getting too close to the truth. You told Ned I'd have to be killed. Did you help him arrange it with McAlpin? Were you there to be sure nothing went wrong? I'm surprised you took such a risk, uncle. I'd have thought you'd be more careful to keep your hands clean."

"My poor child." Daniel's eyes softened with sympathy. "Has Lescaut been feeding you these delusions?"

Paul fixed his gaze on Ned. "You see? Ribard will deny he had anything to do with the attack in Kinrie. Just as he'll deny he had anything to do with the fire and Tom's death."

Ned started, as though Paul had struck him. "Tom killed himself."

"No one can account for why he would have done so. You and Ribard had every reason to want him dead. Was it Ribard's idea to kill him or yours?"

"No." Ned's voice was as taut as a rope about to be rent in two.

"No, it wasn't yours?" Paul asked.

Ned pushed the hair back from his sweaty forehead.

Daniel moved toward him. "He's trying to confuse you, boy. We all know how deeply your brother's death affected you."

"Your own brother," Paul continued. "It must have been difficult. Unless it was Ribard who pulled the trigger. But somehow I doubt it. He's the sort who gets others to do his dirty work. What was your price?"

"Ned?" Charlotte had been watching the scene in silence, her face as white as the marble of the mantel behind her. "Say something."

"Murder." Paul drew out the word. "It's a hanging offense whether or not you have a handle to your name."

Daniel moved to the bellpull. "It's time you left, Lescaut.

Will you have the decency to take yourself off or do I have George throw you out?"

"Just a minute, Ribard." Ned's voice cut the air. "It's my house. I'll decide who gets thrown out."

Daniel released the bellpull and shrugged his elegant, black-clad shoulders. "Suit yourself. For my part I have no desire to listen to more of Lescaut's fantasies. Charlotte—"

"I'm not going anywhere, *Papa*." Charlotte looked at him, her eyes pleading. "Tell them it isn't true. Ned was at Ross-mere the night Tom killed himself. He got the news at the breakfast table with the rest of us."

"Exactly." Daniel nodded. "I'm sure the servants will vouch that he didn't leave the house the entire night."

"But you won't swear to it yourself, will you, Ribard?" Paul turned back to Ned. "You'll get no alibi from him. He'll say the fire was your idea as well. Yours and Tom's. All he'd done was loan you money."

Fresh beads of perspiration broke out on Ned's forehead. Sophie pressed the advantage. "Perhaps that's true. Perhaps Uncle Daniel had nothing to do with the fire. Perhaps it was just you and Tom. Or just you with your friend McAlpin."

"*No.*" The word seemed to be torn from Ned's throat. "He thought of it." Ned waved his arm at Daniel.

The wall of denial was smashed. Sophie released her breath. Charlotte dropped into a chair, her eyes wide and empty.

Daniel shook his head. "Oh, Edward. I should have known at some point you'd start blaming others for your own weakness."

"You're not going to weasel out of this, Ribard. If Lescaut prints any more stories they're going to be my stories. The truth." Ned turned back to Sophie and Paul. "He said the country was on the brink of revolution. We had to nudge Parliament to make sure the appropriate laws were enacted. The Home Secretary employs agents to do this very sort of thing. He implied we had Sidmouth's tacit approval. It was sure to get Tom into the Cabinet. The millworkers were troublemakers anyway. And we'd have the insurance money. He made it sound so simple. It would have been, too, if Tom hadn't threatened to spill the truth like a bloody fool."

"Tom was going to admit the truth about the fire?" Sophie still could not make sense of her husband's actions. "Why?"

"God knows." Ned walked to a table of decanters, picked up a half-filled tumbler of brandy, and downed the contents. "Ribard called me to Rossmere and told me Tom was making trouble. I rode over to Tiverton to reason with him. I brought my pistol, but I only meant to threaten him. Then he grabbed my arm and the damned thing went off. Ribard helped me make it look like suicide."

Daniel laid a hand on Charlotte's shoulder. "It was wrong of me. But the death was accidental. And I knew how much you loved him."

Charlotte stared up at her father, her face a blank.

Ned splashed more brandy into his glass. "It wasn't supposed to be this way. We brought Matt in to help us. He was in need of blunt, and I knew I could trust him. The three of us were supposed to set the bloody fire together so we'd all be equally at risk and no one could blackmail us later. I arranged to have Hagerty there in case we needed someone to vouch for our whereabouts. Stupid idea. I should have realized Hagerty would bungle even that. Then at the last minute Tom claimed he'd been summoned to a meeting in London. Matt and I had to do the dirty work alone. I was angry that Tom didn't do his part, but I never thought he'd turn on us." Ned's voice shook with indignation.

"I begin to see the reason for the fire." Paul gripped the chair back, his gaze going to Daniel. "When the French monarchy was restored, you must have known Tom would start making inquiries about Sophie's estates. So you urged him and Ned to set fire to the mill. That way you'd have a hold on him if he asked embarrassing questions about what happened to the Milvery fortune."

"What?" Ned swung round to look at Daniel.

"Only Tom was cleverer than you gave him credit for,

wasn't he?" Paul continued. "Like you, he knew better than to actually soil his hands with a crime. What happened? Tom challenged you about Sophie's inheritance, you threatened to expose his role in the fire, and he told you he had an alibi? Or perhaps he threatened to reveal the truth about the fire himself and accuse you of complicity. So you got Ned to get rid of him for you."

"By God." Ned flung his glass to the floor and lunged at Daniel. Daniel stepped neatly out of the way. Ned went crashing into the mantel. Charlotte ran to Sophie.

"My poor child." Daniel moved toward the women. His voice was as smooth as fine claret. "I'm so sorry you had to hear this, *ma petite*. I knew Ned was weak, but I had no idea he could turn so vicious. I suppose I should have realized he would try to put the blame on anyone but himself."

Charlotte shrank back in Sophie's arms. "Sophie says she saw you in Kinrie."

"Sophie has been through a great deal." Daniel looked at Sophie. His eyes held a tenderness that made her skin prickle with revulsion. "Lescaut has you bewitched, doesn't he? Don't you know he's hated me since he was a child? Hated all of us. Surely you haven't forgotten what he did to your father? He betrayed him. And D'Epigny and Mouffetard. It's only by the grace of God that I was spared."

Sophie felt Paul go still. She was conscious of the heat of the fire and the smell of spilled brandy. For a moment they were back in Paris, she and Paul and Daniel, on the night that had changed all their lives forever.

A hum of sound outside cut through the memories. Voices. Booted feet against cobblestones. She caught a flash of torchlight through the chinks in the curtains of the windows that ran along the side of the house.

Paul moved to the windows and pushed back the heavy gold curtains. "The protesters have reached your fortress, Rutledge."

Ned ran to the windows as well.

Sophie stayed where she was, arms around Charlotte, eyes

on her uncle. Men marching to the house. Shouts. Torchlight. The same sights and sounds as the night she crept out on the landing to find Paul and saw the soldiers in the foyer below. Paul had forced her to remember her father's death. But she hadn't thought of the subsequent events of that night. Daniel's return home, being bundled into a carriage with her mother and aunt and cousins, the headlong dash to the coast, the way her mother had sat wrapped in her cloak and not touched her, the icy stillness whenever their carriage was stopped.

There must be more to the story than what I wrote, Paul had said. *Something we haven't discovered yet. Something that's worth the risk of killing us to keep secret.*

Sophie looked her uncle directly in the eye, remembering the words he had just spoken. *It's only by the grace of God that I was spared.* The truth burst on her, so blindingly bright she wondered why they had not seen it sooner. "God had nothing to do with it. The night we left France you had a paper you waved whenever our carriage was stopped."

"A forgery. I was lucky." But Daniel's body had gone taut.

"Not a forgery. A reward from the Government for services rendered. It wasn't an accident that you were gone from the house when the soldiers came, was it? You knew exactly when they were coming. Paul didn't betray my father and the others. You did."

Paul turned from the window. Charlotte pulled herself out of Sophie's arms and stumbled backward, looking at her father.

There was a splintering crash. Voices filled the hall. Cries of "Justice" and "the Rutledge Three" battered the door.

"Bastards." Ned moved to his desk and jerked open a drawer. "What's George thinking of?" He pulled a pistol from the drawer.

Daniel moved toward Charlotte. Charlotte ran back to Sophie. Paul moved between Sophie and the door. "Is there a back way out?"

"A servant's door," Sophie said, her arm around Charlotte. "In the wall by the fireplace."

Daniel bolted the door to the hall. "Get Charlotte out of here, Sophie."

Sophie pulled Charlotte toward the servant's door. The hall door shook. There was a blur of movement outside the window behind the desk. The window shattered. A man carrying a club jumped through the hail of glass and grabbed Ned from behind.

Ned aimed his gun at the man. The man hit his arm as he pulled the trigger. There was a loud report. The bullet buried itself in the paneling. The gun thudded to the floor. The man smashed his club into Ned's skull.

"Ned!" Charlotte broke away from Sophie.

The man swung his club again. Ned slumped forward on the desk. Blood pooled onto the ink blotter.

Paul grabbed Charlotte and pushed her back to Sophie. "You can't help him."

The door to the hall crashed open. Men with torches spilled into the study. Smoke and shouts clogged the air. Torchlight glinted off knives and ax handles. Daniel was lost in the melee.

"Rutledge is dead!" the man with the club shouted from the desk.

There was a roar—part approval, part frustration at being deprived of their quarry. Ax blades struck the paneling. Knives slashed upholstery. A glass-fronted bookcase shattered. Someone stuck a torch into one of the chairs, sending up a sheet of flames.

Sophie dragged Charlotte to the servant's door. A man rushed at them, brandishing a burnt spar of wood. Paul upended the table with the decanters and rammed it into their would-be attacker. The man fell to the floor amid smashed crystal and spilled brandy. Paul backed after Sophie and Charlotte, using the table as a shield.

Sophie caught sight of Daniel just as they reached the door. He was stumbling backward. One of the protesters had an ax uplifted to strike him in the head.

A pistol shot cut the air. The man with the ax cried out, dropped his weapon, and clutched his wounded arm. Still holding the smoking pistol, Paul grabbed Daniel and pulled him after the women.

Sophie tugged open the door in the paneling meant to allow the master's valet to slip in and out of the room discreetly. She pulled Charlotte into the musty passage. Paul and Daniel followed.

Sophie had never been in the servants' portion of the house. Going on instinct, she found a door, then a narrow flight of stairs, and then another door opening onto the garden at the back of the house.

Moonlight spilled over shrubs and flower beds and classical statues. A cool, orderly world untouched by madness, save for the shouts that sounded from the street.

"The mews," Paul said. Sophie turned to see that he had slung Daniel over his shoulder. She could not tell how badly her uncle was hurt.

They ran down the gravel paths and out a back gate in the iron railing. Firelight flickered against the night sky. Horses neighed in their stalls, disturbed by the scent of fear and anger in the air.

Charlotte stopped and looked at Paul. Her hair fell about her face. "*Papa*. Is he—"

"He's alive." Paul shifted his hands to get a firmer grip on Daniel. "We have to keep going."

They turned down a side street and made their way through a maze of lanes and alleys. Charlotte moved beside Sophie without protest or hesitation. Paul followed close behind, carrying Daniel, just as he had once carried Sophie through the streets of Kinrie.

They emerged in a narrow street lined with blackened shop fronts. Broken glass and charred embers littered the cobblestones. The looters had moved on. The street was quiet and dark, as if even the families who lived above the shops had fled. Paul stopped and drew a breath. "We can't make it all the way back to Craymere's. This is as good a refuge as any."

Sophie pulled open the smashed door of one of the shops. The scent of yeast mingled with the smell of soot. Flour and crumbs were scattered over the floor along with broken glass. They were in a bakeshop.

Paul eased Daniel to the floor. "Here." He reached in his pocket and tossed Sophie a flint. "Find some candles."

Sophie moved behind the smashed cases, once fronted by glass. She found two candle ends in a drawer and an oil lamp on a shelf. The mantel was cracked, but the wick flared to life. The yellow light revealed the extent of the carnage. The cases had been stripped clean. There was scarcely a scrap of edible food left in the shop. An iron pot and copper skillet lay on the floor along with the wreckage of two chairs. Sophie twitched her skirt away from a sticky mess that looked like raw egg and carried the lamp over to Paul, who was kneeling on the floor by Daniel.

Daniel's head was slumped forward, his eyes closed. Paul had pushed back his coat, revealing a jagged gash in his shoulder that was still bleeding. "Water," Paul said. "And wine or vinegar if you can find it."

Sophie and Charlotte carried the two candles into the kitchen behind the shop. Coals still glowed in the oven. Otherwise the kitchen was a shambles, the long table overturned, the doors ripped from the cupboards, sacks of flour and sugar and broken crockery strewn over the floor.

Charlotte lifted an earthenware ewer. "There's water left in here."

Sophie found a bottle of sherry, broken off at the neck, which had rolled into a corner and still contained a half inch of liquid. They carried their finds to Paul, who had stripped off Daniel's coat and waistcoat and unfastened his shirt.

"It's not a life-threatening wound," Paul told Charlotte, pouring the meager amount of sherry onto a strip torn from his own neckcloth. "He'll recover."

Charlotte said nothing. She was staring down at Daniel as though he were a complete stranger.

Paul cleansed the wound and got Sophie to hold Daniel's arm still while he bound it with the remainder of his neckcloth. How strange, Sophie thought, gripping the warm flesh of Daniel's arm. Her powerful uncle was as helpless as she had once been.

Daniel's head jerked up. His face was ashen. Sophie could swear there were hollows beneath his cheeks and eyes that had not been there an hour since. But the eyes themselves were as sharp as ever. Fear flickered through her. It had been premature to see him as broken.

Daniel turned his head and looked at Paul.

"Rutledge is dead," Paul said. "You'll recover."

Daniel reached up and touched the bandage on his shoulder. "You shot the man who was attacking me."

"A flesh wound." Paul's voice was even. "I wouldn't take a life for your sake."

Daniel regarded Paul for a moment. "Twenty-three years ago you wanted me dead. Why save me now?"

"I'll probably ask myself that question for the rest of my life."

"Careful, boy. Compassion is a costly luxury. You must have inherited it from your mother. Not from me."

Paul sucked in his breath. The fingers of his shattered hand clenched. For a moment he and Daniel stared at each other. The room went so still Sophie could swear she could hear the echoes of the past. "I never thought you'd admit it," Paul said.

The corner of Daniel's mouth lifted in a smile that suddenly reminded Sophie of Paul. "Neither did I."

Paul's face closed. "It would have meant something once." His voice was as cold as the burnt wreckage around them. "It's too late now."

Daniel slowly inclined his head. The lamp cast a small circle of light around him and Paul. Seeing the two men in profile, Sophie was struck by how alike they were. Not their features, but the strength in their faces, the ironic lift of their brows, the determination in the set of mouth and eyes and chin. But Daniel was hard to the core, and she had seen Paul's vulnerability.

"You're her son, aren't you?" Charlotte looked at Paul as though seeking some sign of familiarity. "The other Charlotte's. The little boy *Papa* brought into the house in France."

Paul met her gaze. "The boy who betrayed your father and Sophie's."

"Sophie says it was really *Papa* who did that." Charlotte turned back to her father. Her hands twisted in the velvet folds of her riding habit.

Daniel raised his head. "Charlie—"

"It's true, isn't it?" Charlotte's voice shook. "Everything Sophie and Mr. Lescaut said."

Sophie saw her uncle gather his forces for a denial.

"Don't lie to me, *Papa*." Charlotte's voice was as sharp as broken glass. "Ned did enough of that for a lifetime."

Daniel released his breath. "If it was true you could hardly expect me to admit it, even to you, *ma chère*. But you must believe your happiness has always been my foremost concern, Charlie."

"Oh, God." Charlotte's eyes widened with the full realization. In ten seconds she seemed to age ten years. Sophie sprang to her feet and pulled her trembling cousin into her arms.

"She'll never forgive you," Paul said. Over Charlotte's shoulder, Sophie saw Paul still watching his father. "That's a worse punishment than any I could devise."

"You did devise it." Daniel rested his head against the knife-scarred wall. "You were a clever boy. I was proud of that. But I knew when you came to Rossmere that you'd never let matters rest. I knew I'd have to destroy you or be destroyed."

"I didn't threaten your life." Beneath Paul's quiet tones, Sophie caught an edge of bitterness and a desperate need to understand.

"You threatened everything I'd built in my life. Everything I wanted for Charlotte."

"Charlotte wouldn't thank you for trying to preserve it." Paul sat back on his heels. "I don't know how you did it, but she's good, Ribard. To the core." Paul looked up at Charlotte, then back at Daniel. "Perhaps that was why I saved you. Whatever else you've done, you're my sister's father."

Chapter 29

✦

"Dod." Dugal pulled his feet up on the hearth rug and clasped his arms around his knees. "And we missed all of it. It isna fair."

Paul felt a smile tug at his mouth. They were all gathered in Robert and Emma's parlor. The children on the floor in front of the fireplace; Robert and Emma on a settee with Alison; Sir James, Lady Margaret, and Anne on the sofa; Sophie in an armchair holding Fenella. She hadn't put the baby down since they'd reached the house two hours ago.

Paul had deliberately chosen a chair across the room from Sophie and her daughter. His fingers ached to touch both mother and child, but he knew the time for such intimacy had come to an end.

He looked at the settee where Robert sat with his arm around Emma. Alison was sprawled half on Emma's lap, half on Robert's, cooing at her parents and trying to roll over. Paul had more than one reason to envy his cousin—his loving parents, his belief in humanity, the use of both his arms. But jealousy of Robert had never burned inside him as strongly as it did at this moment.

"Your poor cousin, Sophie." Lady Margaret pushed a ringlet back from her face and glanced up at the plaster ceiling. Charlotte had been put to bed in one of the spare rooms as soon as they reached Old Fishmarket Close. "Does her mother know what happened?"

Sophie was coaxing Fenella to grasp hold of her finger. "I wrote to Aunt Louisa before we left Lancaster. I said that Charlotte had had a shock and was coming back to Edinburgh with us. I told Aunt Louisa she'd have to ask Uncle Daniel for the details."

Emma steadied Alison before she could roll onto the carpet. "Will he tell her?"

"He won't admit a word of it. But Aunt Louisa is no fool. She'll have seen the Tolbooth Story. She must have her own questions about the money Uncle Daniel got out of France. Publicly she'll stand by him. But I wouldn't be surprised if she starts spending most of her time at one of their other houses."

Robert looked at Paul. "Do we print a second story?"

Paul turned to Sophie. These were her family's secrets.

"Yes," Sophie said without hesitation. "The truth deserves an airing."

"It's no' *fair*." Dugal sat up very straight, his body quivering with indignation. "He was behind everythin' and he's no' bein' punished at all."

Amy twisted the end of her braid round her finger. Paul had been worried about how she would take the news of what had happened in Lancaster. Her uncle had paid with his life for Ned and Daniel's crimes. "There's more than one kind of punishment, Dugal," she said. "The marquis has lost his family and his friends."

David squeezed Amy's hand. Dugal looked at Kirsty and rolled his eyes.

Paul reached down to scratch Pauline behind the ears. "I expect the families of d'Epigny and Mouffetard will be interested to learn about Ribard's role in betraying their relatives. I'll write to Adam tomorrow and tell him of our latest discoveries. The d'Epigny and Mouffetard families will listen to a British diplomat. Ribard's credit with the Governments of both countries will be destroyed."

Dugal rested his chin on his knees. "*I'd* rather someone had his guts for garters."

"Never mind," Amy said, still holding David's hand. "You'll understand when you're older."

Dugal made a face at her.

Sir James coughed. "I don't mean to be crass, Lady Rutledge, but Ribard owes you everything he took from your father. With interest, compounded over twenty-three years."

Sophie pulled Fenella closer. "I don't want it."

"But you must take it, for Fenella's sake if not your own." Lady Margaret leaned forward, the apricot ribbons on her sleeves shaking with her insistence. "You have to think of her future, my dear. Not to mention any other children you may have."

Paul felt as if all the attention in the room was suddenly focused on him and Sophie. The lamplight seemed mercilessly bright, the air close and warm. He was reminded of why he had enjoyed having no ties in the world. Letting go of Sophie was painful enough without his family turning a clean cut into a festering wound.

Robert got to his feet. "You both must be exhausted. There'll be plenty of time to talk in the coming days."

Paul sent his cousin a look of silent gratitude.

"Yes, of course, how thoughtless of us." Lady Margaret made a show of gathering up her shawl and reticule and knitting bag. "We'll call again tomorrow, if we may. And you must all come to dinner in Queen Street as soon as you feel equal to it. Oh, it will be so nice to have Sophie and Paul settled in Edinburgh."

"Meg." Sir James gripped his wife's arm.

"For a time at least," Lady Margaret added quickly.

There was a flurry of good nights and farewells to the McClarens. As they were taking candles from the hall table, Sophie touched Paul's arm. "I need to talk. Come to my room."

His throat constricted with an ache at once bittersweet and knife-sharp. But he couldn't deny Sophie. Nor could he deny himself a few more precious moments alone with her. So when the house had settled for the night, he slipped from the room he shared with Dugal and David and tapped at the door of Sophie's chamber. When she bade him come in, he stepped into the room to find her bending over the cradle. She had unpinned her hair and she wore the red silk dressing gown that shimmered with memories. The breath caught in Paul's throat.

Sophie straightened up and smiled at him. "I've fed Fenella, but she's still awake. Don't you want to hold her? You haven't since we got back."

Her face was so open. He had once thought she would never look at him in that way again. "I don't want to disturb her."

"I think she'd like it." Sophie lifted Fenella and walked toward him, so close he could smell her rose fragrance and the milky scent of the baby.

The temptation was too great. He held out his arms and took the baby. Perhaps it was his imagination, but it seemed to him that her body relaxed into his arms as though she remembered his touch. He smiled and she smiled back, piercing his heart. He was sure her smiles were genuine now, not just gas as Lady Margaret had insisted at first. Her eyes were still a clear blue, like Sophie's. He hoped they would stay that way. Then he realized he wouldn't be there to see one way or the other. "She has another sucking blister," he said.

"I know, she's prone to them. But she switched back to my milk without any hesitation. She's a remarkably sturdy child. It must be all the chaos we put her through in the first weeks of her life. Not to mention before she was born." Sophie moved toward the green damask chairs by the fireplace. "Come and sit down. We need to talk."

Her dressing gown fell open as she sat. The firelight shot through the muslin folds of her nightdress, revealing the elegant, familiar outline of her leg. Paul drew a steadying breath and moved to the other chair.

Sophie rested her elbow on the chair arm and cupped her chin in her hand. Her hair streamed over her shoulders, as tousled as when she had woken in his arms. "Sir James and Lady Margaret are right. It's silly to have qualms about taking money from Uncle Daniel."

"You wouldn't be taking it from him. It was yours to begin with."

"It seems tainted by his touch. But we should be practical. There isn't just Fenella to think of. We have Dugal and Amy to provide for as well, not to mention Charlotte, though I assume Uncle Daniel and Aunt Louisa will make her an allowance—"

Paul jerked his head up. "Sophie—"

"She'll have to stay with us, you do see that, don't you? Even if Aunt Louisa leaves Uncle Daniel, I can't see Charlotte wanting to make her home with her. They've never been close. And much as I love Céline, she's no earthly good to anyone in the midst of a crisis. Charlie's always been more like a sister to me than to her own sisters."

"Naturally Charlotte will stay with you." Longing coiled within him. If he wasn't careful it would break free and blind him to reality. "But you haven't thought the rest of this through, Sophie."

"I thought about it for all of that silent journey back from Lancaster, while Charlotte huddled in the corner and you looked resolutely grim. We should find a house in Old Fishmarket Close, because I assume you'll want to work on the paper with Robert. You could start your own, of course, but it seems silly to compete with your cousin. I want you to teach me to set type and work the press. You know how I hate it when you know more about something than I do."

If he hadn't been holding Fenella he would have risen and strode about the room. "It's an appealing fantasy, Sophie. But we both know that's all it is. We've always known we had no future together. We come from different worlds. Nothing we've been through together changes that."

"Robert and Emma come from different worlds. So did Anne and your uncle. Lady Margaret puts up with Argyllshire for Sir James. Sir James puts up with Edinburgh for her."

"There are degrees of difference." He kept his voice harsh because Sophie had a dangerous way of softening him. "You're a comte's daughter. I'm a bastard."

"For shame, Paul, I didn't think such things mattered to you." Sophie shifted her position, causing the dressing gown to fall farther open. "These past weeks haven't made me think much of the life I was born to. Besides, I never really belonged at Rossmere. I've never really belonged anywhere. Until I found you again."

The words and the look in her eyes drove the breath from his lungs. "You've got used to me," he said.

"So I have. All that effort has to be worth something."

He was going to have to say it. He was going to have to open the cesspool and make them both face the ugliness that would always be between them. He stroked his fingers against Fenella's cheek. He didn't want her touched by this. "I betrayed your father, Sophie. The fact that Ribard went to the authorities before I did doesn't make me any less culpable."

Sophie went still. "We've put that behind us."

"It will never be behind us. It made us both who we are." He looked down at his clawed hand, now twisted in Fenella's pink blanket. "I used to lie awake nights wondering about my motives. I'd see your father's bloody body, hear your mother's screams, remember you calling my name. Did I bring about so much suffering only for revenge on my father?"

"Paul, don't." Sophie's voice was strained. "We don't have to talk about it."

"Yes, we do. Because I know now that it was more than revenge. Assassination is wrong. I'd do what I did again." He raised his head and looked at Sophie. He had wrestled to the ground a demon that had haunted him since he was ten years old.

Sophie stood, the silk dressing gown rustling about her. She crossed the room and knelt beside his chair. "You did what you thought was right. If you'd done anything else, you wouldn't be the man I love."

His breathing turned ragged. Happiness was so close he could touch it, yet he knew it was out of his reach.

Sophie placed her hand on his shoulder, her touch warm and firm. "Forget the past, Paul. For once in your life let yourself believe in the future. If you can't let yourself be happy, think of me. Think of Fenella. Think of Dugal and Amy and Charlotte. We all need you. And you need us, deny it as you may."

It was true. She had made a gash in his defenses that would never heal. He looked down at Fenella. Her head had flopped against his arm with the utter abandon of sleep and trust. The thought of her growing to adulthood without him was more than he could bear.

Sophie reached out with her free hand and cupped Fenella's head. "I wouldn't care for myself. But for Fenella's sake, I think you'd better marry me."

Paul breathed in the scent of roses and baby. His resistance was smashed. When the time comes, seize it, Robert had said. His cousin had always been disgustingly acute.

Cradling Fenella in one arm, Paul bent his head and kissed Sophie, making no effort to leash his hunger or his need.

When he raised his head her eyes were glowing, but she said nothing. The next move was up to him. He seized her hand and lifted it to his lips. "I don't deserve you. I have nothing to offer you. But if you marry me I'll spend the rest of my life making sure you never regret it."

Sophie's laughter washed over him. "Of course, Paul. After all, Fenella is almost six weeks old. I think it's high time I married her father."

Historical Note

The riot in Lancaster at the end of *Shadows of the Heart* is fictional, but the poverty and discontent in England and Scotland at the time were very real. Changes in manufacturing, the end of the Napoleonic Wars, and economic depression combined to create massive unemployment, high food prices, and a great deal of dislocation. Arthur Bryant paints a vivid picture of this era in *The Age of Elegance 1812–1822* [New York: Harper & Brothers Publishers, 1950].

Kinrie and Dounfries are both fictional as well.

In the writing of *Shadows of the Heart* I am also indebted to Tom McCulloch for information on the criminal-justice system in nineteenth-century Scotland, and to Devlin Sevy for first-hand experience with a newborn baby.

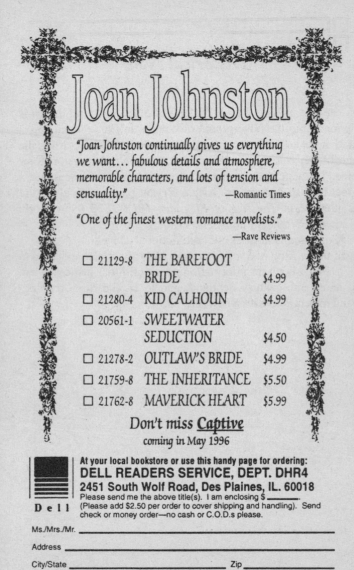

Be sure to read these outstanding historical romances by author:

CHRISTINA SKYE